INVADER ZIM

VOLUME 5

Created by
JHONEN VASQUEZ

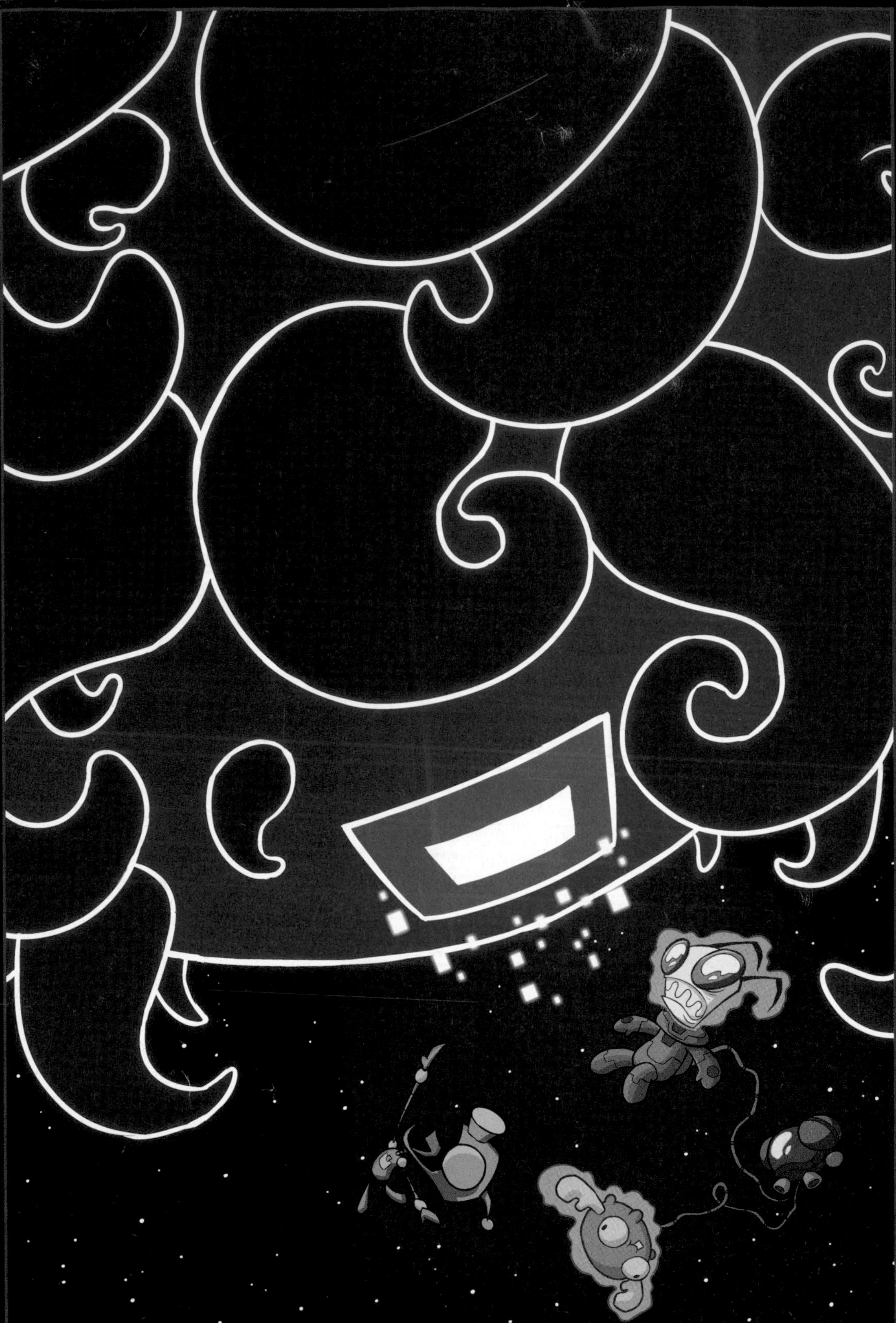

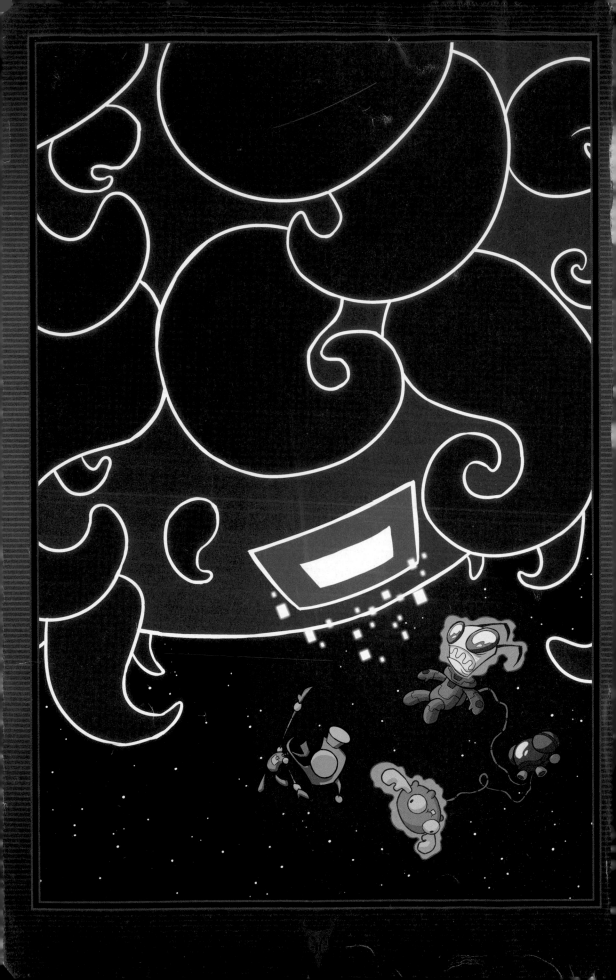

INVADER ZIM

VOLUME 5

Control Brain
JHONEN VASQUEZ

Writer, Chapters 1-4
ERIC TRUEHEART

Writer & Illustrator, Chapter 5
DAVE CROSLAND

Illustrator, Chapters 1-4
Letterer, Chapters 1-5
Colorist, Chapter 5
WARREN WUCINICH

Colorist, Chapters 1-4
FRED C. STRESING

Retail cover illustrated by
WARREN WUCINICH

Oni Press exclusive cover illustrated by
SAM KAYS

ONI PRESS

AN ONI PRESS PUBLICATION

Special thanks to **JOAN HILTY** and **LINDA LEE**

Designed by **KEITH WOOD**

Edited by **ROBIN HERRERA**

Published by Oni Press, Inc.

founder & chief financial officer **JOE NOZEMACK** publisher **JAMES LUCAS JONES**

v.p. of creative & business development **CHARLIE CHU** director of operations **BRAD ROOKS**

marketing manager **RACHEL REED** publicity manager **MELISSA MESZAROS**

director of design & production **TROY LOOK** senior graphic designer **HILARY THOMPSON**

junior graphic designer **KATE Z. STONE** digital prepress technician **ANGIE KNOWLES**

executive editor **ARI YARWOOD** senior editor **ROBIN HERRERA**

associate editor **DESIREE WILSON** administrative assistant **ALISSA SALLAH**

logistics associate **JUNG LEE**

This volume collects issues #21-25 of the
Oni Press series *Invader Zim*.

Oni Press, Inc.
1319 SE Martin Luther King Jr. Blvd.
Suite 240
Portland, OR 97214
USA

onipress.com · facebook.com/onipress · twitter.com/onipress
onipress.tumblr.com · instagram.com/onipress

First edition: February 2018

ISBN: 978-1-62010-478-1 · eISBN: 978-1-62010-479-8
Oni Press Exclusive ISBN: 978-1-62010-489-7

nickelodeon

Library of Congress Control Number: 2015950610

1 3 5 7 9 10 8 6 4 2

PRINTED IN USA.

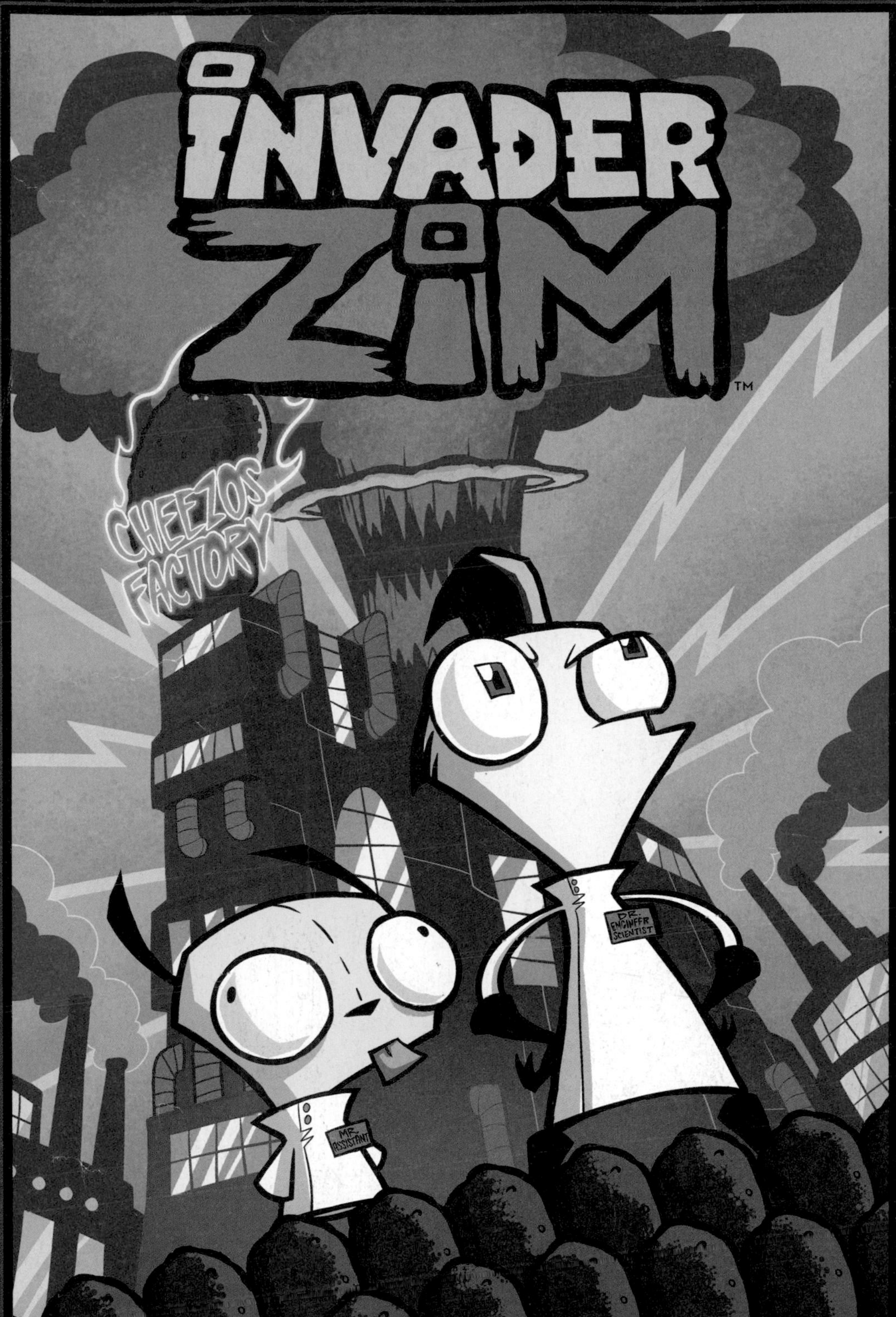
INVADER ZIM
CHEEZOS FACTORY
MR. ASSISTANT

CHAPTER: 1

The Arc of VIROOZ Part One:
The Mark of VIROOZ

illustration by **Warren Wucinich**

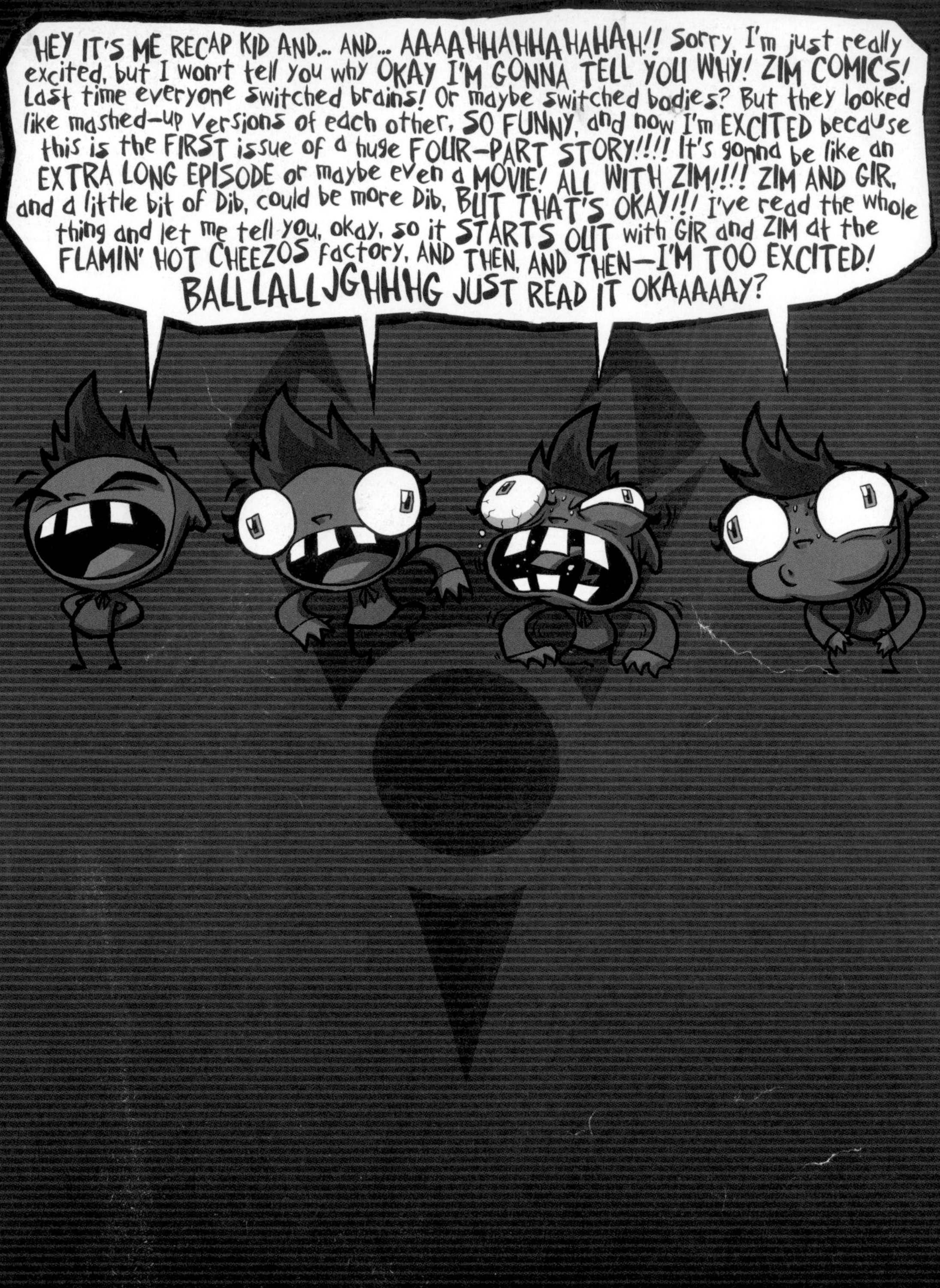
HEY IT'S ME RECAP KID AND... AND... AAAAHHAHHAHAHAH!! Sorry, I'm just really excited, but I won't tell you why OKAY I'M GONNA TELL YOU WHY! ZIM COMICS! Last time everyone switched brains! Or maybe switched bodies? But they looked like mashed-up versions of each other, SO FUNNY, and now I'm EXCITED because this is the FIRST issue of a huge FOUR-PART STORY!!!! It's gonna be like an EXTRA LONG EPISODE or maybe even a MOVIE! ALL WITH ZIM!!!! ZIM AND GIR, and a little bit of Dib, could be more Dib, BUT THAT'S OKAY!!! I've read the whole thing and let me tell you, okay, so it STARTS OUT with GIR and ZIM at the FLAMIN' HOT CHEEZOS factory, AND THEN, AND THEN—I'M TOO EXCITED! BALLLALLJGHHHG JUST READ IT OKAAAAAY?

Recap Kid by **WARREN WUCINICH**

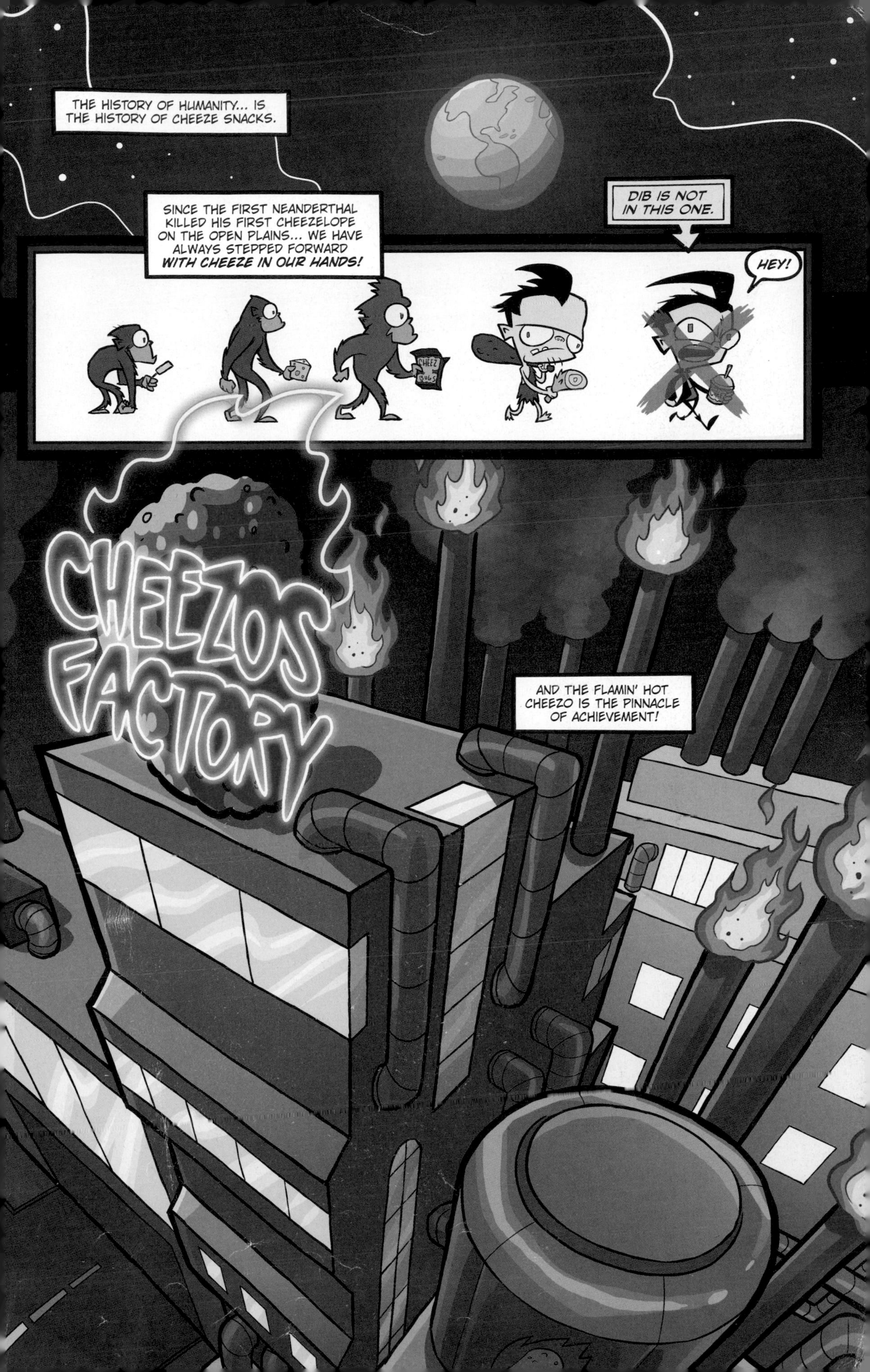
THE HISTORY OF HUMANITY... IS THE HISTORY OF CHEEZE SNACKS.
SINCE THE FIRST NEANDERTHAL KILLED HIS FIRST CHEEZELOPE ON THE OPEN PLAINS... WE HAVE ALWAYS STEPPED FORWARD ***WITH CHEEZE IN OUR HANDS!***
DIB IS NOT IN THIS ONE.
HEY!
CHEEZ BUGS
CHEEZOS FACTORY
AND THE FLAMIN' HOT CHEEZO IS THE PINNACLE OF ACHIEVEMENT!

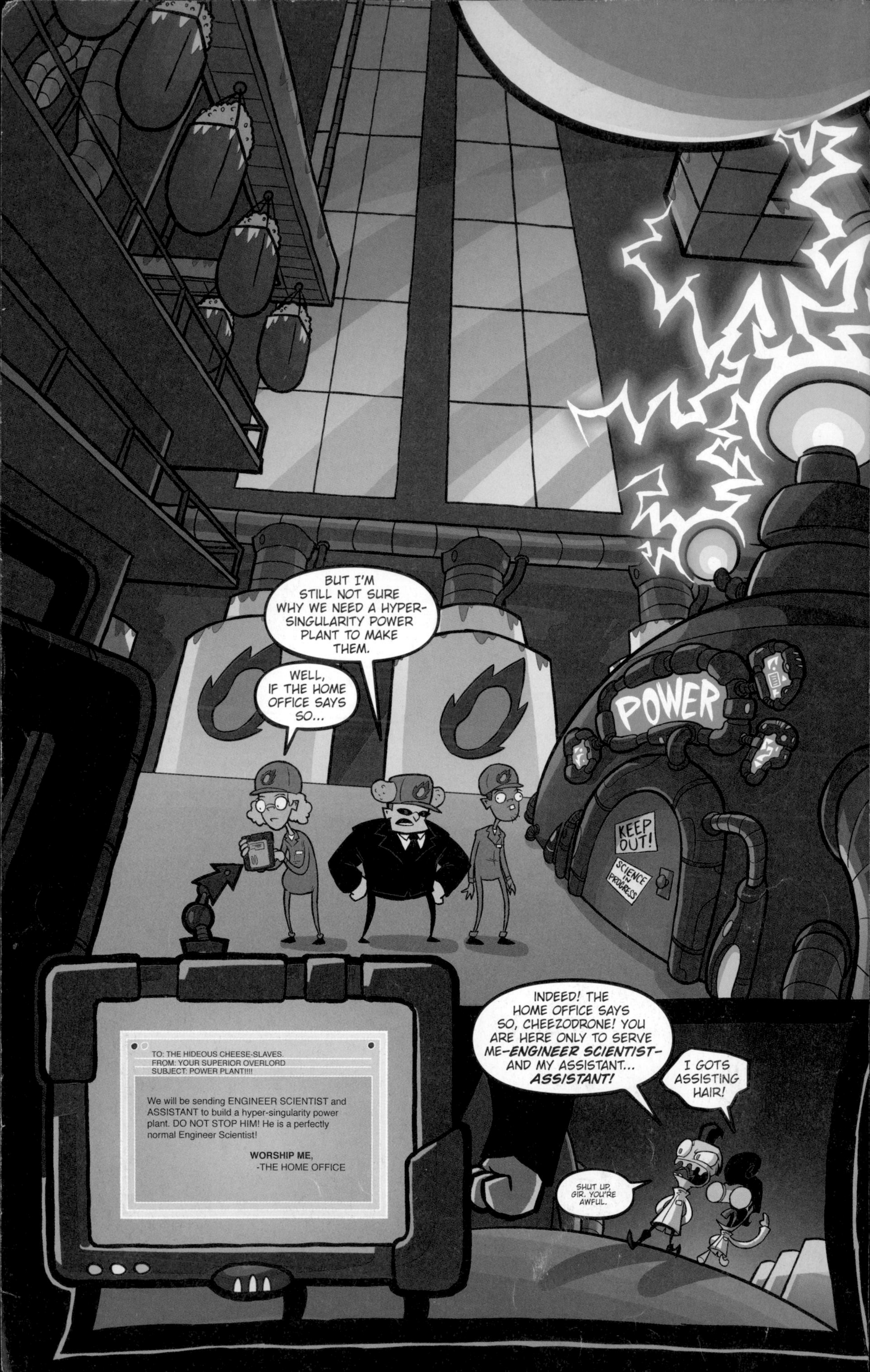
BUT I'M STILL NOT SURE WHY WE NEED A HYPER-SINGULARITY POWER PLANT TO MAKE THEM.
WELL, IF THE HOME OFFICE SAYS SO...
POWER
KEEP OUT!
SCIENCE IN PROGRESS
TO: THE HIDEOUS CHEESE-SLAVES.
FROM: YOUR SUPERIOR OVERLORD
SUBJECT: POWER PLANT!!!!
We will be sending ENGINEER SCIENTIST and ASSISTANT to build a hyper-singularity power plant. DO NOT STOP HIM! He is a perfectly normal Engineer Scientist!
WORSHIP ME,
-THE HOME OFFICE
INDEED! THE HOME OFFICE SAYS SO, CHEEZODRONE! YOU ARE HERE ONLY TO SERVE ME—ENGINEER SCIENTIST—AND MY ASSISTANT... ASSISTANT!
I GOTS ASSISTING HAIR!
SHUT UP, GIR. YOU'RE AWFUL.

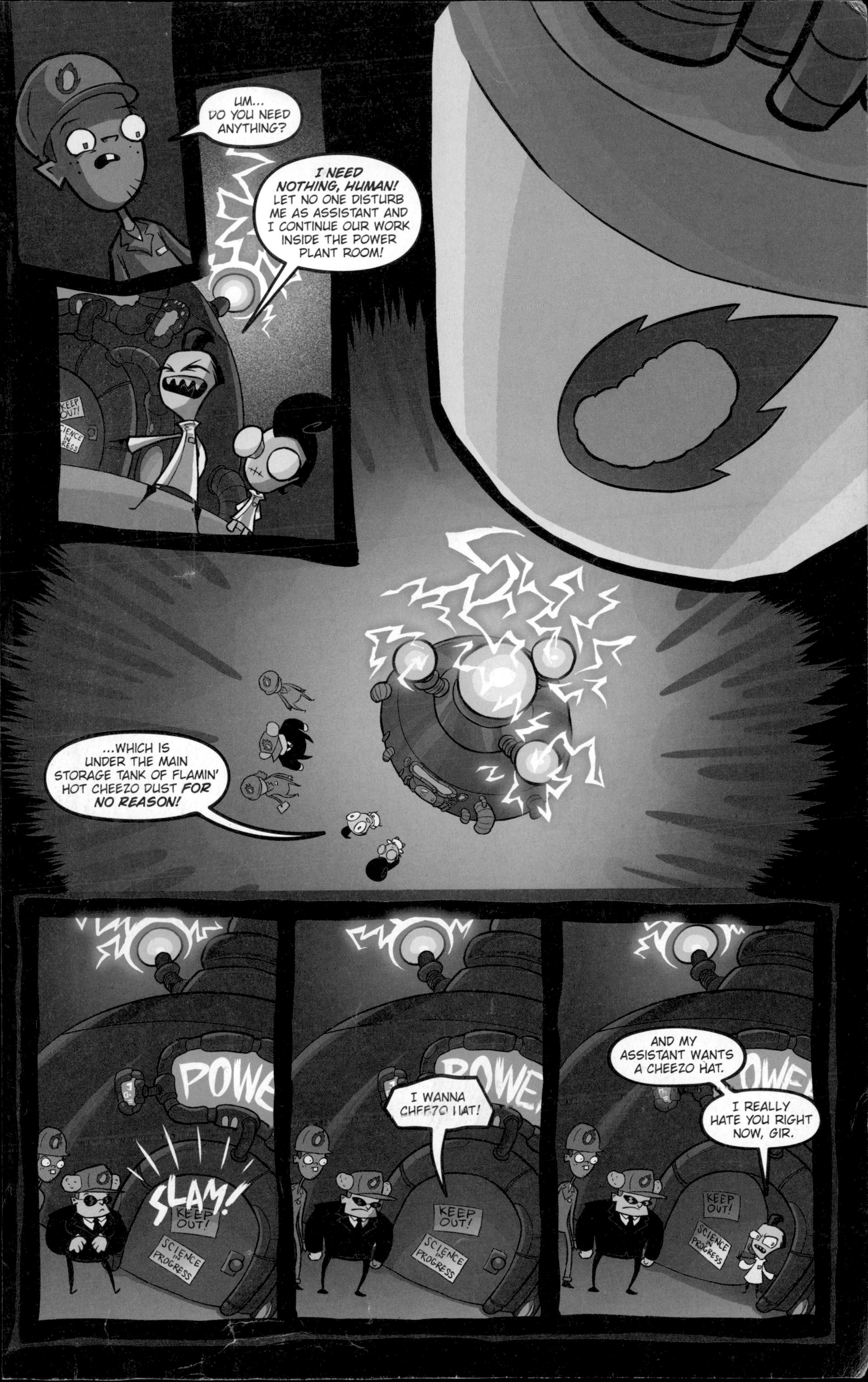
UM... DO YOU NEED ANYTHING?
I NEED NOTHING, HUMAN! LET NO ONE DISTURB ME AS ASSISTANT AND I CONTINUE OUR WORK INSIDE THE POWER PLANT ROOM!
KEEP OUT!
SCIENCE IN PROGRESS
...WHICH IS UNDER THE MAIN STORAGE TANK OF FLAMIN' HOT CHEEZO DUST FOR NO REASON!
POWE
SLAM!
KEEP OUT!
SCIENCE IN PROGRESS
I WANNA CHEEZO HAT!
KEEP OUT!
SCIENCE IN PROGRESS
AND MY ASSISTANT WANTS A CHEEZO HAT.
I REALLY HATE YOU RIGHT NOW, GIR.
KEEP OUT!
SCIENCE IN PROGRESS

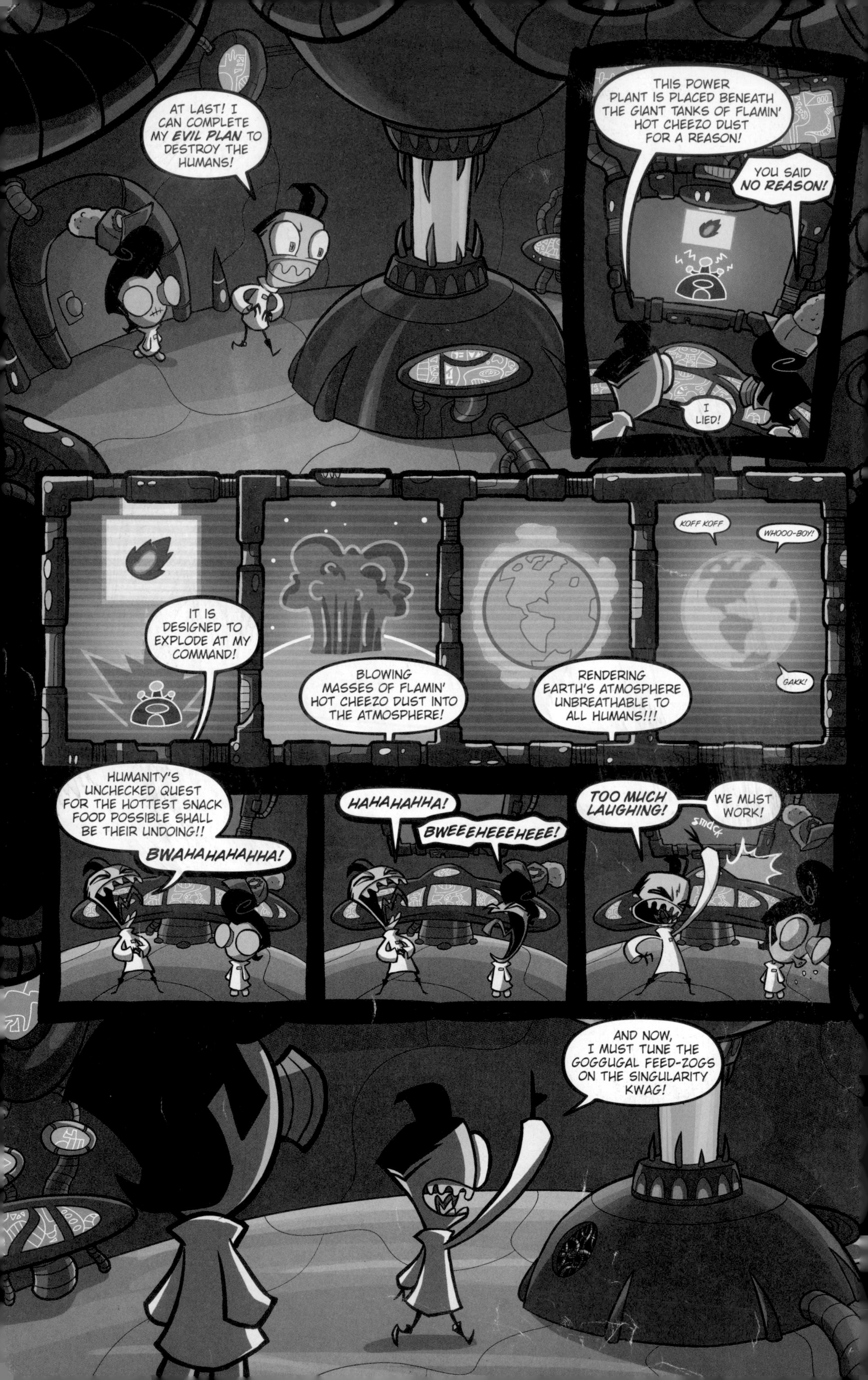

AT LAST! I CAN COMPLETE MY EVIL PLAN TO DESTROY THE HUMANS!
THIS POWER PLANT IS PLACED BENEATH THE GIANT TANKS OF FLAMIN' HOT CHEEZO DUST FOR A REASON!
YOU SAID NO REASON!
I LIED!
IT IS DESIGNED TO EXPLODE AT MY COMMAND!
BLOWING MASSES OF FLAMIN' HOT CHEEZO DUST INTO THE ATMOSPHERE!
RENDERING EARTH'S ATMOSPHERE UNBREATHABLE TO ALL HUMANS!!!
KOFF KOFF
WHOOO-BOY!
GAKK!
HUMANITY'S UNCHECKED QUEST FOR THE HOTTEST SNACK FOOD POSSIBLE SHALL BE THEIR UNDOING!!
BWAHAHAHAHHA!
HAHAHAHHA!
BWEEEHEEEHEEE!
TOO MUCH LAUGHING!
WE MUST WORK!
SMACK
AND NOW, I MUST TUNE THE GOGGUGAL FEED-ZOGS ON THE SINGULARITY KWAG!

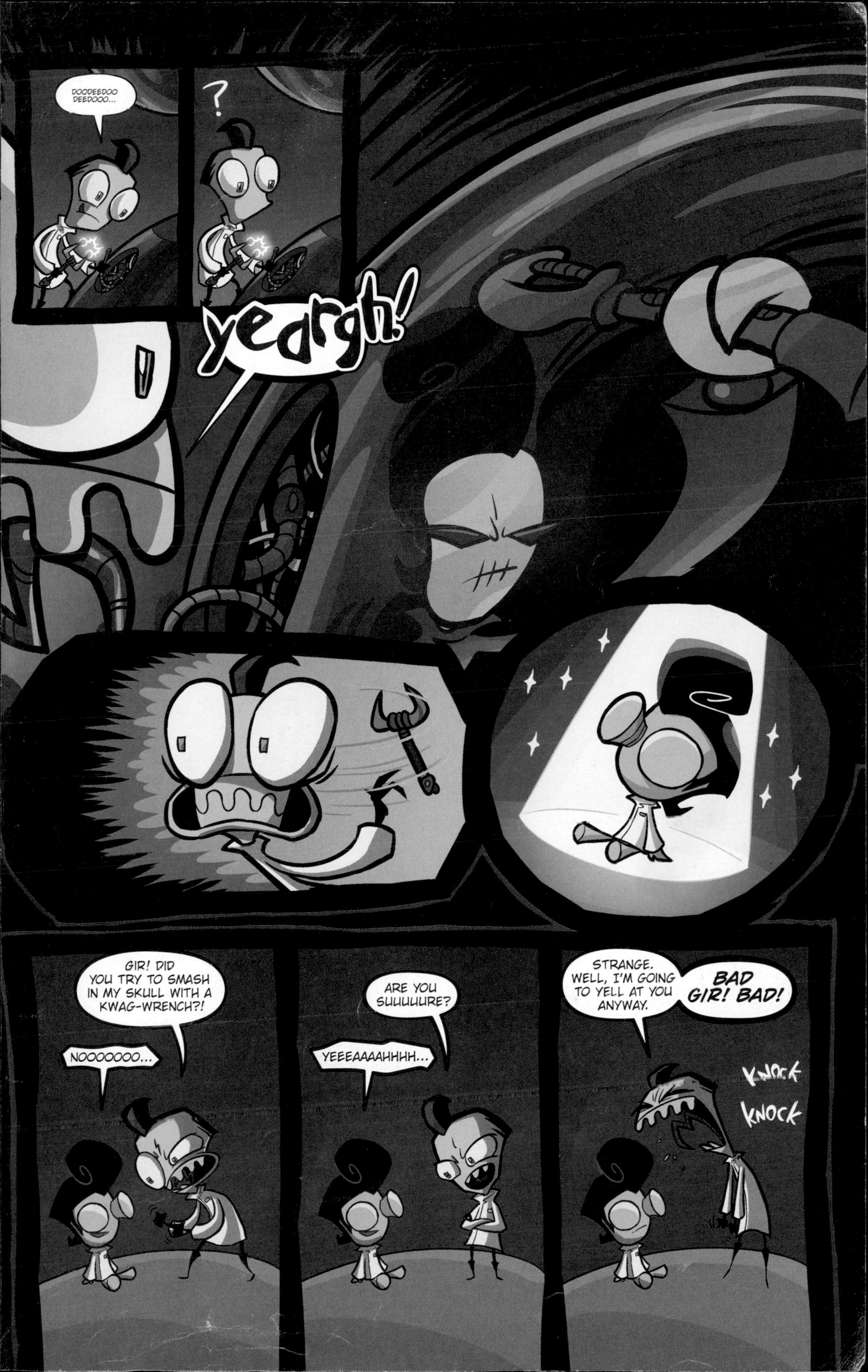
DOODEEDOO DEEDOOO...
?
yeargh!
GIR! DID YOU TRY TO SMASH IN MY SKULL WITH A KWAG-WRENCH?!
NOOOOOOO...
ARE YOU SUUUUURE?
YEEEAAAAHHHH...
STRANGE. WELL, I'M GOING TO YELL AT YOU ANYWAY.
BAD GIR! BAD!
KNOCK
KNOCK

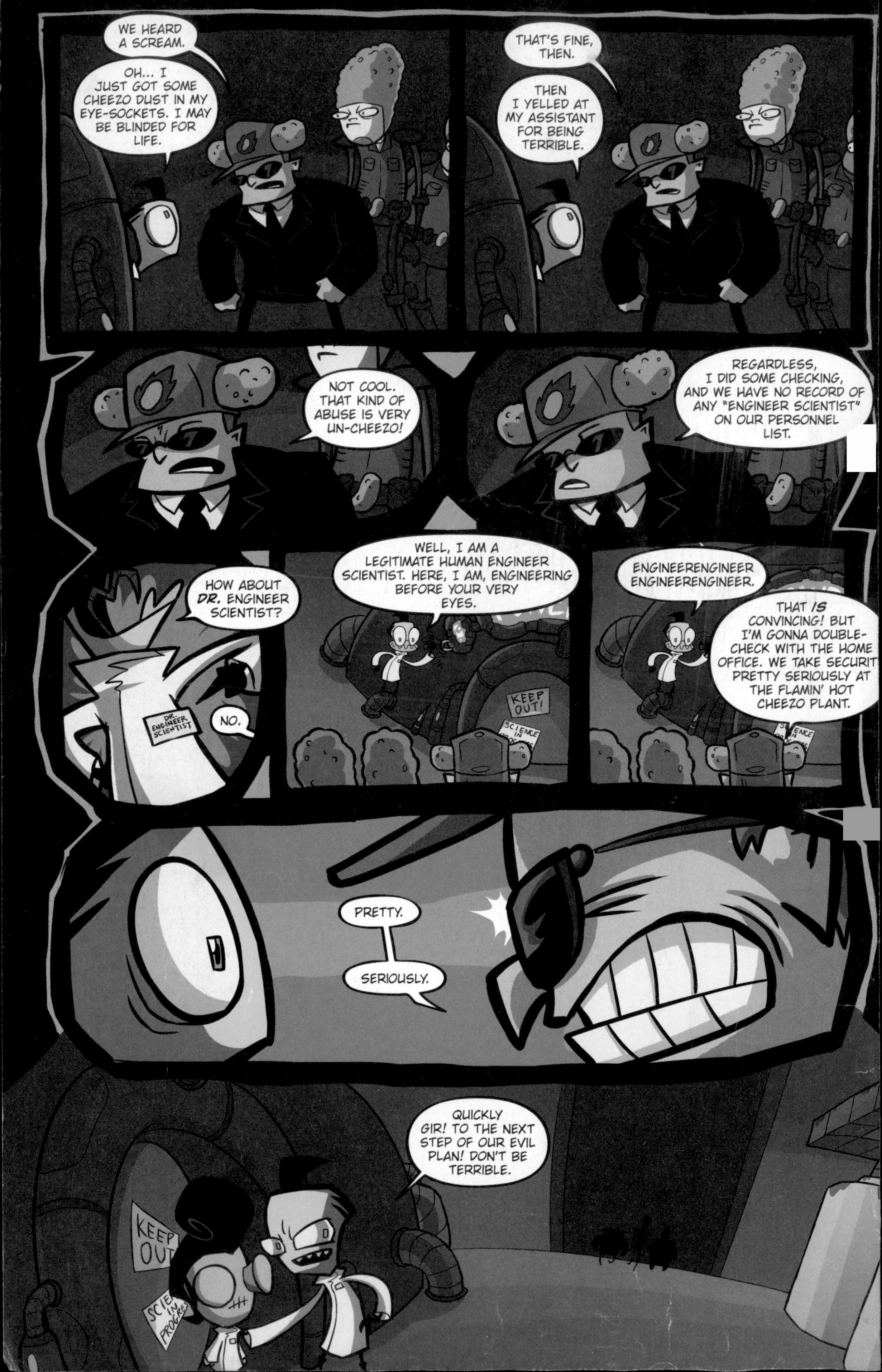
WE HEARD A SCREAM.
OH... I JUST GOT SOME CHEEZO DUST IN MY EYE-SOCKETS. I MAY BE BLINDED FOR LIFE.
THAT'S FINE, THEN.
THEN I YELLED AT MY ASSISTANT FOR BEING TERRIBLE.
NOT COOL. THAT KIND OF ABUSE IS VERY UN-CHEEZO!
REGARDLESS, I DID SOME CHECKING, AND WE HAVE NO RECORD OF ANY "ENGINEER SCIENTIST" ON OUR PERSONNEL LIST.
HOW ABOUT DR. ENGINEER SCIENTIST?
DR. ENGINEER SCIENTIST
NO.
WELL, I AM A LEGITIMATE HUMAN ENGINEER SCIENTIST. HERE, I AM, ENGINEERING BEFORE YOUR VERY EYES.
KEEP OUT!
ENGINEERENGINEER ENGINEERENGINEER.
THAT IS CONVINCING! BUT I'M GONNA DOUBLE-CHECK WITH THE HOME OFFICE. WE TAKE SECURIT PRETTY SERIOUSLY AT THE FLAMIN' HOT CHEEZO PLANT.
PRETTY.
SERIOUSLY.
QUICKLY GIR! TO THE NEXT STEP OF OUR EVIL PLAN! DON'T BE TERRIBLE.
KEEP OUT

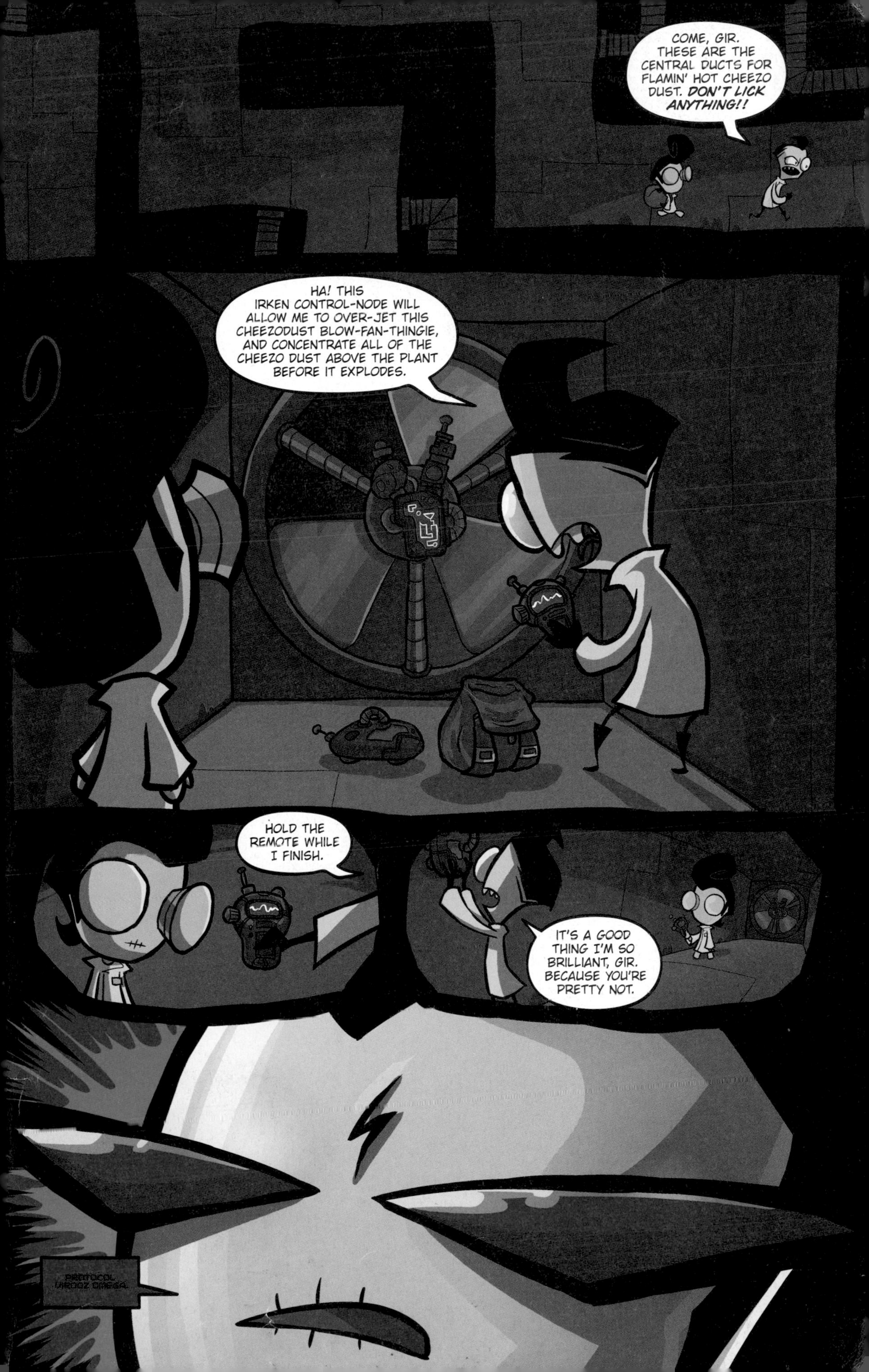
COME, GIR. THESE ARE THE CENTRAL DUCTS FOR FLAMIN' HOT CHEEZO DUST. ***DON'T LICK ANYTHING!!***
HA! THIS IRKEN CONTROL-NODE WILL ALLOW ME TO OVER-JET THIS CHEEZODUST BLOW-FAN-THINGIE, AND CONCENTRATE ALL OF THE CHEEZO DUST ABOVE THE PLANT BEFORE IT EXPLODES.
HOLD THE REMOTE WHILE I FINISH.
IT'S A GOOD THING I'M SO BRILLIANT, GIR. BECAUSE YOU'RE PRETTY NOT.

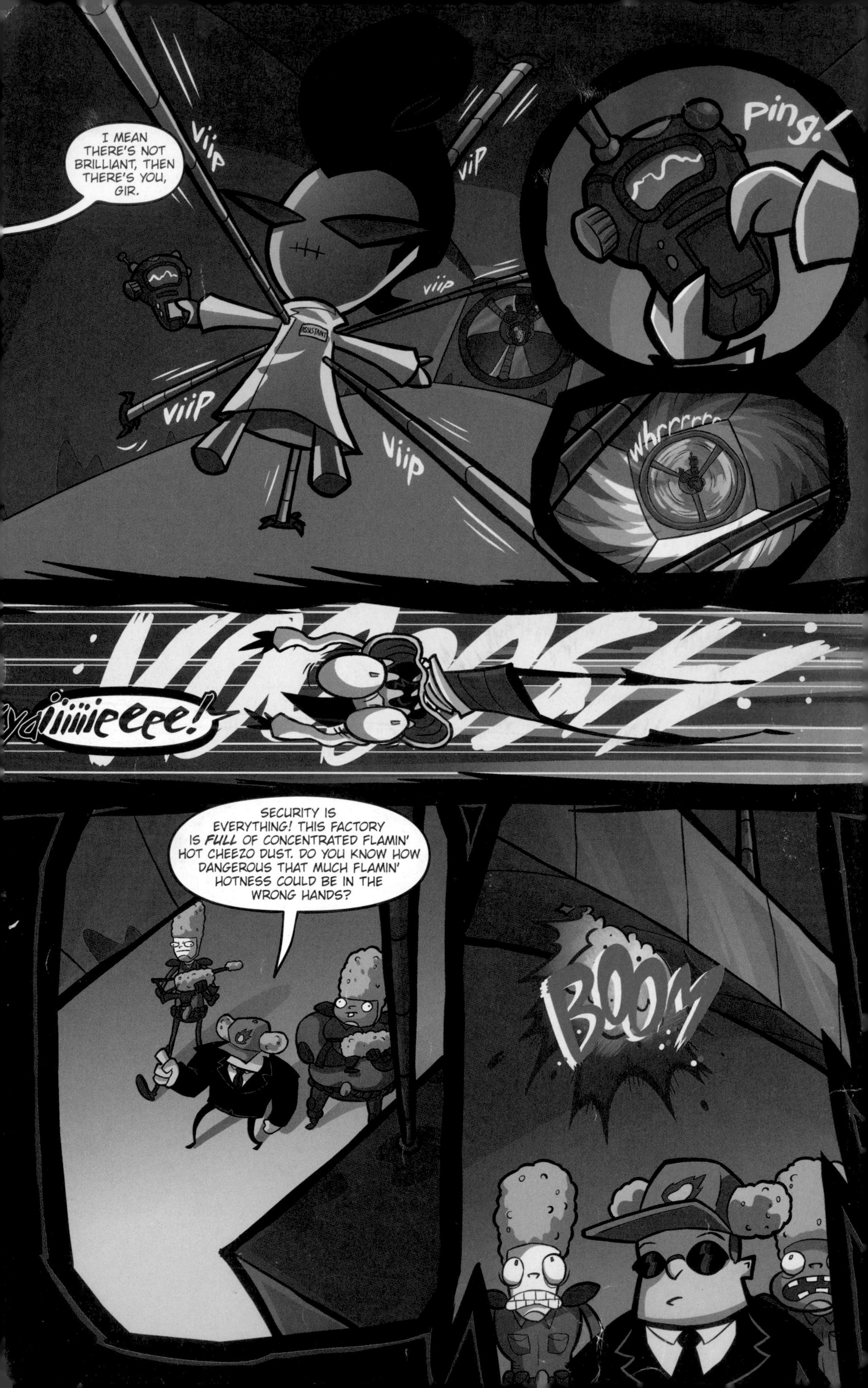
I MEAN THERE'S NOT BRILLIANT, THEN THERE'S YOU, GIR.
viip
viip
viip
viip
viip
Ping!
whrrrrrr
yaiiiiieeee!
SECURITY IS EVERYTHING! THIS FACTORY IS FULL OF CONCENTRATED FLAMIN' HOT CHEEZO DUST. DO YOU KNOW HOW DANGEROUS THAT MUCH FLAMIN' HOTNESS COULD BE IN THE WRONG HANDS?
BOOM

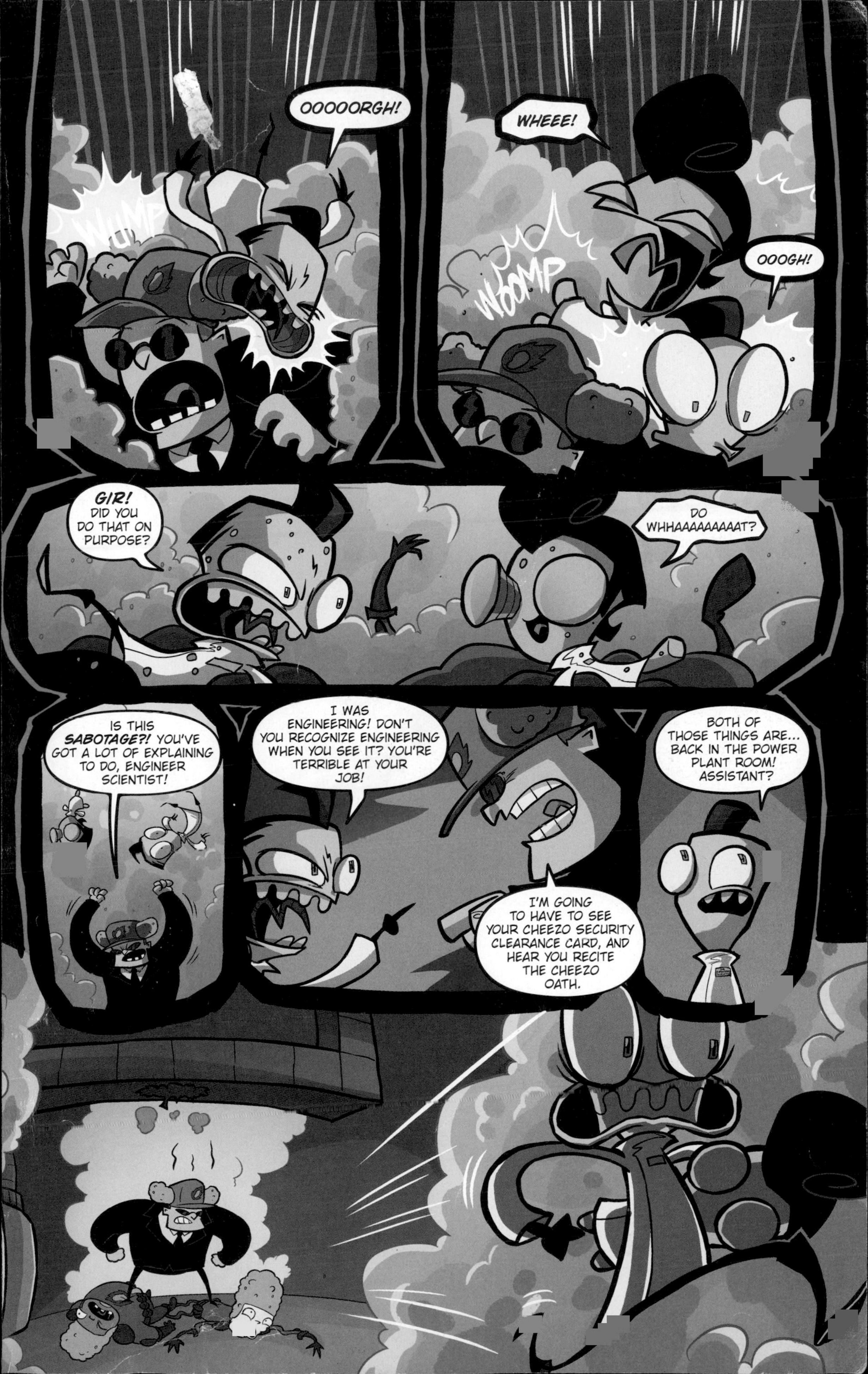

WUMP
OOOORGH!
WHEEE!
WOOMP
OOOGH!
GIR! DID YOU DO THAT ON PURPOSE?
DO WHHAAAAAAAAAT?
IS THIS SABOTAGE?! YOU'VE GOT A LOT OF EXPLAINING TO DO, ENGINEER SCIENTIST!
I WAS ENGINEERING! DON'T YOU RECOGNIZE ENGINEERING WHEN YOU SEE IT? YOU'RE TERRIBLE AT YOUR JOB!
I'M GOING TO HAVE TO SEE YOUR CHEEZO SECURITY CLEARANCE CARD, AND HEAR YOU RECITE THE CHEEZO OATH.
BOTH OF THOSE THINGS ARE... BACK IN THE POWER PLANT ROOM! ASSISTANT?

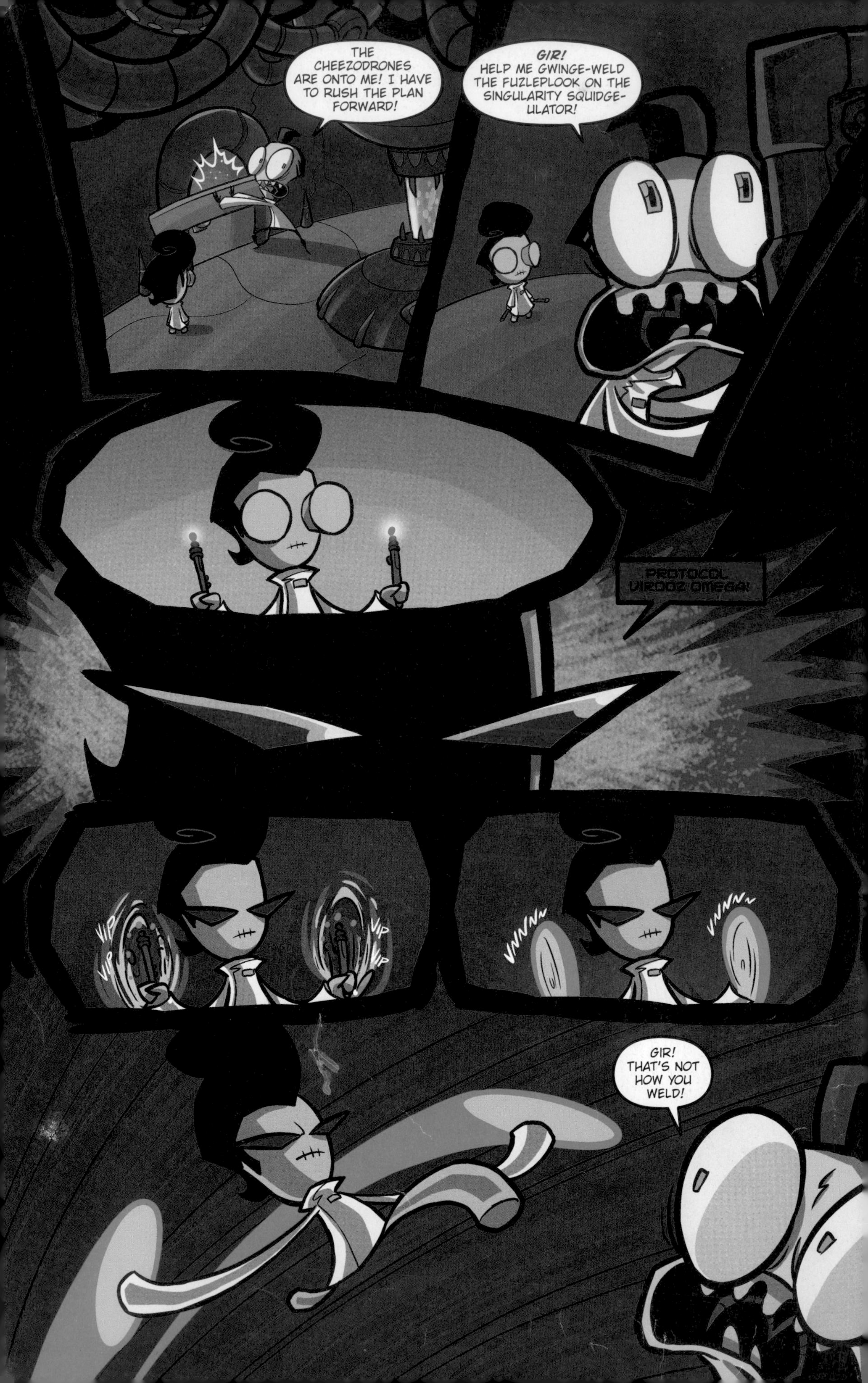
THE CHEEZODRONES ARE ONTO ME! I HAVE TO RUSH THE PLAN FORWARD!
GIR! HELP ME GWINGE-WELD THE FUZLEPLOOK ON THE SINGULARITY SQUIDGE-ULATOR!
PROTOCOL VIROOZ OMEGA!
VIP VIP VIP VIP
VNNNN VNNNN
GIR! THAT'S NOT HOW YOU WELD!

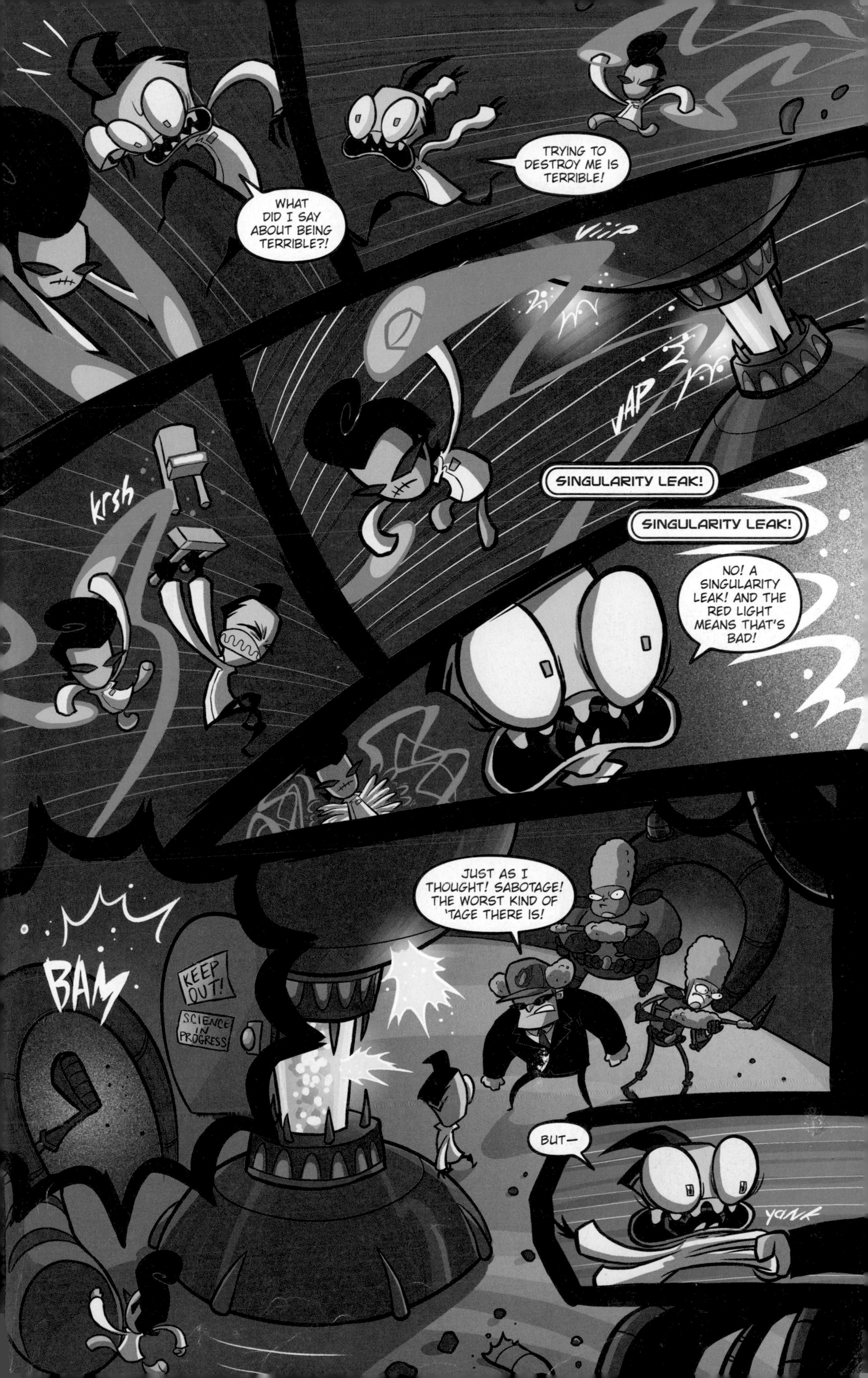
WHAT DID I SAY ABOUT BEING TERRIBLE?!
TRYING TO DESTROY ME IS TERRIBLE!
VIIP
krsh
VAP
SINGULARITY LEAK!
SINGULARITY LEAK!
NO! A SINGULARITY LEAK! AND THE RED LIGHT MEANS THAT'S BAD!
BAM
KEEP OUT!
SCIENCE IN PROGRESS
JUST AS I THOUGHT! SABOTAGE! THE WORST KIND OF 'TAGE THERE IS!
BUT—
yank

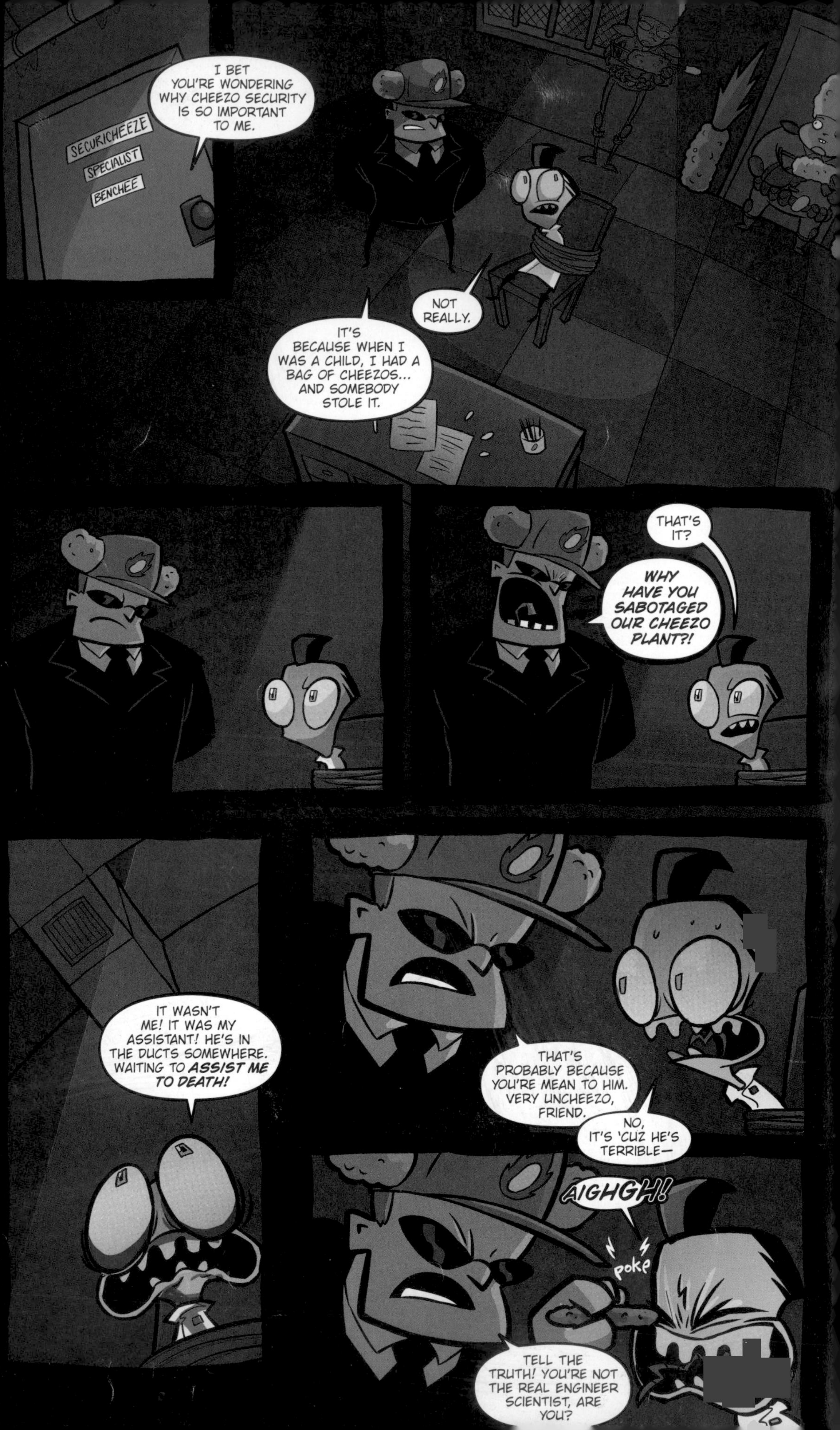

SECURICHEEZE
SPECIALIST
BENCHEE
I BET YOU'RE WONDERING WHY CHEEZO SECURITY IS SO IMPORTANT TO ME.
NOT REALLY.
IT'S BECAUSE WHEN I WAS A CHILD, I HAD A BAG OF CHEEZOS... AND SOMEBODY STOLE IT.
THAT'S IT?
WHY HAVE YOU SABOTAGED OUR CHEEZO PLANT?!
IT WASN'T ME! IT WAS MY ASSISTANT! HE'S IN THE DUCTS SOMEWHERE. WAITING TO ASSIST ME TO DEATH!
THAT'S PROBABLY BECAUSE YOU'RE MEAN TO HIM. VERY UNCHEEZO, FRIEND.
NO, IT'S 'CUZ HE'S TERRIBLE—
AIGHGH!
poke
TELL THE TRUTH! YOU'RE NOT THE REAL ENGINEER SCIENTIST, ARE YOU?

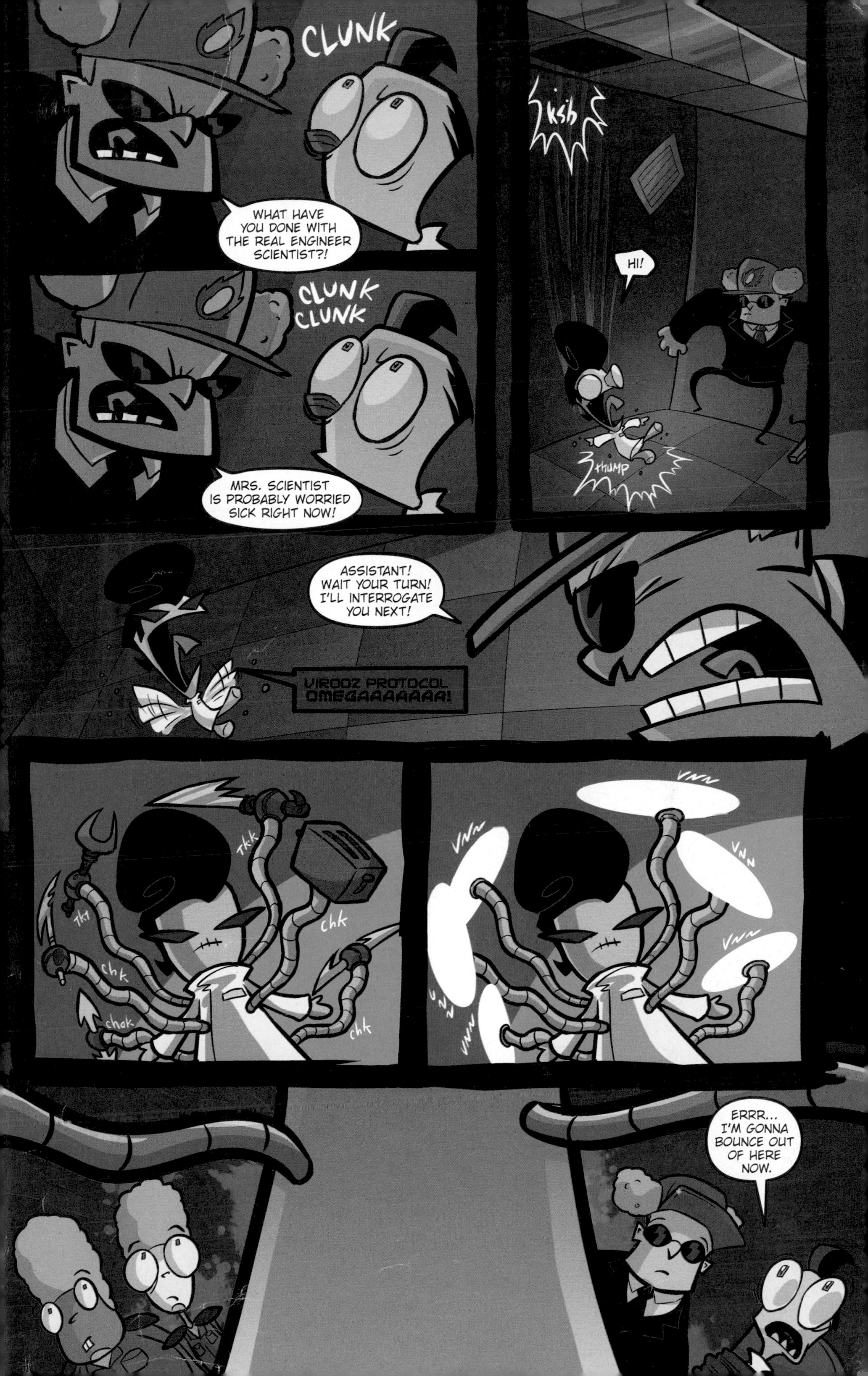
CLUNK
WHAT HAVE YOU DONE WITH THE REAL ENGINEER SCIENTIST?!
ksh
CLUNK CLUNK
MRS. SCIENTIST IS PROBABLY WORRIED SICK RIGHT NOW!
HI!
thump
ASSISTANT! WAIT YOUR TURN! I'LL INTERROGATE YOU NEXT!
VIROOZ PROTOCOL OMEGAAAAAAA!
tkk
tkt
chk
chk
chak
chk
VNN
VNN
VNN
VNN
VNN
VNN
ERRR... I'M GONNA BOUNCE OUT OF HERE NOW.

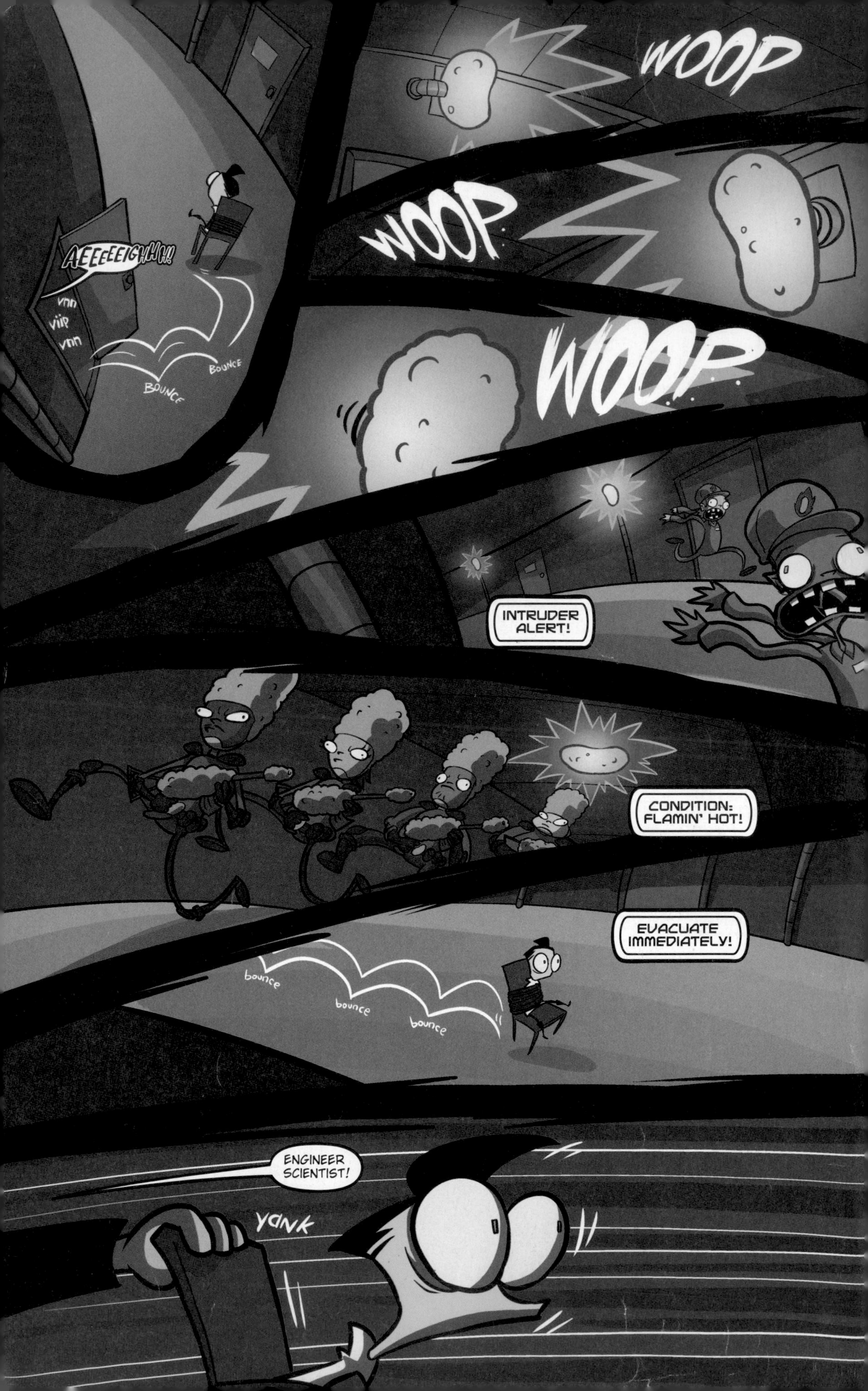

AEEEEEIGHHH!!
vnn
viip
vnn
BOUNCE
BOUNCE
WOOP
WOOP
WOOP
INTRUDER ALERT!
CONDITION: FLAMIN' HOT!
EVACUATE IMMEDIATELY!
bounce
bounce
bounce
ENGINEER SCIENTIST!
YANK

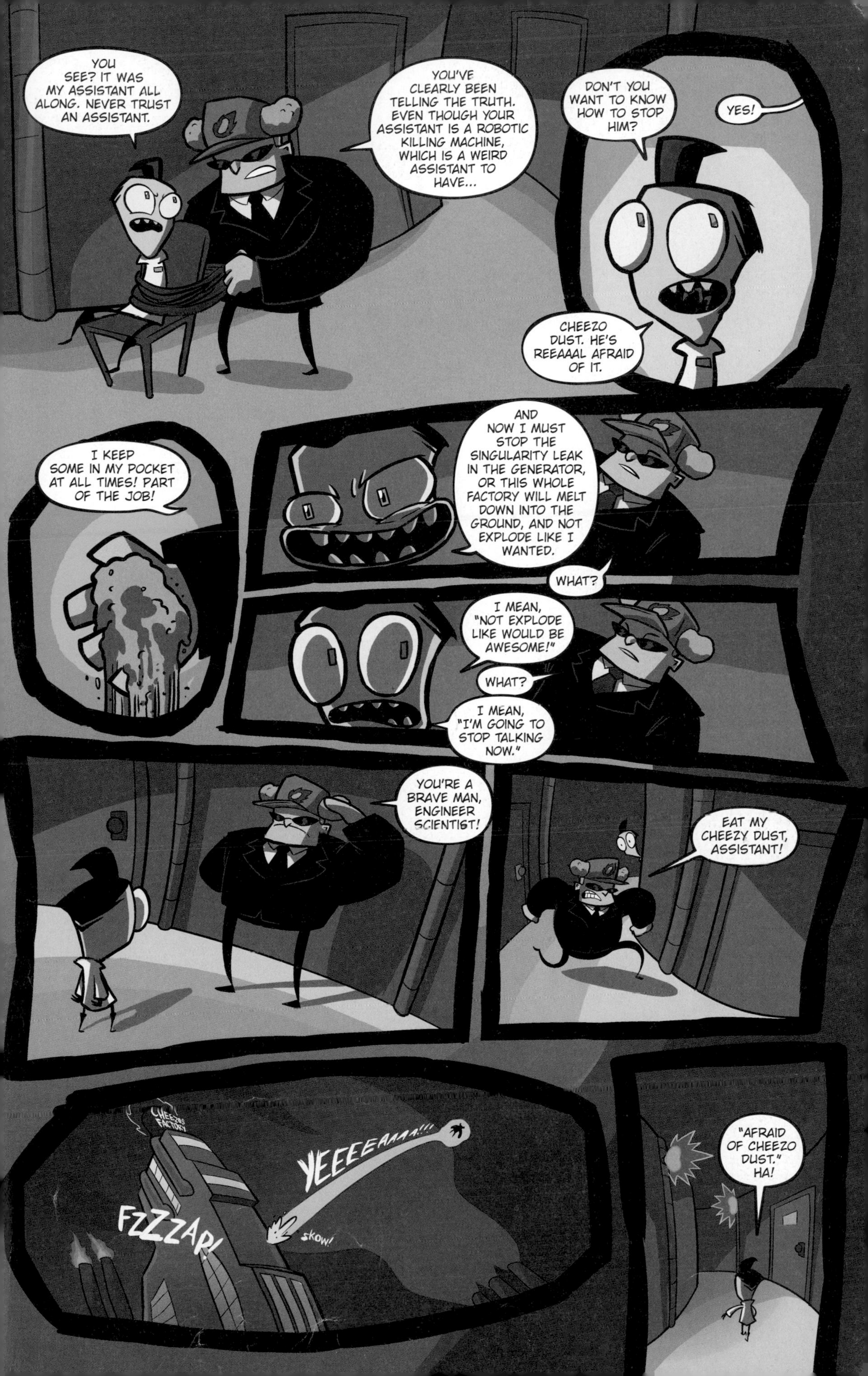
YOU SEE? IT WAS MY ASSISTANT ALL ALONG. NEVER TRUST AN ASSISTANT.
YOU'VE CLEARLY BEEN TELLING THE TRUTH. EVEN THOUGH YOUR ASSISTANT IS A ROBOTIC KILLING MACHINE, WHICH IS A WEIRD ASSISTANT TO HAVE...
DON'T YOU WANT TO KNOW HOW TO STOP HIM?
YES!
CHEEZO DUST. HE'S REEAAAL AFRAID OF IT.
I KEEP SOME IN MY POCKET AT ALL TIMES! PART OF THE JOB!
AND NOW I MUST STOP THE SINGULARITY LEAK IN THE GENERATOR, OR THIS WHOLE FACTORY WILL MELT DOWN INTO THE GROUND, AND NOT EXPLODE LIKE I WANTED.
WHAT?
I MEAN, "NOT EXPLODE LIKE WOULD BE AWESOME!"
WHAT?
I MEAN, "I'M GOING TO STOP TALKING NOW."
YOU'RE A BRAVE MAN, ENGINEER SCIENTIST!
EAT MY CHEEZY DUST, ASSISTANT!
YEEEEAAAAA!!!
FZZZAP!
SKOW!
"AFRAID OF CHEEZO DUST." HA!

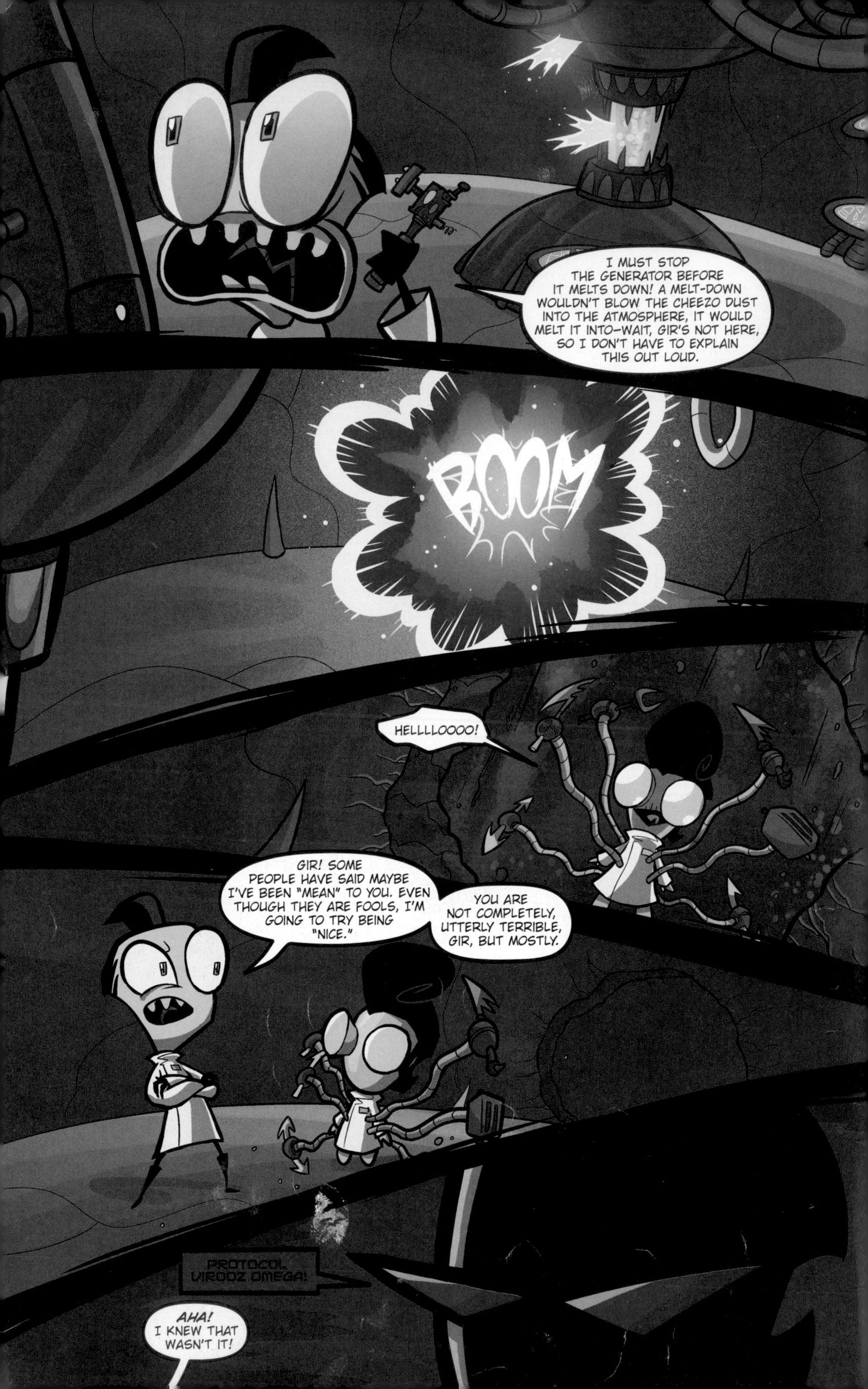
I MUST STOP THE GENERATOR BEFORE IT MELTS DOWN! A MELT-DOWN WOULDN'T BLOW THE CHEEZO DUST INTO THE ATMOSPHERE, IT WOULD MELT IT INTO—WAIT, GIR'S NOT HERE, SO I DON'T HAVE TO EXPLAIN THIS OUT LOUD.
BOOM
HELLLLOOOO!
GIR! SOME PEOPLE HAVE SAID MAYBE I'VE BEEN "MEAN" TO YOU. EVEN THOUGH THEY ARE FOOLS, I'M GOING TO TRY BEING "NICE."
YOU ARE NOT COMPLETELY, UTTERLY TERRIBLE, GIR, BUT MOSTLY.
PROTOCOL VIROOZ OMEGA!
AHA! I KNEW THAT WASN'T IT!

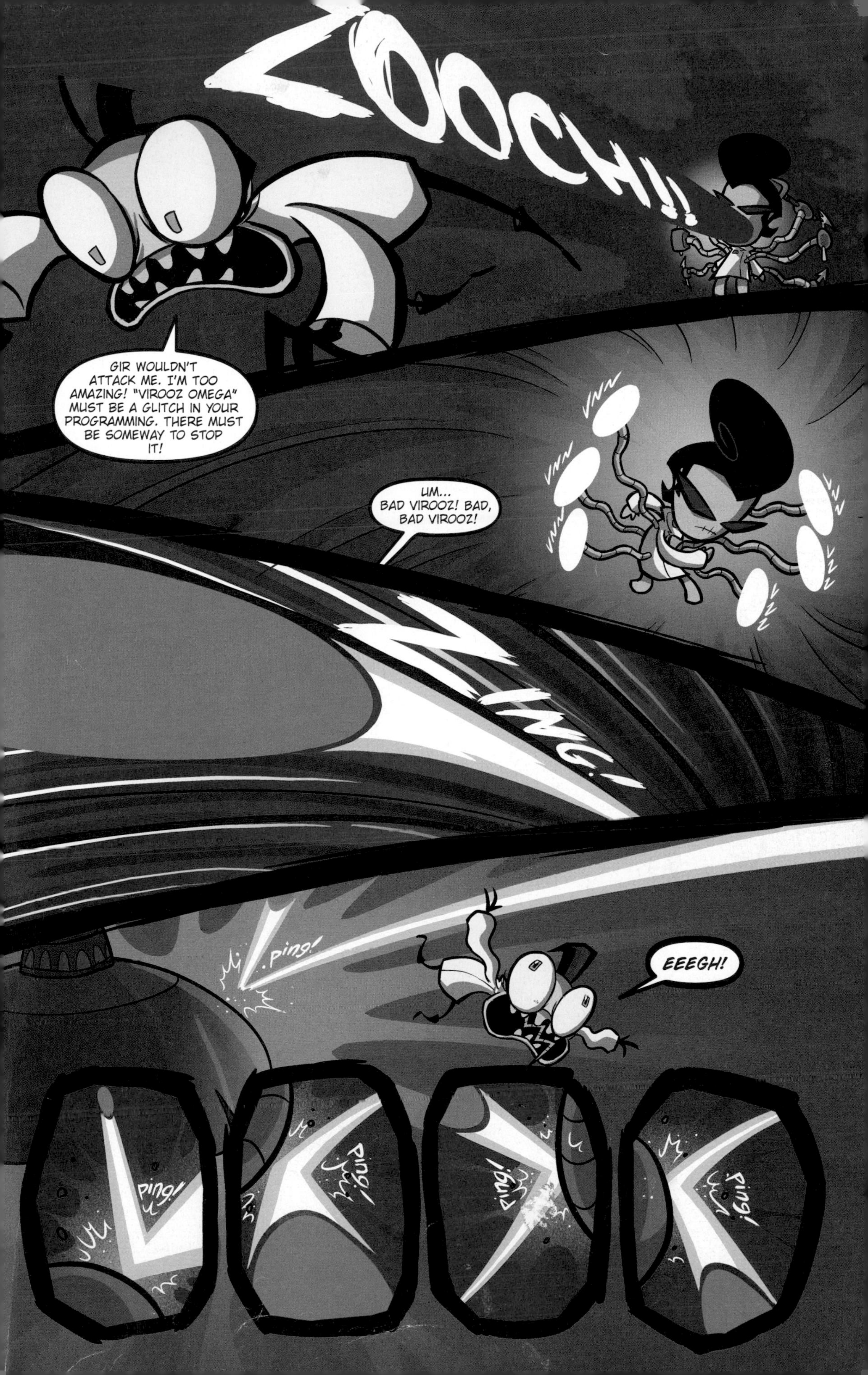
ZOOOCH!!
GIR WOULDN'T ATTACK ME. I'M TOO AMAZING! "VIROOZ OMEGA" MUST BE A GLITCH IN YOUR PROGRAMMING. THERE MUST BE SOMEWAY TO STOP IT!
VNN
VNN
VNN
UM... BAD VIROOZ! BAD, BAD VIROOZ!
ZING!
ping!
EEEGH!
ping!
ping!
ping!
ping!

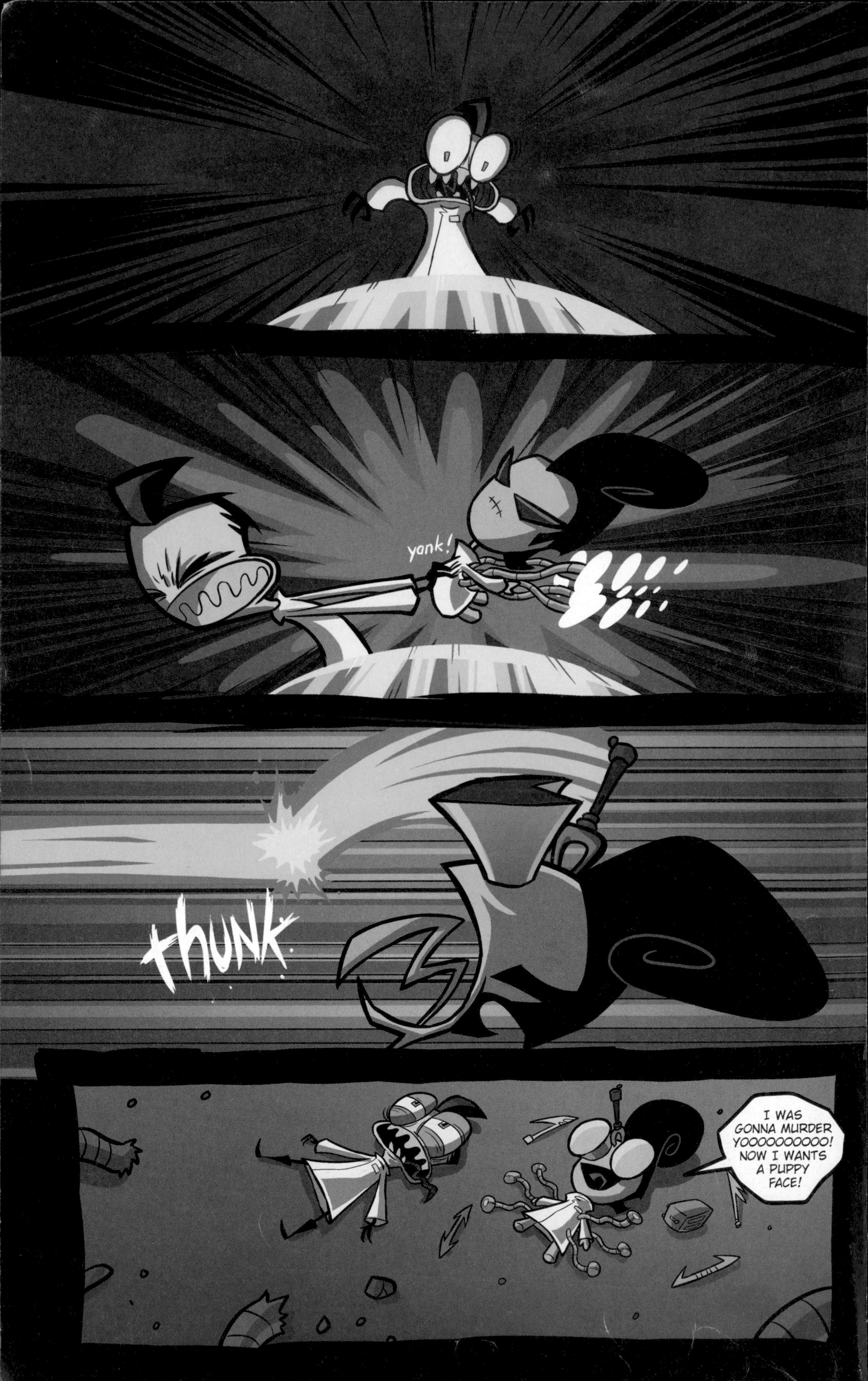
yank!
thunk
I WAS GONNA MURDER YOOOOOOOOOO! NOW I WANTS A PUPPY FACE!

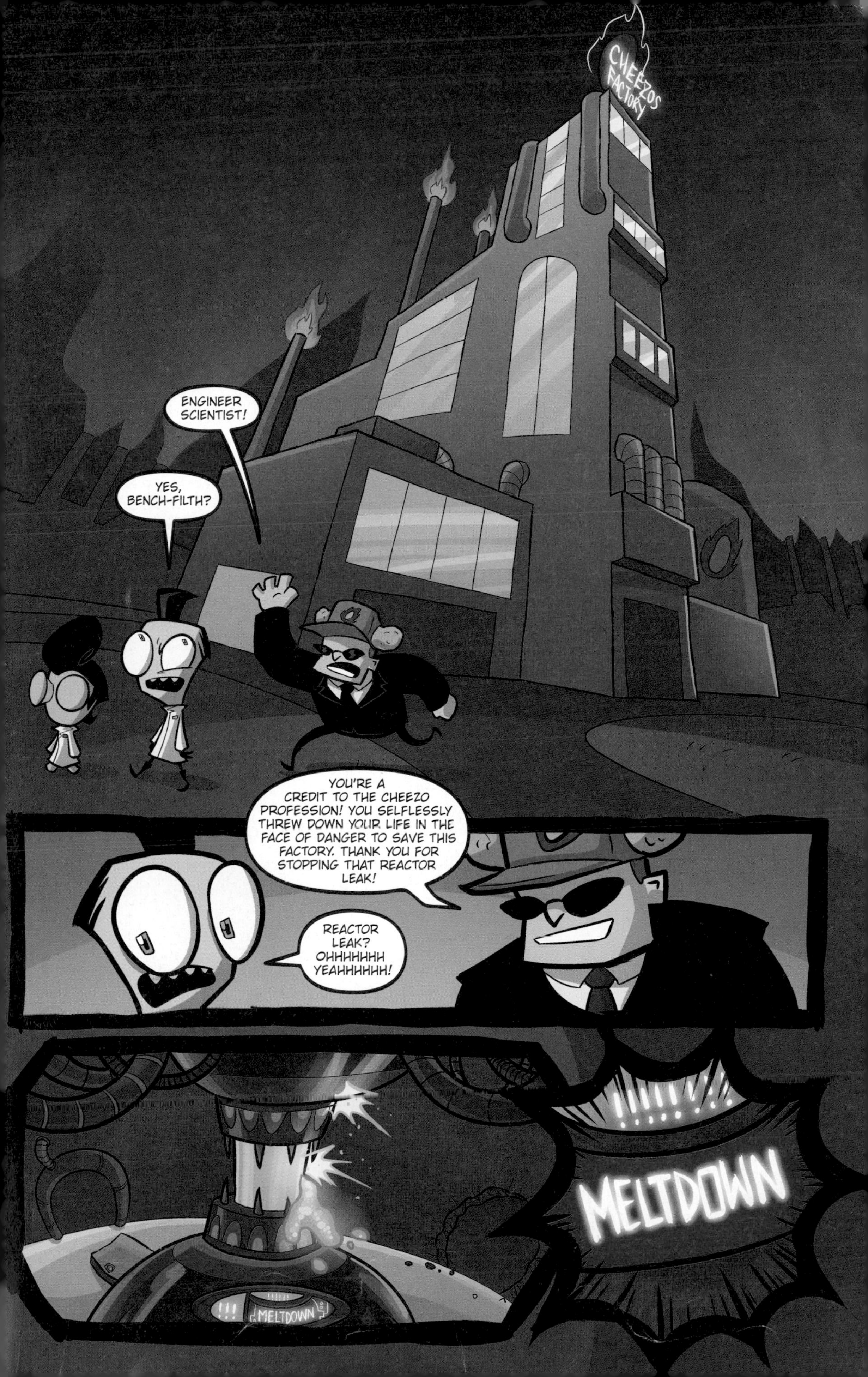
CHEEZOS FACTORY
ENGINEER SCIENTIST!
YES, BENCH-FILTH?
YOU'RE A CREDIT TO THE CHEEZO PROFESSION! YOU SELFLESSLY THREW DOWN YOUR LIFE IN THE FACE OF DANGER TO SAVE THIS FACTORY. THANK YOU FOR STOPPING THAT REACTOR LEAK!
REACTOR LEAK? OHHHHHHH YEAHHHHHH!
!!!!!!!!!
MELTDOWN
!!! MELTDOWN

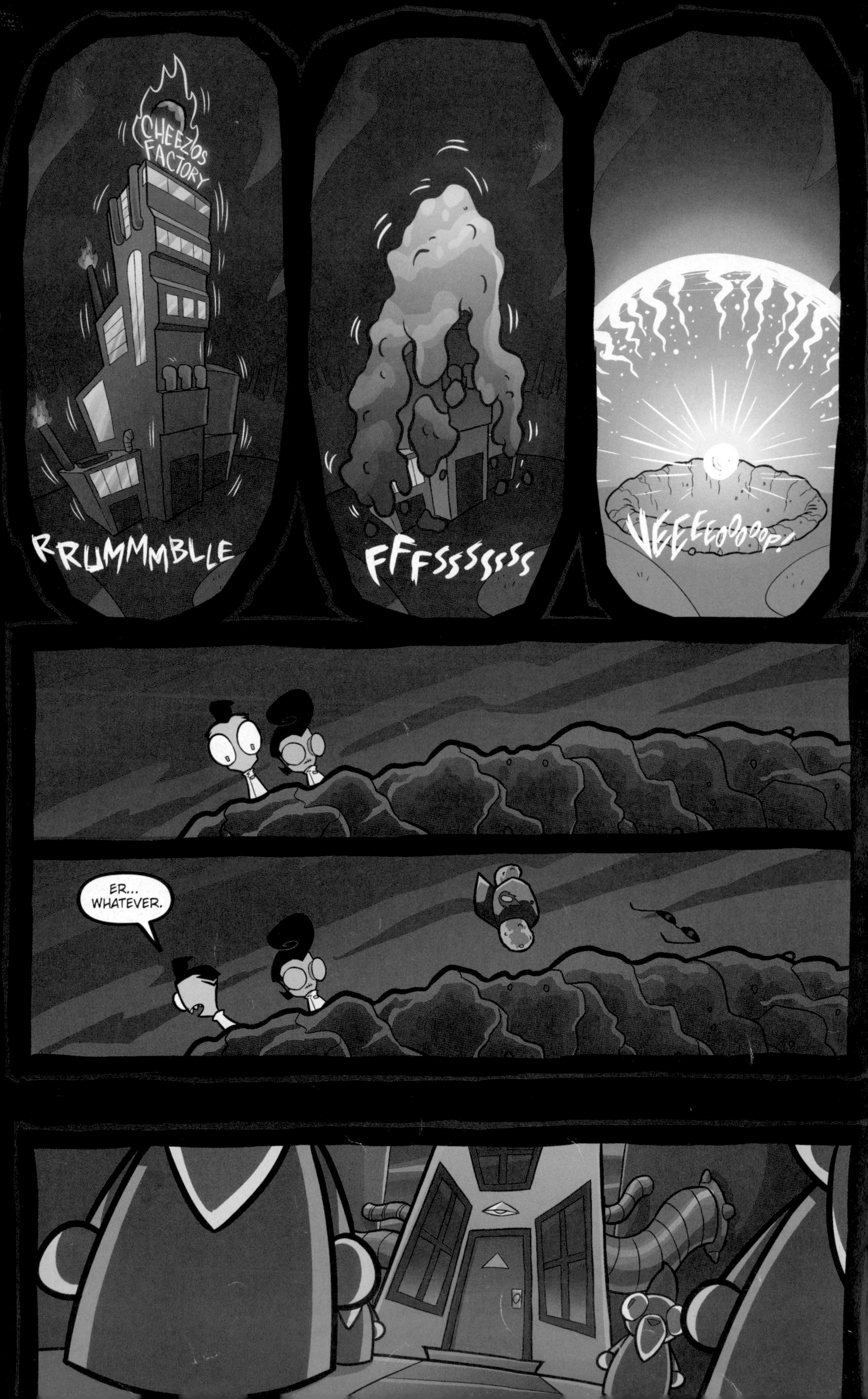
CHEEZOS FACTORY
RRUMMMBLLE
FFFSSSSSSS
VEEEEOOOOOP!
ER... WHATEVER.

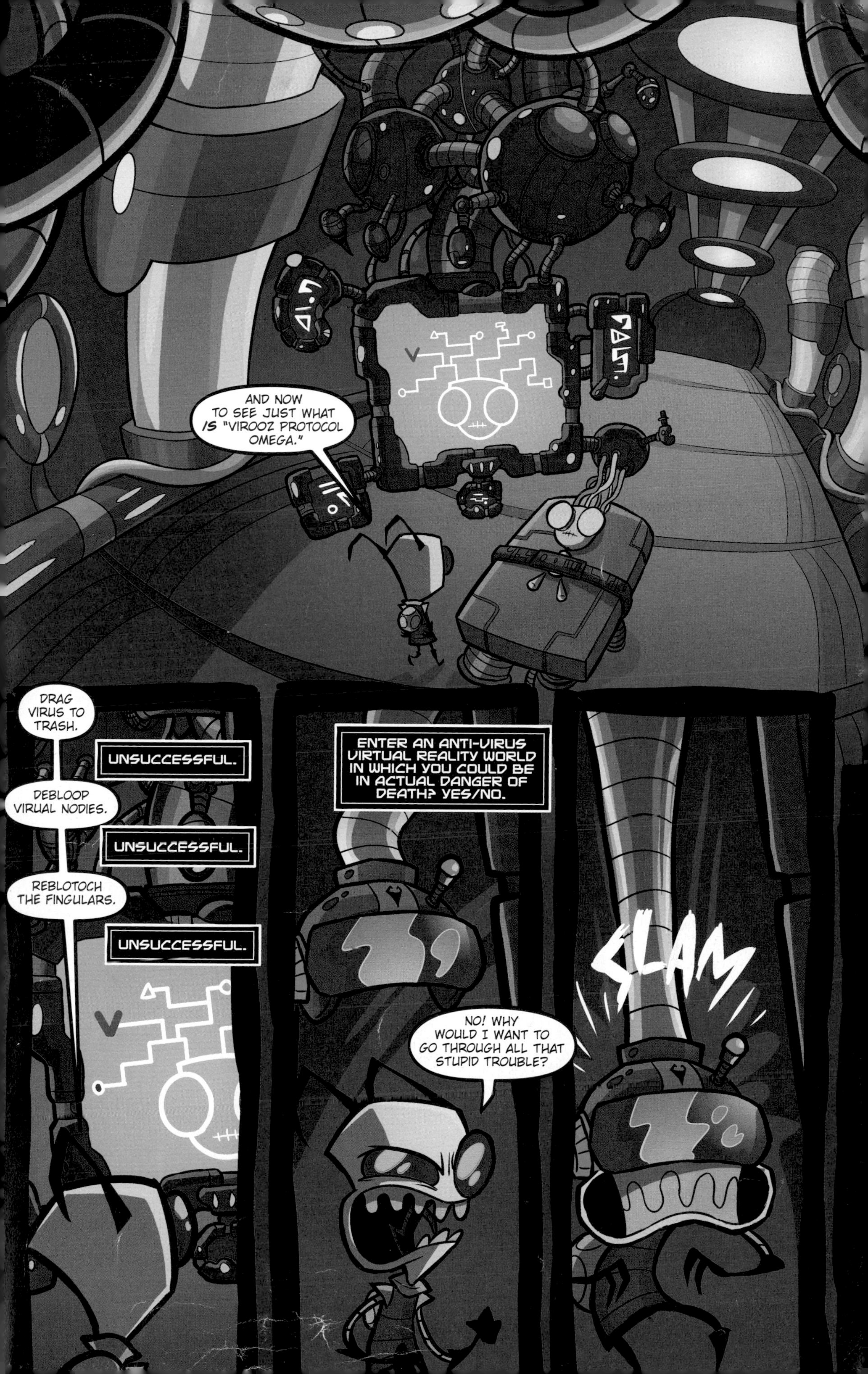
AND NOW TO SEE JUST WHAT IS "VIROOZ PROTOCOL OMEGA."
DRAG VIRUS TO TRASH.
UNSUCCESSFUL.
DEBLOOP VIRUAL NODIES.
UNSUCCESSFUL.
REBLOTOCH THE FINGULARS.
UNSUCCESSFUL.
ENTER AN ANTI-VIRUS VIRTUAL REALITY WORLD IN WHICH YOU COULD BE IN ACTUAL DANGER OF DEATH? YES/NO.
NO! WHY WOULD I WANT TO GO THROUGH ALL THAT STUPID TROUBLE?
SLAM

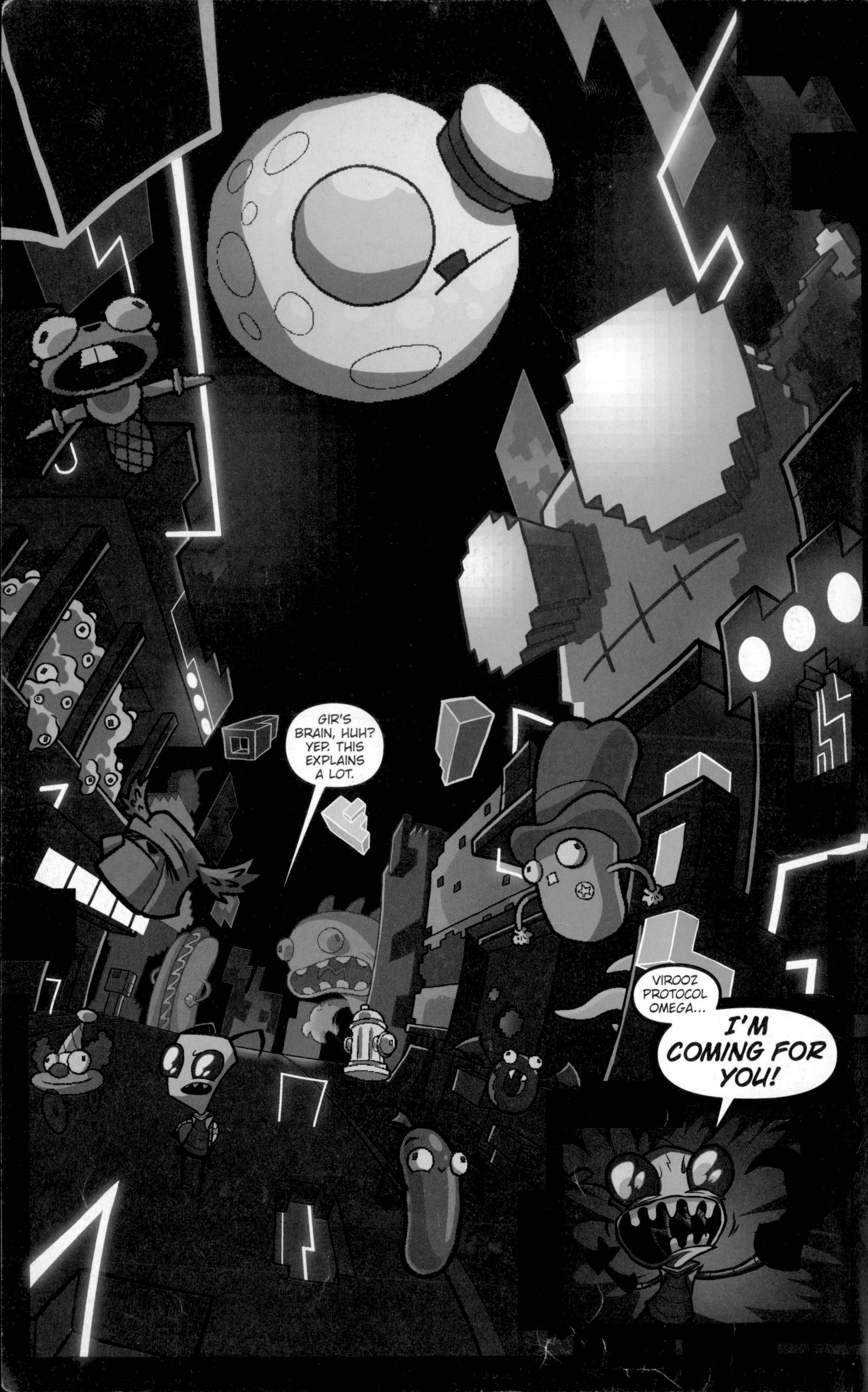
GIR'S BRAIN, HUH? YEP. THIS EXPLAINS A LOT.
VIROOZ PROTOCOL OMEGA...
I'M COMING FOR YOU!

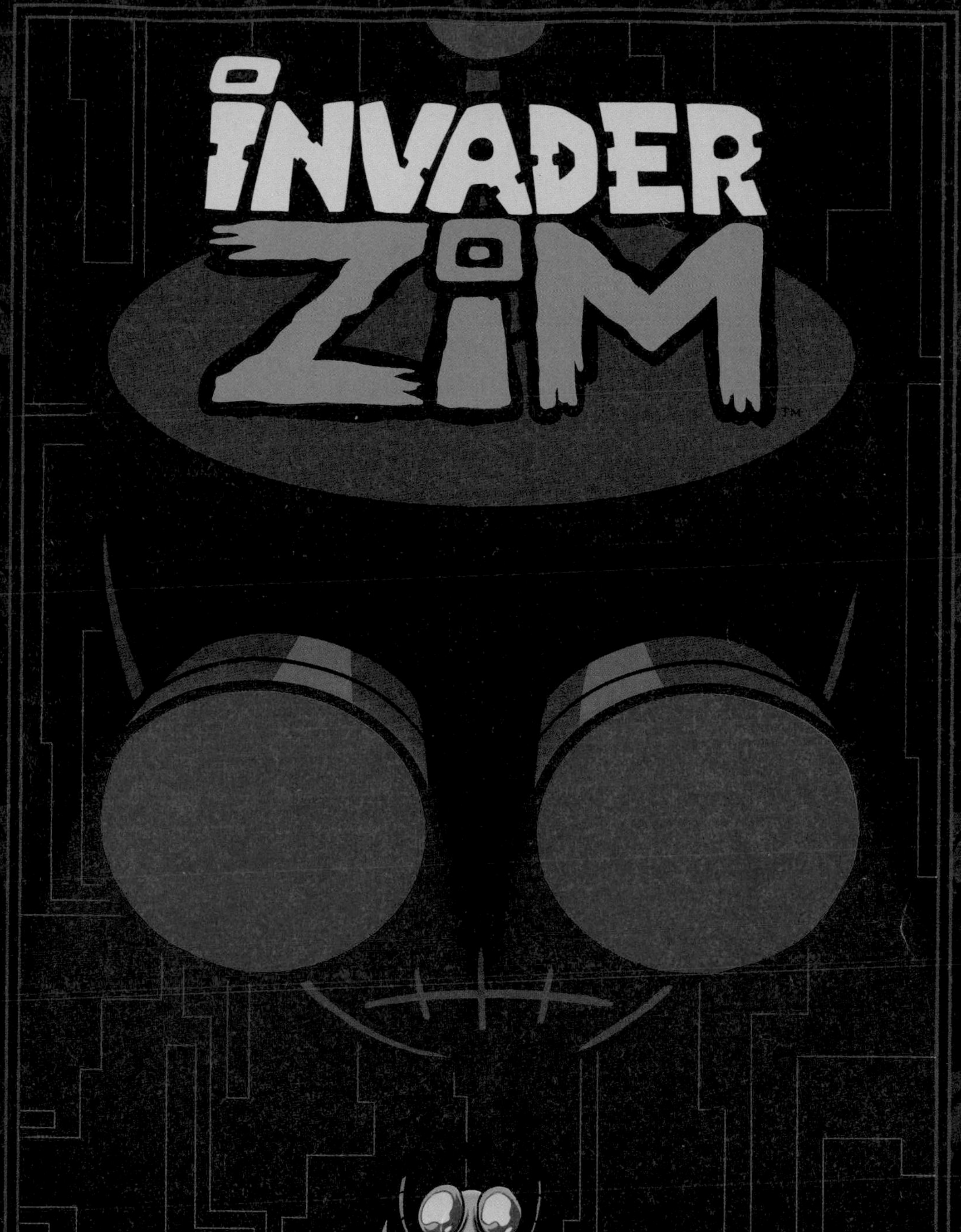
INVADER ZIM

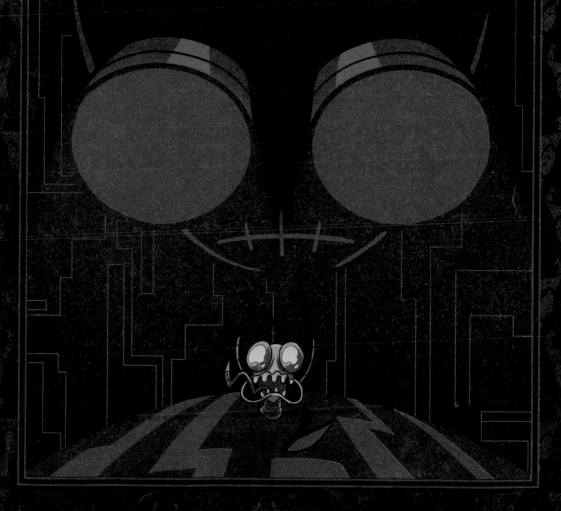

CHAPTER: 2

**The Arc of VIROOZ Part Two:
The Spark of VIROOZ**

illustration by **Warren Wucinich**

WOW, okay, Recap Kid here again, back in action!!! Are you ready to read some ZIM COMICS? I KNOW I AM! Every time the NEW issue comes out I read all the OLD issues TEN TIMES. ELEVEN, SOMETIMES. And now we're in PART TWO of this HUGE BIG GIANT ZIM STORY! Last time, GIR went WHAOOOAOOO NUTS and tried to KILL ZIM!!! And if you watch the show you know that's a BIG FAT NO!!!! GIR WOULD NEVER DO THAT! SO something was WRONG WITH GIR!!! Something like GIR HAS A VIRUS!!!! AAHAHHHHhbhbhbhbh well in THIS ONE ZIM's gonna GET RID of that VIRUS! BY GOING IN GIR'S HEAD!! AHHhbhbhbhHHHbhb WHAT'S GONNA HAPPEN? I ALREADY KNOW BUT I'M GONNA READ IT AGAIN, OKAY? BYEEEeeeee!

Recap Kid by WARREN WUCINICH

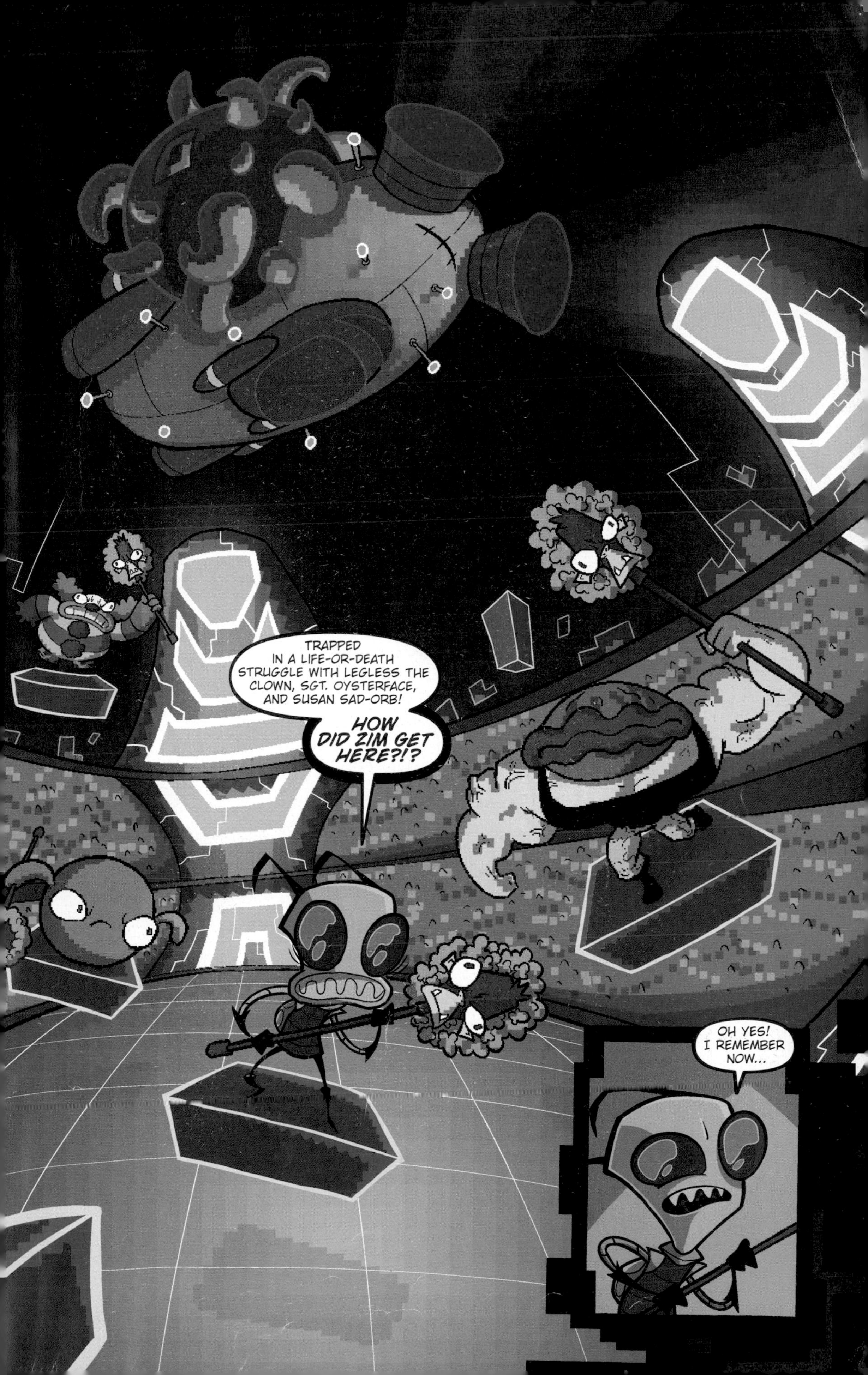
TRAPPED IN A LIFE-OR-DEATH STRUGGLE WITH LEGLESS THE CLOWN, SGT. OYSTERFACE, AND SUSAN SAD-ORB!
HOW DID ZIM GET HERE?!?
OH YES! I REMEMBER NOW...

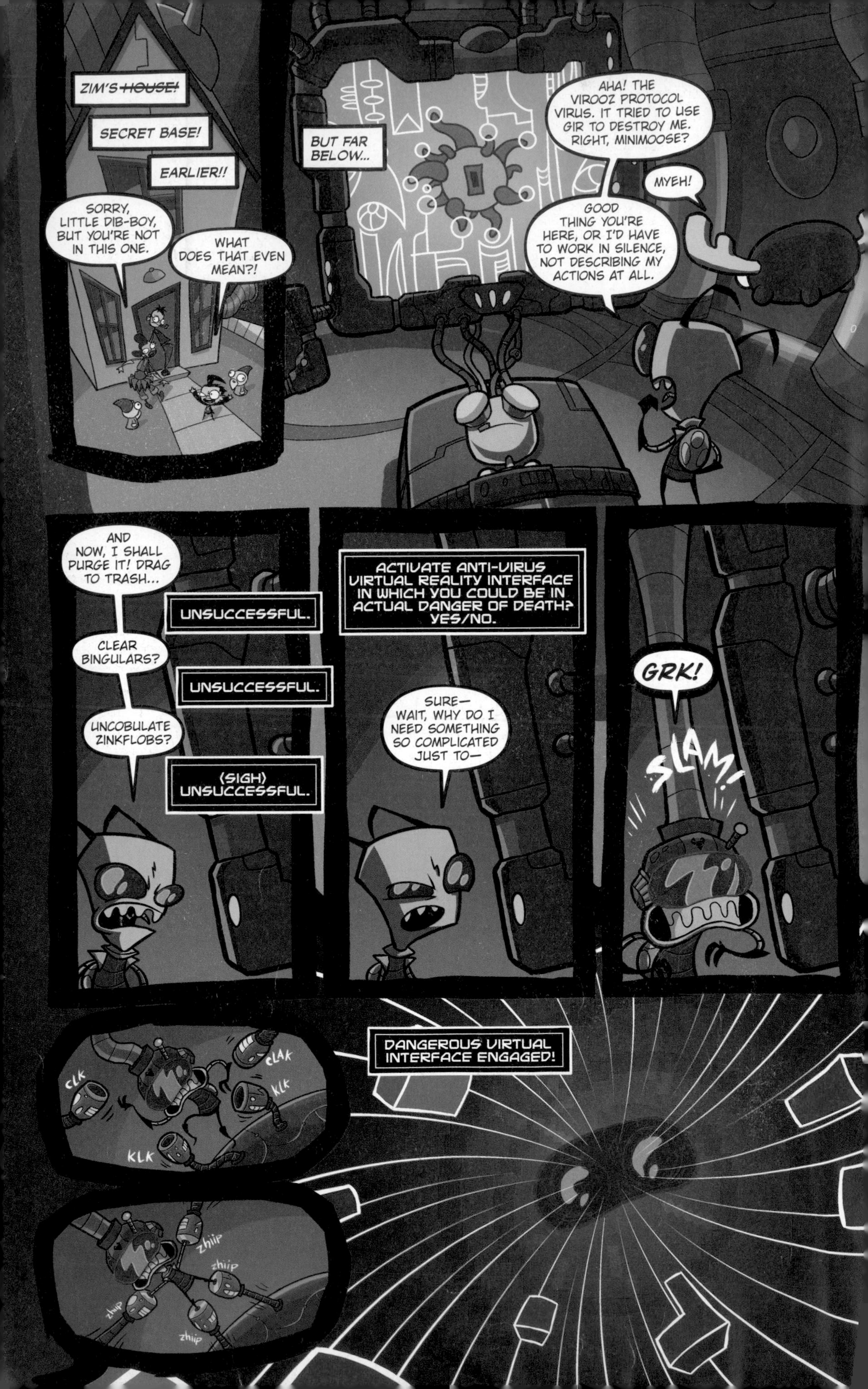
ZIM'S ~~HOUSE!~~
SECRET BASE!
EARLIER!!
SORRY, LITTLE DIB-BOY, BUT YOU'RE NOT IN THIS ONE.
WHAT DOES THAT EVEN MEAN?!
BUT FAR BELOW...
AHA! THE VIROOZ PROTOCOL VIRUS. IT TRIED TO USE GIR TO DESTROY ME. RIGHT, MINIMOOSE?
MYEH!
GOOD THING YOU'RE HERE, OR I'D HAVE TO WORK IN SILENCE, NOT DESCRIBING MY ACTIONS AT ALL.
AND NOW, I SHALL PURGE IT! DRAG TO TRASH...
UNSUCCESSFUL.
CLEAR BINGULARS?
UNSUCCESSFUL.
UNCOBULATE ZINKFLOBS?
(SIGH) UNSUCCESSFUL.
ACTIVATE ANTI-VIRUS VIRTUAL REALITY INTERFACE IN WHICH YOU COULD BE IN ACTUAL DANGER OF DEATH? YES/NO.
SURE— WAIT, WHY DO I NEED SOMETHING SO COMPLICATED JUST TO—
GRK!
SLAM!
CLK
CLAK
KLK
KLK
DANGEROUS VIRTUAL INTERFACE ENGAGED!
zhiip
zhiip
zhiip
zhiip

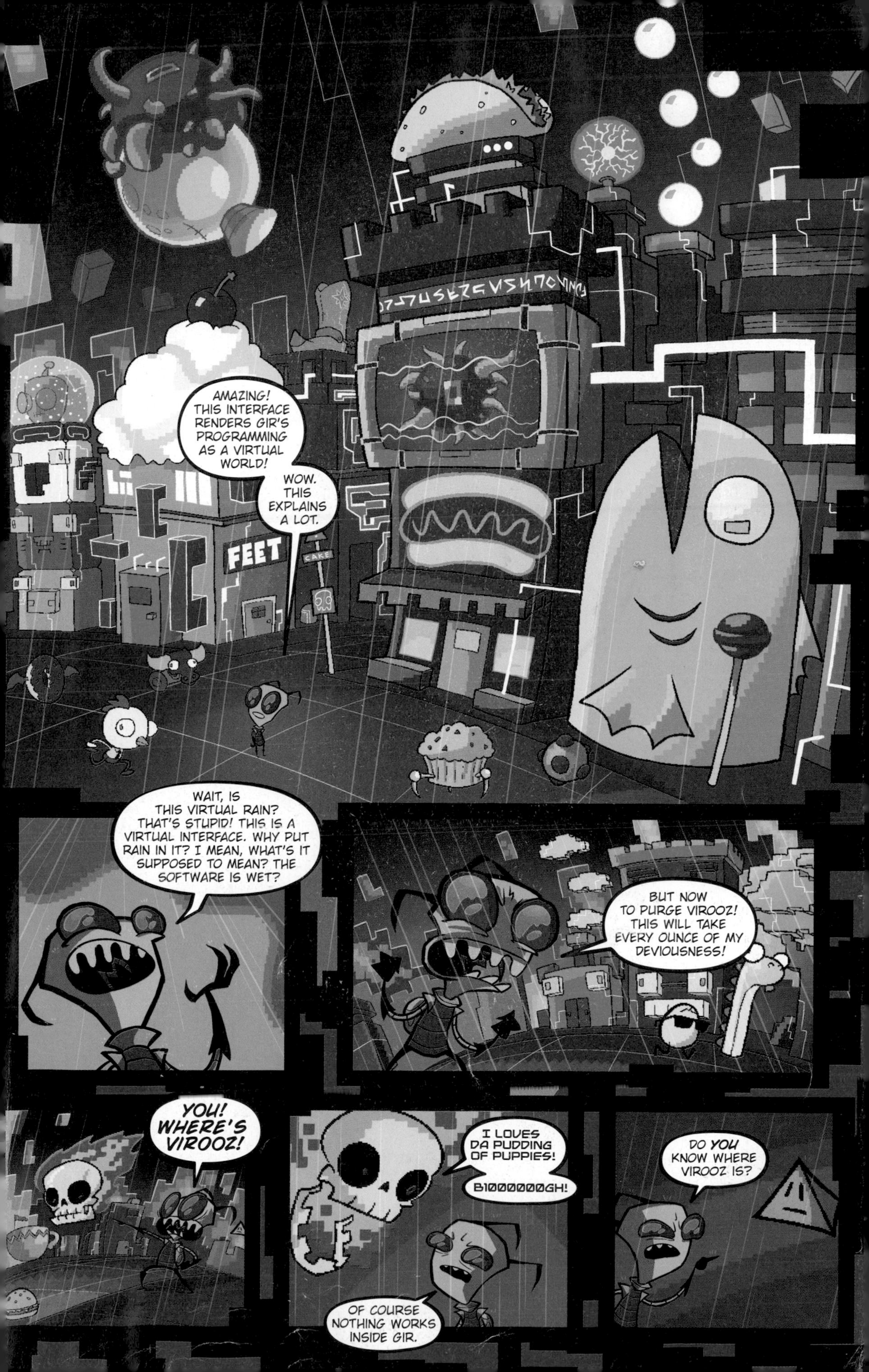
AMAZING! THIS INTERFACE RENDERS GIR'S PROGRAMMING AS A VIRTUAL WORLD!
WOW. THIS EXPLAINS A LOT.
FEET
CAKE
WAIT, IS THIS VIRTUAL RAIN? THAT'S STUPID! THIS IS A VIRTUAL INTERFACE. WHY PUT RAIN IN IT? I MEAN, WHAT'S IT SUPPOSED TO MEAN? THE SOFTWARE IS WET?
BUT NOW TO PURGE VIROOZ! THIS WILL TAKE EVERY OUNCE OF MY DEVIOUSNESS!
YOU! WHERE'S VIROOZ!
I LOVES DA PUDDING OF PUPPIES!
BLOOOOOOGH!
OF COURSE NOTHING WORKS INSIDE GIR.
DO YOU KNOW WHERE VIROOZ IS?

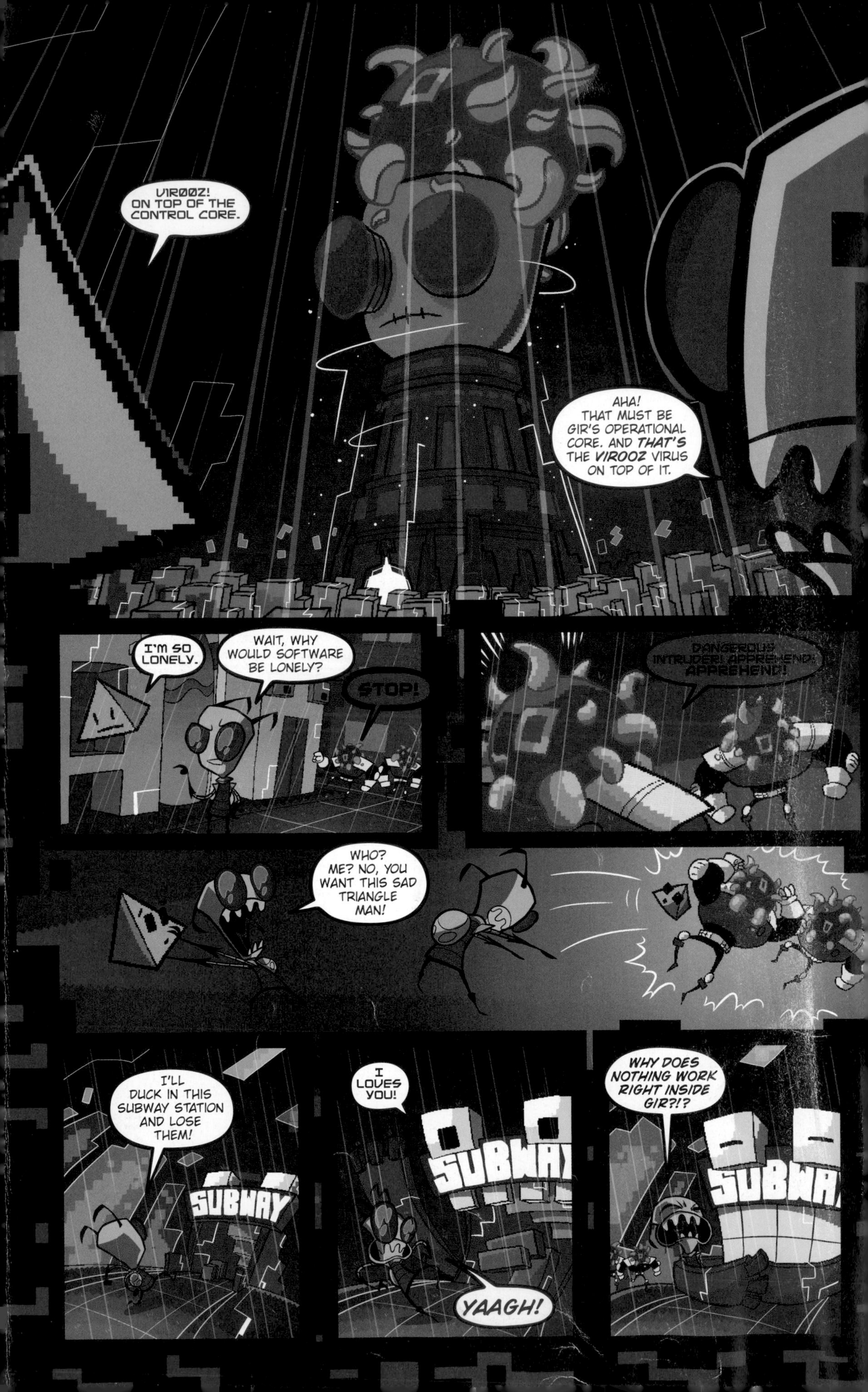
VIRØØZ! ON TOP OF THE CONTROL CORE.
AHA! THAT MUST BE GIR'S OPERATIONAL CORE. AND *THAT'S* THE *VIROOZ* VIRUS ON TOP OF IT.
I'M SO LONELY.
WAIT, WHY WOULD SOFTWARE BE LONELY?
STOP!
DANGEROUS INTRUDER! APPREHEND! APPREHEND!
WHO? ME? NO, YOU WANT THIS SAD TRIANGLE MAN!
I'LL DUCK IN THIS SUBWAY STATION AND LOSE THEM!
SUBWAY
I LOVES YOU!
SUBWAY
YAAGH!
WHY DOES NOTHING WORK RIGHT INSIDE GIR?!?
SUBWAY

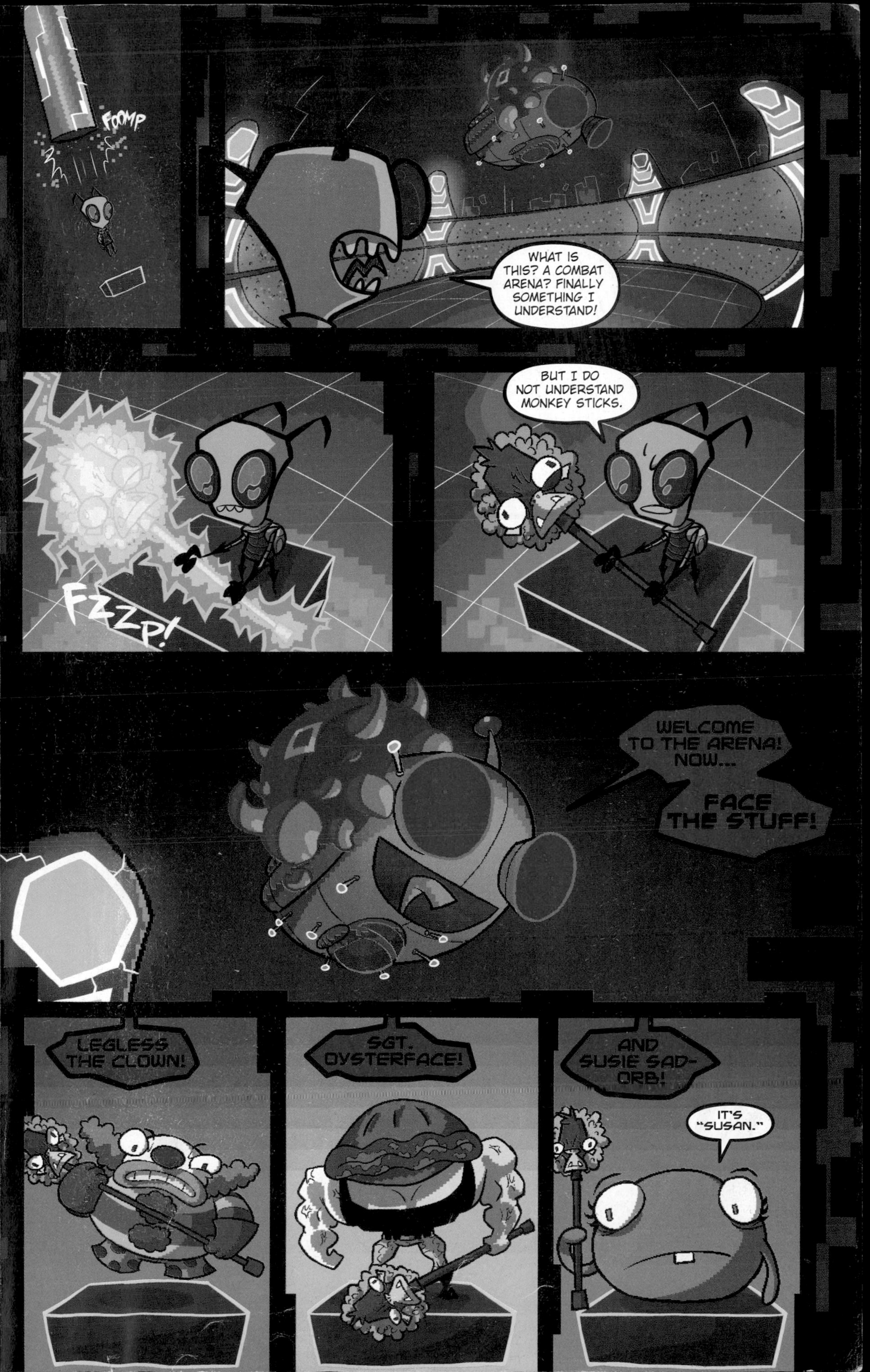
FOOMP
WHAT IS THIS? A COMBAT ARENA? FINALLY SOMETHING I UNDERSTAND!
FZZZP!
BUT I DO NOT UNDERSTAND MONKEY STICKS.
WELCOME TO THE ARENA! NOW...
FACE THE STUFF!
LEGLESS THE CLOWN!
SGT. OYSTERFACE!
AND SUSIE SAD-ORB!
IT'S "SUSAN."

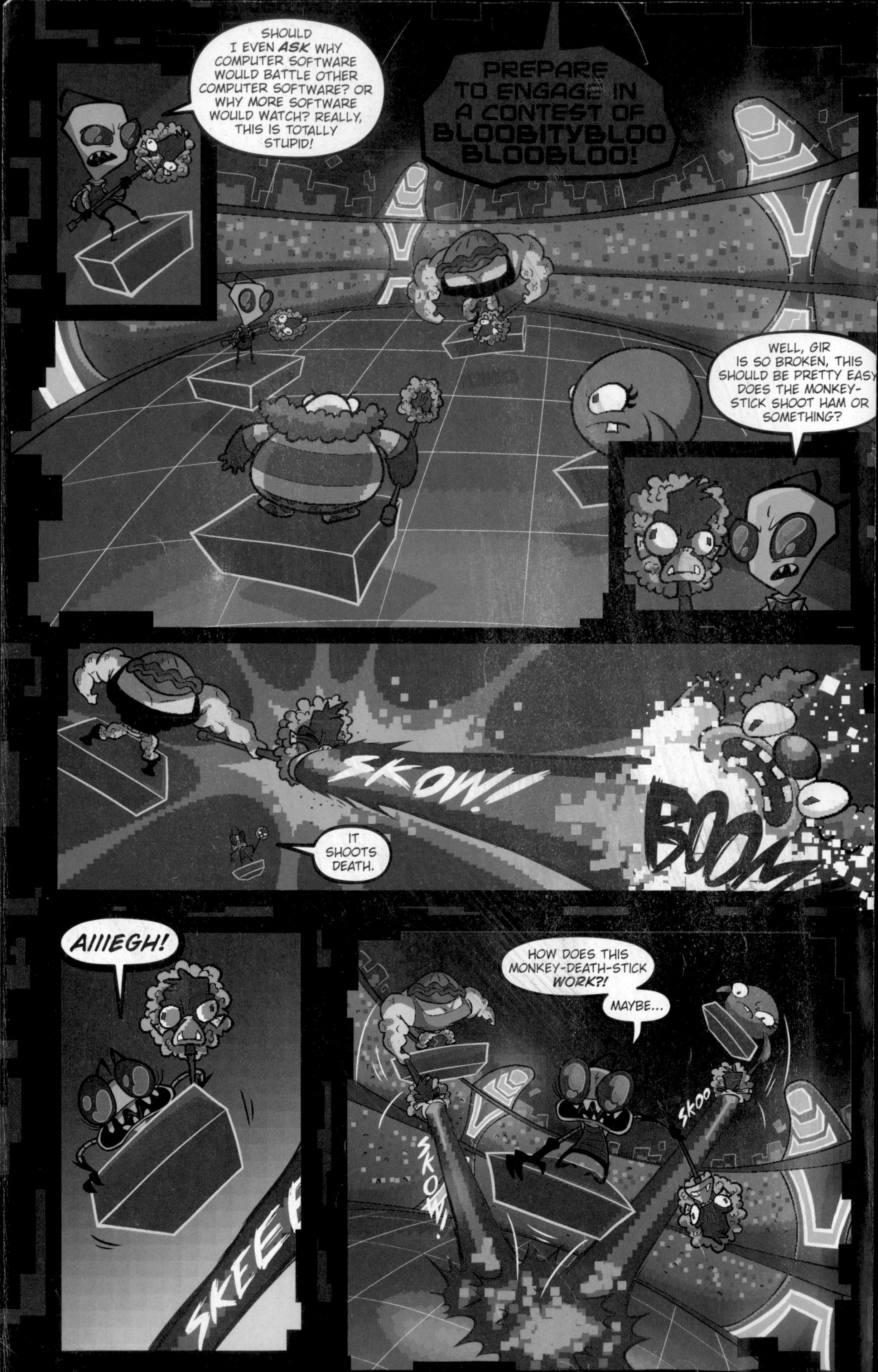
SHOULD I EVEN ASK WHY COMPUTER SOFTWARE WOULD BATTLE OTHER COMPUTER SOFTWARE? OR WHY MORE SOFTWARE WOULD WATCH? REALLY, THIS IS TOTALLY STUPID!
PREPARE TO ENGAGE IN A CONTEST OF BLOOBITYBLOO BLOOBLOO!
WELL, GIR IS SO BROKEN, THIS SHOULD BE PRETTY EASY. DOES THE MONKEY-STICK SHOOT HAM OR SOMETHING?
SKOW!
IT SHOOTS DEATH.
AIIIEGH!
HOW DOES THIS MONKEY-DEATH-STICK WORK?!
MAYBE...
SKOO
SKOW!

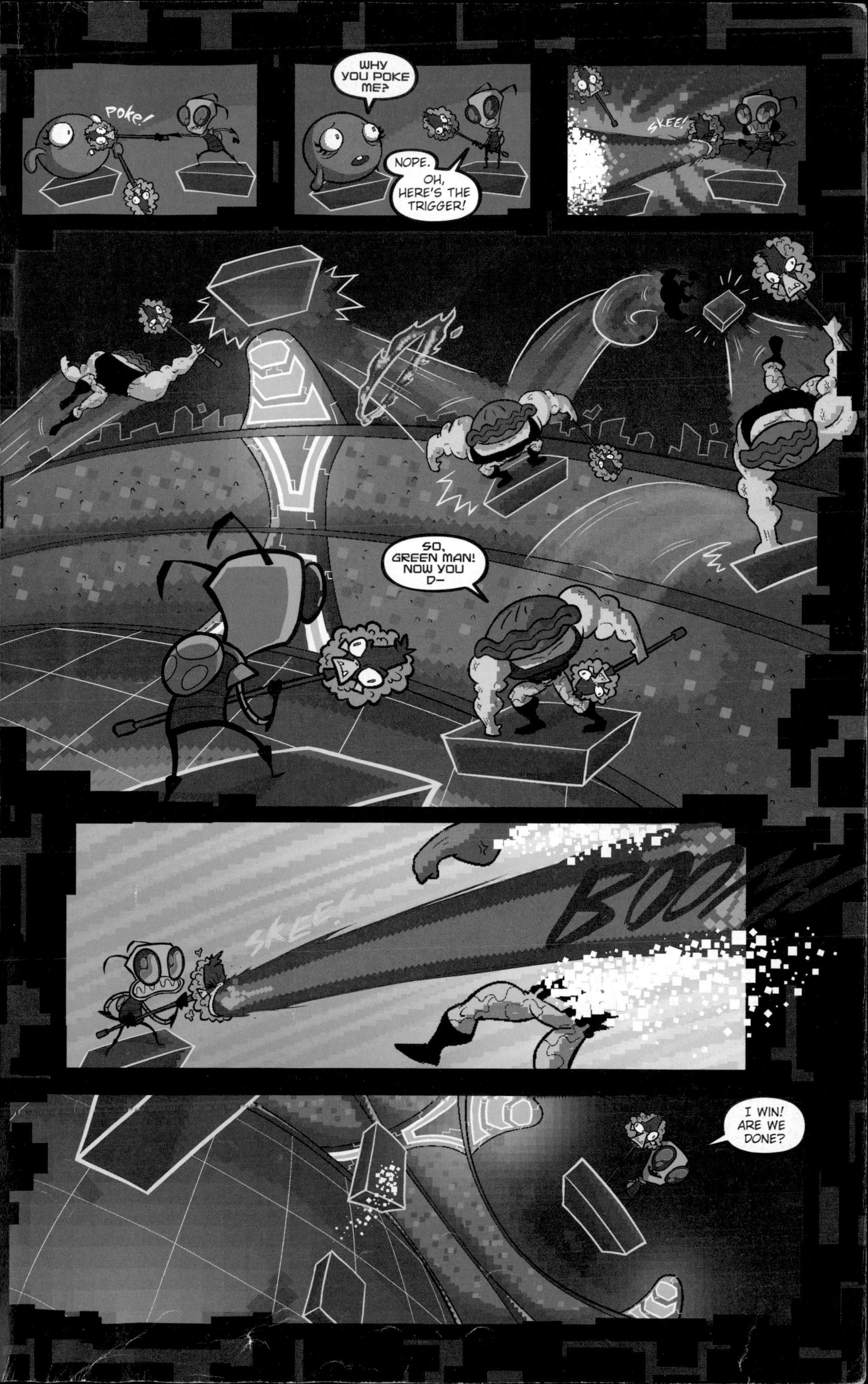
POKE!
WHY YOU POKE ME?
NOPE.
OH, HERE'S THE TRIGGER!
SKEE!
SO, GREEN MAN! NOW YOU D–
SKEE!
BOOM!
I WIN! ARE WE DONE?

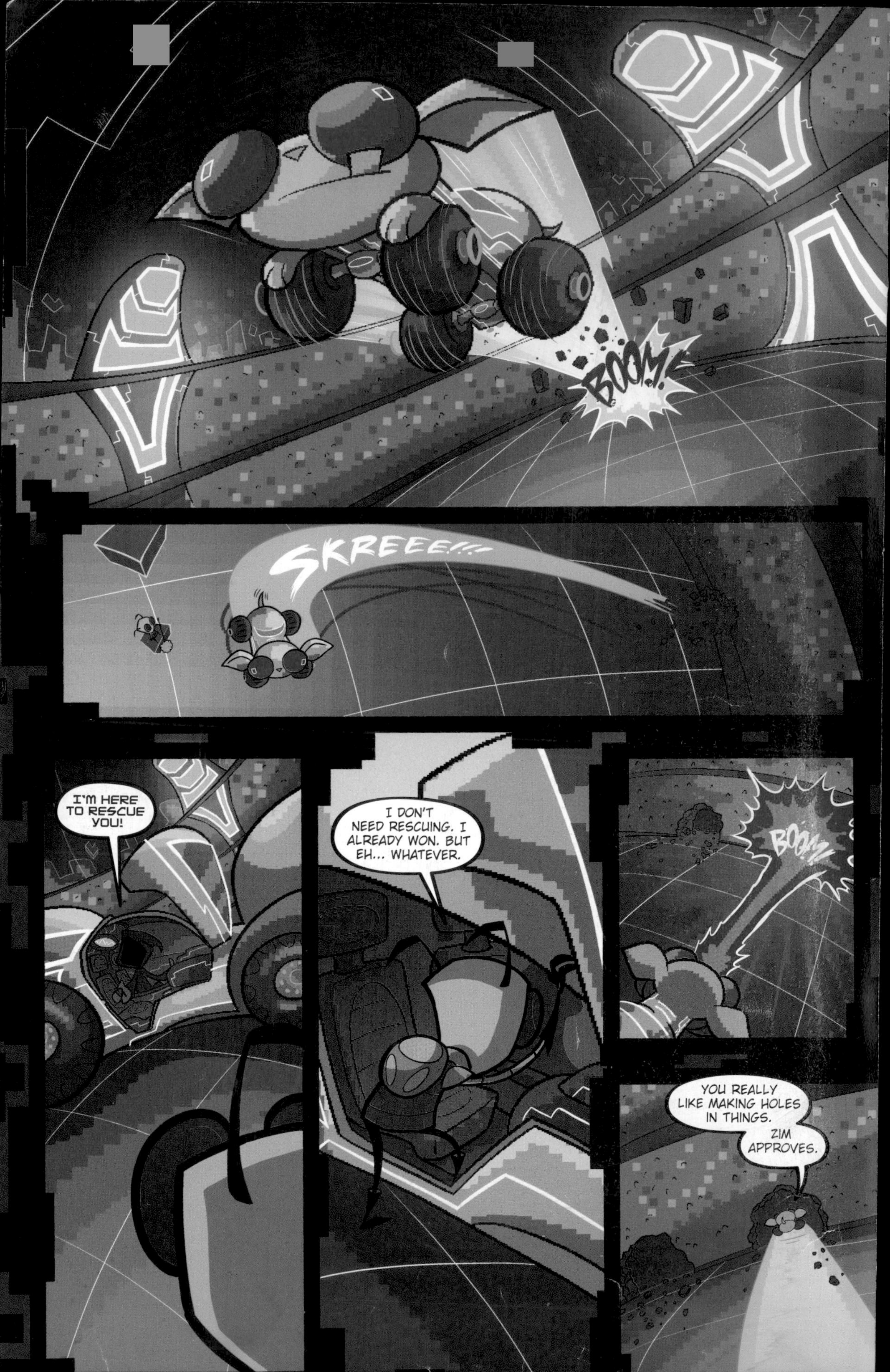
BOOM!
SKREEE!!!
I'M HERE TO RESCUE YOU!
I DON'T NEED RESCUING. I ALREADY WON. BUT EH... WHATEVER.
BOOM!
YOU REALLY LIKE MAKING HOLES IN THINGS.
ZIM APPROVES.

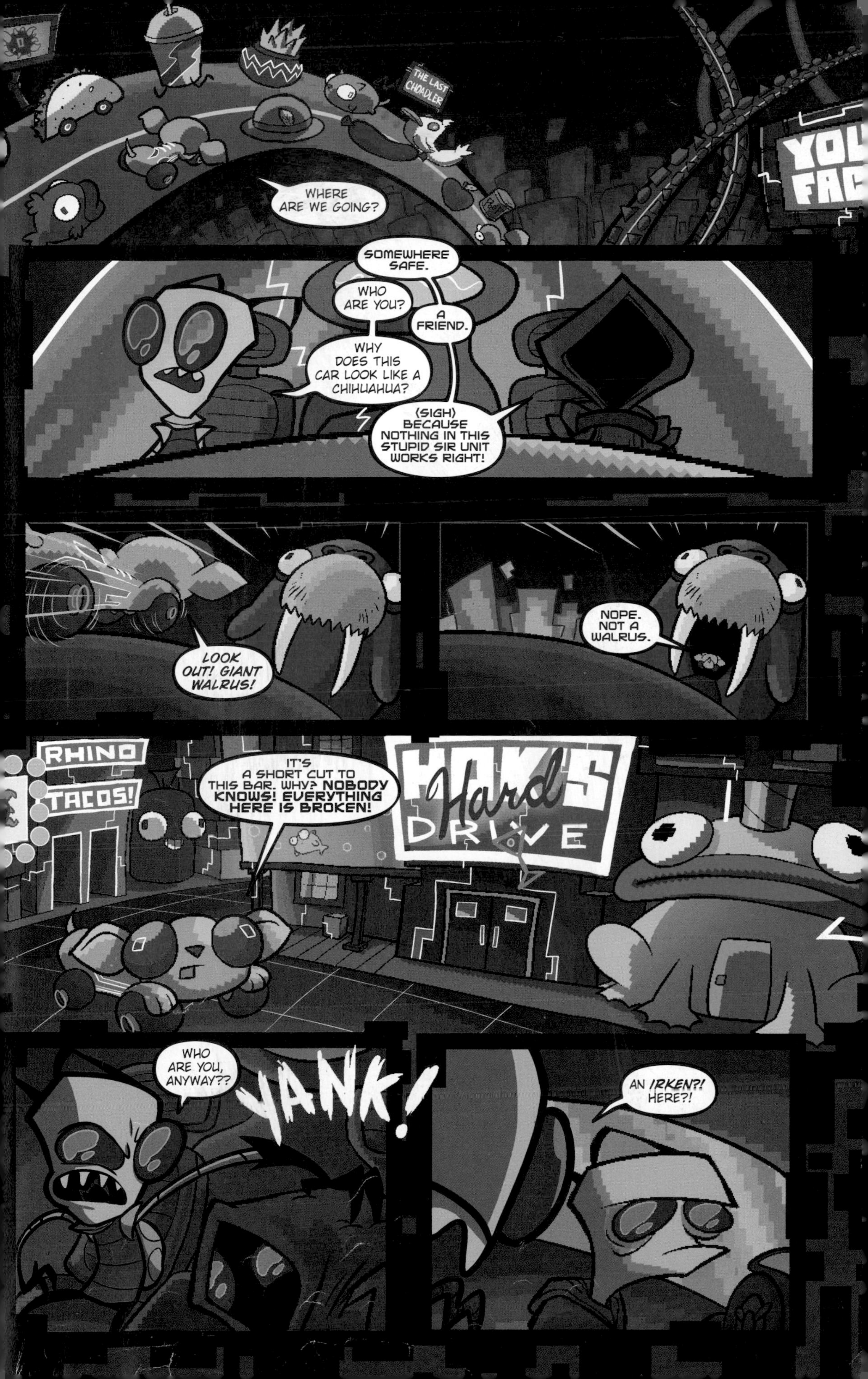
THE LAST CHOADLER
YOU FAC
WHERE ARE WE GOING?
SOMEWHERE SAFE.
WHO ARE YOU?
A FRIEND.
WHY DOES THIS CAR LOOK LIKE A CHIHUAHUA?
(SIGH) BECAUSE NOTHING IN THIS STUPID SIR UNIT WORKS RIGHT!
LOOK OUT! GIANT WALRUS!
NOPE. NOT A WALRUS.
RHINO TACOS!
IT'S A SHORT CUT TO THIS BAR. WHY? NOBODY KNOWS! EVERYTHING HERE IS BROKEN!
Hard DRIVE
WHO ARE YOU, ANYWAY??
YANK!
AN IRKEN?! HERE?!

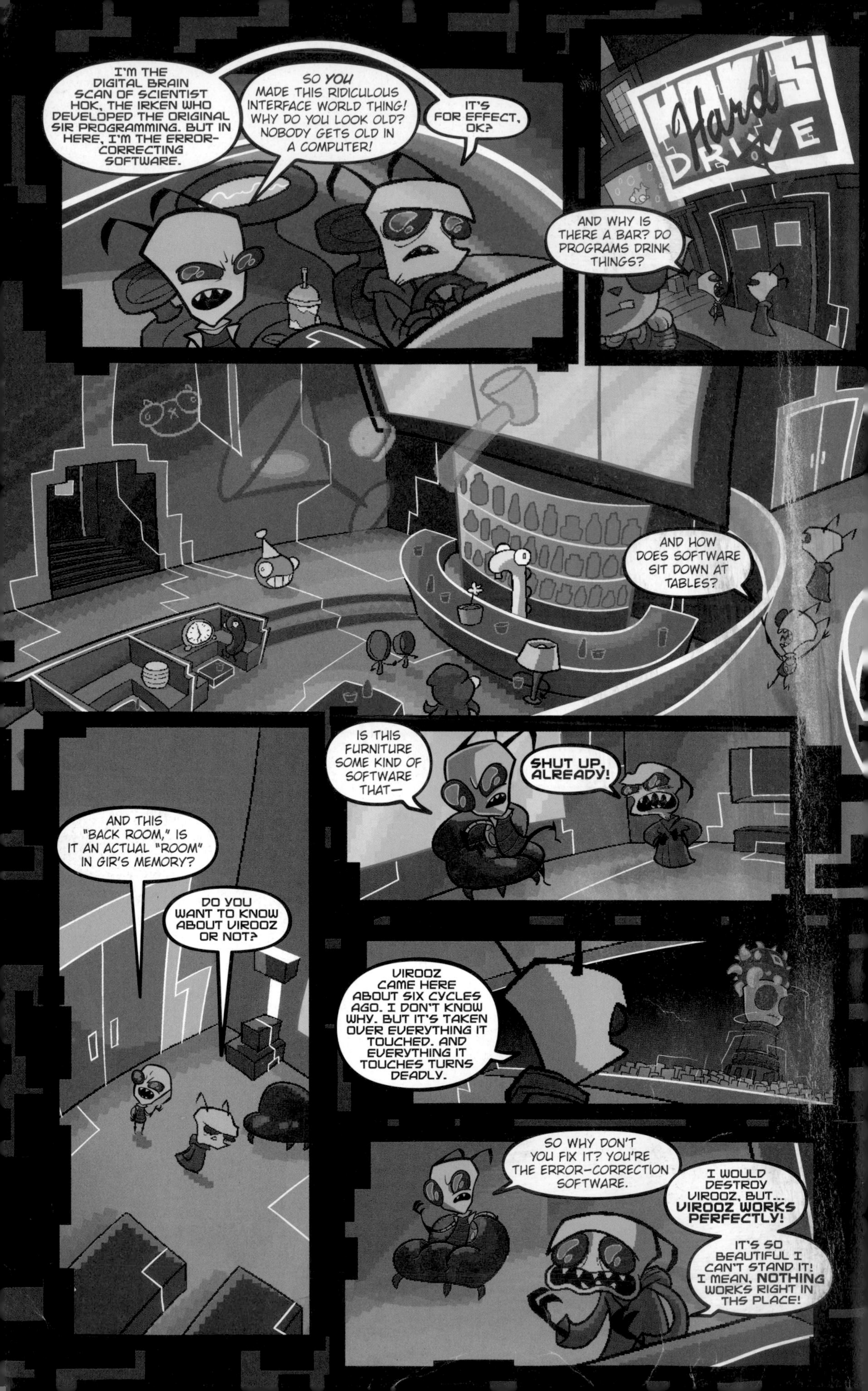
I'M THE DIGITAL BRAIN SCAN OF SCIENTIST HOK, THE IRKEN WHO DEVELOPED THE ORIGINAL SIR PROGRAMMING. BUT IN HERE, I'M THE ERROR-CORRECTING SOFTWARE.
SO YOU MADE THIS RIDICULOUS INTERFACE WORLD THING! WHY DO YOU LOOK OLD? NOBODY GETS OLD IN A COMPUTER!
IT'S FOR EFFECT, OK?
HOK'S Hard DRIVE
AND WHY IS THERE A BAR? DO PROGRAMS DRINK THINGS?
AND HOW DOES SOFTWARE SIT DOWN AT TABLES?
AND THIS "BACK ROOM," IS IT AN ACTUAL "ROOM" IN GIR'S MEMORY?
DO YOU WANT TO KNOW ABOUT VIROOZ OR NOT?
IS THIS FURNITURE SOME KIND OF SOFTWARE THAT—
SHUT UP, ALREADY!
VIROOZ CAME HERE ABOUT SIX CYCLES AGO. I DON'T KNOW WHY. BUT IT'S TAKEN OVER EVERYTHING IT TOUCHED. AND EVERYTHING IT TOUCHES TURNS DEADLY.
SO WHY DON'T YOU FIX IT? YOU'RE THE ERROR-CORRECTION SOFTWARE.
I WOULD DESTROY VIROOZ, BUT... VIROOZ WORKS PERFECTLY!
IT'S SO BEAUTIFUL I CAN'T STAND IT! I MEAN, NOTHING WORKS RIGHT IN THS PLACE!

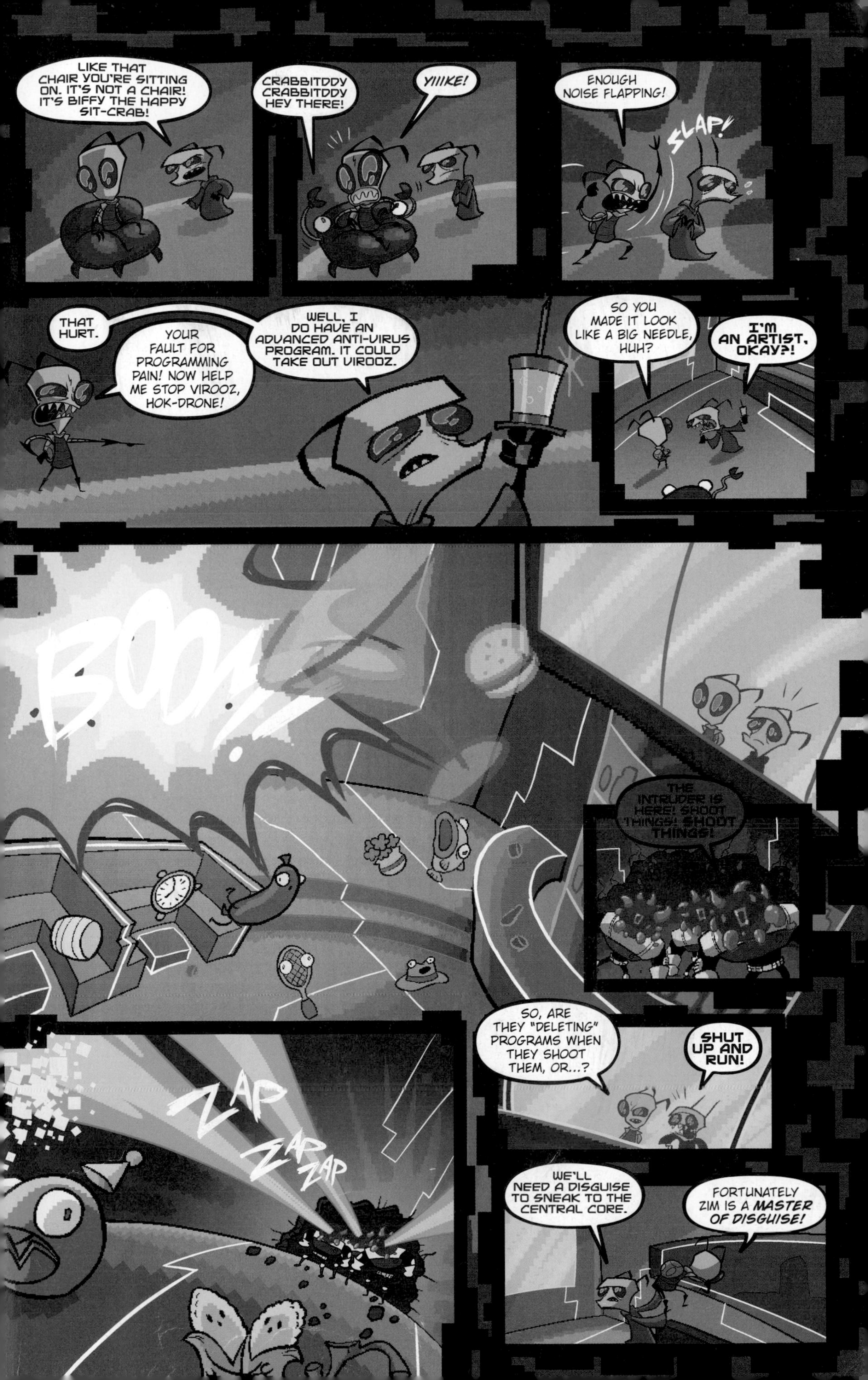

LIKE THAT CHAIR YOU'RE SITTING ON. IT'S NOT A CHAIR! IT'S BIFFY THE HAPPY SIT-CRAB!
CRABBITDDY CRABBITDDY HEY THERE!
YIIIKE!
ENOUGH NOISE FLAPPING!
SLAP!
THAT HURT.
YOUR FAULT FOR PROGRAMMING PAIN! NOW HELP ME STOP VIROOZ, HOK-DRONE!
WELL, I DO HAVE AN ADVANCED ANTI-VIRUS PROGRAM. IT COULD TAKE OUT VIROOZ.
SO YOU MADE IT LOOK LIKE A BIG NEEDLE, HUH?
I'M AN ARTIST, OKAY?!
BOOM!
THE INTRUDER IS HERE! SHOOT THINGS! SHOOT THINGS!
ZAP
ZAP
ZAP
SO, ARE THEY "DELETING" PROGRAMS WHEN THEY SHOOT THEM, OR...?
SHUT UP AND RUN!
WE'LL NEED A DISGUISE TO SNEAK TO THE CENTRAL CORE.
FORTUNATELY ZIM IS A MASTER OF DISGUISE!

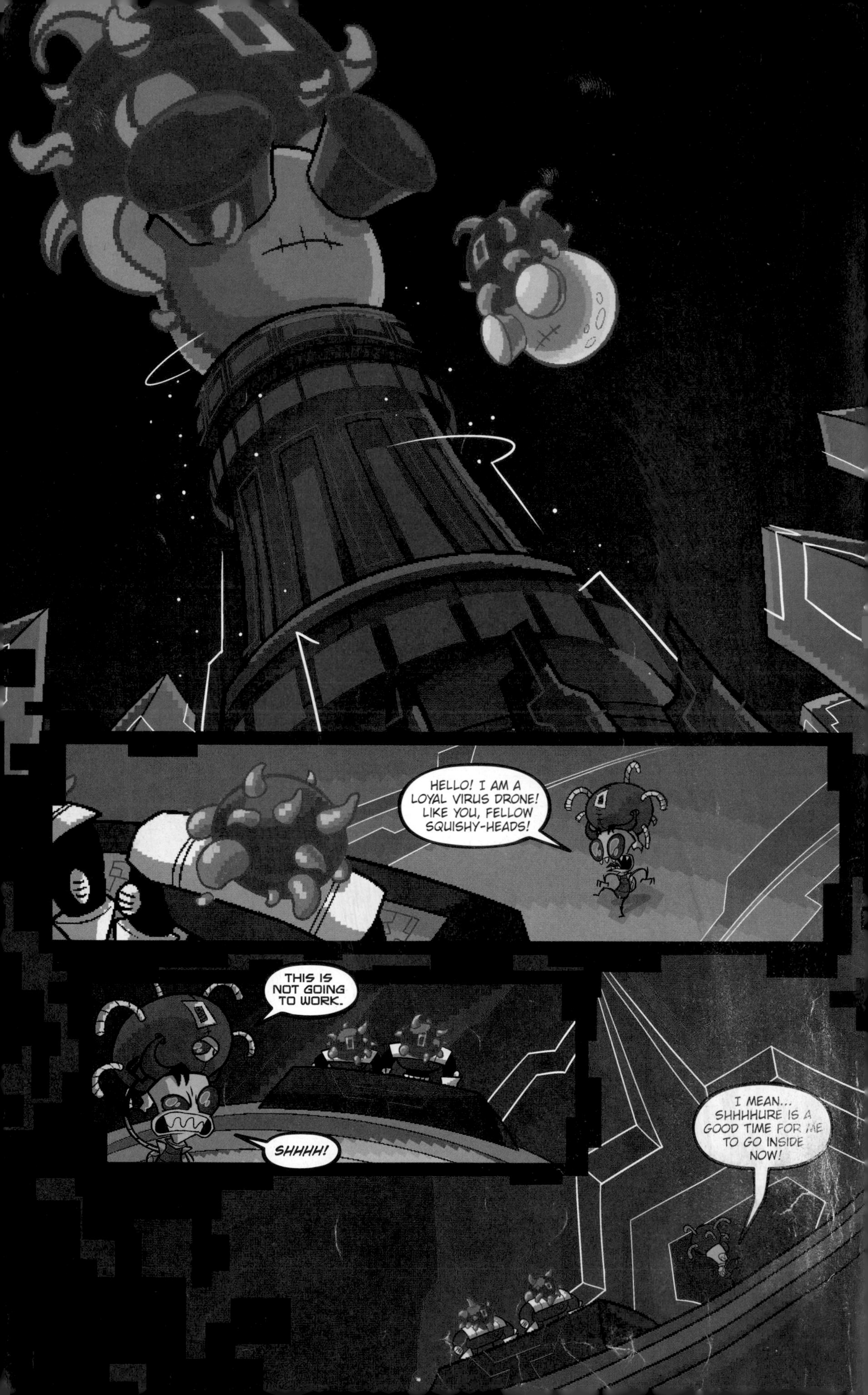
HELLO! I AM A LOYAL VIRUS DRONE! LIKE YOU, FELLOW SQUISHY-HEADS!
THIS IS NOT GOING TO WORK.
SHHHH!
I MEAN... SHHHHURE IS A GOOD TIME FOR ME TO GO INSIDE NOW!

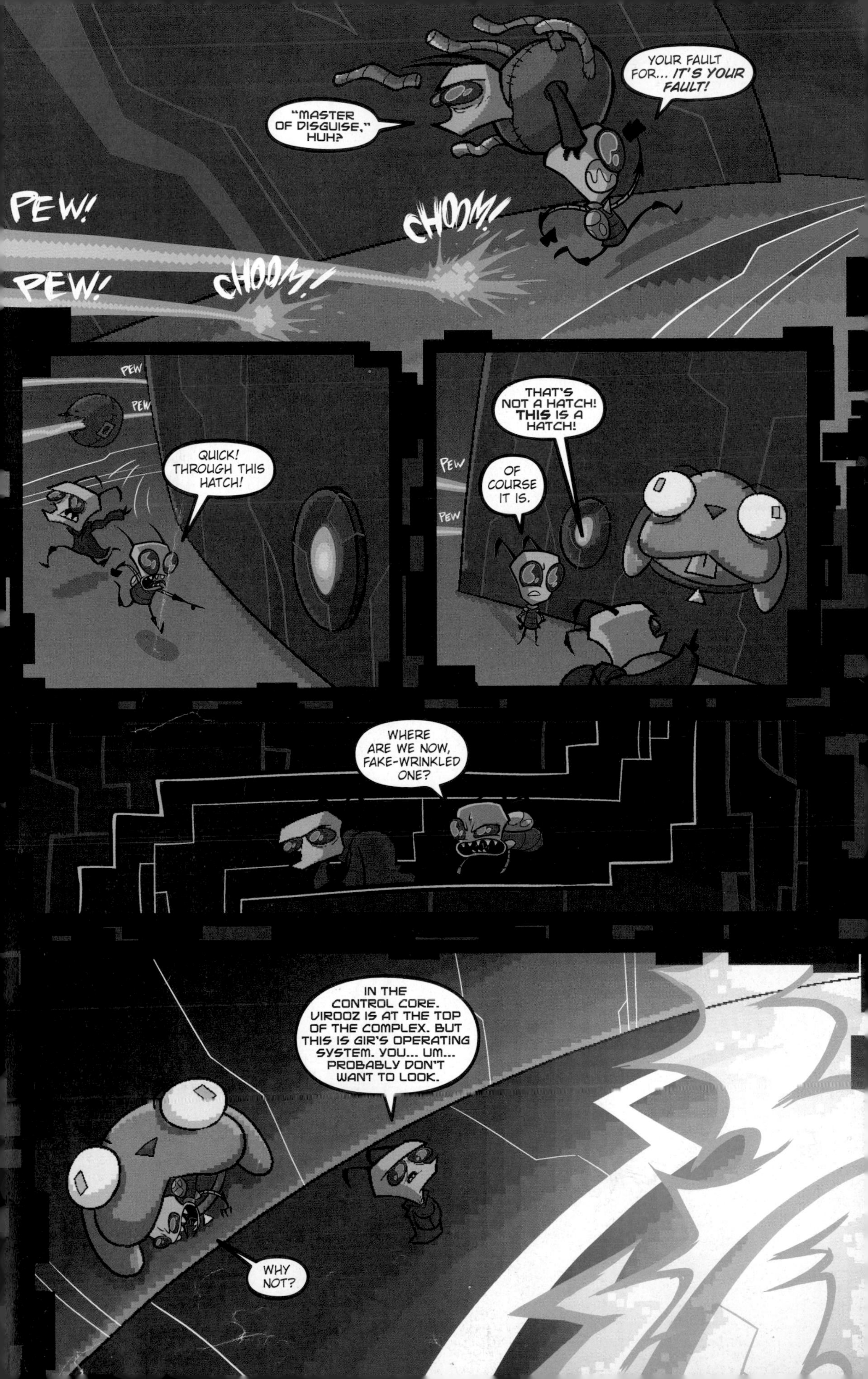
"MASTER OF DISGUISE," HUH?
YOUR FAULT FOR... IT'S YOUR FAULT!
PEW!
PEW!
CHOOM!
CHOOM!
PEW
PEW
QUICK! THROUGH THIS HATCH!
THAT'S NOT A HATCH! THIS IS A HATCH!
OF COURSE IT IS.
PEW
PEW
WHERE ARE WE NOW, FAKE-WRINKLED ONE?
IN THE CONTROL CORE. VIROOZ IS AT THE TOP OF THE COMPLEX. BUT THIS IS GIR'S OPERATING SYSTEM. YOU... UM... PROBABLY DON'T WANT TO LOOK.
WHY NOT?

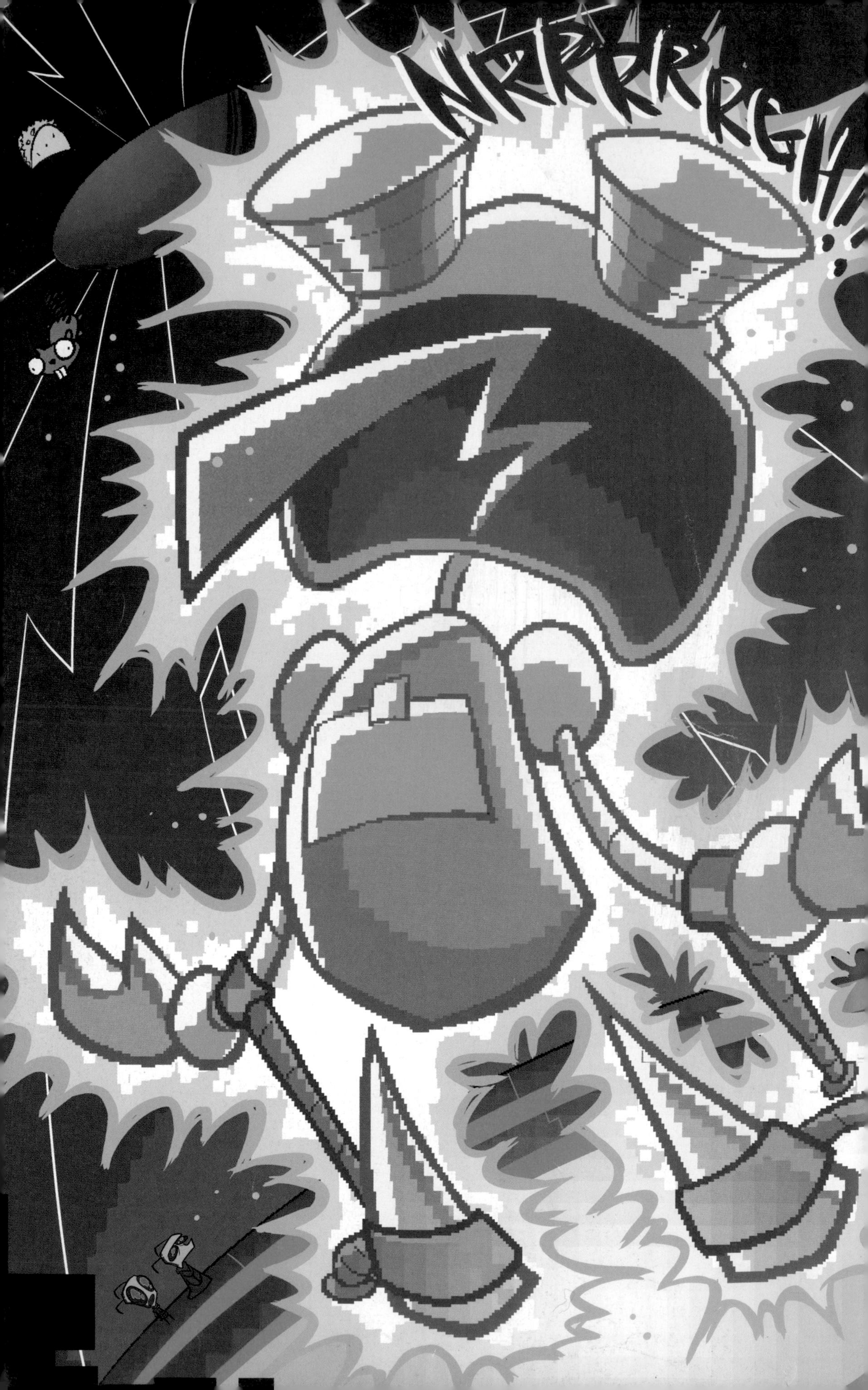
NRRRRRGH!!!

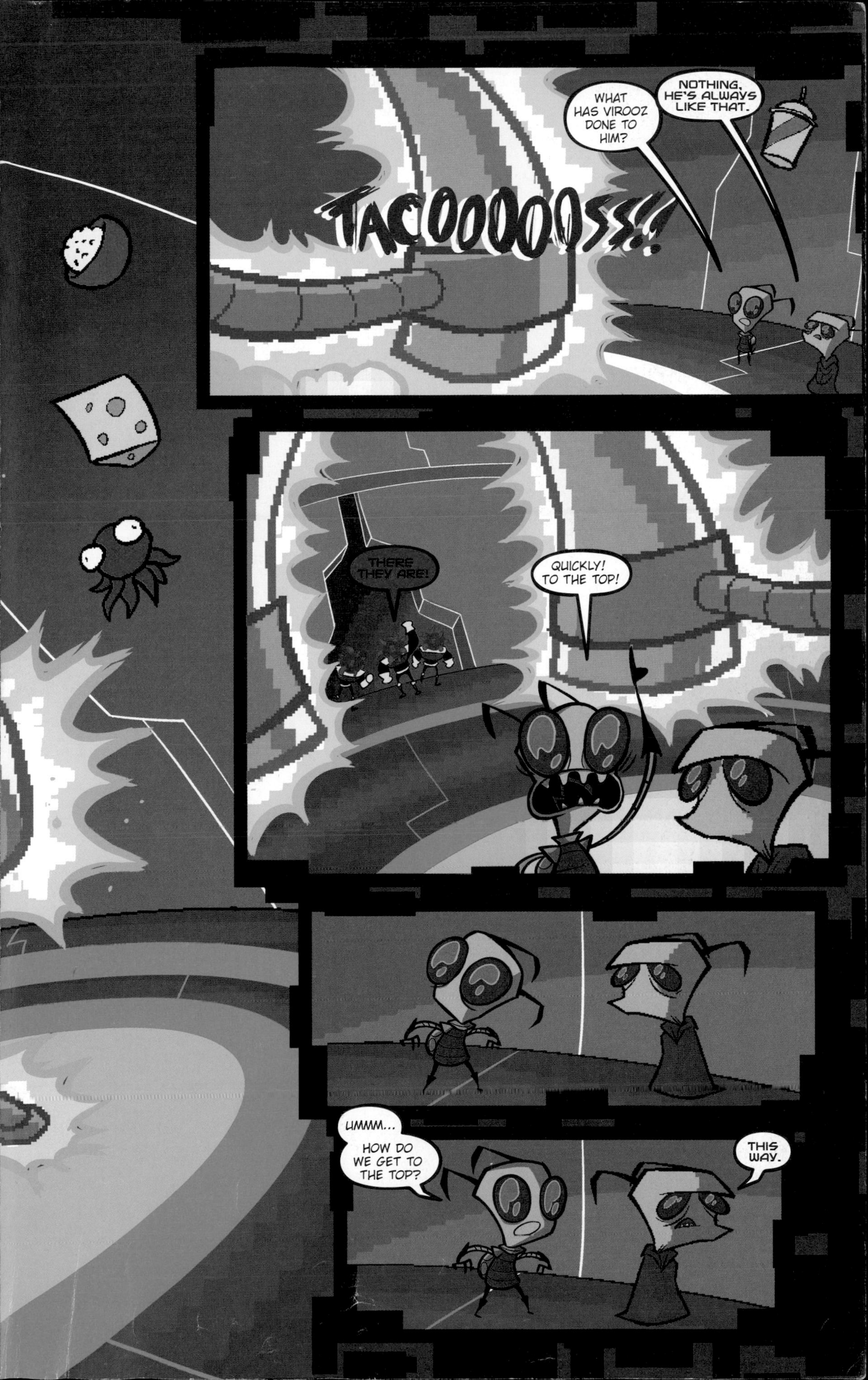
TACOOOOOOSSS!!
WHAT HAS VIROOZ DONE TO HIM?
NOTHING, HE'S ALWAYS LIKE THAT.
THERE THEY ARE!
QUICKLY! TO THE TOP!
UMMM... HOW DO WE GET TO THE TOP?
THIS WAY.

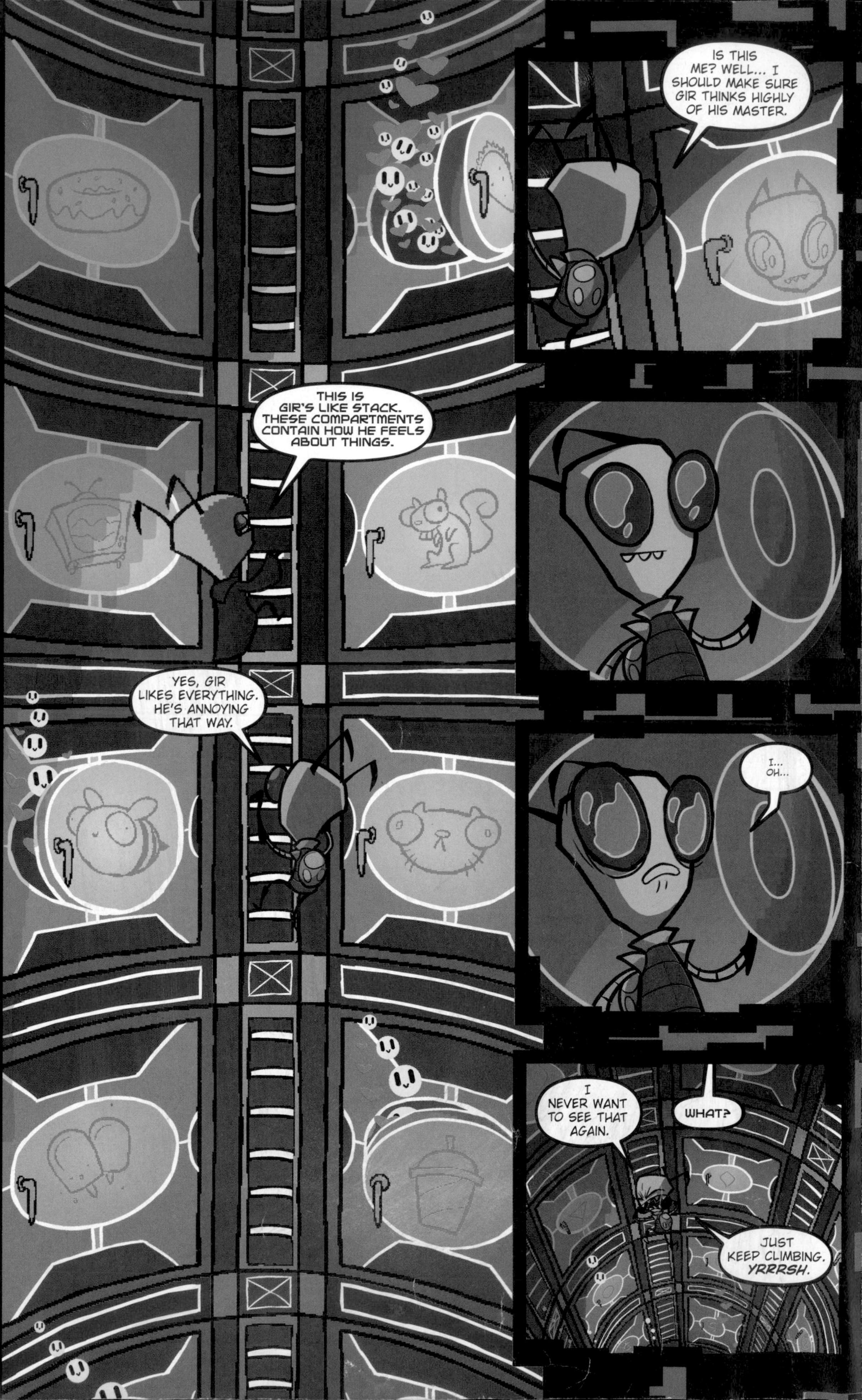
THIS IS GIR'S LIKE STACK. THESE COMPARTMENTS CONTAIN HOW HE FEELS ABOUT THINGS.
YES, GIR LIKES EVERYTHING. HE'S ANNOYING THAT WAY.
IS THIS ME? WELL... I SHOULD MAKE SURE GIR THINKS HIGHLY OF HIS MASTER.
I... OH...
I NEVER WANT TO SEE THAT AGAIN.
WHAT?
JUST KEEP CLIMBING. YRRRSH.

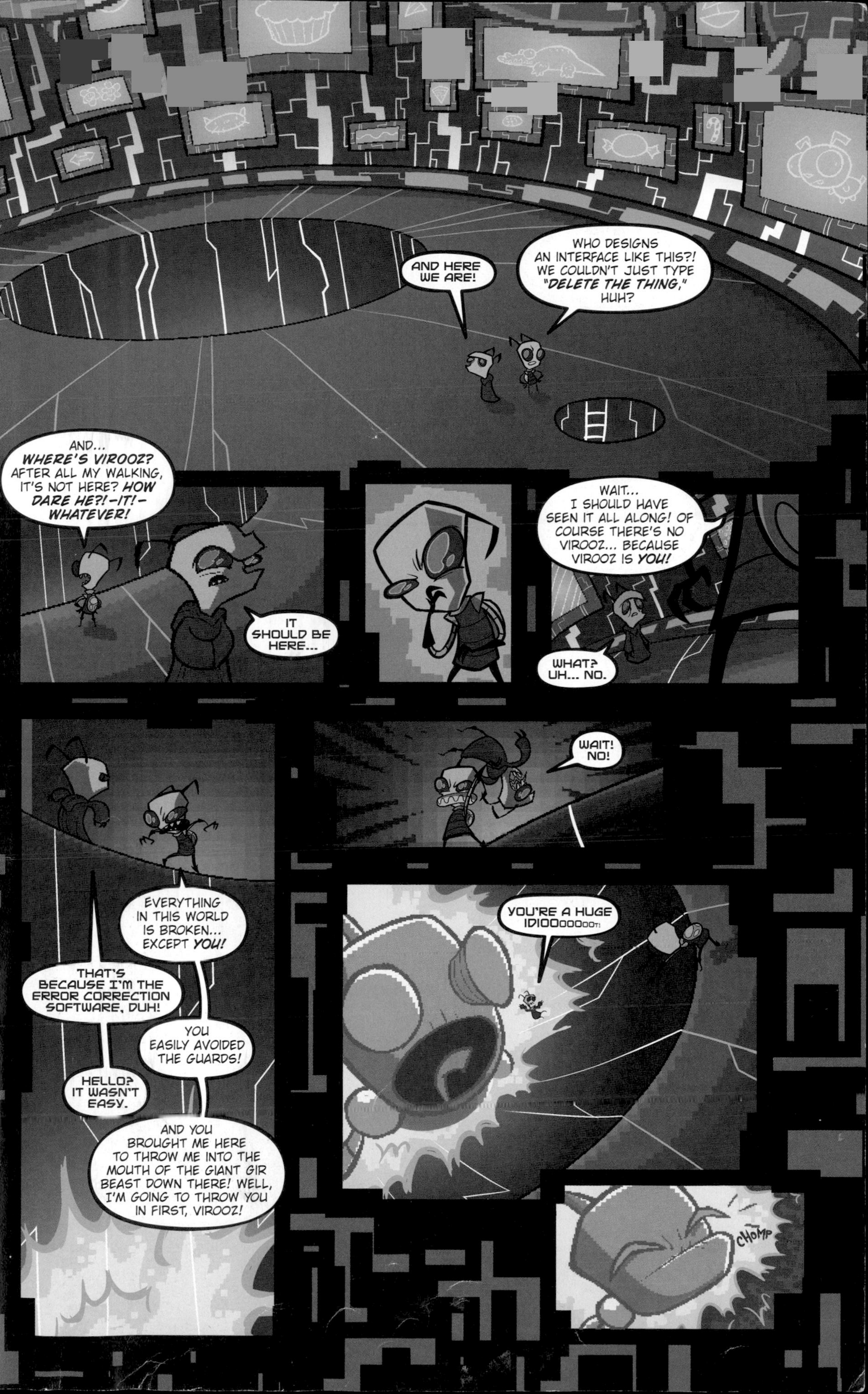
AND HERE WE ARE!
WHO DESIGNS AN INTERFACE LIKE THIS?! WE COULDN'T JUST TYPE "DELETE THE THING," HUH?
AND... WHERE'S VIROOZ? AFTER ALL MY WALKING, IT'S NOT HERE? HOW DARE HE?! –IT! –WHATEVER!
IT SHOULD BE HERE...
WAIT... I SHOULD HAVE SEEN IT ALL ALONG! OF COURSE THERE'S NO VIROOZ... BECAUSE VIROOZ IS YOU!
WHAT? UH... NO.
EVERYTHING IN THIS WORLD IS BROKEN... EXCEPT YOU!
THAT'S BECAUSE I'M THE ERROR CORRECTION SOFTWARE, DUH!
YOU EASILY AVOIDED THE GUARDS!
HELLO? IT WASN'T EASY.
AND YOU BROUGHT ME HERE TO THROW ME INTO THE MOUTH OF THE GIANT GIR BEAST DOWN THERE! WELL, I'M GOING TO THROW YOU IN FIRST, VIROOZ!
WAIT! NO!
YOU'RE A HUGE IDIOOOOOOOT!
CHOMP

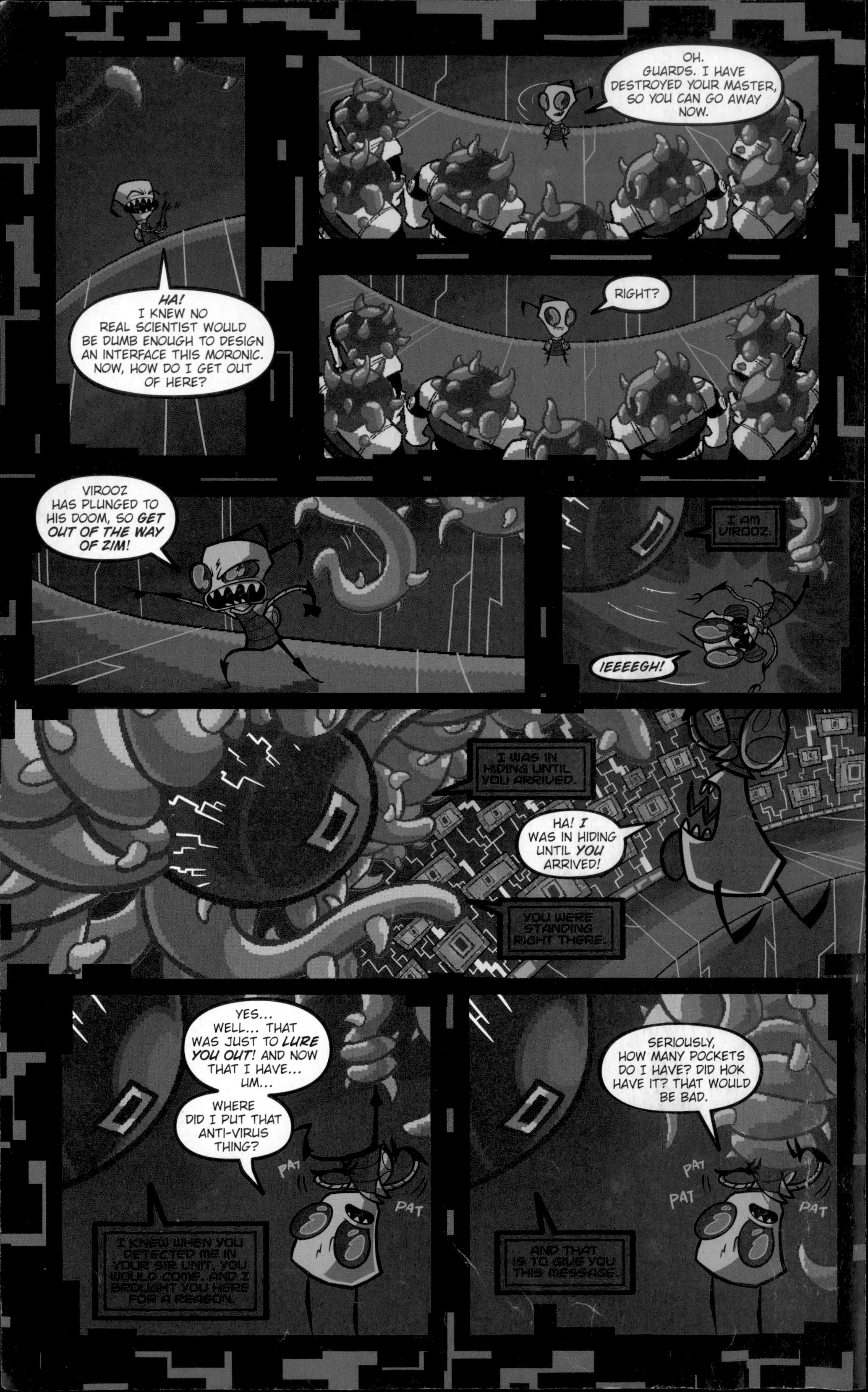
HA! I KNEW NO REAL SCIENTIST WOULD BE DUMB ENOUGH TO DESIGN AN INTERFACE THIS MORONIC. NOW, HOW DO I GET OUT OF HERE?
OH. GUARDS. I HAVE DESTROYED YOUR MASTER, SO YOU CAN GO AWAY NOW.
RIGHT?
VIROOZ HAS PLUNGED TO HIS DOOM, SO GET OUT OF THE WAY OF ZIM!
I AM VIROOZ.
IEEEEGH!
I WAS IN HIDING UNTIL YOU ARRIVED.
HA! I WAS IN HIDING UNTIL YOU ARRIVED!
YOU WERE STANDING RIGHT THERE.
YES... WELL... THAT WAS JUST TO LURE YOU OUT! AND NOW THAT I HAVE... UM...
WHERE DID I PUT THAT ANTI-VIRUS THING?
PAT
PAT
I KNEW WHEN YOU DETECTED ME IN YOUR SIR UNIT, YOU WOULD COME. AND I BROUGHT YOU HERE FOR A REASON.
SERIOUSLY, HOW MANY POCKETS DO I HAVE? DID HOK HAVE IT? THAT WOULD BE BAD.
PAT
PAT
PAT
AND THAT IS TO GIVE YOU THIS MESSAGE.

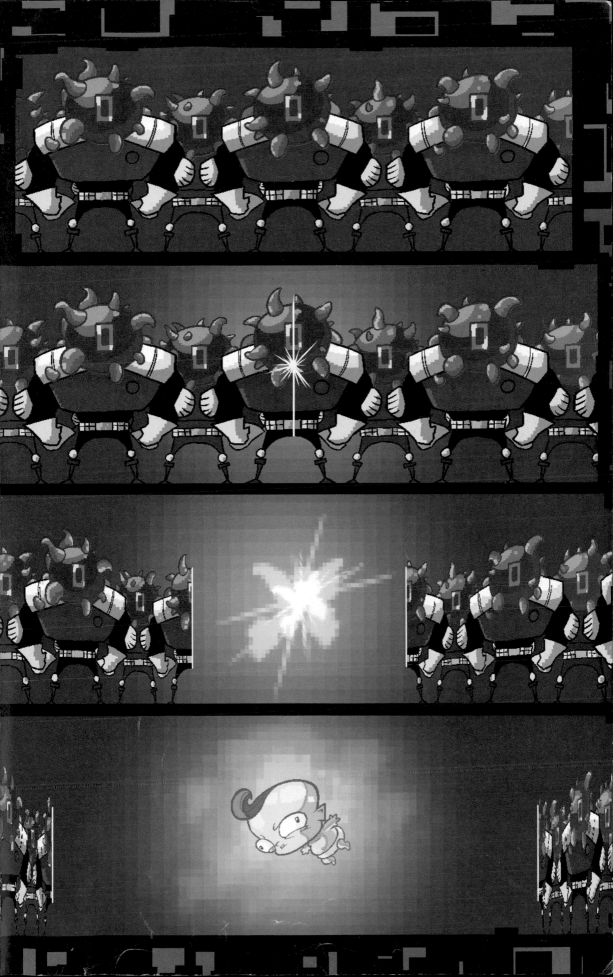

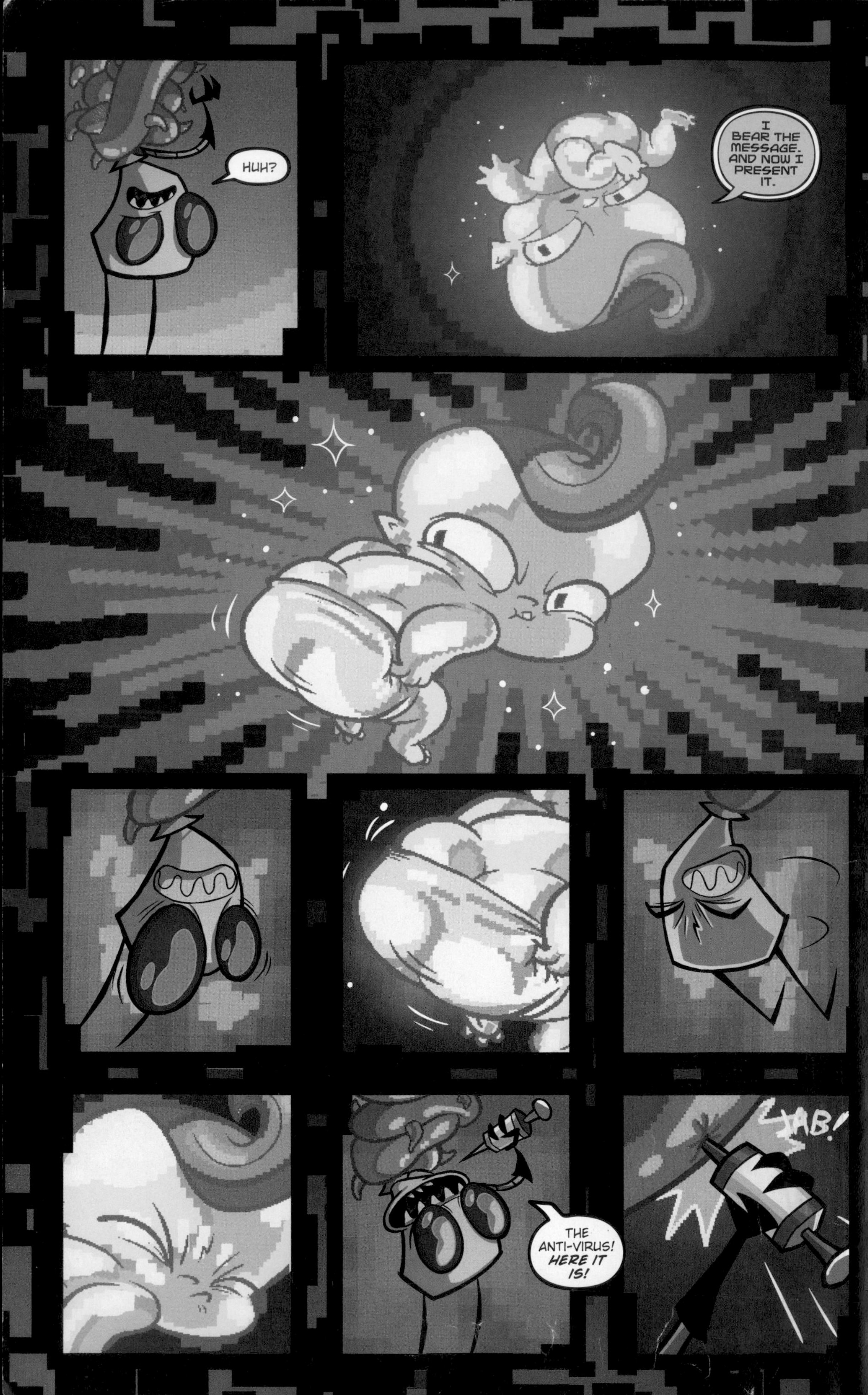
HUH?
I BEAR THE MESSAGE. AND NOW I PRESENT IT.
THE ANTI-VIRUS! HERE IT IS!
JAB!

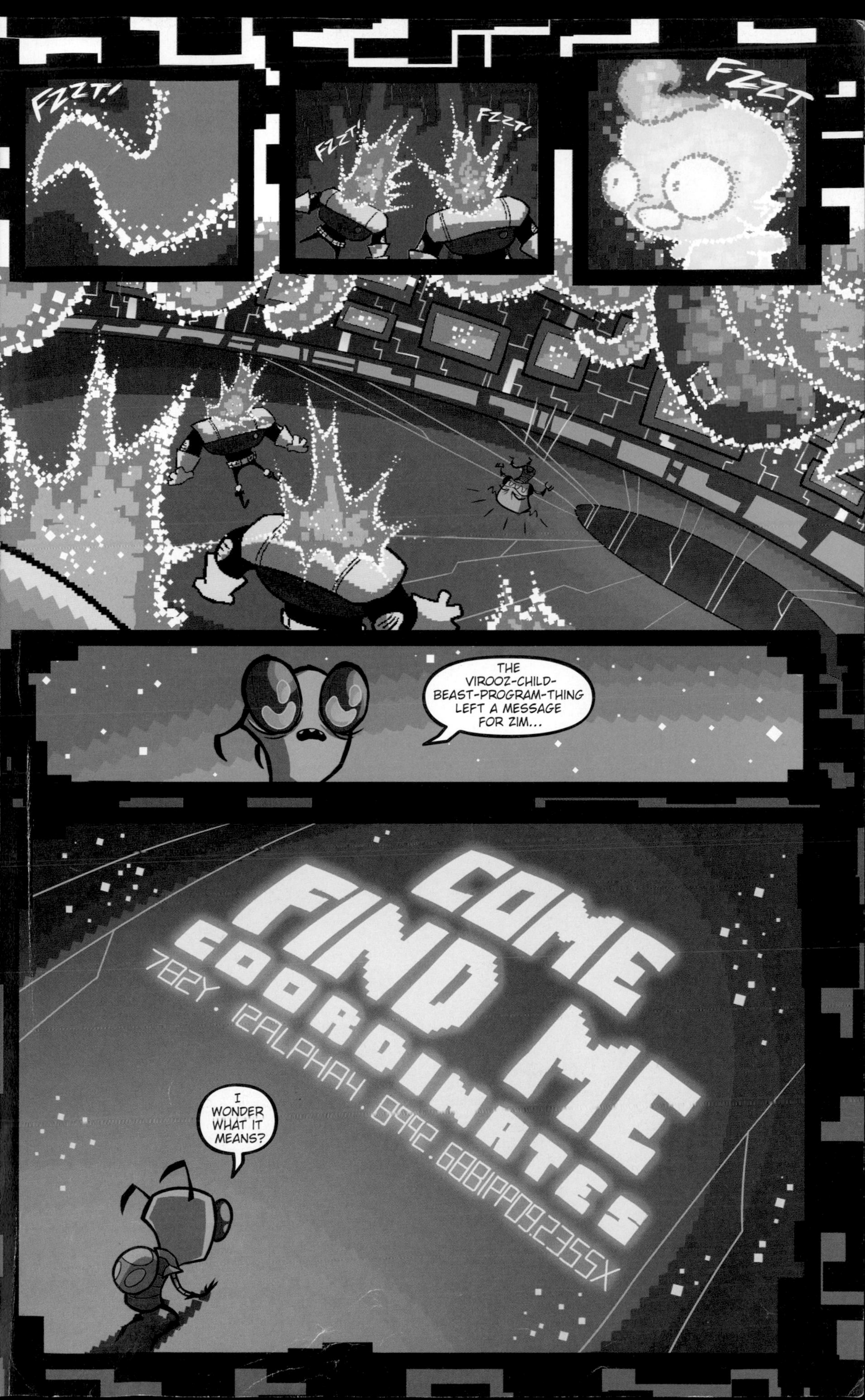
FZZT!
FZZT!
FZZT!
FZZT
THE VIROOZ-CHILD-BEAST-PROGRAM-THING LEFT A MESSAGE FOR ZIM...
COME FIND ME
COORDINATES
782Y. 12ALPHA4. 6992. 6881PP09.2355X
I WONDER WHAT IT MEANS?

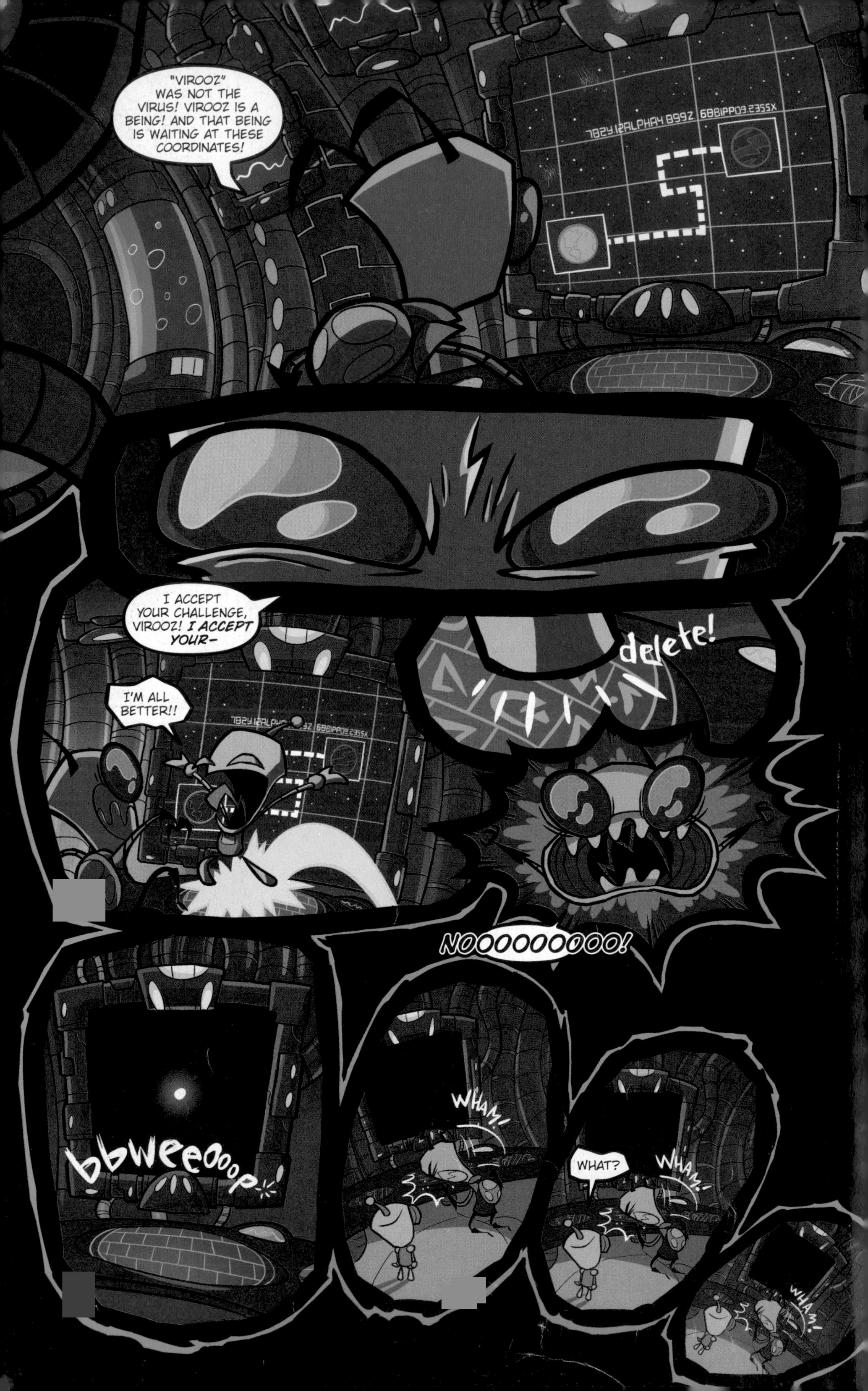
"VIROOZ" WAS NOT THE VIRUS! VIROOZ IS A BEING! AND THAT BEING IS WAITING AT THESE COORDINATES!
7B2Y.12ALPHA4 B99Z 6B8IPP09.2355X
I ACCEPT YOUR CHALLENGE, VIROOZ! I ACCEPT YOUR-
I'M ALL BETTER!!
delete!
NOOOOOOOOO!
bbweeooop
WHAM!
WHAT?
WHAM!
WHAM!

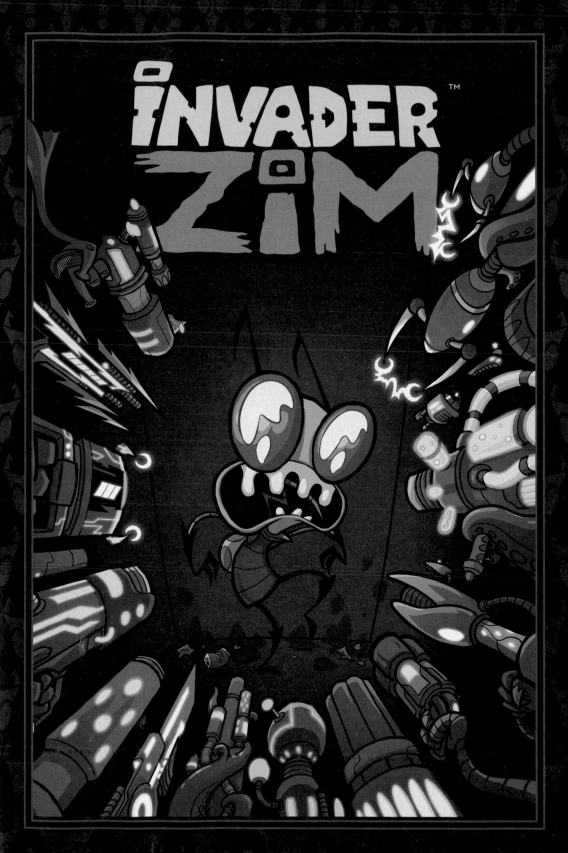

CHAPTER: 3

The Arc of VIROOZ Part Three:
The Shquark of VIROOZ

illustration by **Warren Wucinich**

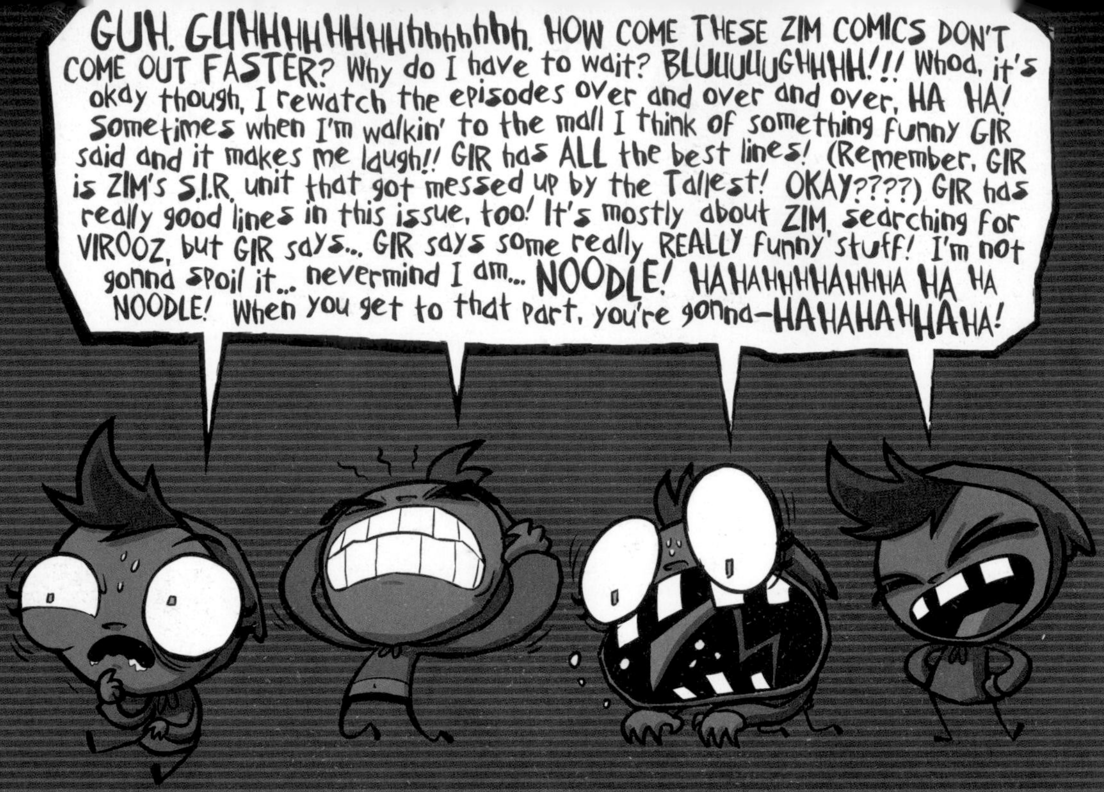
GUH. GUHHHHHHHHhhhhhhh. HOW COME THESE ZIM COMICS DON'T COME OUT FASTER? Why do I have to wait? BLUUUUUGHHHH!!! Whoa, it's okay though, I rewatch the episodes over and over and over, HA HA! Sometimes when I'm walkin' to the mall I think of something funny GIR said and it makes me laugh!! GIR has ALL the best lines! (Remember, GIR is ZIM's S.I.R. unit that got messed up by the Tallest! OKAY????) GIR has really good lines in this issue, too! It's mostly about ZIM, searching for VIROOZ, but GIR says... GIR says some really REALLY funny stuff! I'm not gonna spoil it... nevermind I am... NOODLE! HAHAHHHAHHHA HA HA NOODLE! When you get to that part, you're gonna-HAHAHAHHAHA!

Recap Kid by WARREN WUCINICH

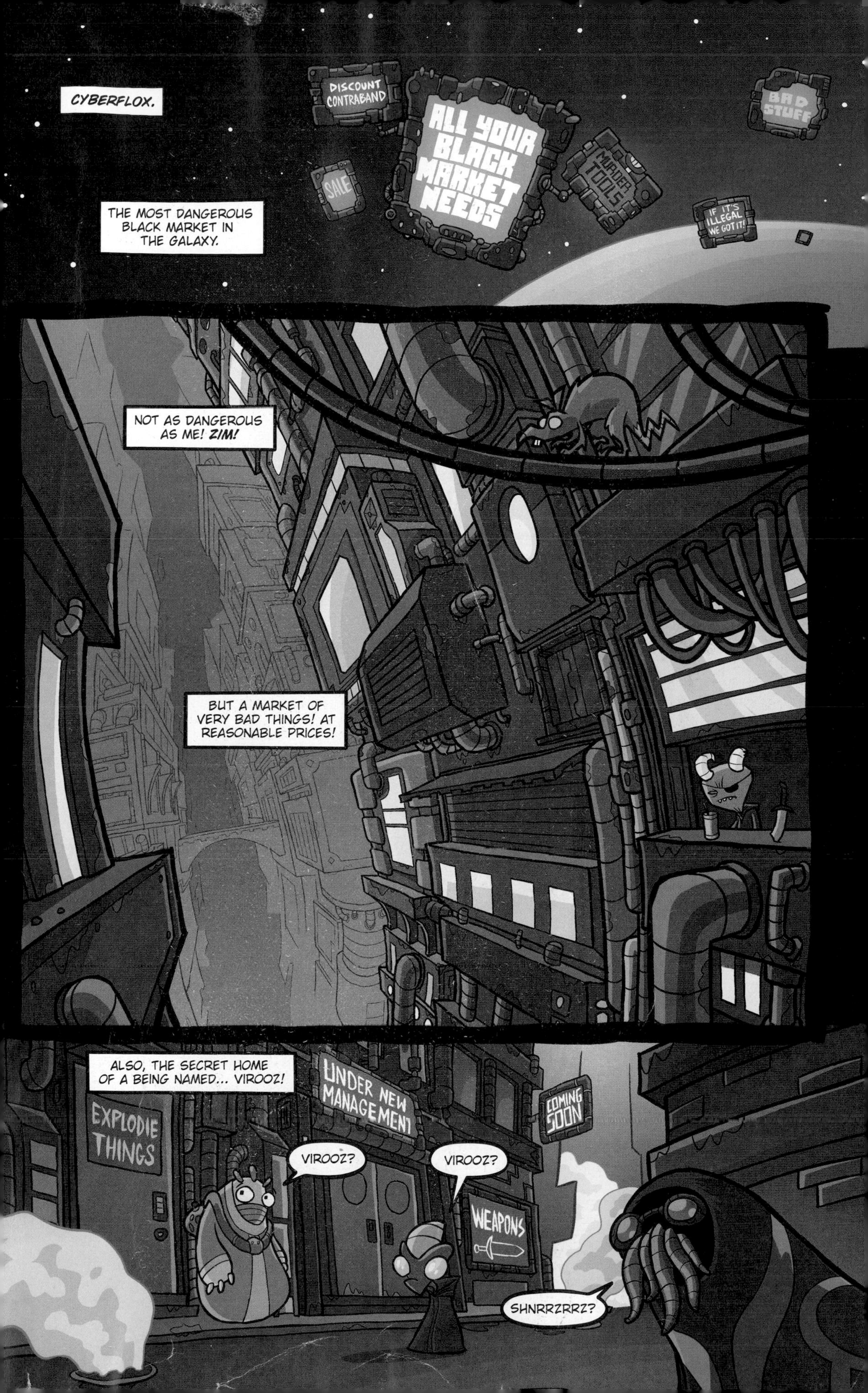
CYBERFLOX.
DISCOUNT CONTRABAND
ALL YOUR BLACK MARKET NEEDS
BAD STUFF
SALE
MURDER TOOLS
IF IT'S ILLEGAL WE GOT IT!
THE MOST DANGEROUS BLACK MARKET IN THE GALAXY.
NOT AS DANGEROUS AS ME! ZIM!
BUT A MARKET OF VERY BAD THINGS! AT REASONABLE PRICES!
ALSO, THE SECRET HOME OF A BEING NAMED... VIROOZ!
UNDER NEW MANAGEMENT
COMING SOON
EXPLODIE THINGS
VIROOZ?
VIROOZ?
WEAPONS
SHNRRZRRZ?

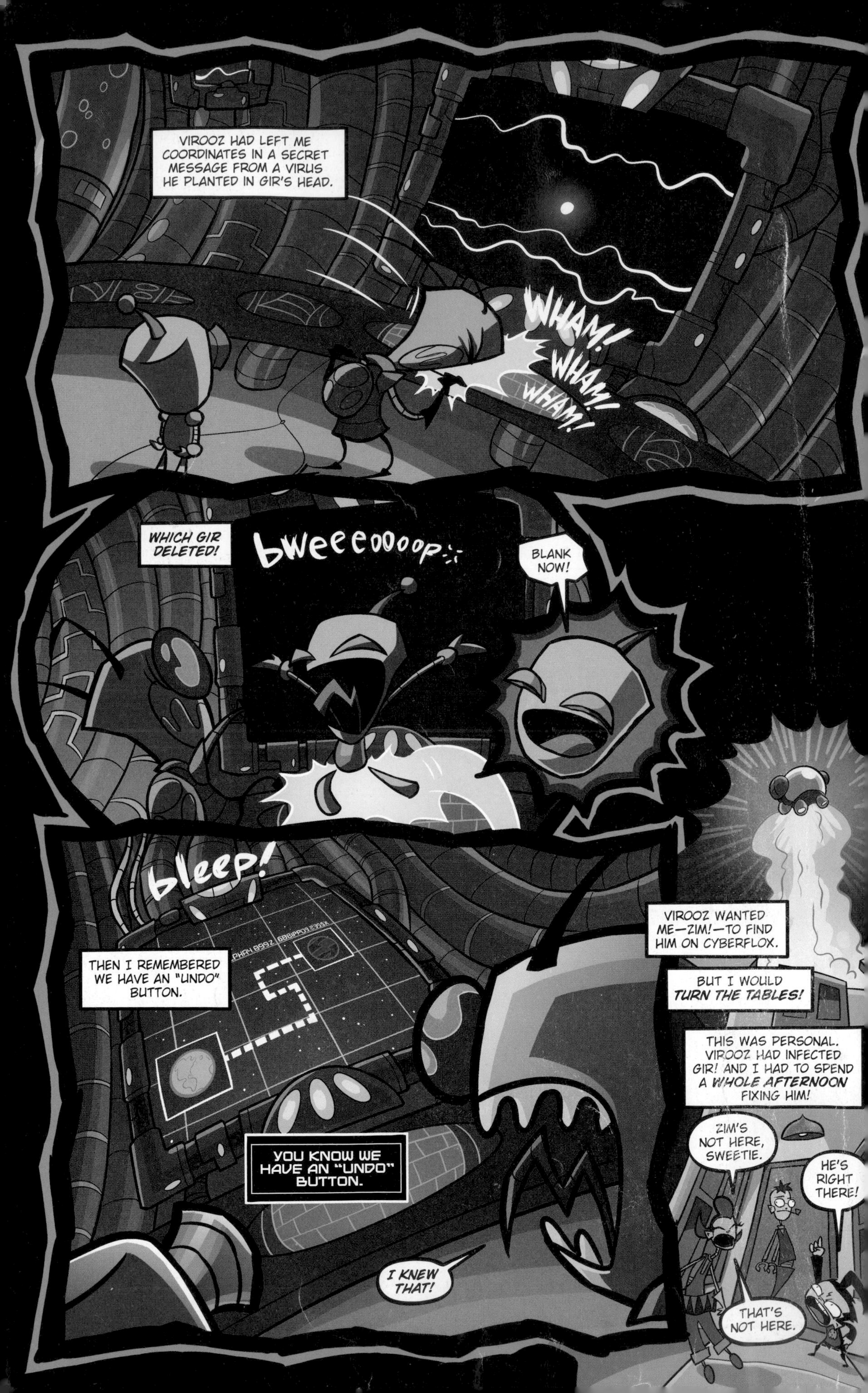

VIROOZ HAD LEFT ME COORDINATES IN A SECRET MESSAGE FROM A VIRUS HE PLANTED IN GIR'S HEAD.
WHAM! WHAM! WHAM!
WHICH GIR DELETED!
bweeeoooop
BLANK NOW!
bleep!
THEN I REMEMBERED WE HAVE AN "UNDO" BUTTON.
YOU KNOW WE HAVE AN "UNDO" BUTTON.
I KNEW THAT!
VIROOZ WANTED ME—ZIM!—TO FIND HIM ON CYBERFLOX.
BUT I WOULD *TURN THE TABLES!*
THIS WAS PERSONAL. VIROOZ HAD INFECTED GIR! AND I HAD TO SPEND A *WHOLE AFTERNOON* FIXING HIM!
ZIM'S NOT HERE, SWEETIE.
HE'S RIGHT THERE!
THAT'S NOT HERE.

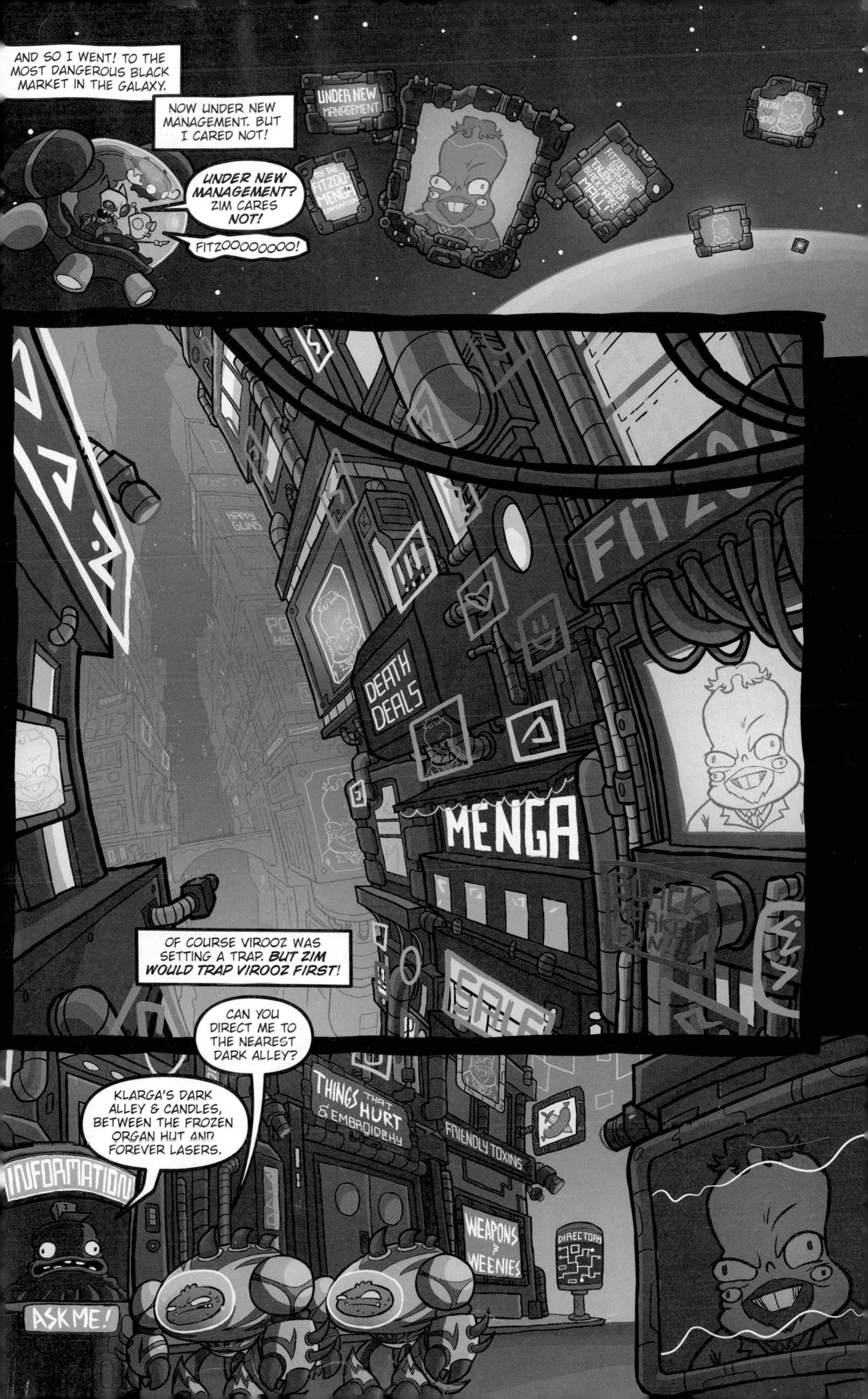
AND SO I WENT! TO THE MOST DANGEROUS BLACK MARKET IN THE GALAXY.
NOW UNDER NEW MANAGEMENT. BUT I CARED NOT!
UNDER NEW MANAGEMENT
BY THE FITZOO-MENGA CORPORATION
FITZOO-MENGA SAYS "ENJOY YOUR BLACK MARKET MALL!"
FITZOO YOU!
UNDER NEW MANAGEMENT? ZIM CARES NOT!
FITZOOOOOOOO!
HAPPY GUNS
FITZOO
DEATH DEALS
MENGA
SALE
OF COURSE VIROOZ WAS SETTING A TRAP. BUT ZIM WOULD TRAP VIROOZ FIRST!
CAN YOU DIRECT ME TO THE NEAREST DARK ALLEY?
KLARGA'S DARK ALLEY & CANDLES, BETWEEN THE FROZEN ORGAN HUT AND FOREVER LASERS.
INFORMATION
ASK ME!
THINGS THAT HURT & EMBROIDERY
FRIENDLY TOXINS
WEAPONS & WEENIES
DIRECTORY

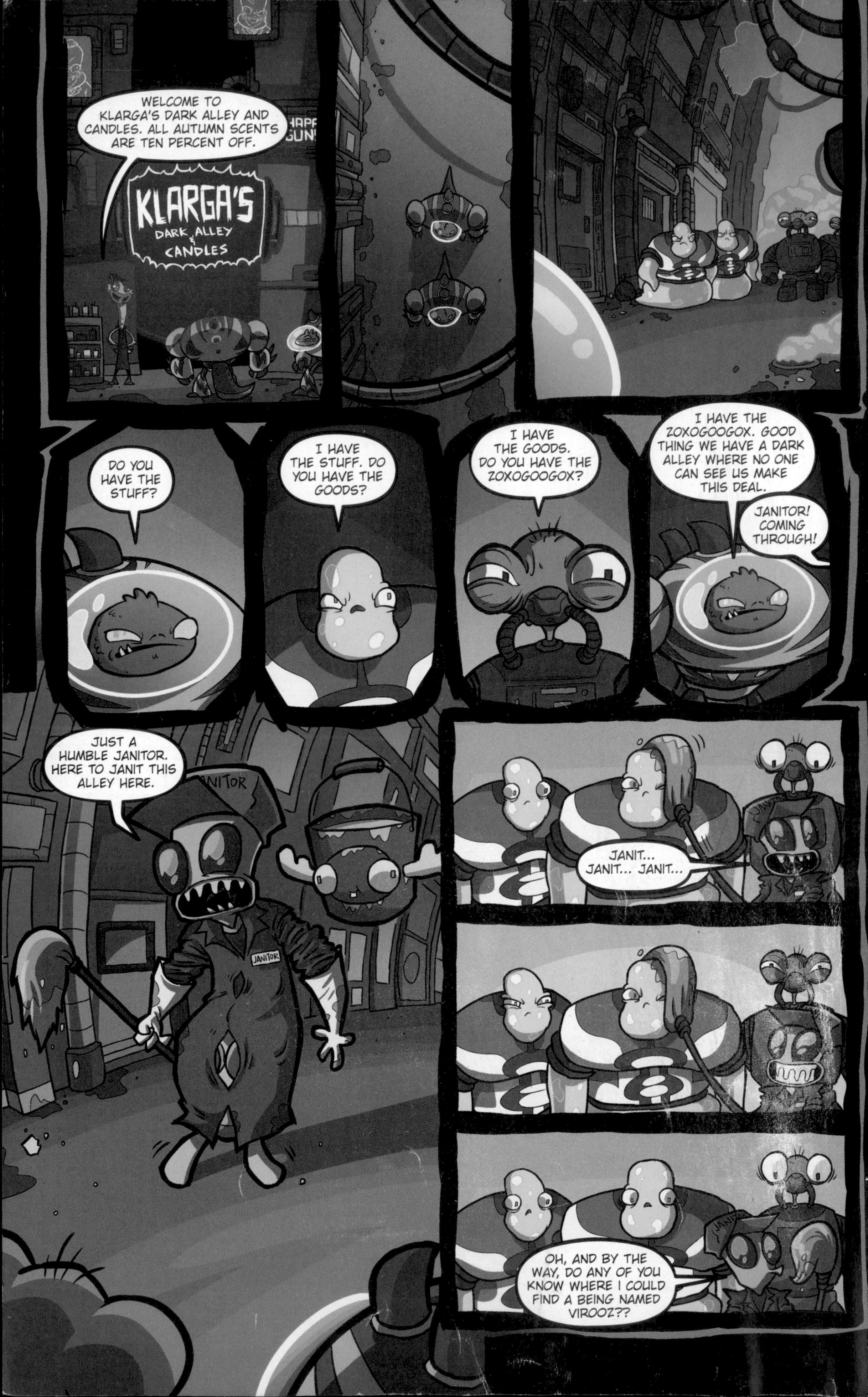
WELCOME TO KLARGA'S DARK ALLEY AND CANDLES. ALL AUTUMN SCENTS ARE TEN PERCENT OFF.
KLARGA'S DARK ALLEY & CANDLES
DO YOU HAVE THE STUFF?
I HAVE THE STUFF. DO YOU HAVE THE GOODS?
I HAVE THE GOODS. DO YOU HAVE THE ZOXOGOOGOX?
I HAVE THE ZOXOGOOGOX. GOOD THING WE HAVE A DARK ALLEY WHERE NO ONE CAN SEE US MAKE THIS DEAL.
JANITOR! COMING THROUGH!
JUST A HUMBLE JANITOR. HERE TO JANIT THIS ALLEY HERE.
JANITOR
JANITOR
JANIT... JANIT... JANIT...
OH, AND BY THE WAY, DO ANY OF YOU KNOW WHERE I COULD FIND A BEING NAMED VIROOZ??

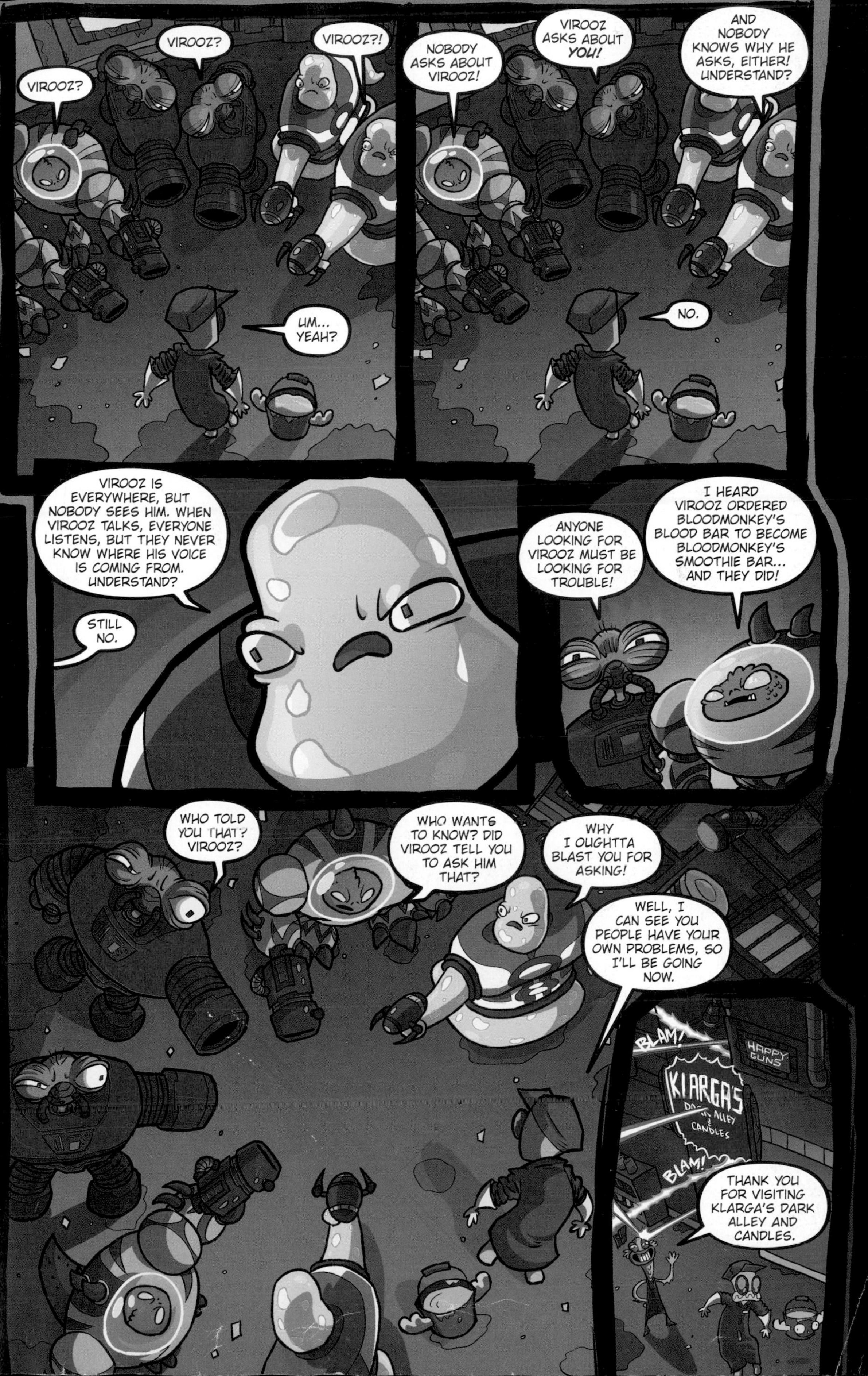
VIROOZ?
VIROOZ?
VIROOZ?!
UM... YEAH?
NOBODY ASKS ABOUT VIROOZ!
VIROOZ ASKS ABOUT *YOU!*
AND NOBODY KNOWS WHY HE ASKS, EITHER! UNDERSTAND?
NO.
VIROOZ IS EVERYWHERE, BUT NOBODY SEES HIM. WHEN VIROOZ TALKS, EVERYONE LISTENS, BUT THEY NEVER KNOW WHERE HIS VOICE IS COMING FROM. UNDERSTAND?
STILL NO.
ANYONE LOOKING FOR VIROOZ MUST BE LOOKING FOR TROUBLE!
I HEARD VIROOZ ORDERED BLOODMONKEY'S BLOOD BAR TO BECOME BLOODMONKEY'S SMOOTHIE BAR... AND THEY DID!
WHO TOLD YOU THAT? VIROOZ?
WHO WANTS TO KNOW? DID VIROOZ TELL YOU TO ASK HIM THAT?
WHY I OUGHTTA BLAST YOU FOR ASKING!
WELL, I CAN SEE YOU PEOPLE HAVE YOUR OWN PROBLEMS, SO I'LL BE GOING NOW.
BLAM!
HAPPY GUNS
KLARGA'S
CANDLES
BLAM!
THANK YOU FOR VISITING KLARGA'S DARK ALLEY AND CANDLES.

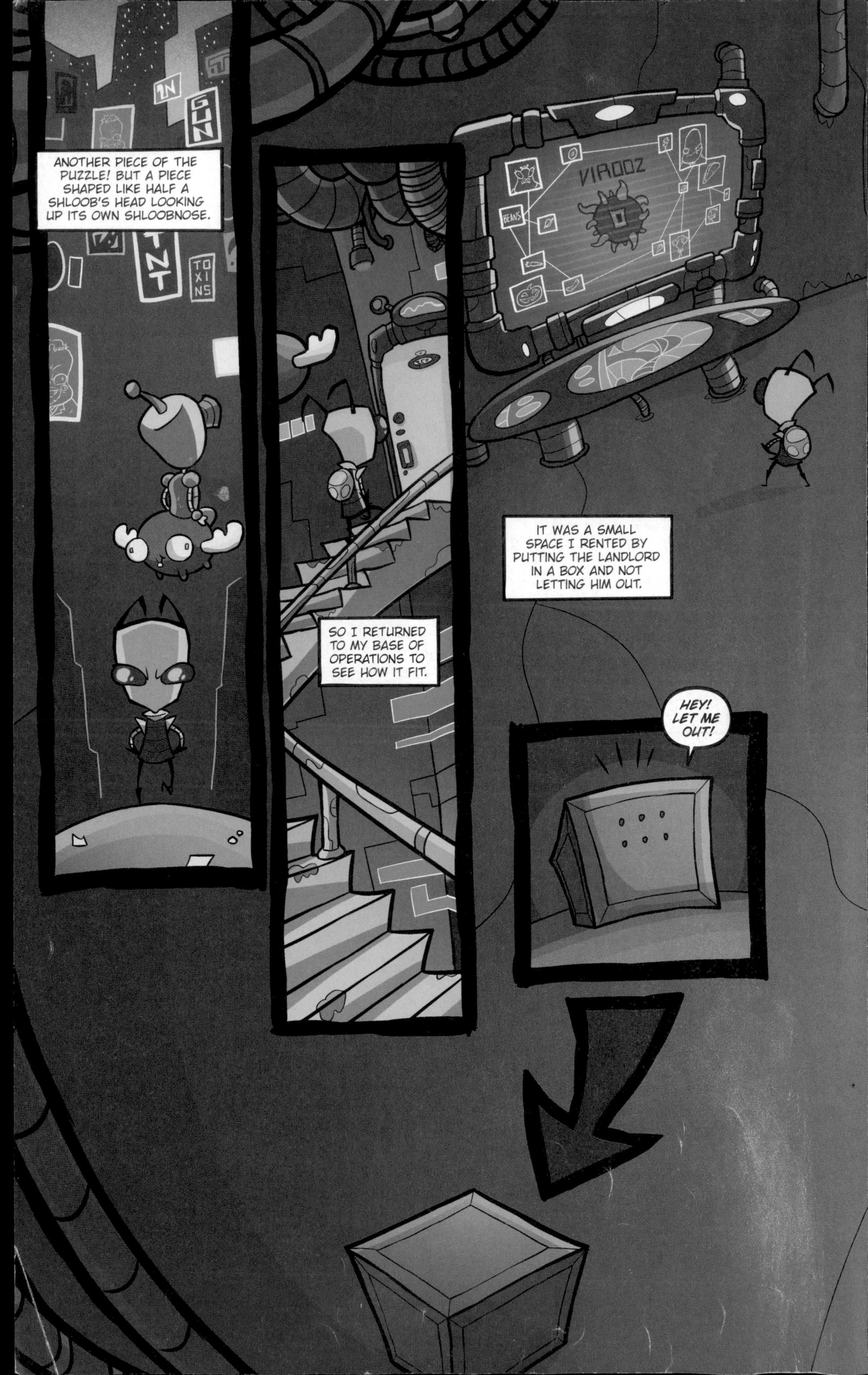

ANOTHER PIECE OF THE PUZZLE! BUT A PIECE SHAPED LIKE HALF A SHLOOB'S HEAD LOOKING UP ITS OWN SHLOOBNOSE.
GUN
TNT
TOXINS
SO I RETURNED TO MY BASE OF OPERATIONS TO SEE HOW IT FIT.
VIROOZ
BEANS
IT WAS A SMALL SPACE I RENTED BY PUTTING THE LANDLORD IN A BOX AND NOT LETTING HIM OUT.
HEY! LET ME OUT!

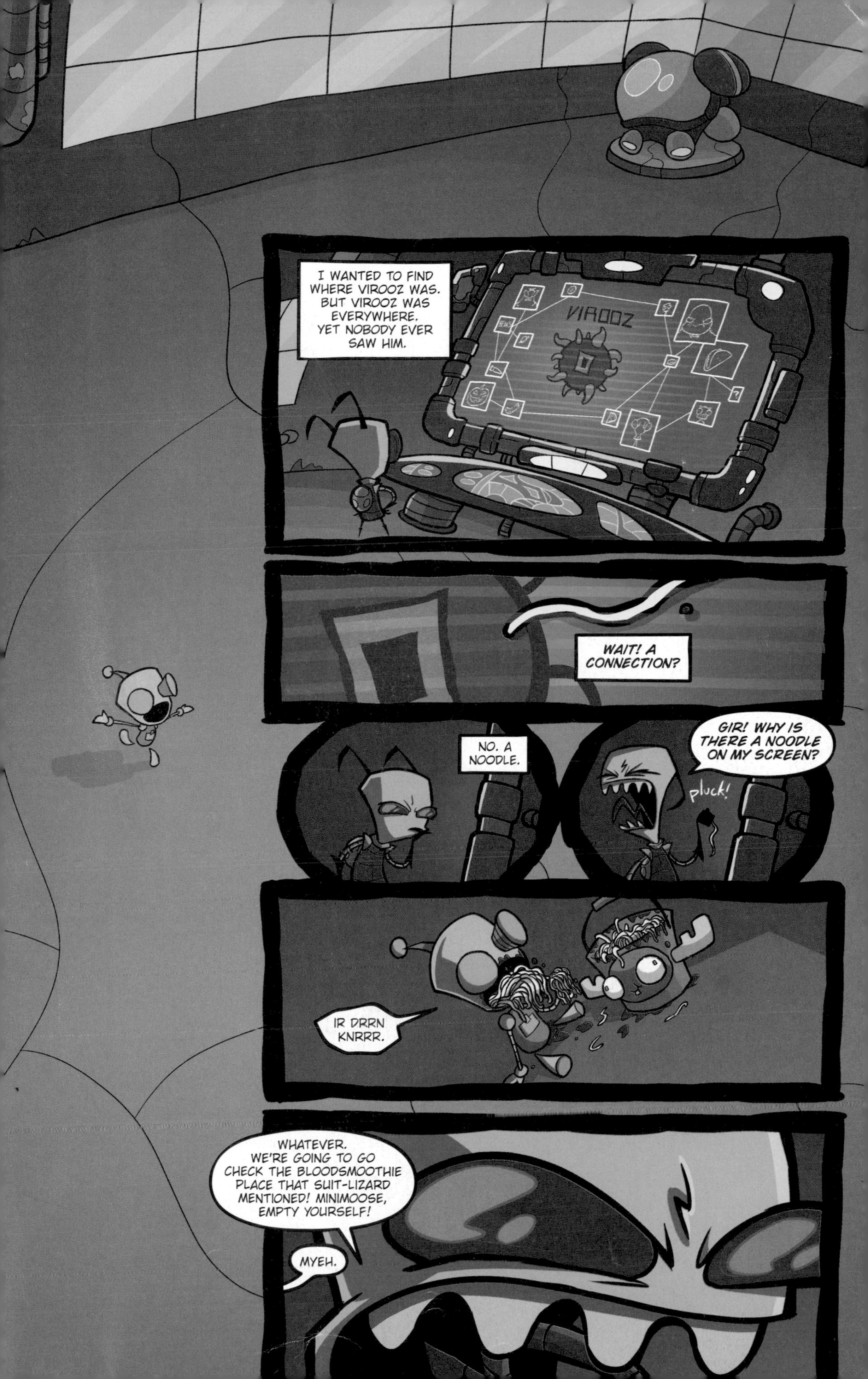
I WANTED TO FIND WHERE VIROOZ WAS. BUT VIROOZ WAS EVERYWHERE. YET NOBODY EVER SAW HIM.
VIROOZ
WAIT! A CONNECTION?
NO. A NOODLE.
GIR! WHY IS THERE A NOODLE ON MY SCREEN?
pluck!
IR DRRN KNRRR.
WHATEVER. WE'RE GOING TO GO CHECK THE BLOODSMOOTHIE PLACE THAT SUIT-LIZARD MENTIONED! MINIMOOSE, EMPTY YOURSELF!
MYEH.

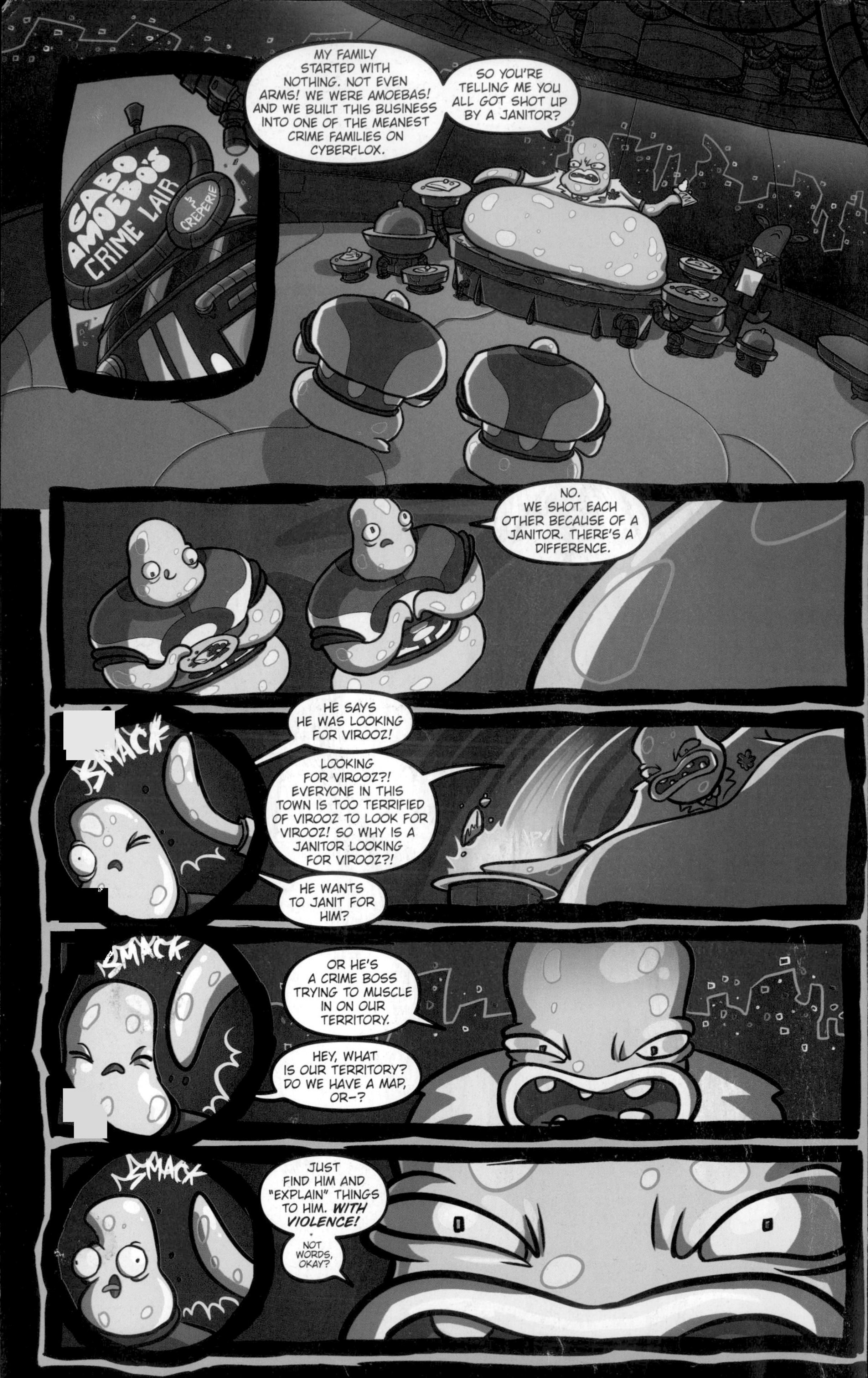
CABO AMOEBO'S CRIME LAIR & CREPERIE
MY FAMILY STARTED WITH NOTHING. NOT EVEN ARMS! WE WERE AMOEBAS! AND WE BUILT THIS BUSINESS INTO ONE OF THE MEANEST CRIME FAMILIES ON CYBERFLOX.
SO YOU'RE TELLING ME YOU ALL GOT SHOT UP BY A JANITOR?
NO. WE SHOT EACH OTHER BECAUSE OF A JANITOR. THERE'S A DIFFERENCE.
SMACK
HE SAYS HE WAS LOOKING FOR VIROOZ!
LOOKING FOR VIROOZ?! EVERYONE IN THIS TOWN IS TOO TERRIFIED OF VIROOZ TO LOOK FOR VIROOZ! SO WHY IS A JANITOR LOOKING FOR VIROOZ?!
HE WANTS TO JANIT FOR HIM?
SMACK
OR HE'S A CRIME BOSS TRYING TO MUSCLE IN ON OUR TERRITORY.
HEY, WHAT IS OUR TERRITORY? DO WE HAVE A MAP, OR–?
SMACK
JUST FIND HIM AND "EXPLAIN" THINGS TO HIM. WITH VIOLENCE!
NOT WORDS, OKAY?

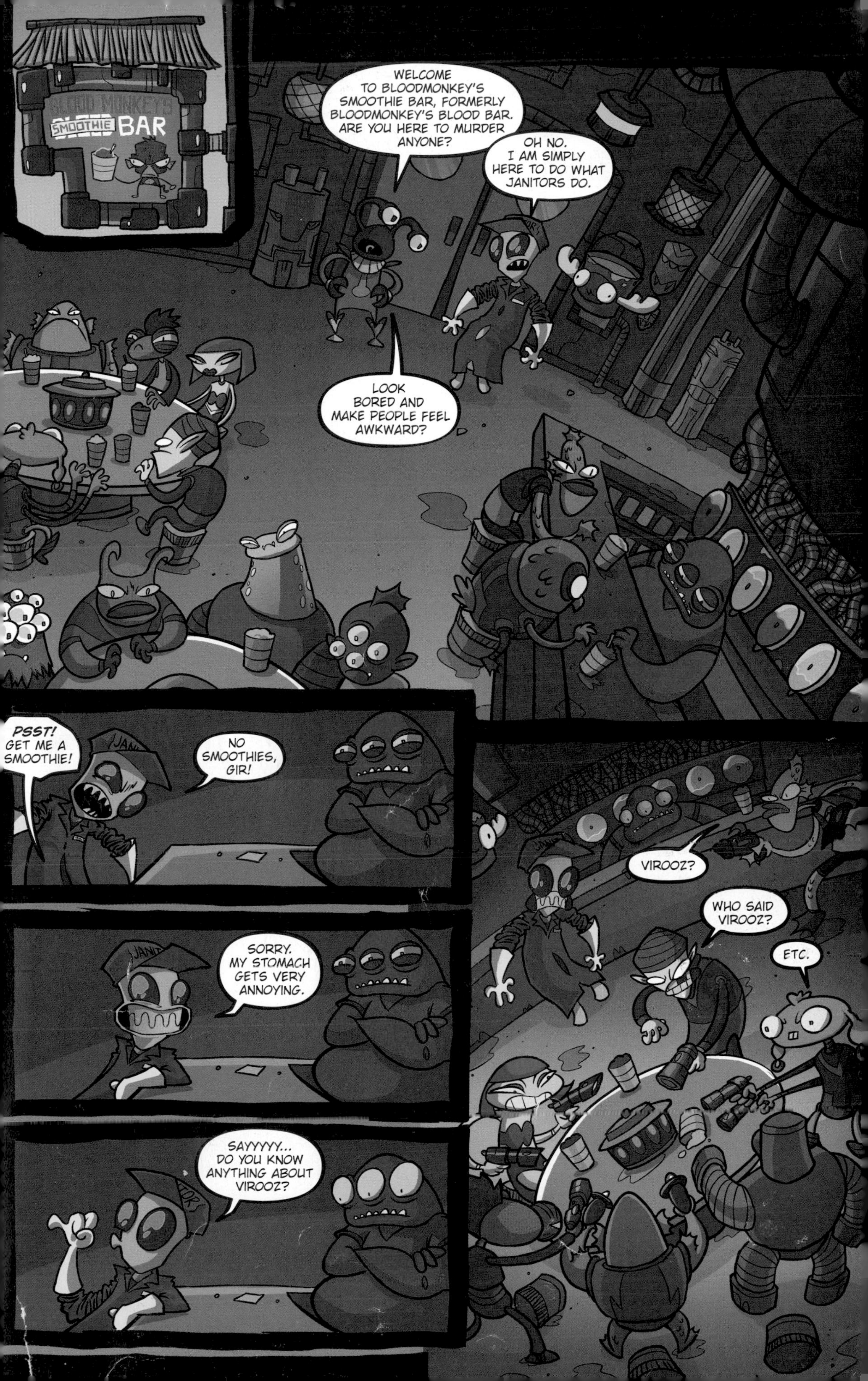
BLOOD MONKEY'S SMOOTHIE BAR
WELCOME TO BLOODMONKEY'S SMOOTHIE BAR, FORMERLY BLOODMONKEY'S BLOOD BAR. ARE YOU HERE TO MURDER ANYONE?
OH NO. I AM SIMPLY HERE TO DO WHAT JANITORS DO.
LOOK BORED AND MAKE PEOPLE FEEL AWKWARD?
PSST! GET ME A SMOOTHIE!
NO SMOOTHIES, GIR!
SORRY. MY STOMACH GETS VERY ANNOYING.
SAYYYYY... DO YOU KNOW ANYTHING ABOUT VIROOZ?
VIROOZ?
WHO SAID VIROOZ?
ETC.

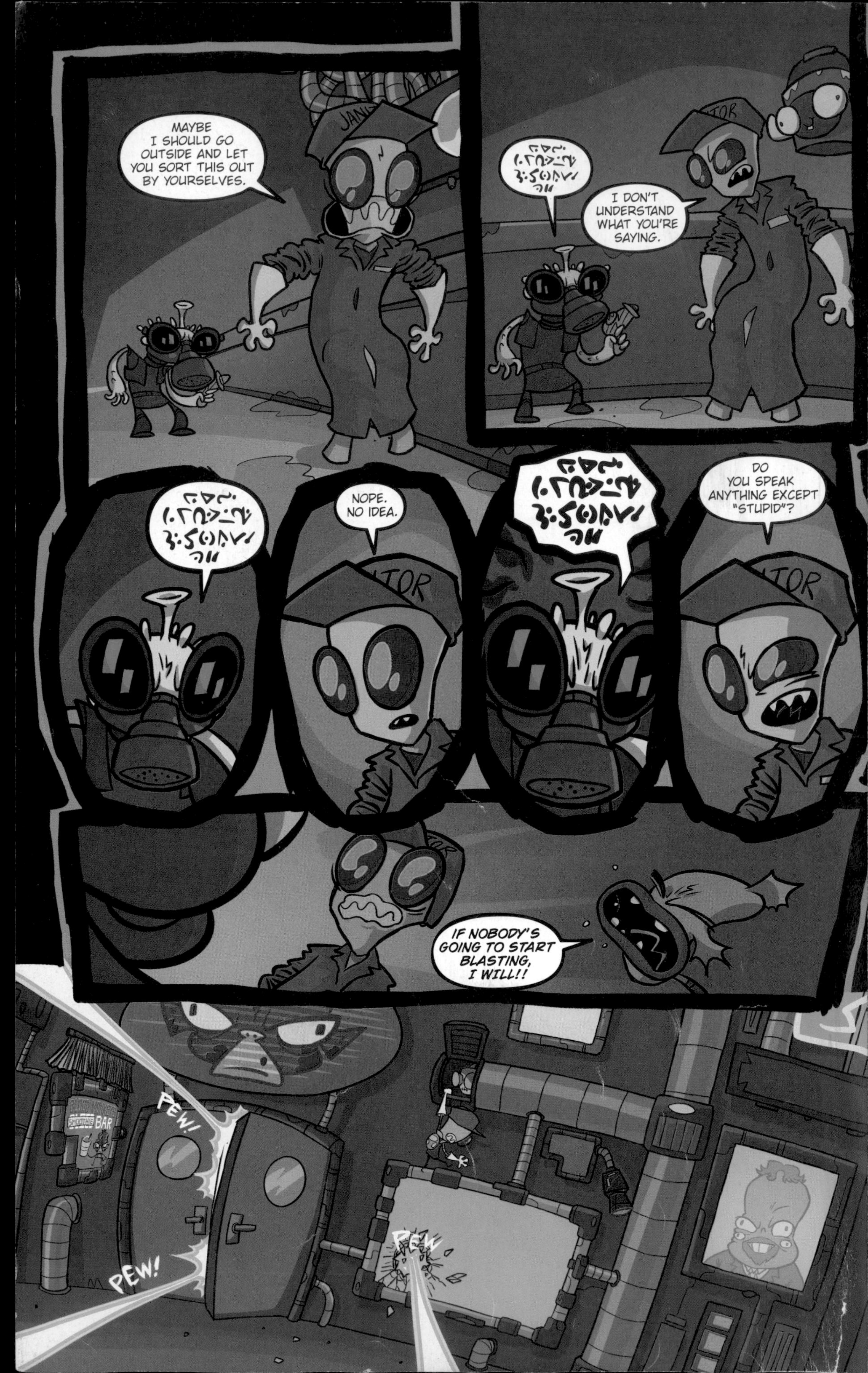
MAYBE I SHOULD GO OUTSIDE AND LET YOU SORT THIS OUT BY YOURSELVES.
I DON'T UNDERSTAND WHAT YOU'RE SAYING.
NOPE. NO IDEA.
DO YOU SPEAK ANYTHING EXCEPT "STUPID"?
IF NOBODY'S GOING TO START BLASTING, I WILL!!
PEW!
PEW!
PEW
SMOOTHIE BAR

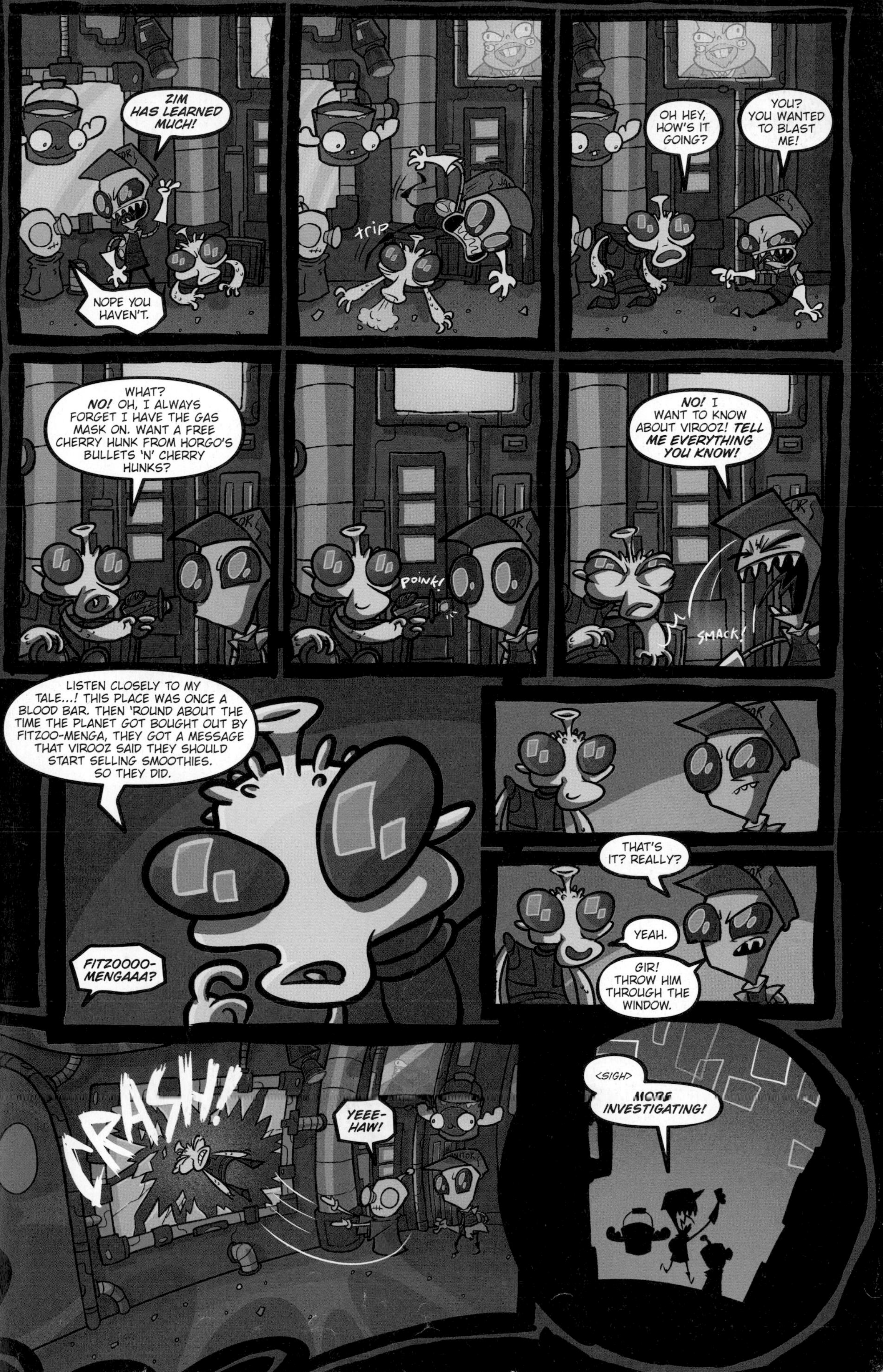

ZIM HAS LEARNED MUCH!
NOPE YOU HAVEN'T.
trip
OH HEY, HOW'S IT GOING?
YOU? YOU WANTED TO BLAST ME!
WHAT? NO! OH, I ALWAYS FORGET I HAVE THE GAS MASK ON. WANT A FREE CHERRY HUNK FROM HORGO'S BULLETS 'N' CHERRY HUNKS?
POINK!
NO! I WANT TO KNOW ABOUT VIROOZ! TELL ME EVERYTHING YOU KNOW!
SMACK!
LISTEN CLOSELY TO MY TALE...! THIS PLACE WAS ONCE A BLOOD BAR. THEN 'ROUND ABOUT THE TIME THE PLANET GOT BOUGHT OUT BY FITZOO-MENGA, THEY GOT A MESSAGE THAT VIROOZ SAID THEY SHOULD START SELLING SMOOTHIES. SO THEY DID.
FITZOOOO-MENGAAA?
THAT'S IT? REALLY?
YEAH.
GIR! THROW HIM THROUGH THE WINDOW.
CRASH!
YEEE-HAW!
<SIGH>
MORE INVESTIGATING!

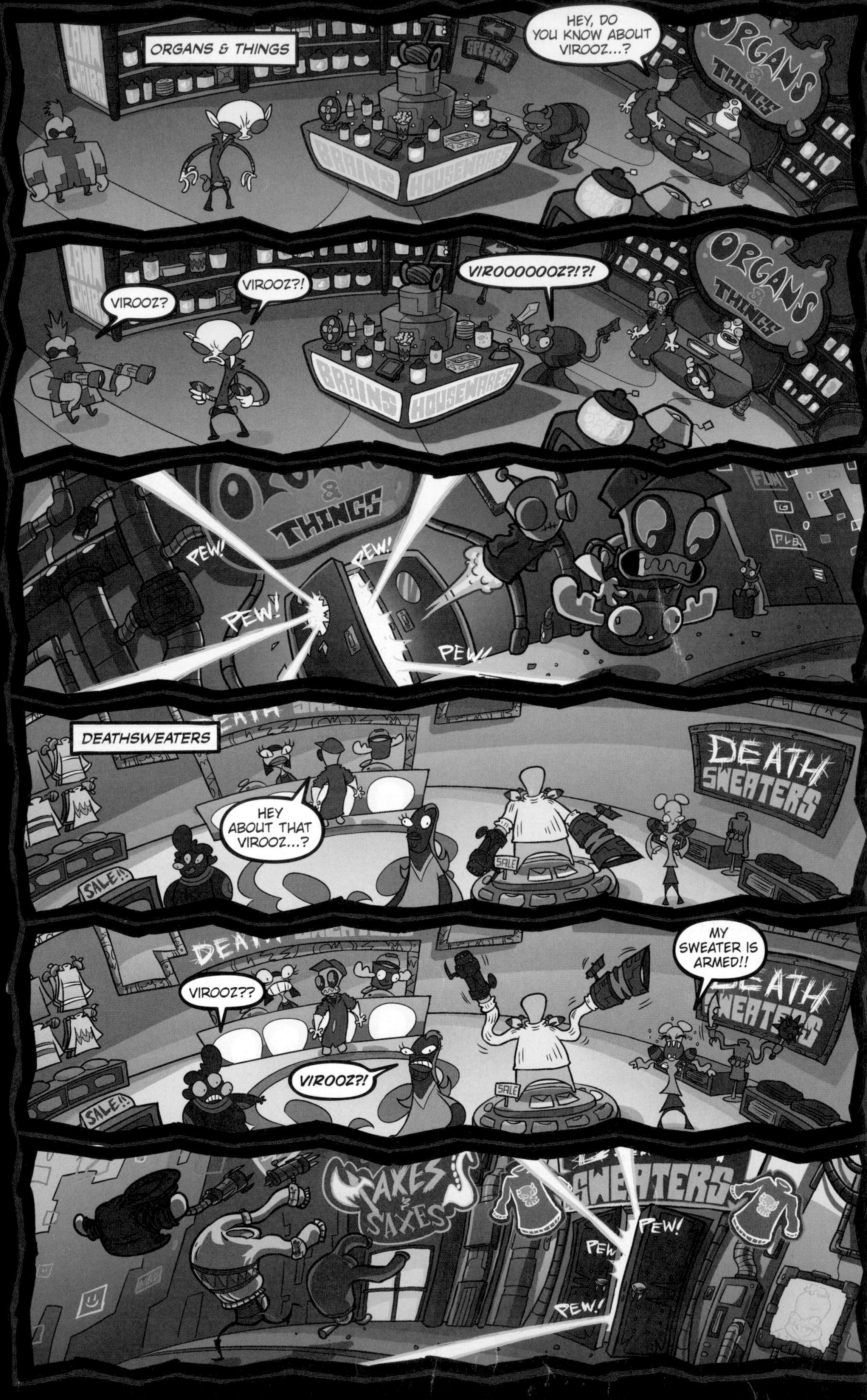
ORGANS & THINGS
HEY, DO YOU KNOW ABOUT VIROOZ...?
LAWN CHAIRS
SPLEENS
ORGANS & THINGS
BRAINS
HOUSEWARES
VIROOZ?
VIROOZ?!
VIROOOOOOZ?!?!
PEW!
PEW!
PEW!
PEW!
DEATHSWEATERS
HEY ABOUT THAT VIROOZ...?
DEATH SWEATERS
SALE!!
VIROOZ??
VIROOZ?!
MY SWEATER IS ARMED!!
AXES & SAXES
SWEATERS
PEW!
PEW
PEW!

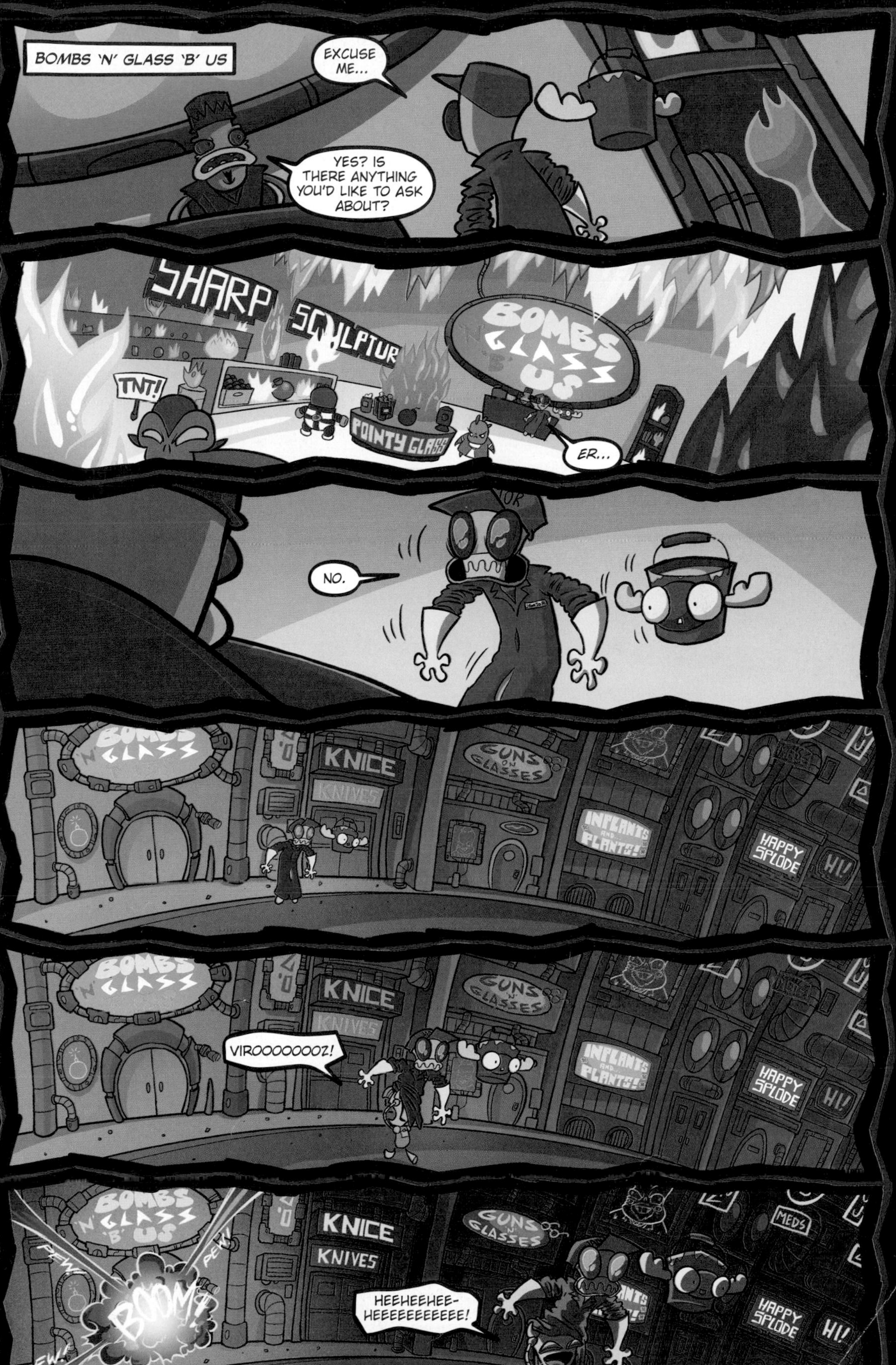
BOMBS 'N' GLASS 'B' US
EXCUSE ME...
YES? IS THERE ANYTHING YOU'D LIKE TO ASK ABOUT?
SHARP SCULPTUR
TNT!
BOMBS 'N' GLASS 'B' US
POINTY GLASS
ER...
NO.
BOMBS 'N' GLASS
KNICE KNIVES
GUNS ON GLASSES
INFLANTS AND PLANTS!
HAPPY SPLODE
HI!
VIROOOOOOOZ!
BOMBS 'N' GLASS 'B' US
KNICE KNIVES
GUNS 'N' GLASSES
MEDS
PEW!
PEW!
BOOM!
PEW!
HEEHEEHEE-HEEEEEEEEEEE!
HAPPY SPLODE
HI!

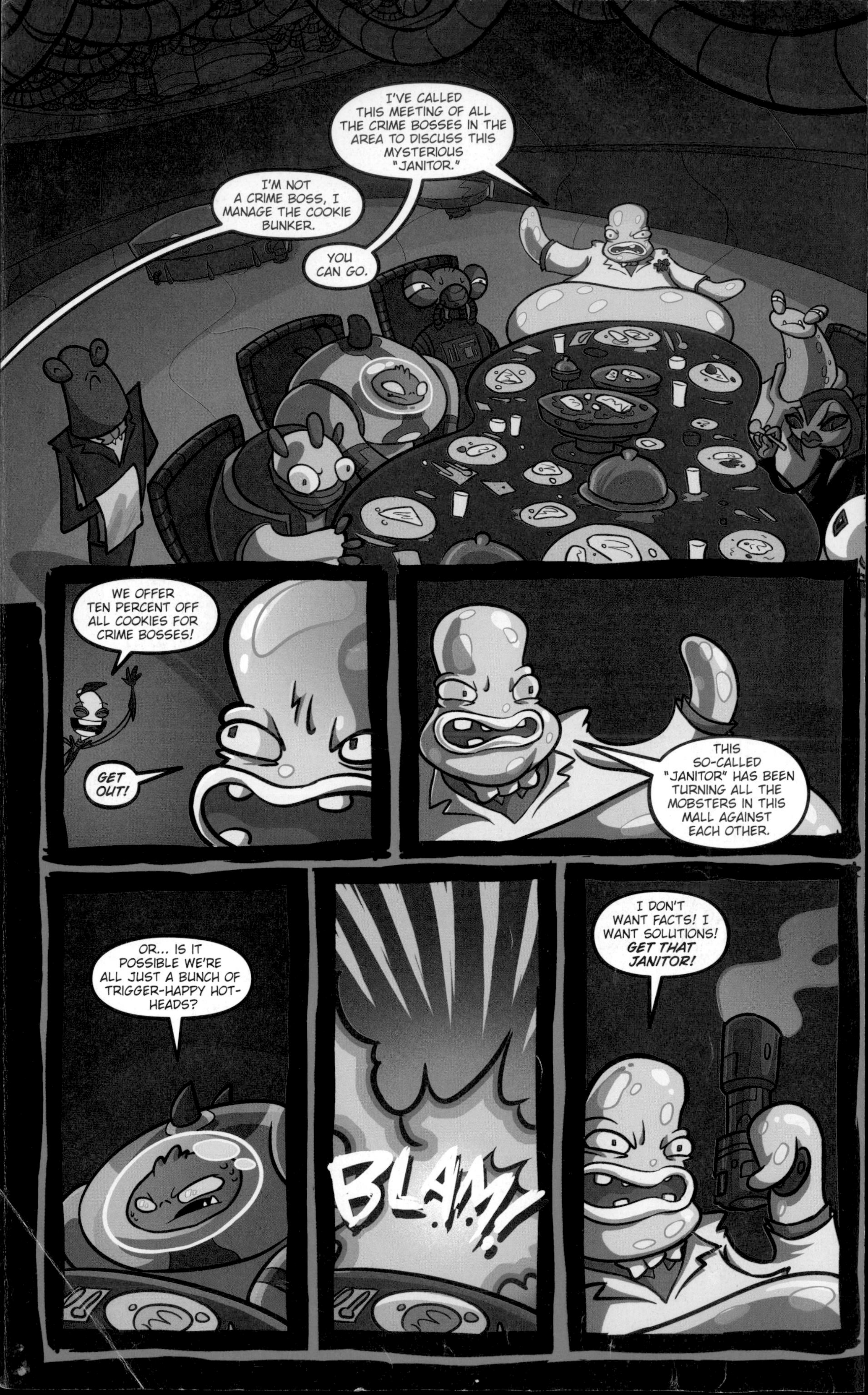
I'VE CALLED THIS MEETING OF ALL THE CRIME BOSSES IN THE AREA TO DISCUSS THIS MYSTERIOUS "JANITOR."
I'M NOT A CRIME BOSS, I MANAGE THE COOKIE BUNKER.
YOU CAN GO.
WE OFFER TEN PERCENT OFF ALL COOKIES FOR CRIME BOSSES!
GET OUT!
THIS SO-CALLED "JANITOR" HAS BEEN TURNING ALL THE MOBSTERS IN THIS MALL AGAINST EACH OTHER.
OR... IS IT POSSIBLE WE'RE ALL JUST A BUNCH OF TRIGGER-HAPPY HOT-HEADS?
BLAM!!
I DON'T WANT FACTS! I WANT SOLUTIONS! GET THAT JANITOR!

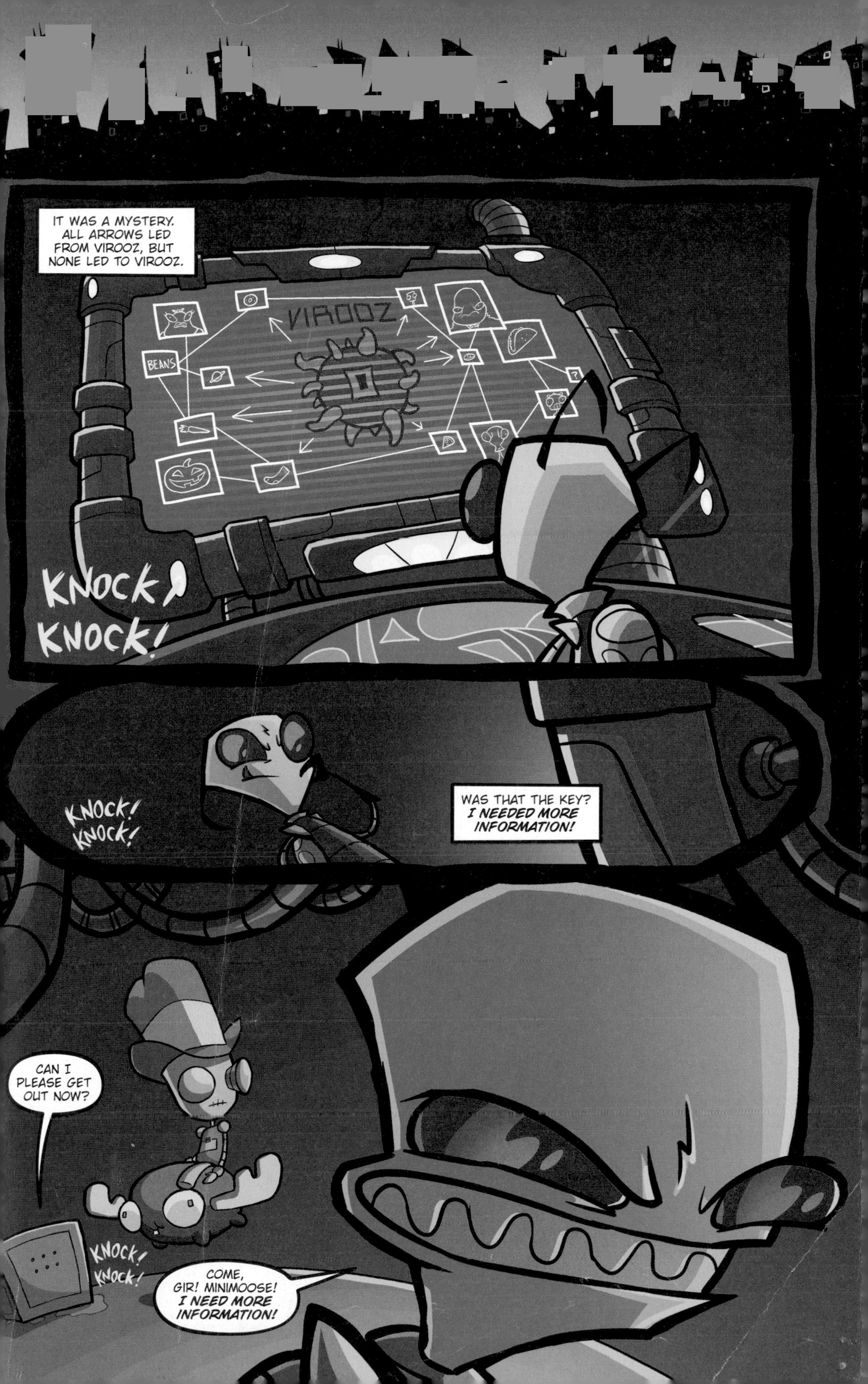
IT WAS A MYSTERY. ALL ARROWS LED FROM VIROOZ, BUT NONE LED TO VIROOZ.
VIROOZ
BEANS
?
KNOCK! KNOCK!
KNOCK! KNOCK!
WAS THAT THE KEY? *I NEEDED MORE INFORMATION!*
CAN I PLEASE GET OUT NOW?
KNOCK! KNOCK!
COME, GIR! MINIMOOSE! *I NEED MORE INFORMATION!*

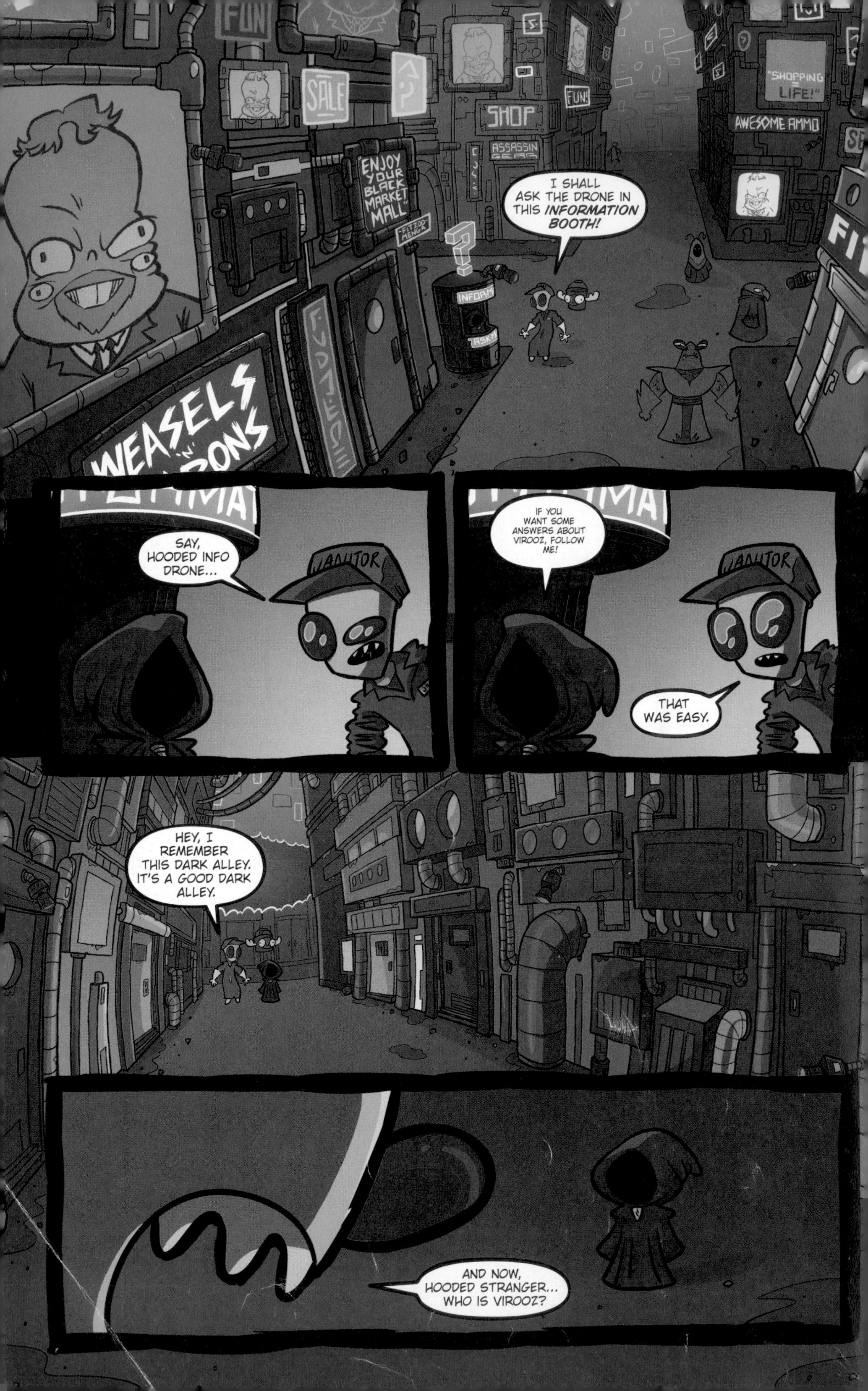
FUN
SALE
SHOP
FUN!
"SHOPPING = LIFE!"
AWESOME AMMO
ASSASSIN GEAR
ENJOY YOUR BLACK MARKET MALL
WEASELS 'N' IRONS
INFORM
ASK
I SHALL ASK THE DRONE IN THIS *INFORMATION BOOTH!*
SAY, HOODED INFO DRONE...
JANITOR
IF YOU WANT SOME ANSWERS ABOUT VIROOZ, FOLLOW ME!
THAT WAS EASY.
HEY, I REMEMBER THIS DARK ALLEY. IT'S A GOOD DARK ALLEY.
AND NOW, HOODED STRANGER... WHO IS VIROOZ?

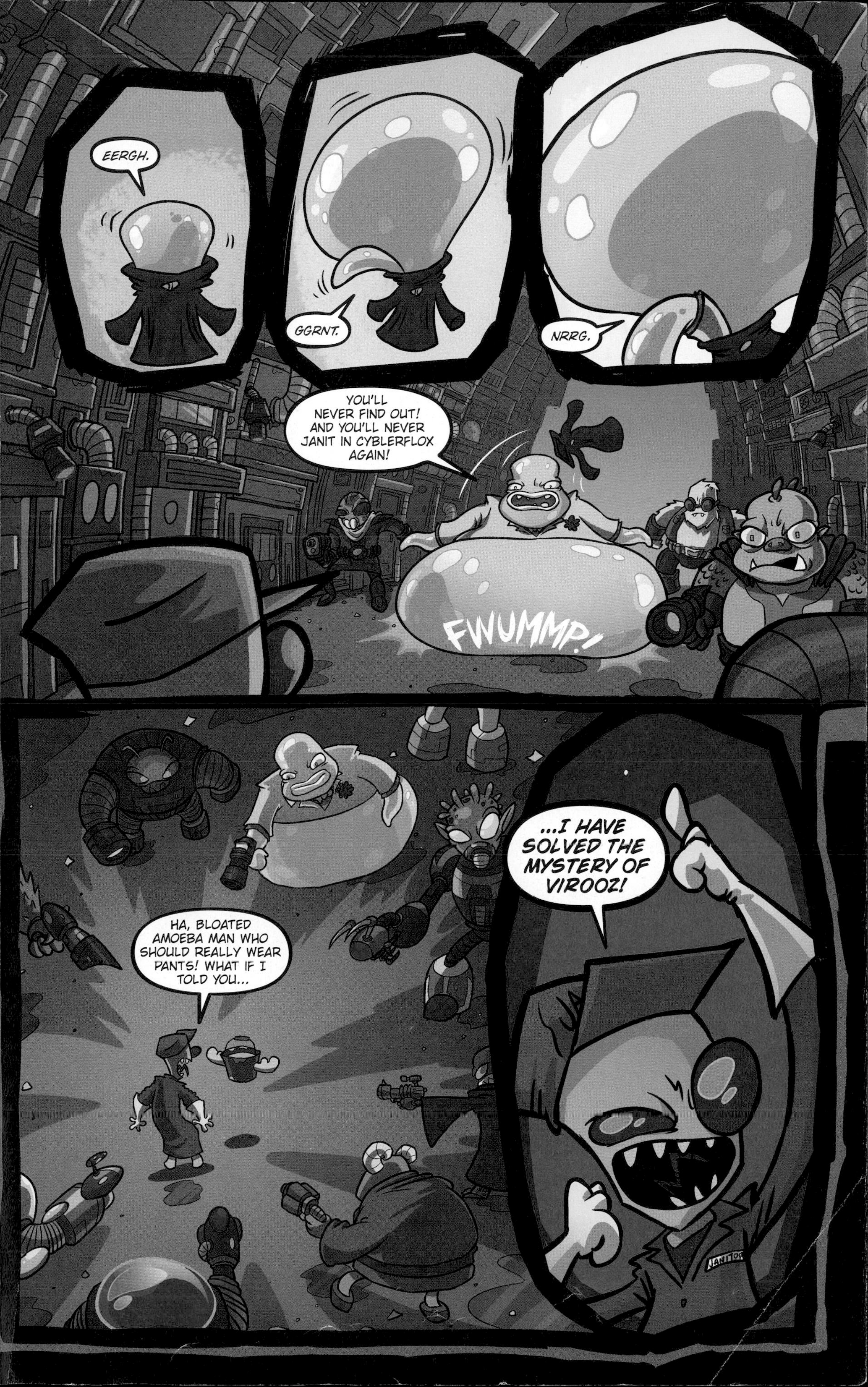
EERGH.
GGRNT.
NRRG.
YOU'LL NEVER FIND OUT! AND YOU'LL NEVER JANIT IN CYBLERFLOX AGAIN!
FWUMMP!
HA, BLOATED AMOEBA MAN WHO SHOULD REALLY WEAR PANTS! WHAT IF I TOLD YOU...
...I HAVE SOLVED THE MYSTERY OF VIROOZ!
JANITOR

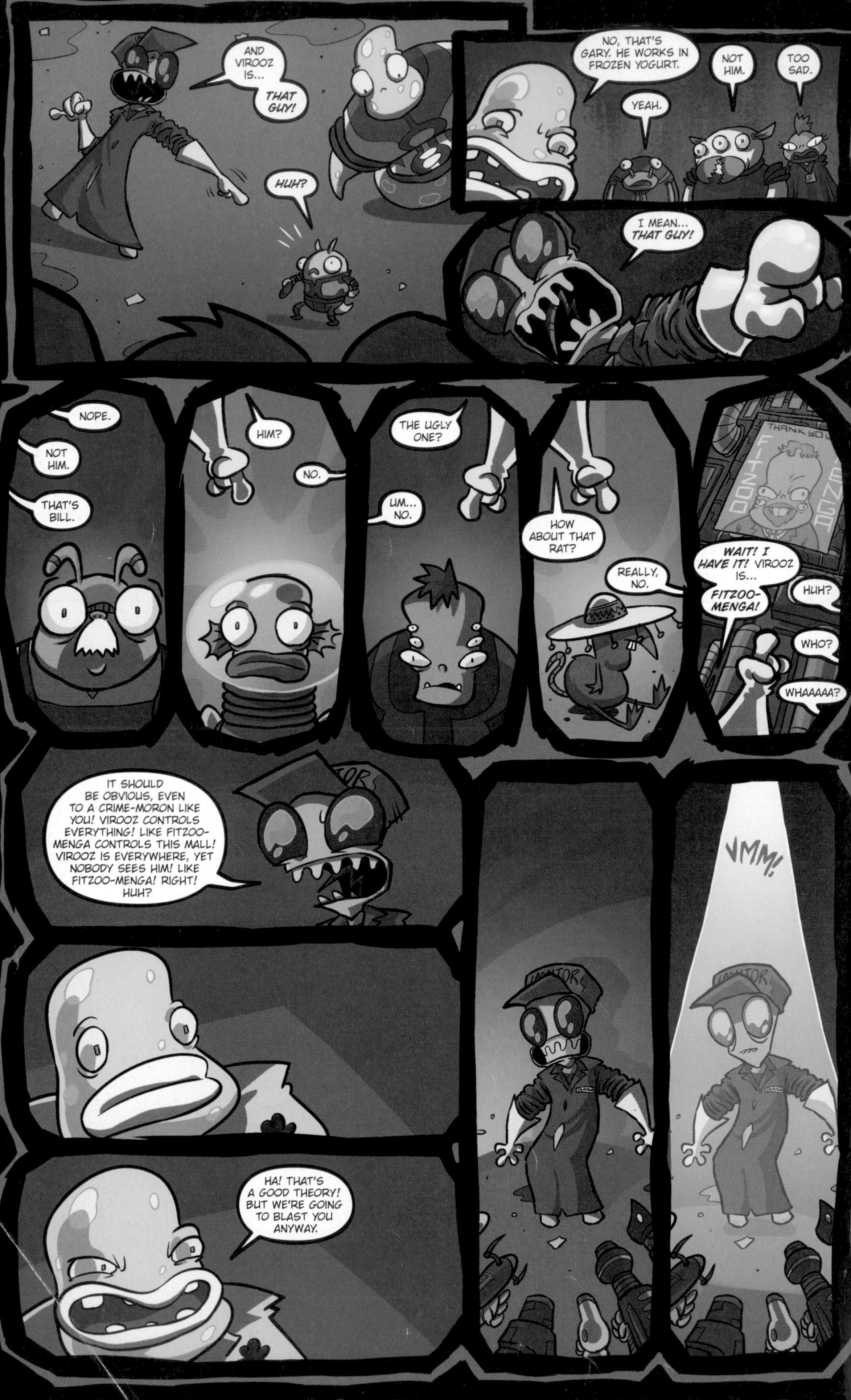
AND VIROOZ IS... THAT GUY!
HUH?
NO, THAT'S GARY. HE WORKS IN FROZEN YOGURT.
YEAH.
NOT HIM.
TOO SAD.
I MEAN... THAT GUY!
NOPE.
NOT HIM.
THAT'S BILL.
HIM?
NO.
THE UGLY ONE?
UM... NO.
HOW ABOUT THAT RAT?
REALLY, NO.
THANK YOU FITZOO-MENGA
WAIT! I HAVE IT! VIROOZ IS... FITZOO-MENGA!
HUH?
WHO?
WHAAAAA?
IT SHOULD BE OBVIOUS, EVEN TO A CRIME-MORON LIKE YOU! VIROOZ CONTROLS EVERYTHING! LIKE FITZOO-MENGA CONTROLS THIS MALL! VIROOZ IS EVERYWHERE, YET NOBODY SEES HIM! LIKE FITZOO-MENGA! RIGHT! HUH?
HA! THAT'S A GOOD THEORY! BUT WE'RE GOING TO BLAST YOU ANYWAY.
VMM!

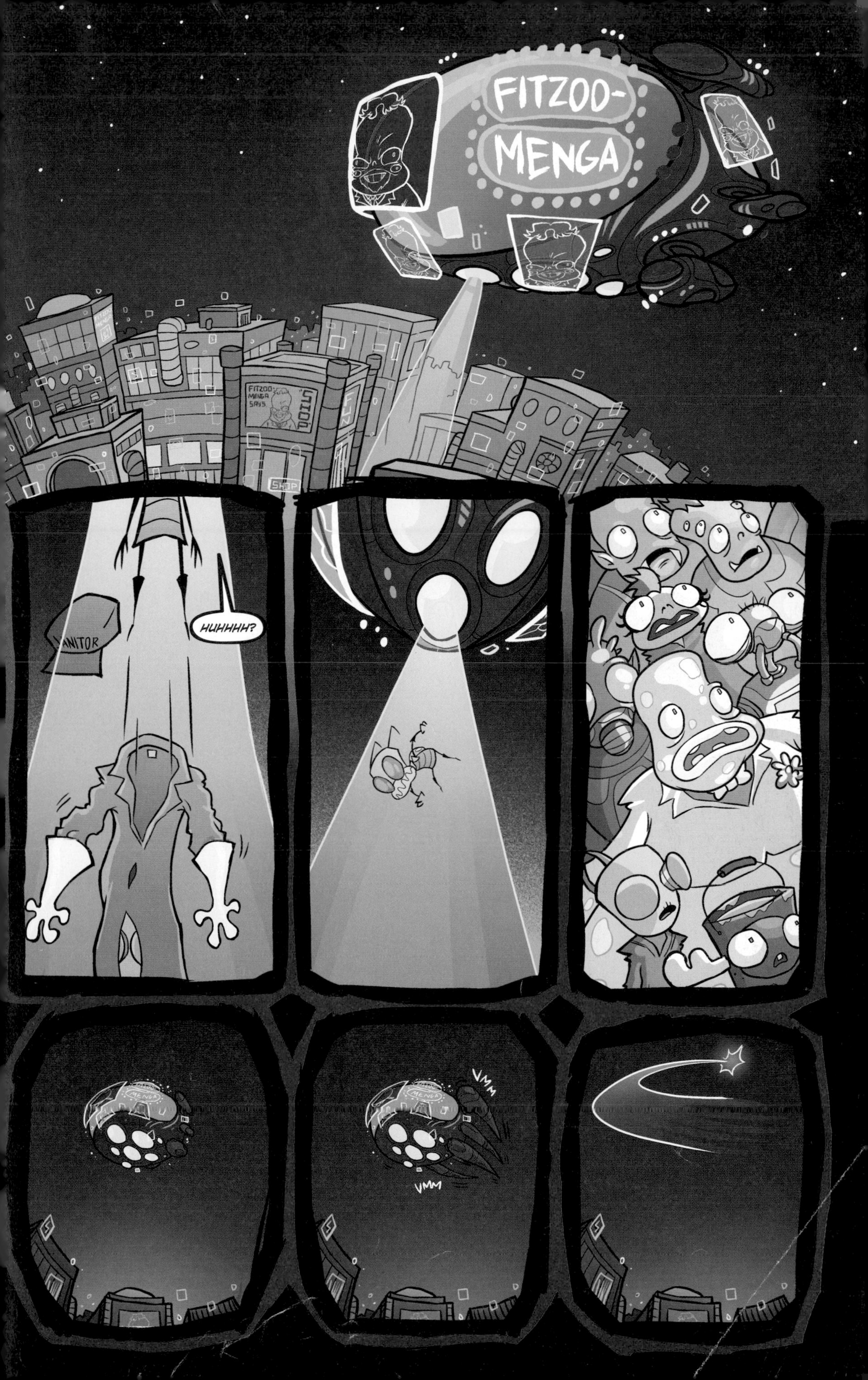
FITZOO-
MENGA
FITZOO-
MENGA
SAYS.
SHOP
SHOP
FUN
JANITOR
HUHHHH?
MENGA
MENGA
VMM
VMM

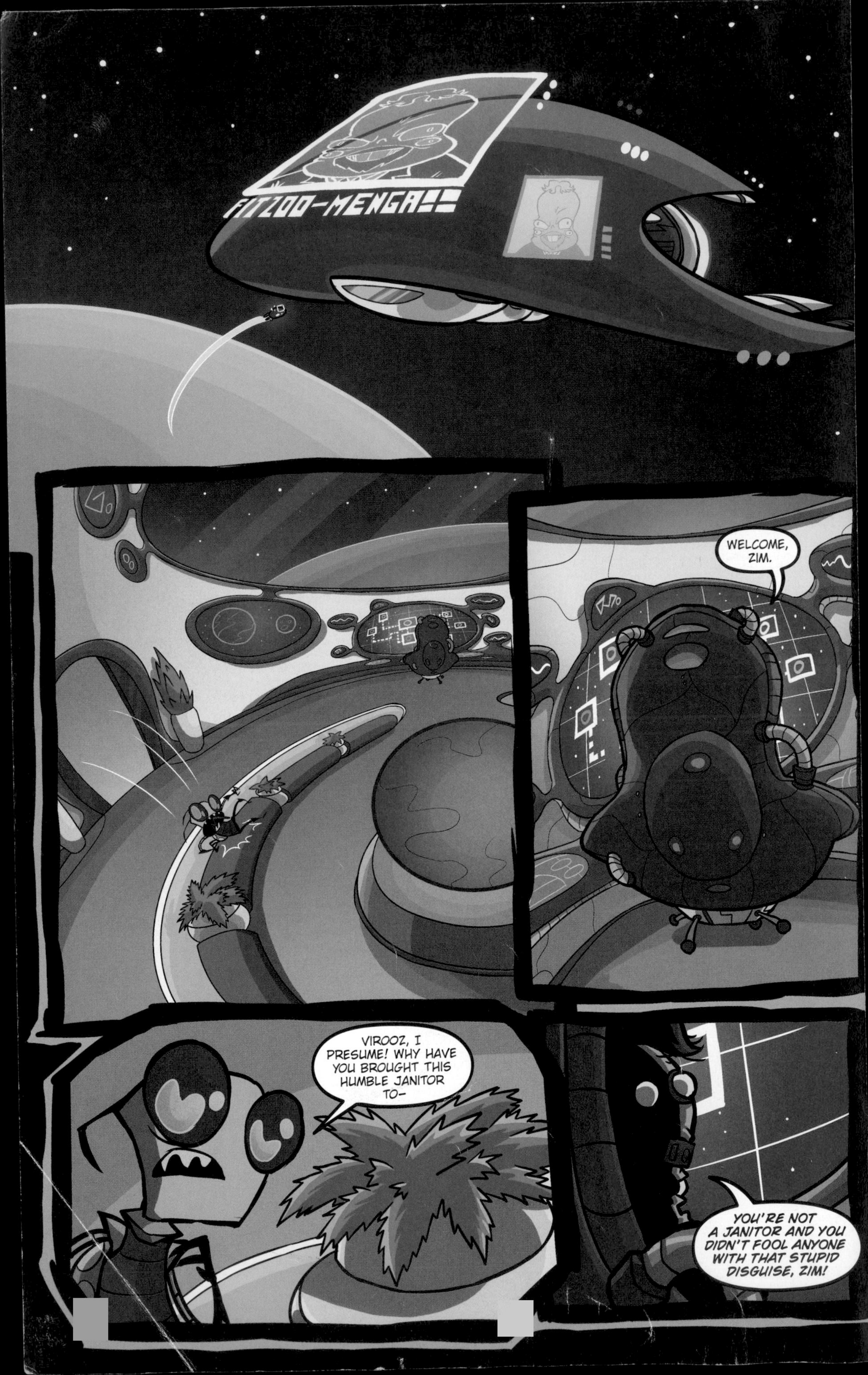
FITZOO-MENGA!!
WELCOME, ZIM.
VIROOZ, I PRESUME! WHY HAVE YOU BROUGHT THIS HUMBLE JANITOR TO—
YOU'RE NOT A JANITOR AND YOU DIDN'T FOOL ANYONE WITH THAT STUPID DISGUISE, ZIM!

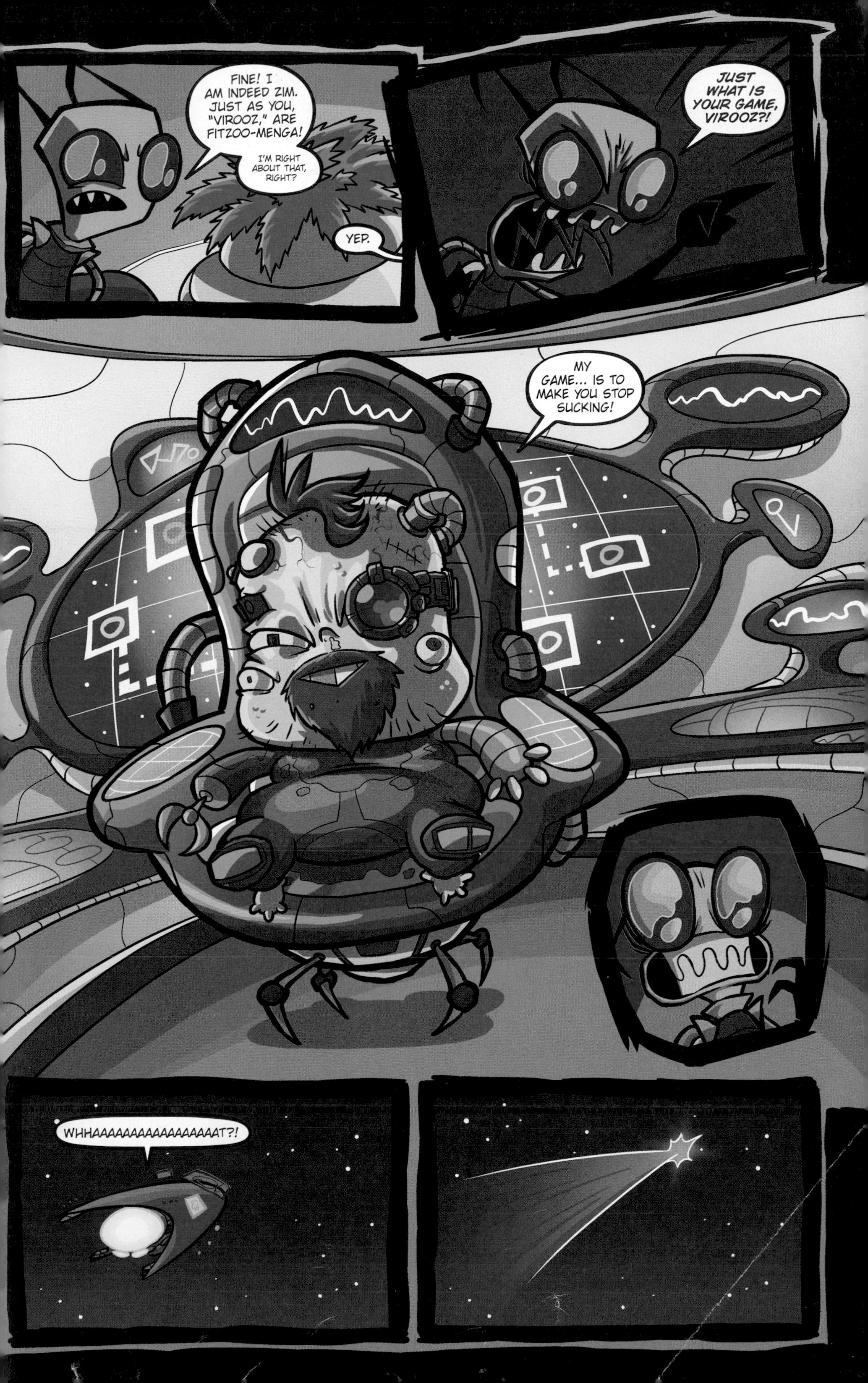

FINE! I AM INDEED ZIM. JUST AS YOU, "VIROOZ," ARE FITZOO-MENGA!
I'M RIGHT ABOUT THAT, RIGHT?
YEP.
JUST WHAT IS YOUR GAME, VIROOZ?!
MY GAME... IS TO MAKE YOU STOP SUCKING!
WHHAAAAAAAAAAAAAAAAAT?!

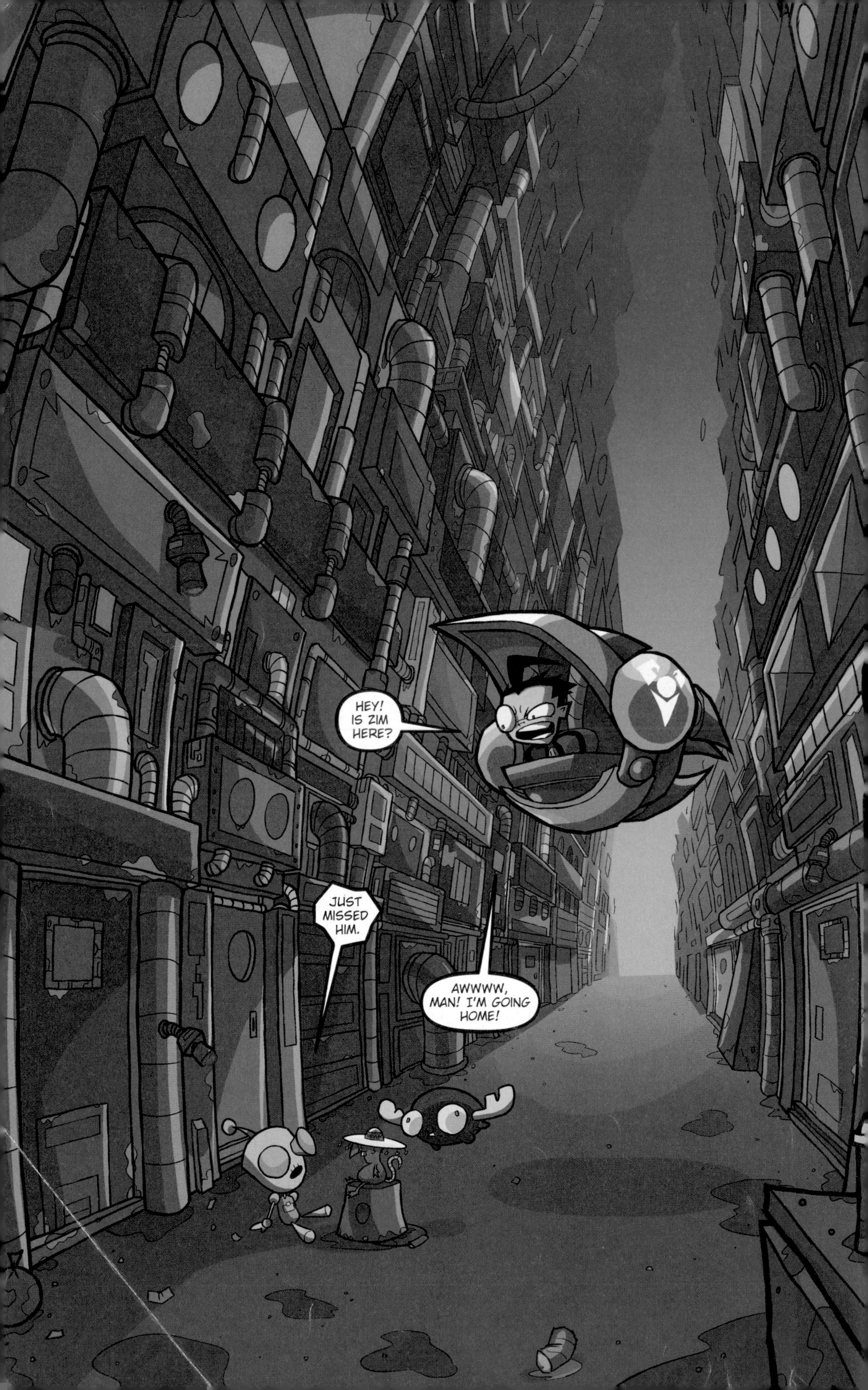
HEY! IS ZIM HERE?
JUST MISSED HIM.
AWWWW, MAN! I'M GOING HOME!

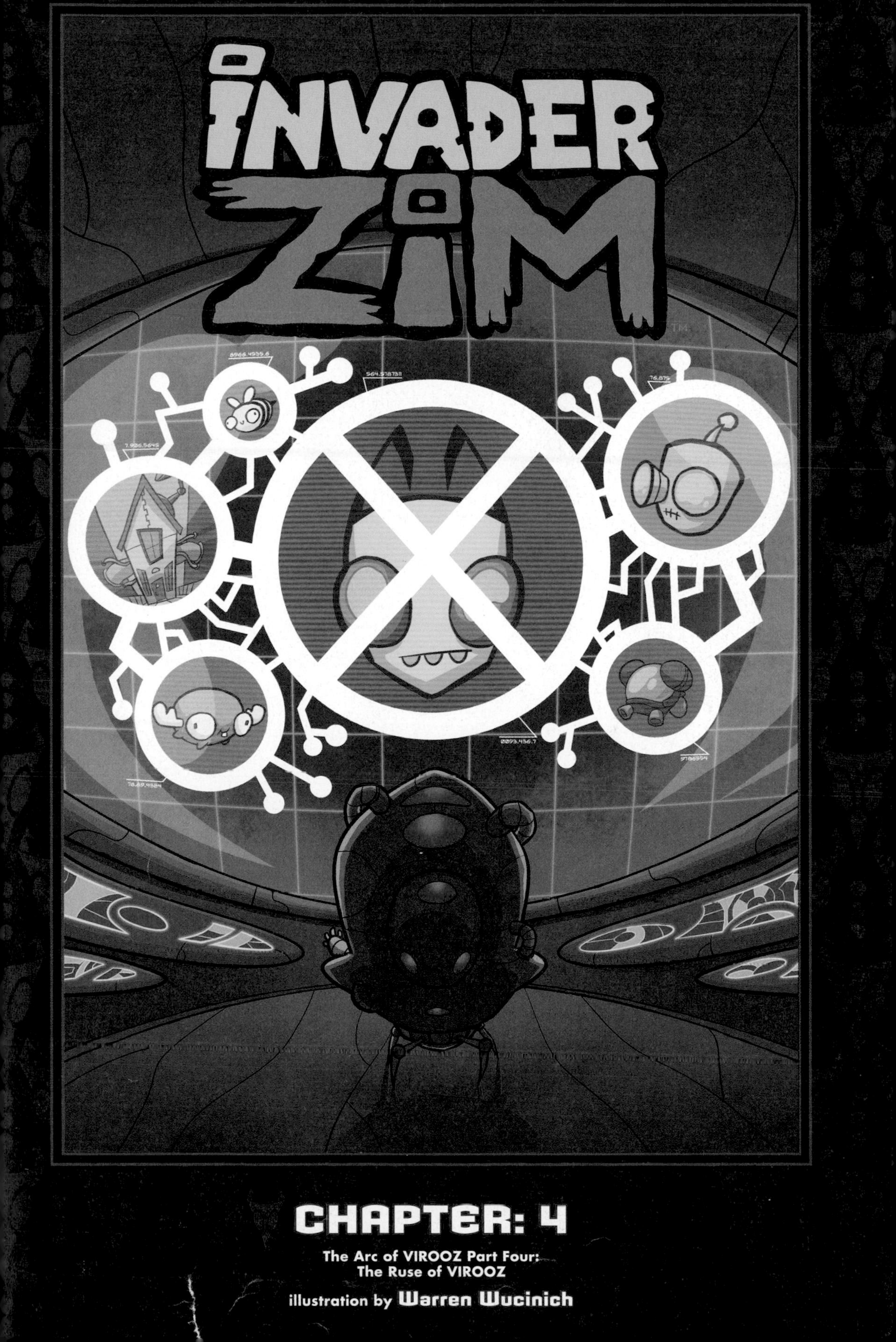
INVADER
ZIM

CHAPTER: 4

The Arc of VIROOZ Part Four:
The Ruse of VIROOZ

illustration by **Warren Wucinich**

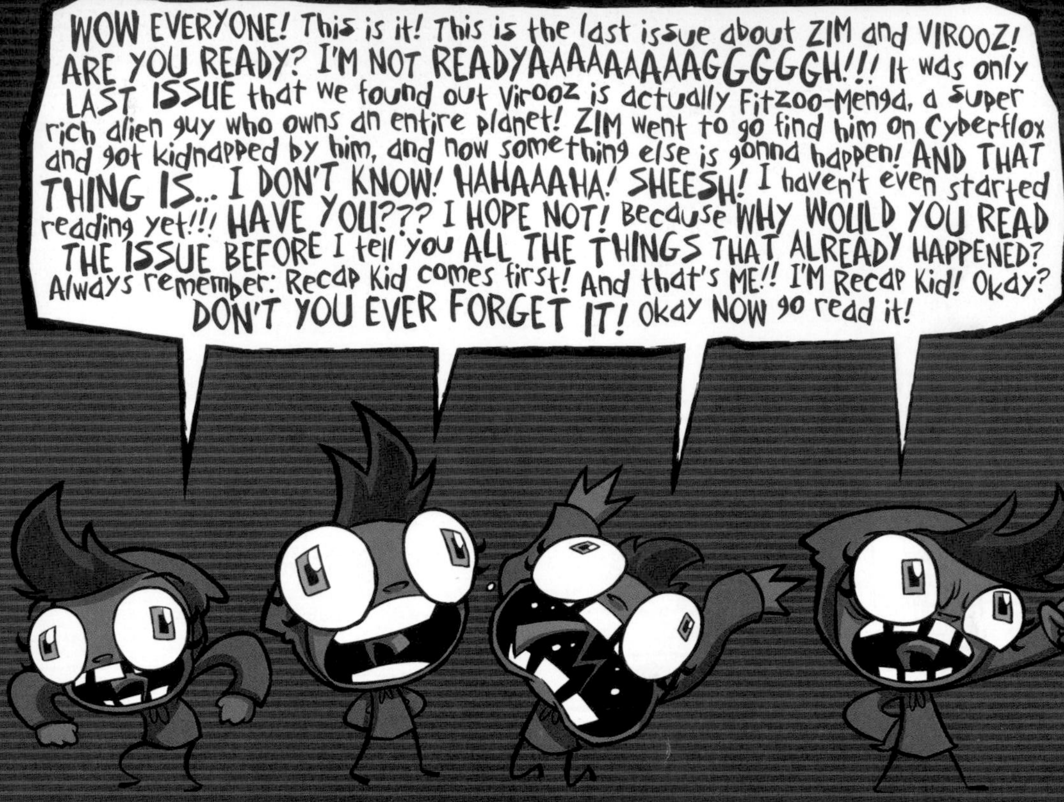
WOW EVERYONE! This is it! This is the last issue about ZIM and VIROOZ! ARE YOU READY? I'M NOT READYAAAAAAAAAGGGGGH!!! It was only LAST ISSUE that we found out Virooz is actually Fitzoo-Menga, a super rich alien guy who owns an entire planet! ZIM went to go find him on Cyberflox and got kidnapped by him, and now something else is gonna happen! AND THAT THING IS... I DON'T KNOW! HAHAAAHA! SHEESH! I haven't even started reading yet!!! HAVE YOU??? I HOPE NOT! Because WHY WOULD YOU READ THE ISSUE BEFORE I tell you ALL THE THINGS THAT ALREADY HAPPENED? Always remember: Recap Kid comes first! And that's ME!! I'M Recap Kid! Okay? DON'T YOU EVER FORGET IT! Okay NOW go read it!

Recap Kid by WARREN WUCINICH

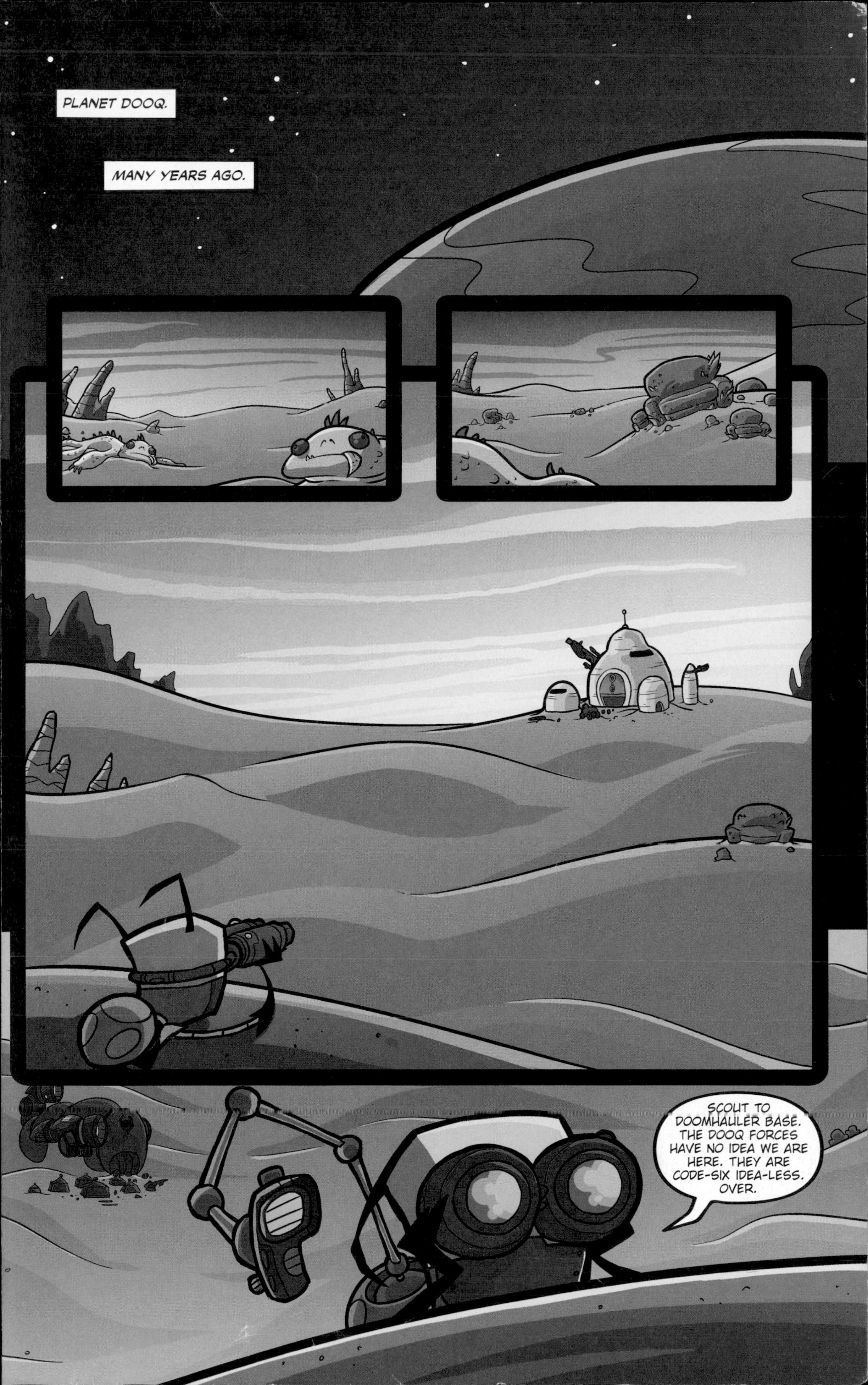
PLANET DOOQ.
MANY YEARS AGO.
SCOUT TO DOOMHAULER BASE. THE DOOQ FORCES HAVE NO IDEA WE ARE HERE. THEY ARE CODE-SIX IDEA-LESS. OVER.

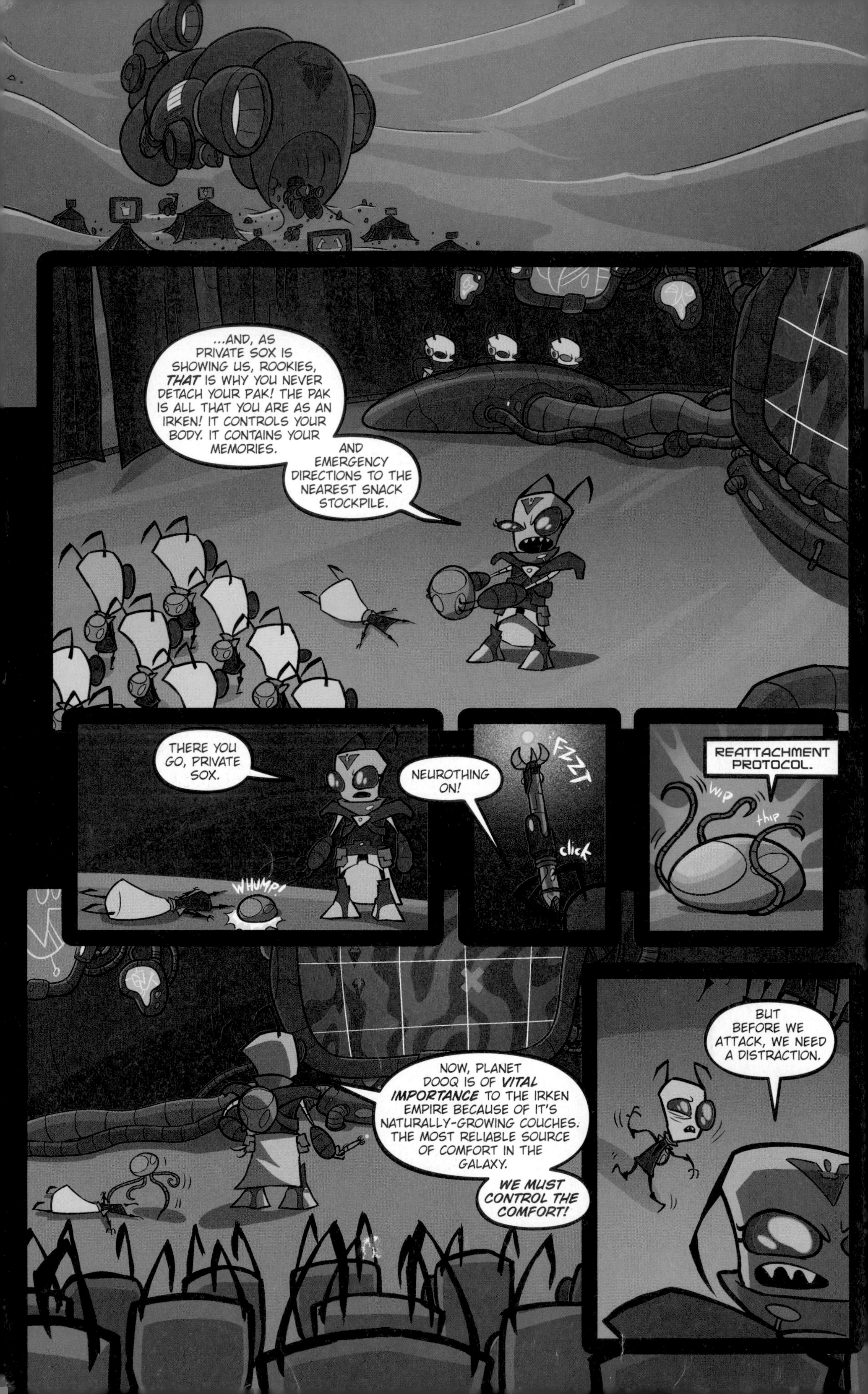

...AND, AS PRIVATE SOX IS SHOWING US, ROOKIES, *THAT* IS WHY YOU NEVER DETACH YOUR PAK! THE PAK IS ALL THAT YOU ARE AS AN IRKEN! IT CONTROLS YOUR BODY. IT CONTAINS YOUR MEMORIES.
AND EMERGENCY DIRECTIONS TO THE NEAREST SNACK STOCKPILE.
THERE YOU GO, PRIVATE SOX.
WHUMP!
NEUROTHING ON!
FZZT
click
REATTACHMENT PROTOCOL.
wip
thip
NOW, PLANET DOOQ IS OF *VITAL IMPORTANCE* TO THE IRKEN EMPIRE BECAUSE OF IT'S NATURALLY-GROWING COUCHES. THE MOST RELIABLE SOURCE OF COMFORT IN THE GALAXY.
WE MUST CONTROL THE COMFORT!
BUT BEFORE WE ATTACK, WE NEED A DISTRACTION.

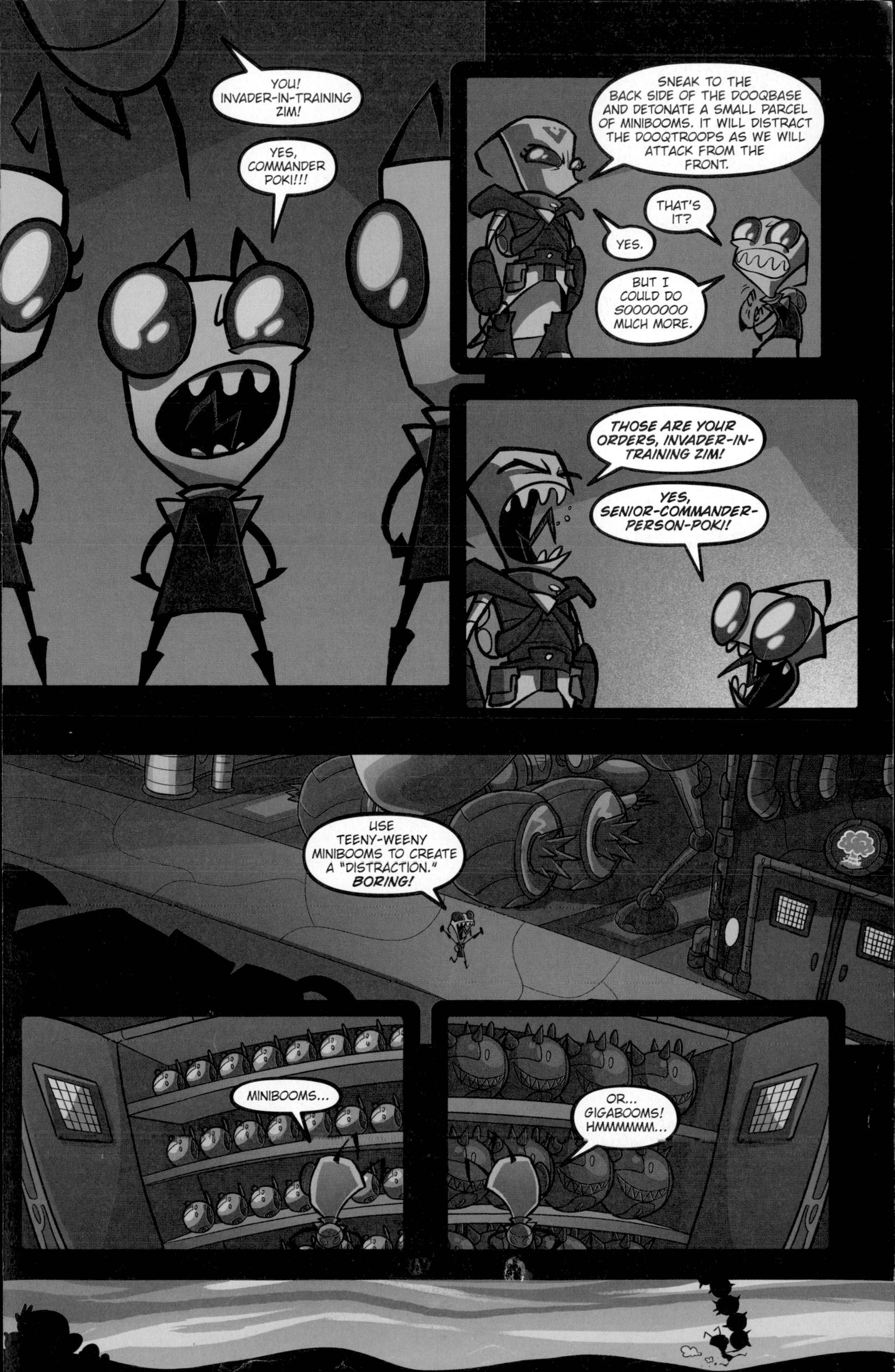
YOU! INVADER-IN-TRAINING ZIM!
YES, COMMANDER POKI!!!
SNEAK TO THE BACK SIDE OF THE DOOQBASE AND DETONATE A SMALL PARCEL OF MINIBOOMS. IT WILL DISTRACT THE DOOQTROOPS AS WE WILL ATTACK FROM THE FRONT.
THAT'S IT?
YES.
BUT I COULD DO SOOOOOOO MUCH MORE.
THOSE ARE YOUR ORDERS, INVADER-IN-TRAINING ZIM!
YES, SENIOR-COMMANDER-PERSON-POKI!
USE TEENY-WEENY MINIBOOMS TO CREATE A "DISTRACTION." BORING!
MINIBOOMS...
OR... GIGABOOMS! HMMMMMM...

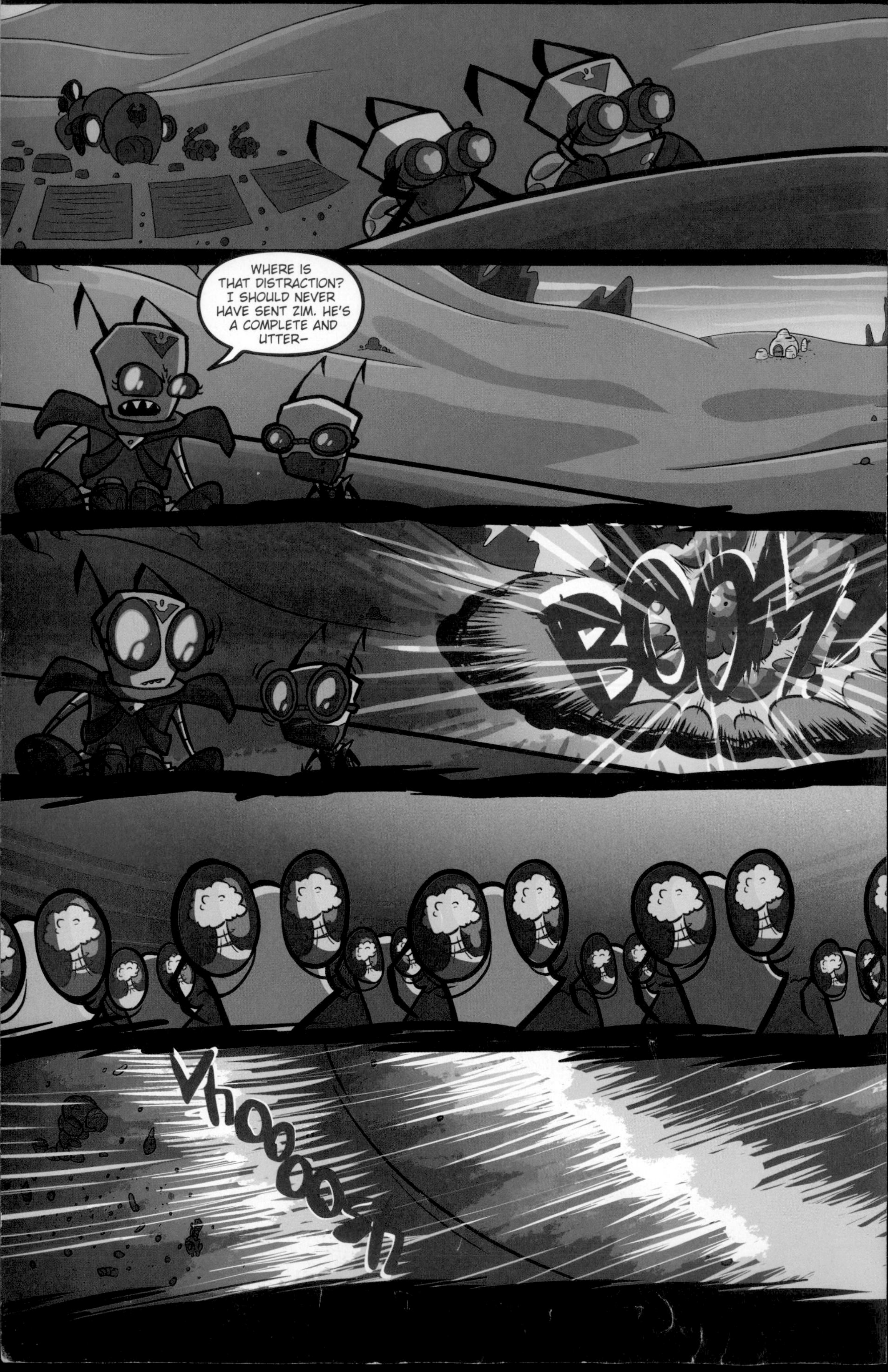
WHERE IS THAT DISTRACTION? I SHOULD NEVER HAVE SENT ZIM. HE'S A COMPLETE AND UTTER-
BOOM!
Vhooooosh

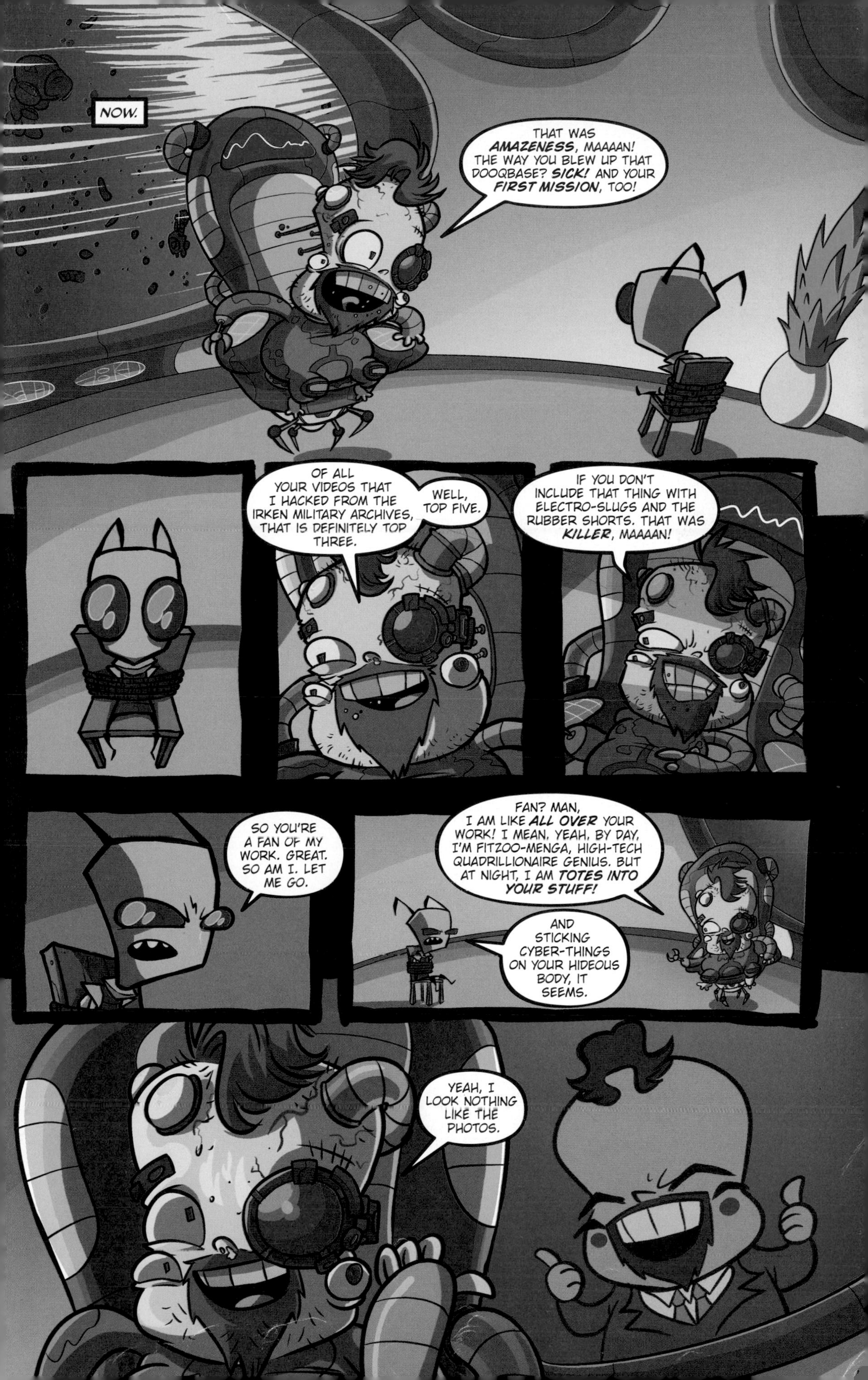
NOW.
THAT WAS AMAZENESS, MAAAAN! THE WAY YOU BLEW UP THAT DOOQBASE? SICK! AND YOUR FIRST MISSION, TOO!
OF ALL YOUR VIDEOS THAT I HACKED FROM THE IRKEN MILITARY ARCHIVES, THAT IS DEFINITELY TOP THREE.
WELL, TOP FIVE.
IF YOU DON'T INCLUDE THAT THING WITH ELECTRO-SLUGS AND THE RUBBER SHORTS. THAT WAS KILLER, MAAAAN!
SO YOU'RE A FAN OF MY WORK. GREAT. SO AM I. LET ME GO.
FAN? MAN, I AM LIKE ALL OVER YOUR WORK! I MEAN, YEAH, BY DAY, I'M FITZOO-MENGA, HIGH-TECH QUADRILLIONAIRE GENIUS. BUT AT NIGHT, I AM TOTES INTO YOUR STUFF!
AND STICKING CYBER-THINGS ON YOUR HIDEOUS BODY, IT SEEMS.
YEAH, I LOOK NOTHING LIKE THE PHOTOS.

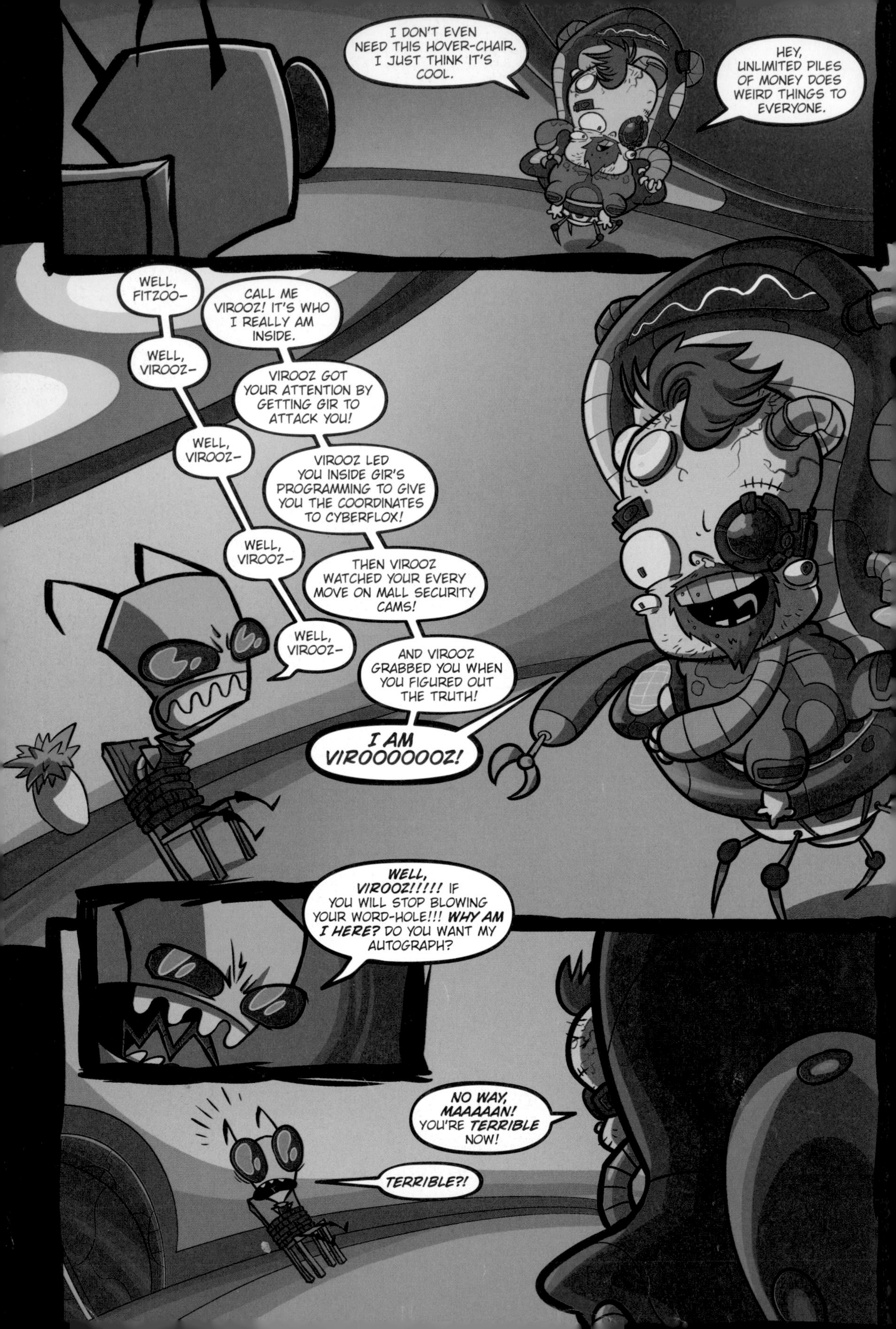
I DON'T EVEN NEED THIS HOVER-CHAIR. I JUST THINK IT'S COOL.
HEY, UNLIMITED PILES OF MONEY DOES WEIRD THINGS TO EVERYONE.
WELL, FITZOO-
CALL ME VIROOZ! IT'S WHO I REALLY AM INSIDE.
WELL, VIROOZ-
VIROOZ GOT YOUR ATTENTION BY GETTING GIR TO ATTACK YOU!
WELL, VIROOZ-
VIROOZ LED YOU INSIDE GIR'S PROGRAMMING TO GIVE YOU THE COORDINATES TO CYBERFLOX!
WELL, VIROOZ-
THEN VIROOZ WATCHED YOUR EVERY MOVE ON MALL SECURITY CAMS!
WELL, VIROOZ-
AND VIROOZ GRABBED YOU WHEN YOU FIGURED OUT THE TRUTH!
I AM VIROOOOOOZ!
WELL, VIROOZ!!!!! IF YOU WILL STOP BLOWING YOUR WORD-HOLE!!! WHY AM I HERE? DO YOU WANT MY AUTOGRAPH?
NO WAY, MAAAAAN! YOU'RE TERRIBLE NOW!
TERRIBLE?!

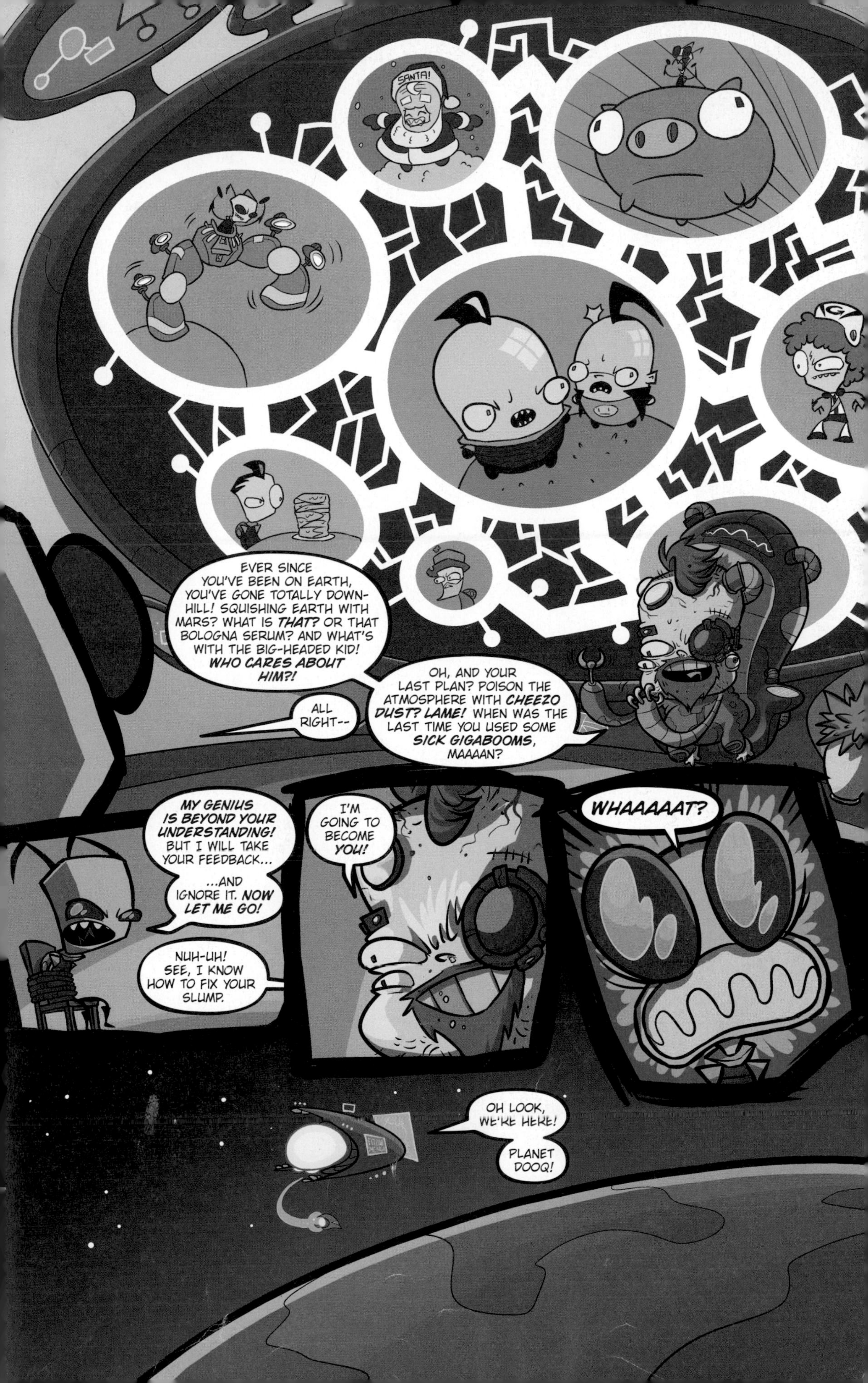

SANTA!
EVER SINCE YOU'VE BEEN ON EARTH, YOU'VE GONE TOTALLY DOWN-HILL! SQUISHING EARTH WITH MARS? WHAT IS THAT? OR THAT BOLOGNA SERUM? AND WHAT'S WITH THE BIG-HEADED KID! WHO CARES ABOUT HIM?!
OH, AND YOUR LAST PLAN? POISON THE ATMOSPHERE WITH CHEEZO DUST? LAME! WHEN WAS THE LAST TIME YOU USED SOME SICK GIGABOOMS, MAAAAN?
ALL RIGHT--
MY GENIUS IS BEYOND YOUR UNDERSTANDING! BUT I WILL TAKE YOUR FEEDBACK...
...AND IGNORE IT. NOW LET ME GO!
NUH-UH! SEE, I KNOW HOW TO FIX YOUR SLUMP.
I'M GOING TO BECOME YOU!
WHAAAAAT?
OH LOOK, WE'RE HERE!
PLANET DOOQ!

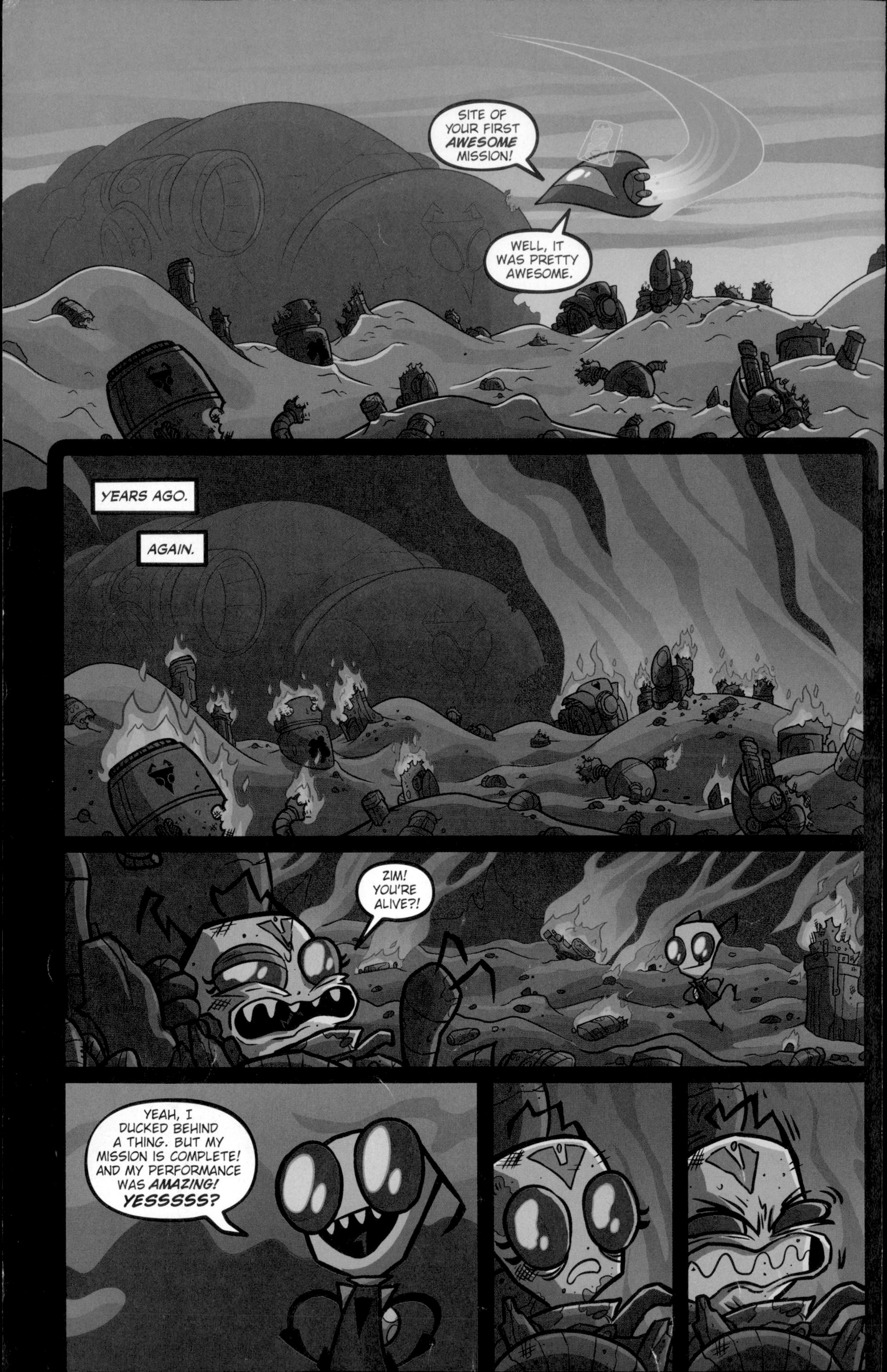
SITE OF YOUR FIRST AWESOME MISSION!
WELL, IT WAS PRETTY AWESOME.
YEARS AGO.
AGAIN.
ZIM! YOU'RE ALIVE?!
YEAH, I DUCKED BEHIND A THING. BUT MY MISSION IS COMPLETE! AND MY PERFORMANCE WAS AMAZING! YESSSSS?

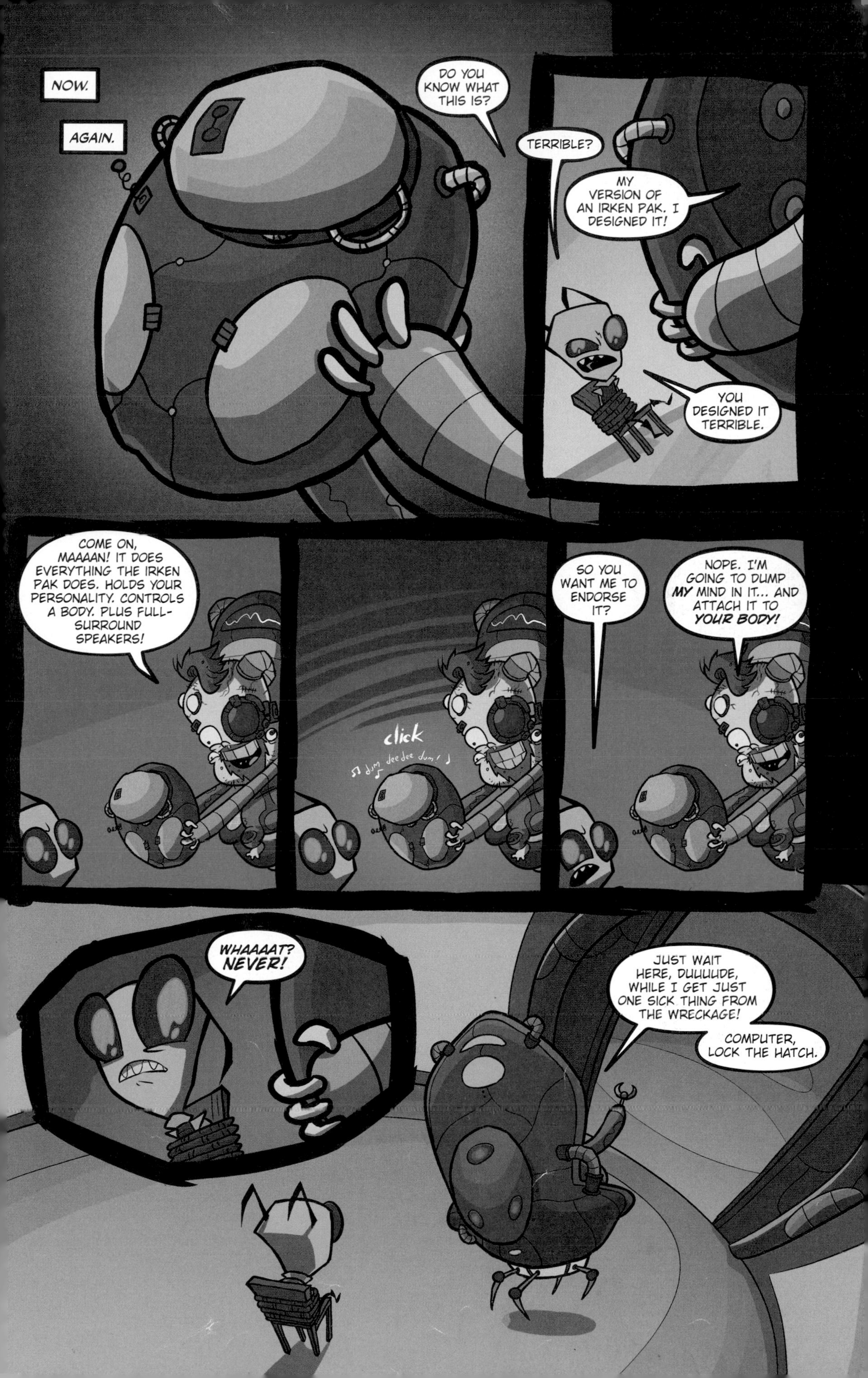
NOW.
AGAIN.
DO YOU KNOW WHAT THIS IS?
TERRIBLE?
MY VERSION OF AN IRKEN PAK. I DESIGNED IT!
YOU DESIGNED IT TERRIBLE.
COME ON, MAAAAN! IT DOES EVERYTHING THE IRKEN PAK DOES. HOLDS YOUR PERSONALITY. CONTROLS A BODY. PLUS FULL-SURROUND SPEAKERS!
click
dum deedee dum!
SO YOU WANT ME TO ENDORSE IT?
NOPE. I'M GOING TO DUMP MY MIND IN IT... AND ATTACH IT TO YOUR BODY!
WHAAAAT? NEVER!
JUST WAIT HERE, DUUUUDE, WHILE I GET JUST ONE SICK THING FROM THE WRECKAGE!
COMPUTER, LOCK THE HATCH.

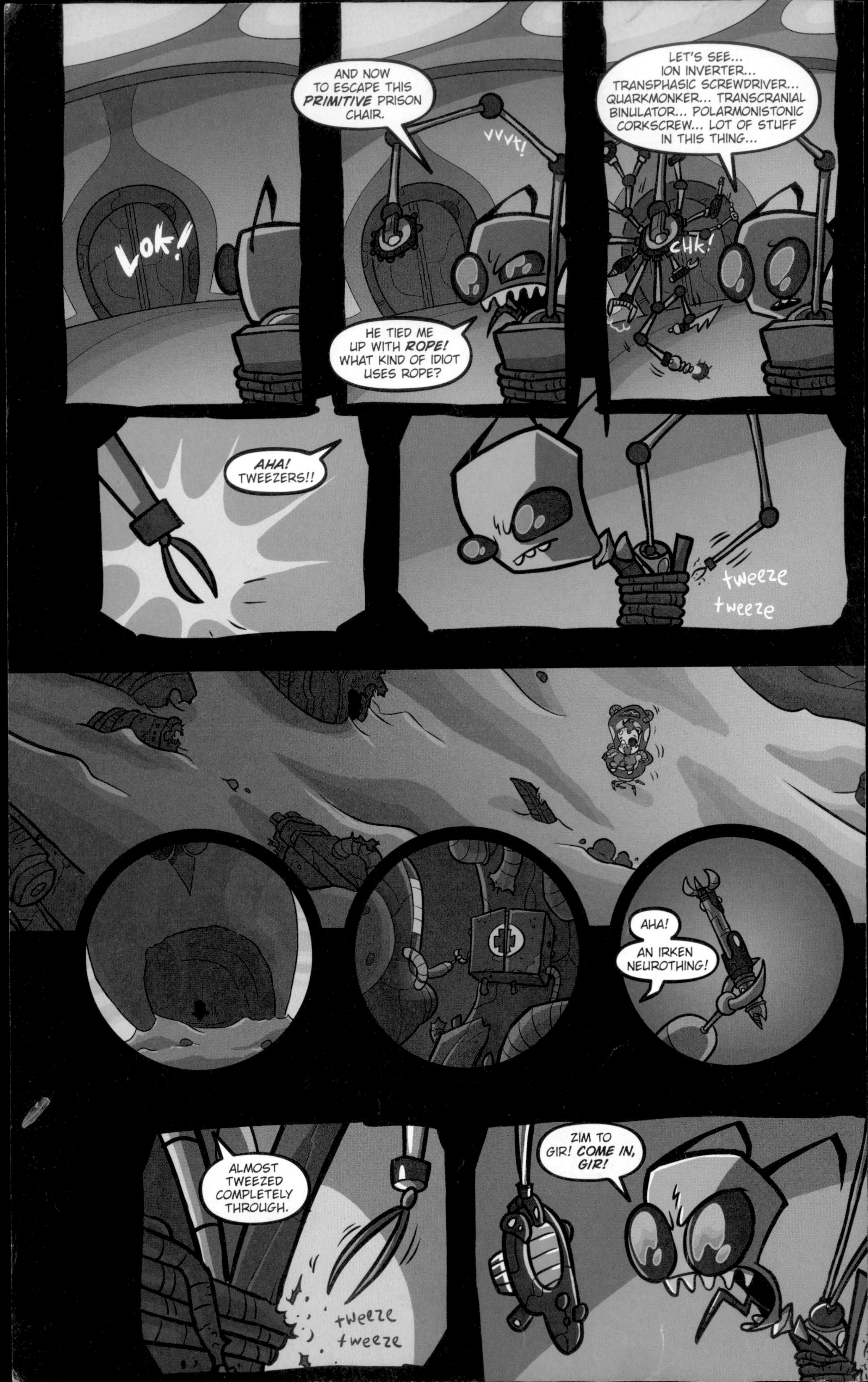
LOK!
AND NOW TO ESCAPE THIS PRIMITIVE PRISON CHAIR.
VVVT!
HE TIED ME UP WITH ROPE! WHAT KIND OF IDIOT USES ROPE?
LET'S SEE... ION INVERTER... TRANSPHASIC SCREWDRIVER... QUARKMONKER... TRANSCRANIAL BINULATOR... POLARMONISTONIC CORKSCREW... LOT OF STUFF IN THIS THING...
CHK!
AHA! TWEEZERS!!
tweeze tweeze
AHA! AN IRKEN NEUROTHING!
ALMOST TWEEZED COMPLETELY THROUGH.
tweeze tweeze
ZIM TO GIR! COME IN, GIR!

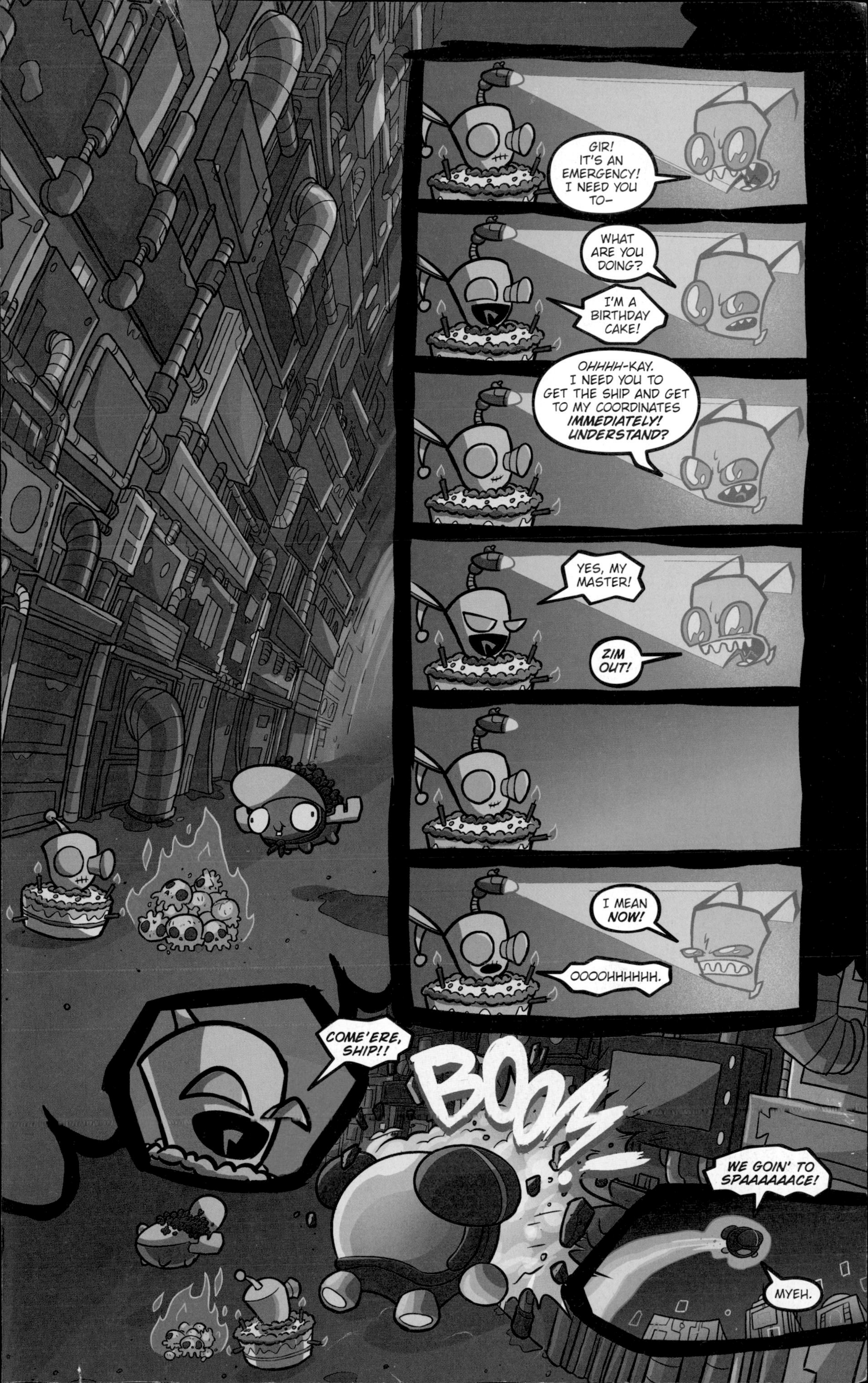
GIR! IT'S AN EMERGENCY! I NEED YOU TO–
WHAT ARE YOU DOING?
I'M A BIRTHDAY CAKE!
OHHHH-KAY. I NEED YOU TO GET THE SHIP AND GET TO MY COORDINATES IMMEDIATELY! UNDERSTAND?
YES, MY MASTER!
ZIM OUT!
I MEAN NOW!
OOOOHHHHHH.
COME'ERE, SHIP!!
BOOM!
WE GOIN' TO SPAAAAAACE!
MYEH.

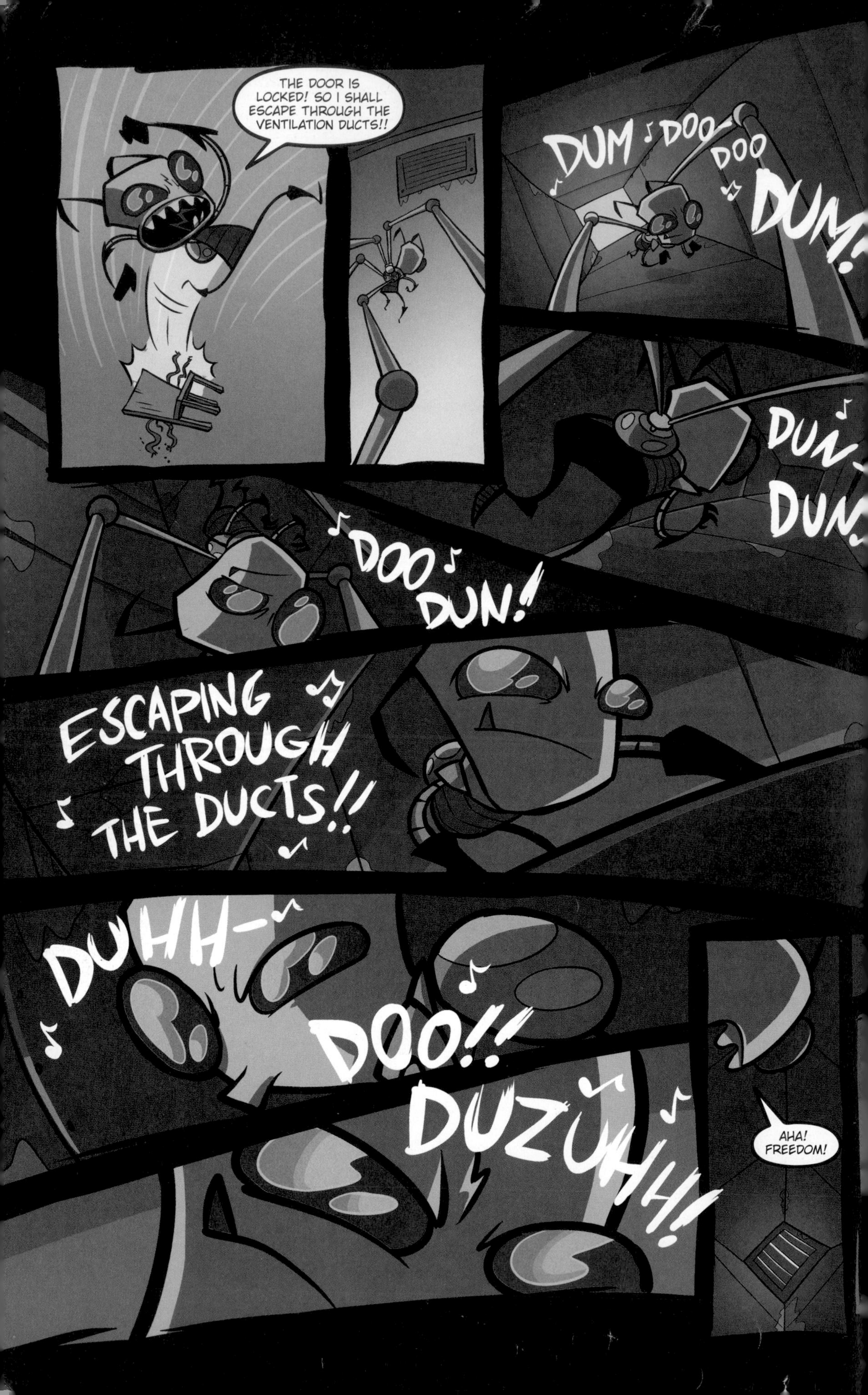
THE DOOR IS LOCKED! SO I SHALL ESCAPE THROUGH THE VENTILATION DUCTS!!
DUM DOO-DOO DUM!
DUN-DUN
DOO DUN!
ESCAPING THROUGH THE DUCTS!!
DUHH-
DOO!!
DUZUHH!!
AHA! FREEDOM!

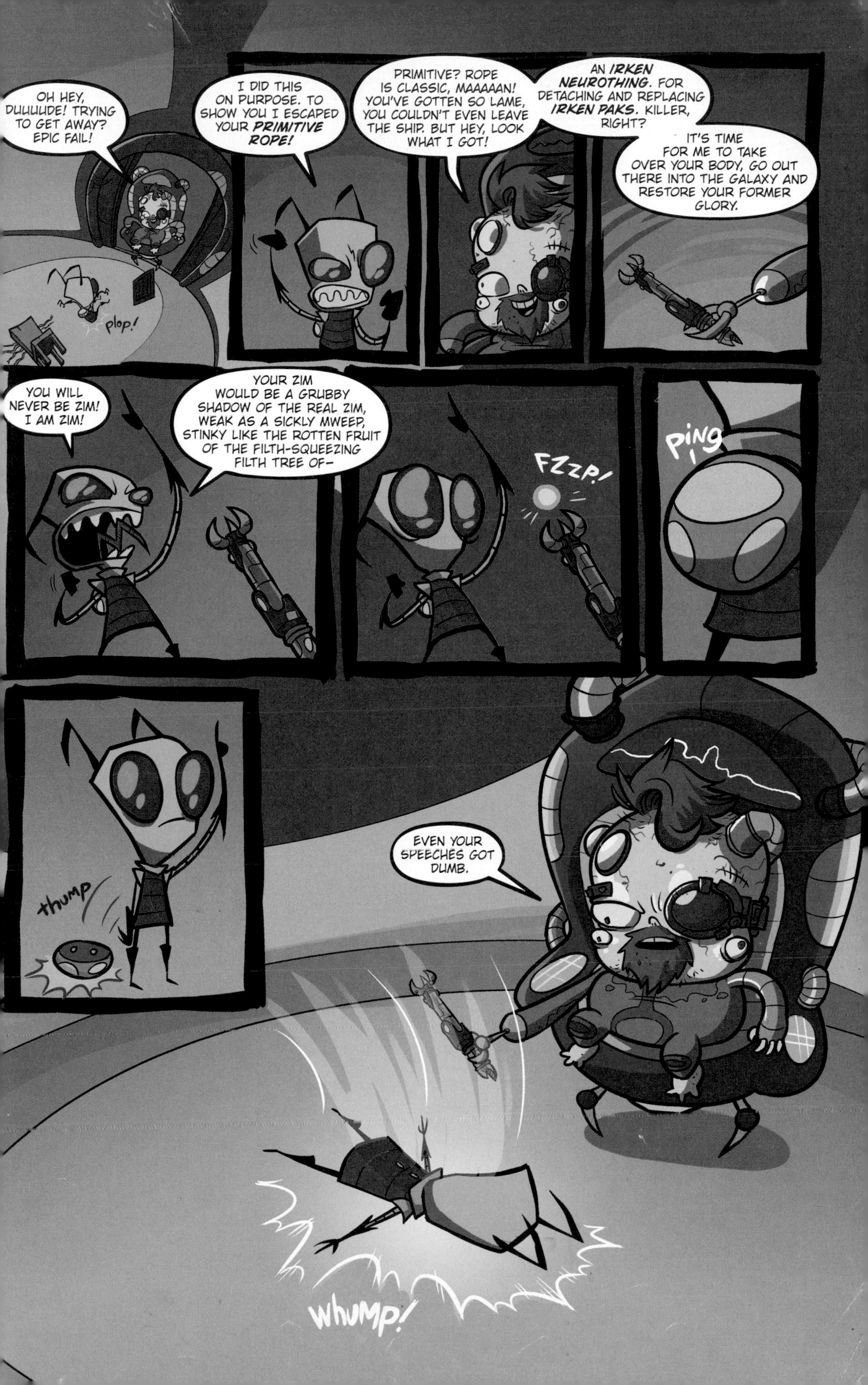
OH HEY, DUUUUDE! TRYING TO GET AWAY? EPIC FAIL!
plop!
I DID THIS ON PURPOSE. TO SHOW YOU I ESCAPED YOUR PRIMITIVE ROPE!
PRIMITIVE? ROPE IS CLASSIC, MAAAAAN! YOU'VE GOTTEN SO LAME, YOU COULDN'T EVEN LEAVE THE SHIP. BUT HEY, LOOK WHAT I GOT!
AN IRKEN NEUROTHING. FOR DETACHING AND REPLACING IRKEN PAKS. KILLER, RIGHT?
IT'S TIME FOR ME TO TAKE OVER YOUR BODY, GO OUT THERE INTO THE GALAXY AND RESTORE YOUR FORMER GLORY.
YOU WILL NEVER BE ZIM! I AM ZIM!
YOUR ZIM WOULD BE A GRUBBY SHADOW OF THE REAL ZIM, WEAK AS A SICKLY MWEEP, STINKY LIKE THE ROTTEN FRUIT OF THE FILTH-SQUEEZING FILTH TREE OF-
FZZP!
PING
thump
EVEN YOUR SPEECHES GOT DUMB.
WHUMP!

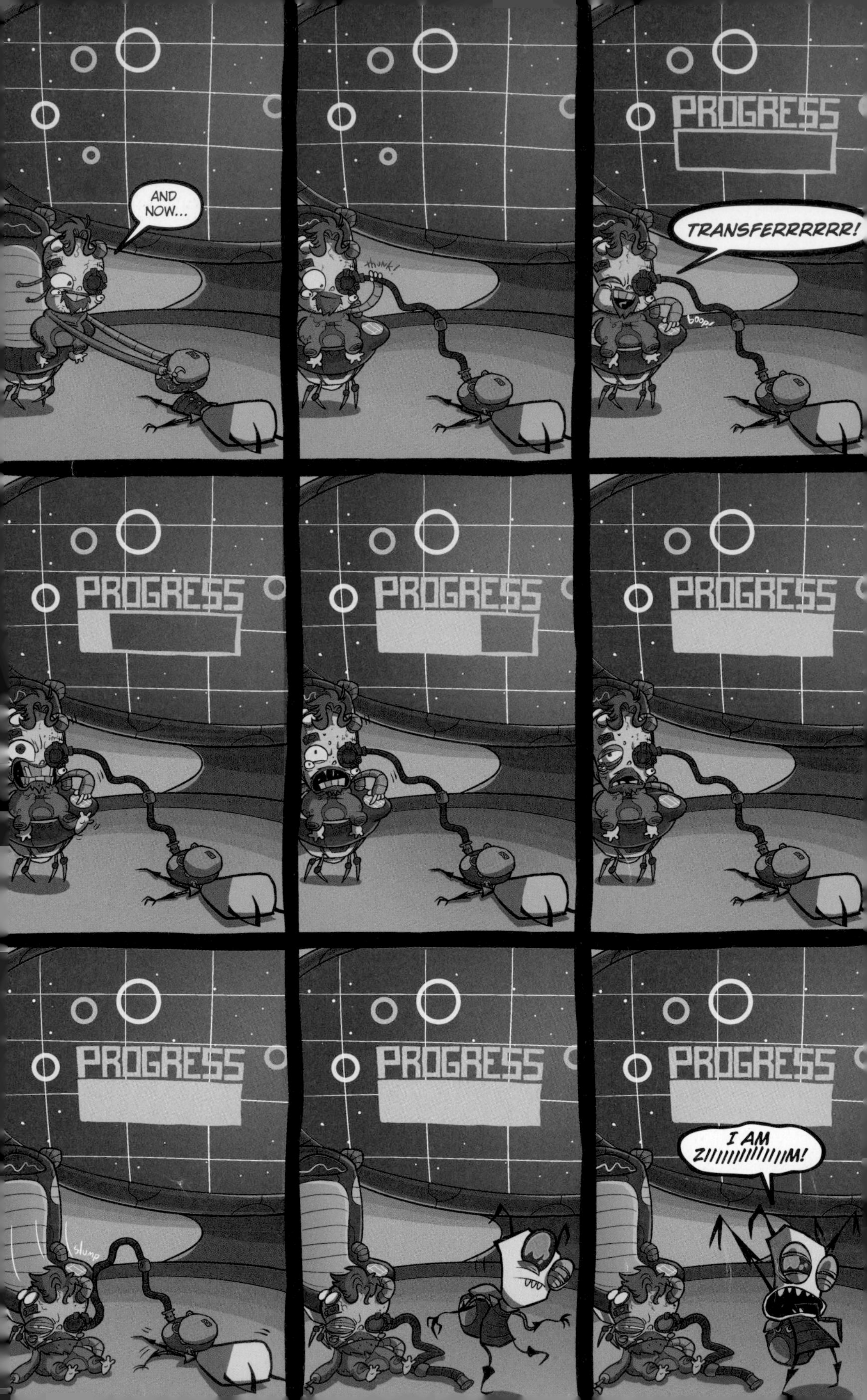
AND NOW...
THUNK!
PROGRESS
TRANSFERRRRRR!
BOOP!
PROGRESS
PROGRESS
PROGRESS
PROGRESS
SLUMP
PROGRESS
PROGRESS
I AM ZIIIIIIIIIIIIIIM!

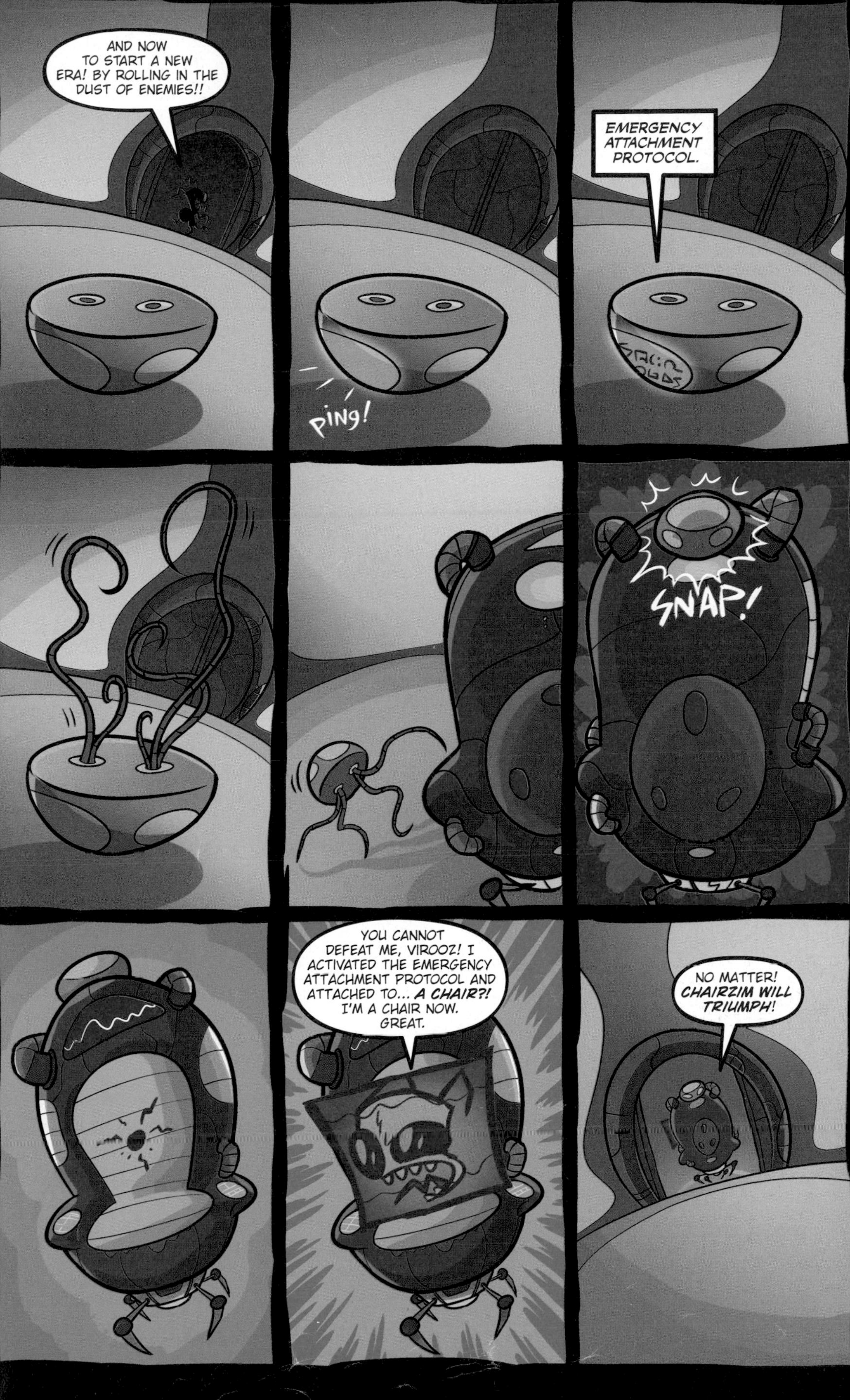
AND NOW TO START A NEW ERA! BY ROLLING IN THE DUST OF ENEMIES!!
PING!
EMERGENCY ATTACHMENT PROTOCOL.
SNAP!
YOU CANNOT DEFEAT ME, VIROOZ! I ACTIVATED THE EMERGENCY ATTACHMENT PROTOCOL AND ATTACHED TO... *A CHAIR?!* I'M A CHAIR NOW. GREAT.
NO MATTER! *CHAIRZIM WILL TRIUMPH!*

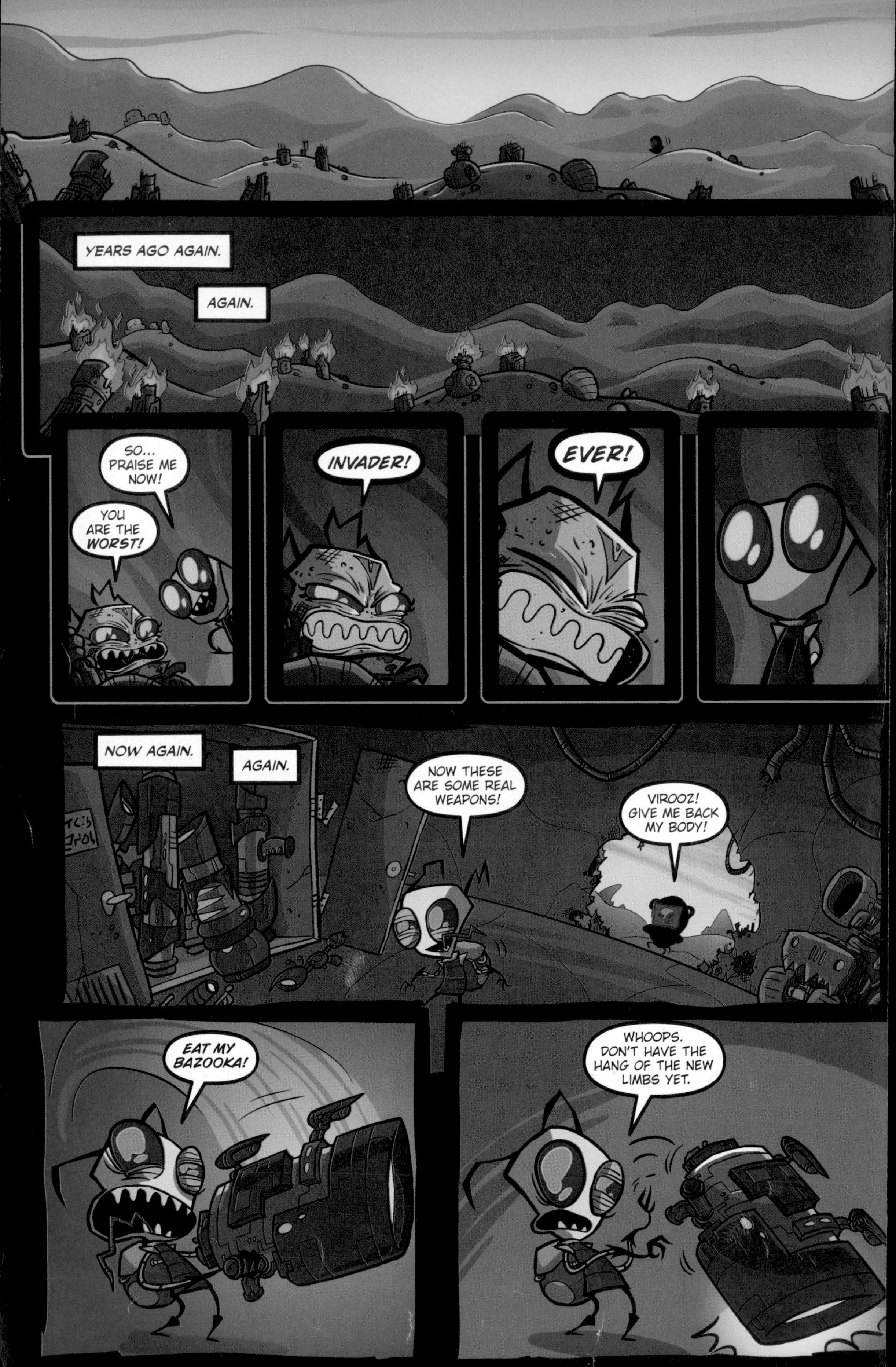
YEARS AGO AGAIN.
AGAIN.
SO... PRAISE ME NOW!
YOU ARE THE WORST!
INVADER!
EVER!
NOW AGAIN.
AGAIN.
NOW THESE ARE SOME REAL WEAPONS!
VIROOZ! GIVE ME BACK MY BODY!
EAT MY BAZOOKA!
WHOOPS. DON'T HAVE THE HANG OF THE NEW LIMBS YET.

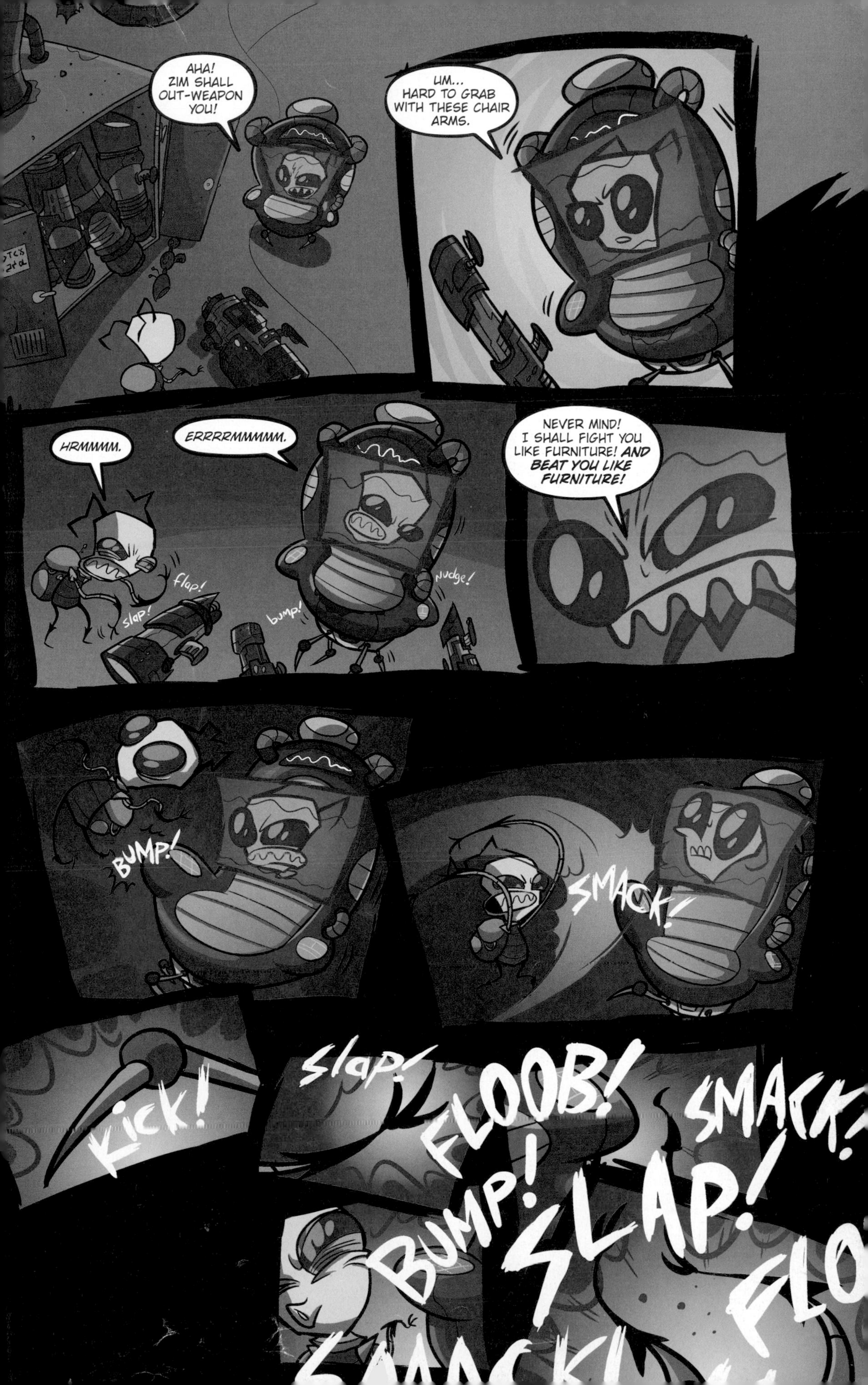
AHA! ZIM SHALL OUT-WEAPON YOU!
UM... HARD TO GRAB WITH THESE CHAIR ARMS.
HRMMMM.
ERRRRMMMMM.
flap!
slap!
bump!
nudge!
NEVER MIND! I SHALL FIGHT YOU LIKE FURNITURE! AND BEAT YOU LIKE FURNITURE!
BUMP!
SMACK!
KICK!
slap!
FLOOB!
SMACK!
BUMP!
SLAP!

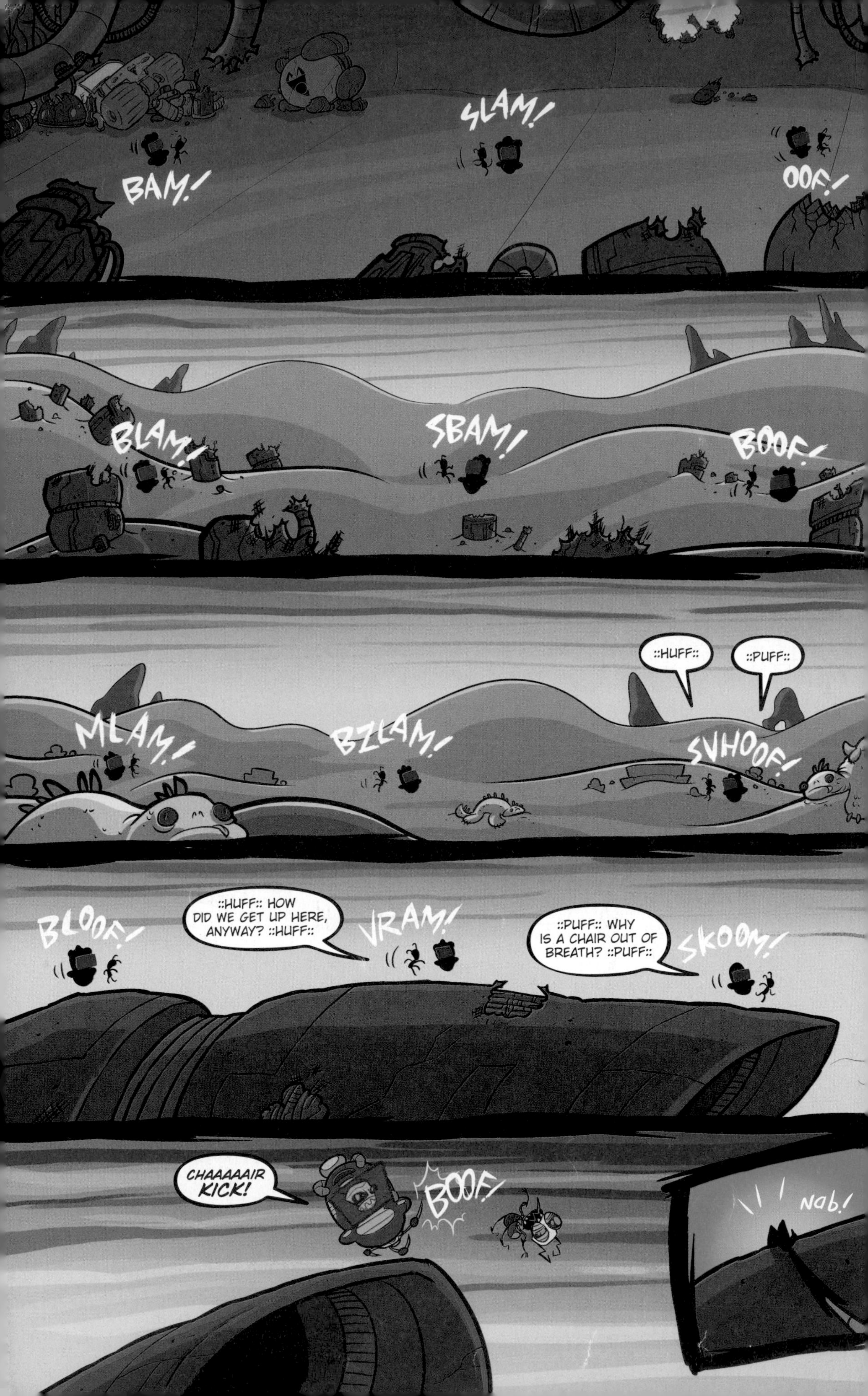

SLAM!
BAM!
OOF!
BLAM!
SBAM!
BOOF!
::HUFF::
::PUFF::
MLAM!
BZLAM!
SVHOOF!
BLOOF!
::HUFF:: HOW DID WE GET UP HERE, ANYWAY? ::HUFF::
VRAM!
::PUFF:: WHY IS A CHAIR OUT OF BREATH? ::PUFF::
SKOOM!
CHAAAAAIR KICK!
BOOF!
Nab!

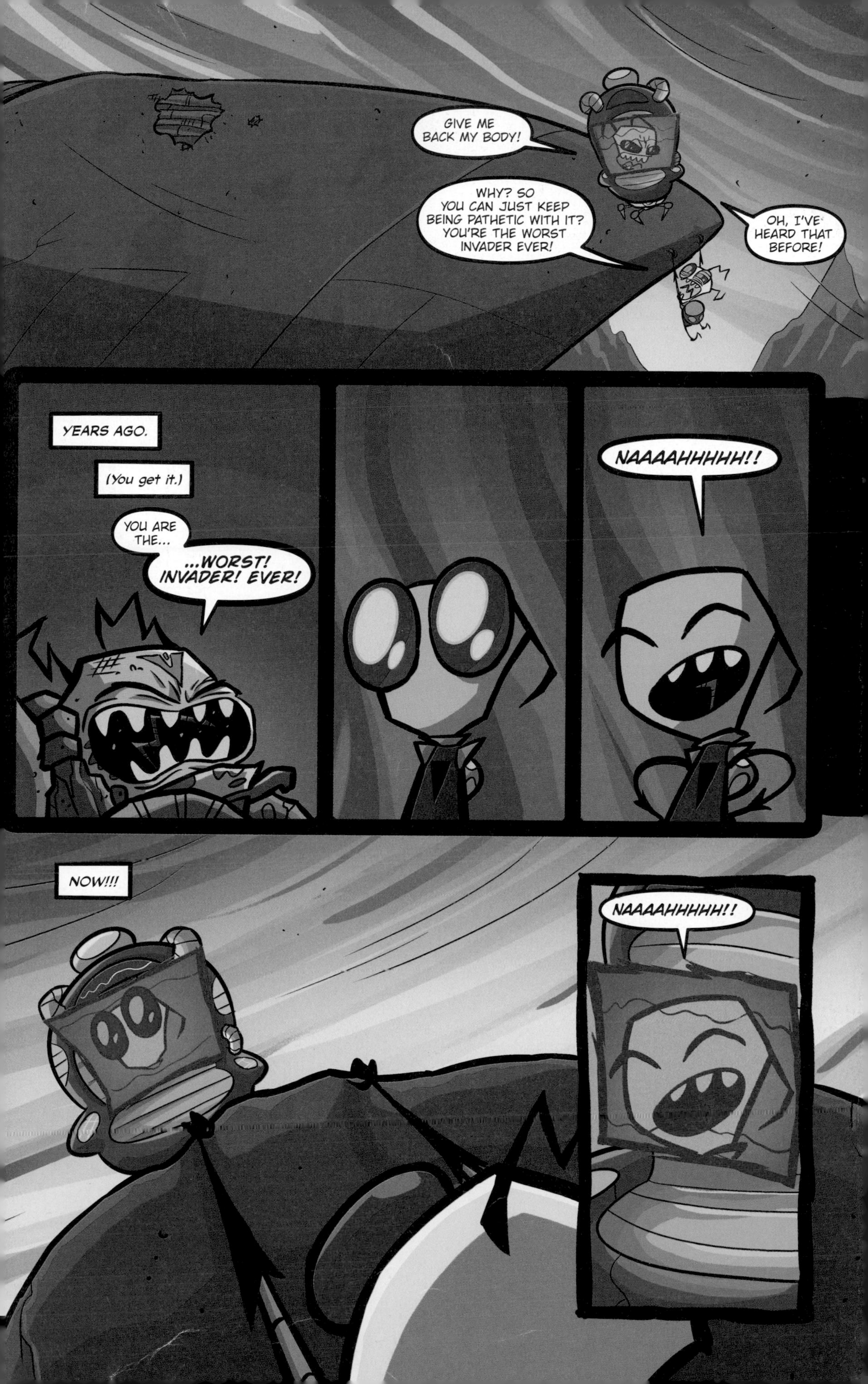
GIVE ME BACK MY BODY!
WHY? SO YOU CAN JUST KEEP BEING PATHETIC WITH IT? YOU'RE THE WORST INVADER EVER!
OH, I'VE HEARD THAT BEFORE!
YEARS AGO.
(You get it.)
YOU ARE THE...
...WORST! INVADER! EVER!
NAAAAHHHHH!!
NOW!!!
NAAAAHHHHH!!

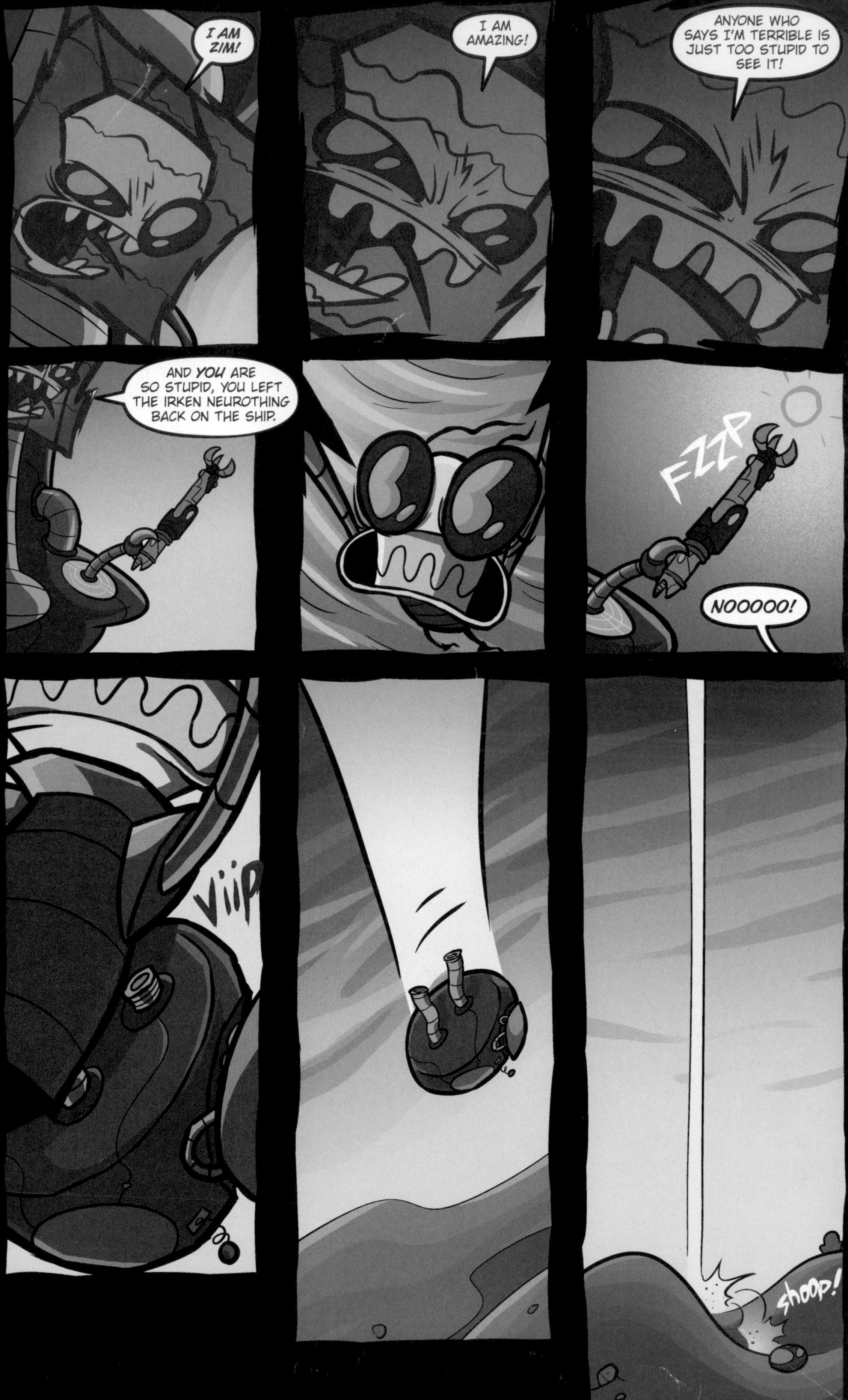
I AM ZIM!
I AM AMAZING!
ANYONE WHO SAYS I'M TERRIBLE IS JUST TOO STUPID TO SEE IT!
AND YOU ARE SO STUPID, YOU LEFT THE IRKEN NEUROTHING BACK ON THE SHIP.
FZZP
NOOOOO!
VIIP
SHOOP!

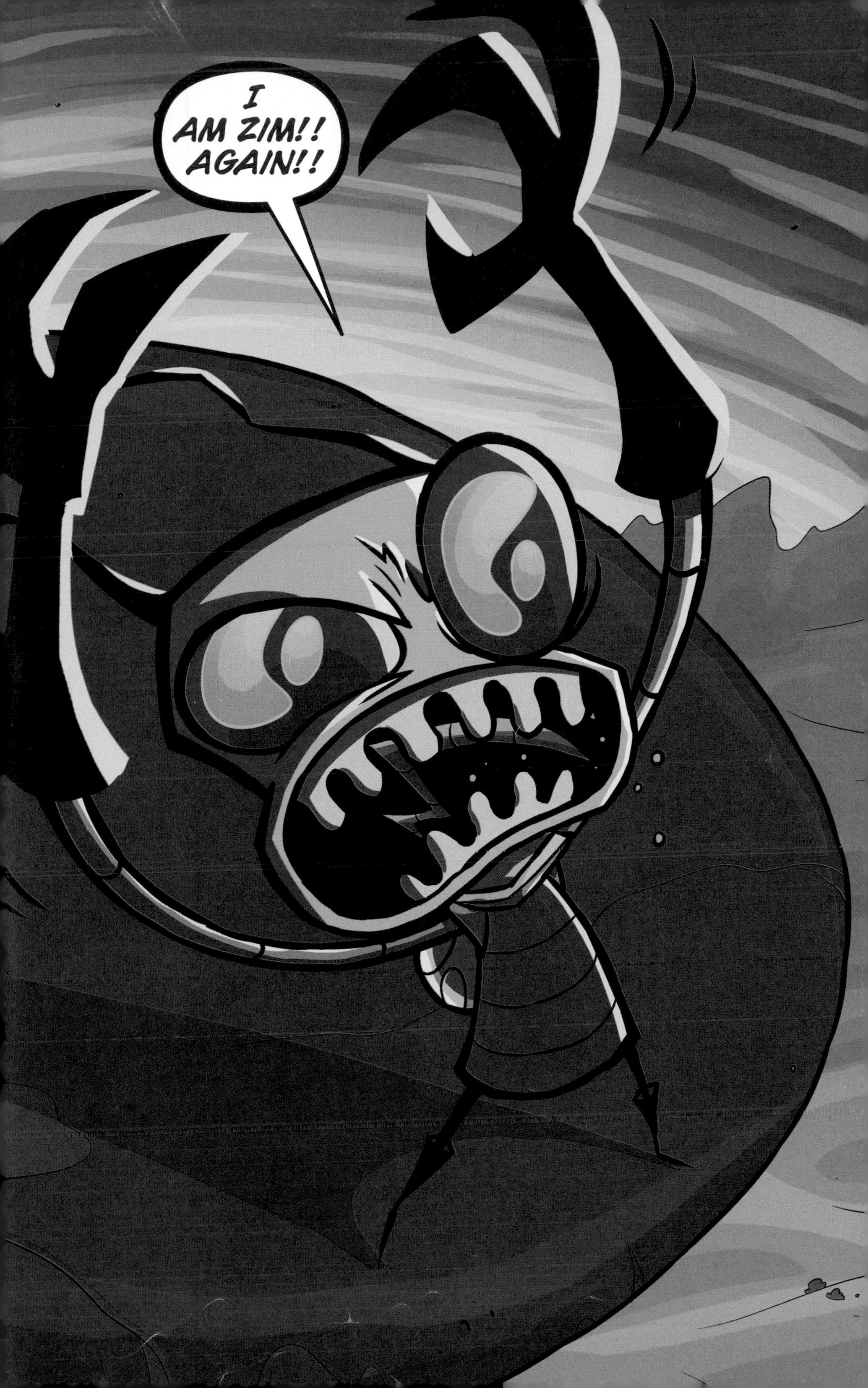
I AM ZIM!! AGAIN!!

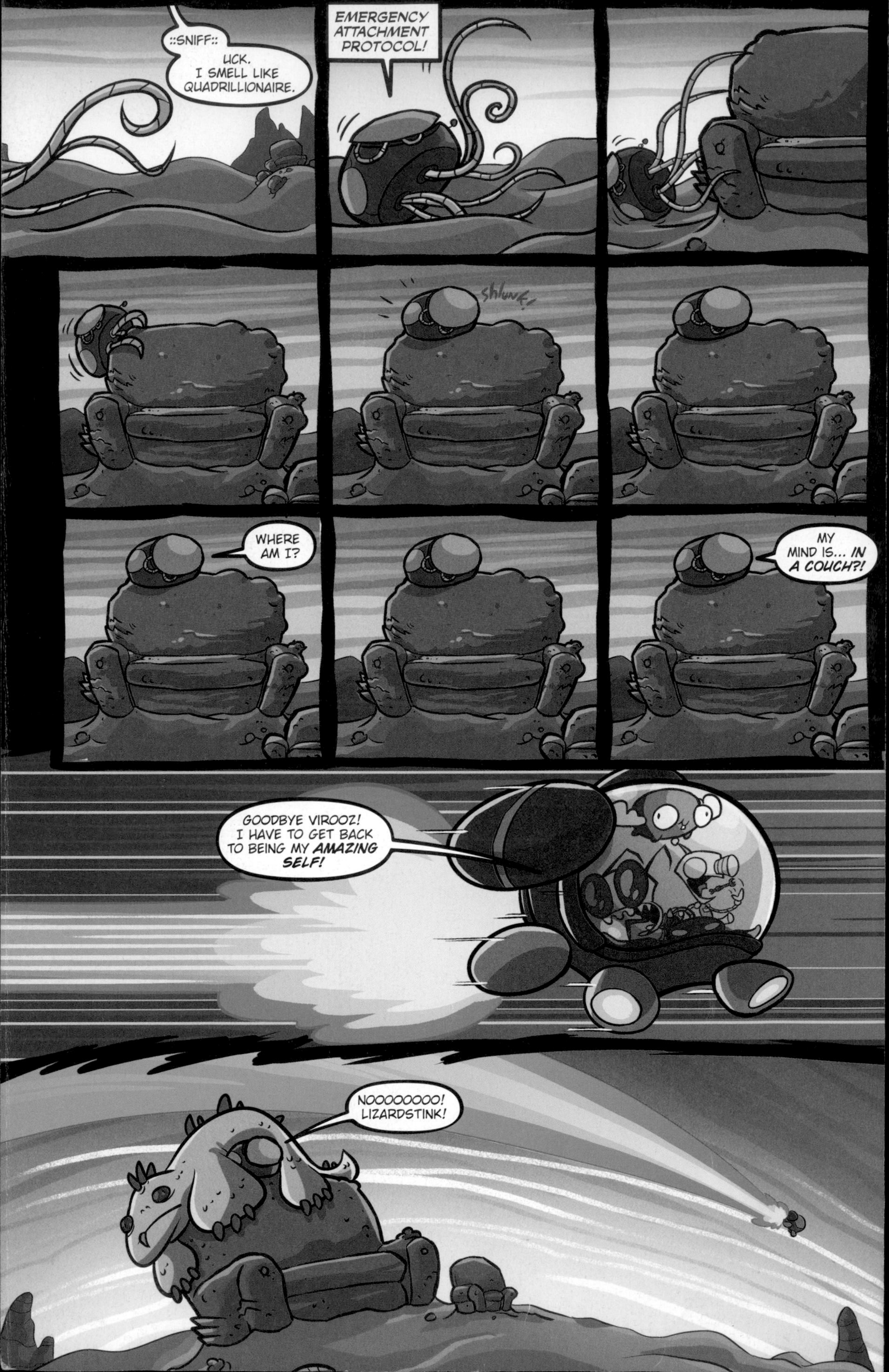
::SNIFF::
UCK. I SMELL LIKE QUADRILLIONAIRE.
EMERGENCY ATTACHMENT PROTOCOL!
SHLUNK!
WHERE AM I?
MY MIND IS... IN A COUCH?!
GOODBYE VIROOZ! I HAVE TO GET BACK TO BEING MY AMAZING SELF!
NOOOOOOOO! LIZARDSTINK!

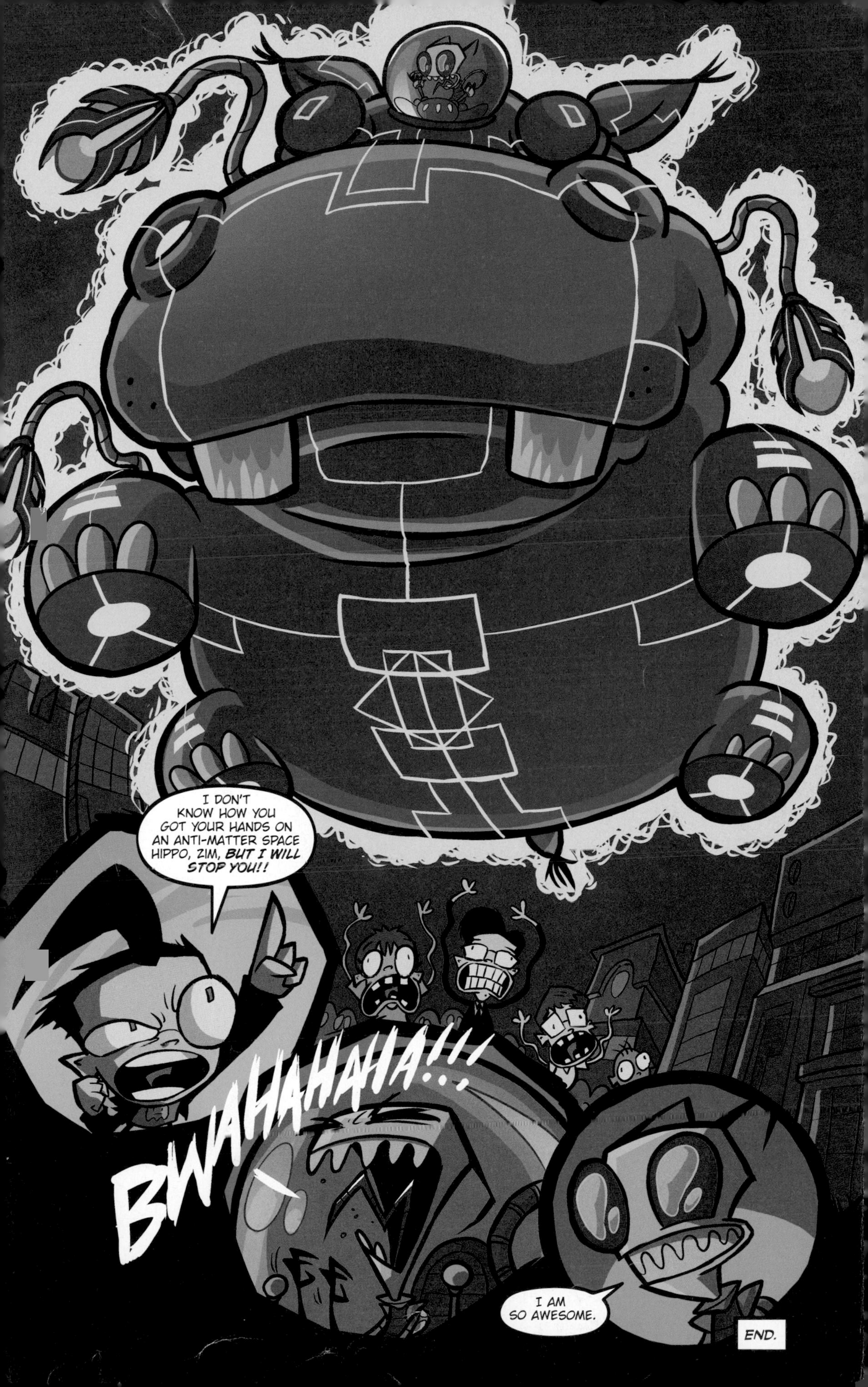
I DON'T KNOW HOW YOU GOT YOUR HANDS ON AN ANTI-MATTER SPACE HIPPO, ZIM, BUT I WILL STOP YOU!!
BWAHAHAHA!!!
I AM SO AWESOME.
END.

INVADER ZIM™

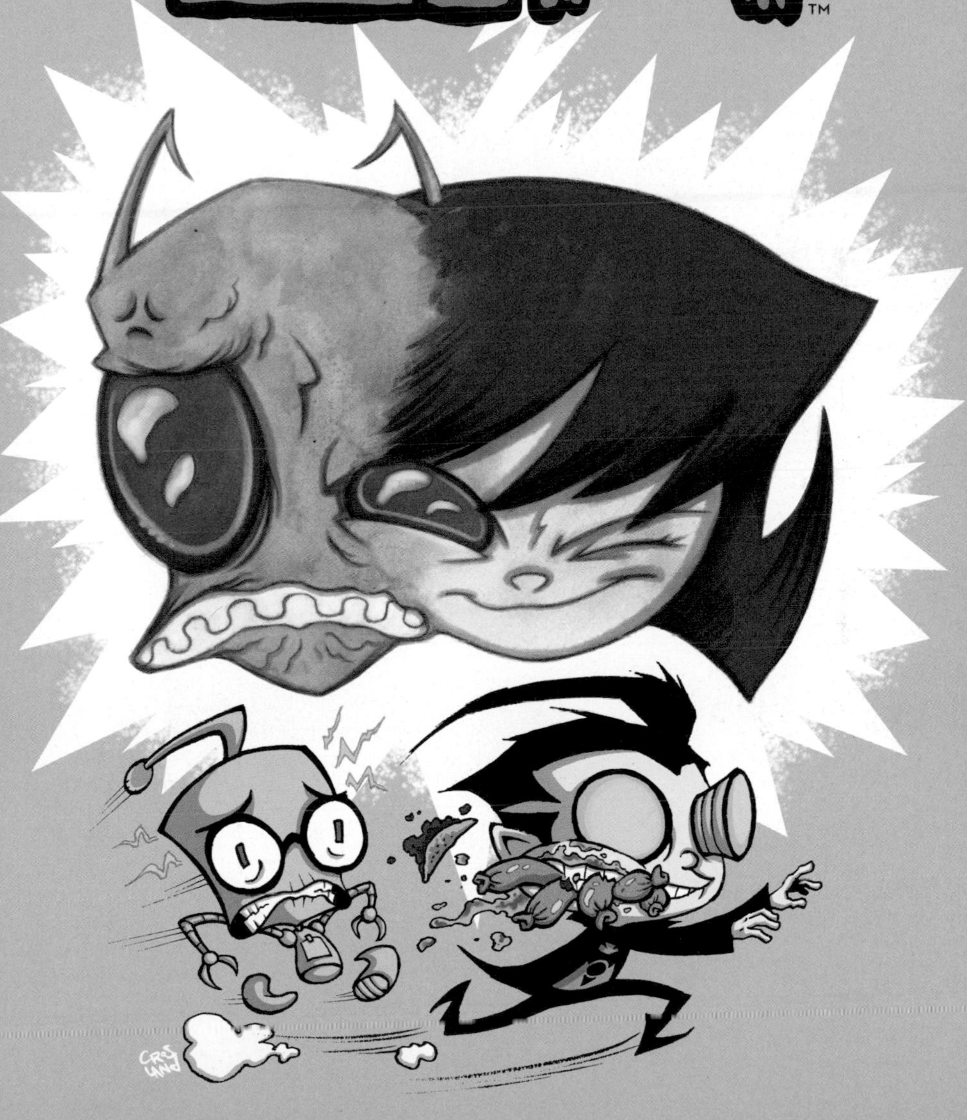
CROSLAND

CHAPTER: 5

HELLO AGAIN, people! WOW! Recap Kid here, just bein' me, which means bein' THE BIGGEST INVADER ZIM FAN EVER TO WALK THE EARTH! That's why I read these comics, ya know? HA! HA HA HA! HA! So last time ZIM and GIR sat on the couch watching TV getting gross and smelly! There weren't any stink lines or anything BUT YOU COULD DEFINITELY TELL, and maybe I threw up a bit! Maybe just thinking about it is making me REAL SICK, OKAY? AH HA HA HA (cough) It was funny, though! THEY DIDN'T MOVE FOR THE WHOLE ISSUE!!! Now this new issue is about everyone's BRAINS getting SWAPPED! Dib and GIR swap brains and I'm thinkin' about that... I'm thinkin' about it REAL HARD... because it's REAL FUNNY! REAL FUNNY TO ME!!! I just LOVE IT! SO MUCH! AAAAAH HA HA HA (cough)

Recap Kid by DAVE CROSLAND
with WARREN WUCINICH

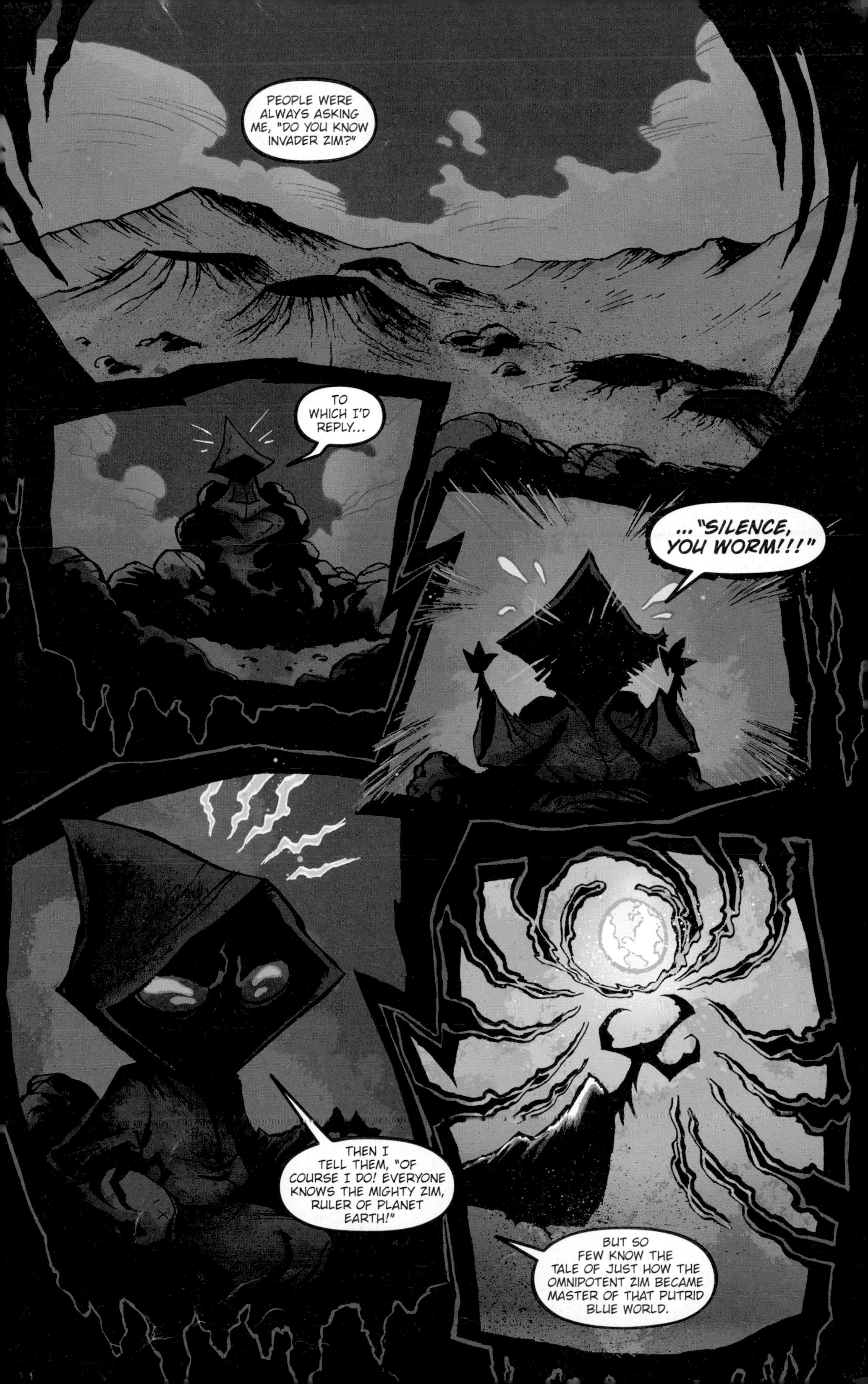
PEOPLE WERE ALWAYS ASKING ME, "DO YOU KNOW INVADER ZIM?"
TO WHICH I'D REPLY...
..."SILENCE, YOU WORM!!!"
THEN I TELL THEM, "OF COURSE I DO! EVERYONE KNOWS THE MIGHTY ZIM, RULER OF PLANET EARTH!"
BUT SO FEW KNOW THE TALE OF JUST HOW THE OMNIPOTENT ZIM BECAME MASTER OF THAT PUTRID BLUE WORLD.

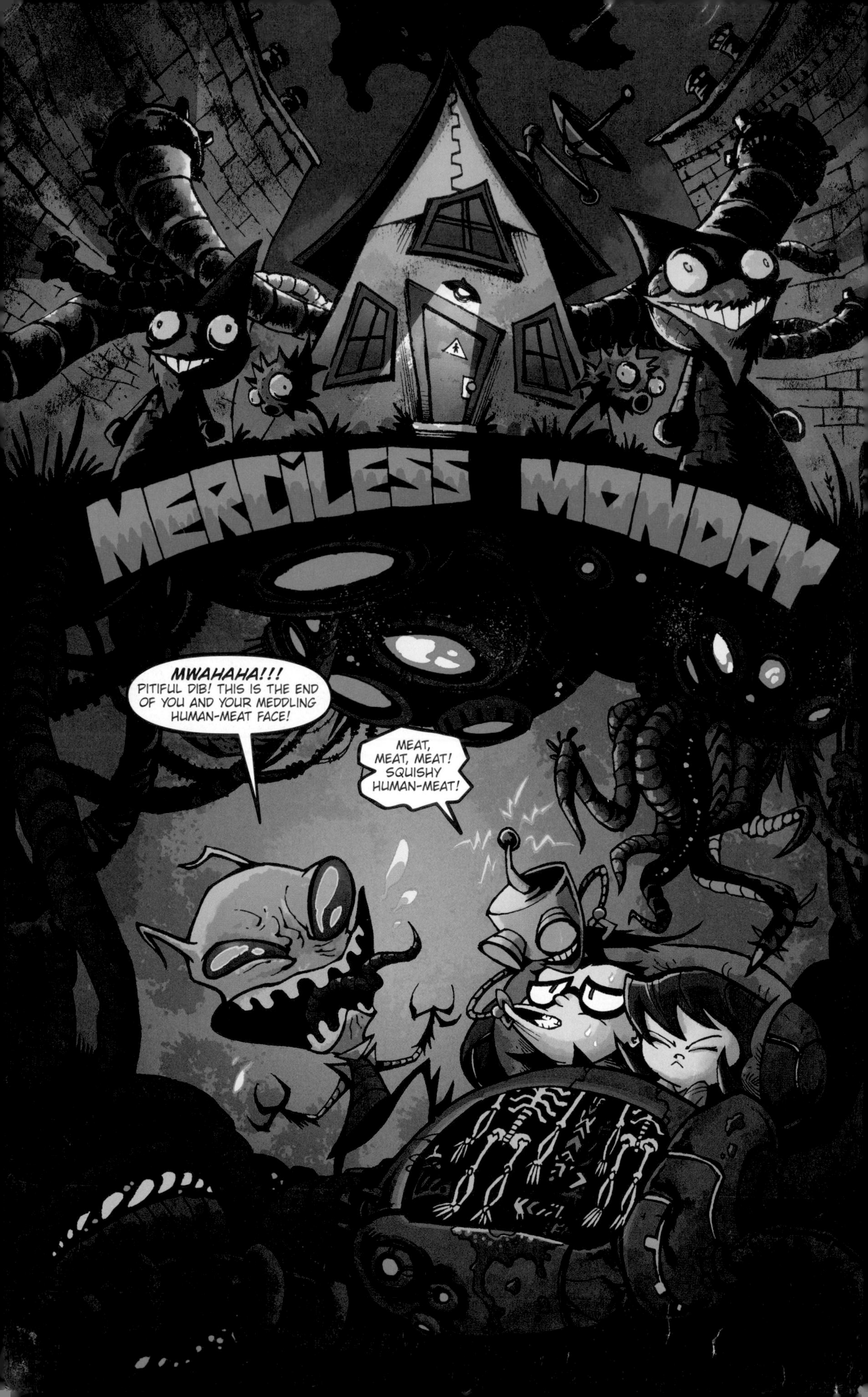
MERCILESS MONDAY
MWAHAHA!!! PITIFUL DIB! THIS IS THE END OF YOU AND YOUR MEDDLING HUMAN-MEAT FACE!
MEAT, MEAT, MEAT! SQUISHY HUMAN-MEAT!

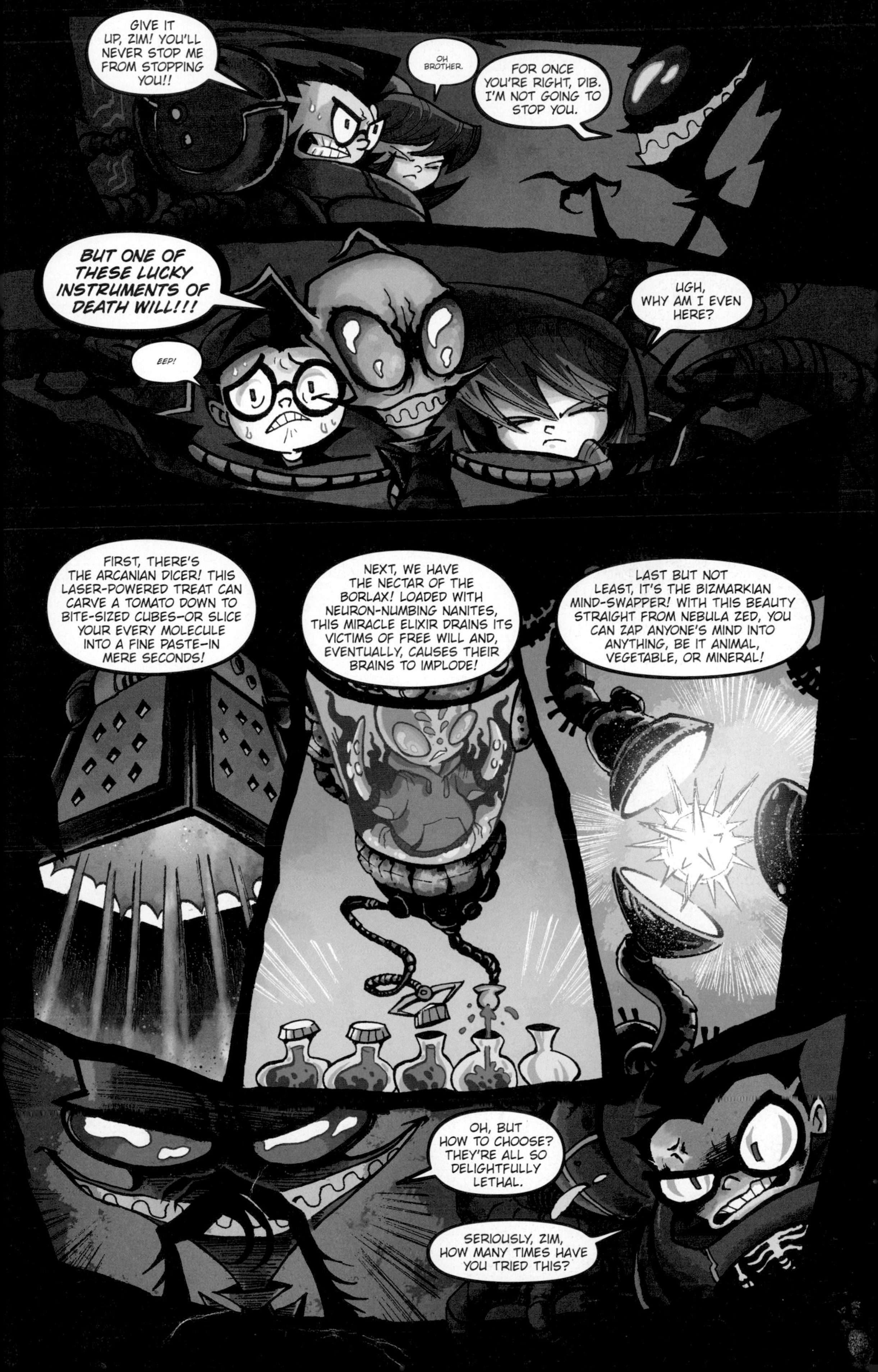
GIVE IT UP, ZIM! YOU'LL NEVER STOP ME FROM STOPPING YOU!!
OH BROTHER.
FOR ONCE YOU'RE RIGHT, DIB. I'M NOT GOING TO STOP YOU.
BUT ONE OF THESE LUCKY INSTRUMENTS OF DEATH WILL!!!
UGH, WHY AM I EVEN HERE?
EEP!
FIRST, THERE'S THE ARCANIAN DICER! THIS LASER-POWERED TREAT CAN CARVE A TOMATO DOWN TO BITE-SIZED CUBES—OR SLICE YOUR EVERY MOLECULE INTO A FINE PASTE—IN MERE SECONDS!
NEXT, WE HAVE THE NECTAR OF THE BORLAX! LOADED WITH NEURON-NUMBING NANITES, THIS MIRACLE ELIXIR DRAINS ITS VICTIMS OF FREE WILL AND, EVENTUALLY, CAUSES THEIR BRAINS TO IMPLODE!
LAST BUT NOT LEAST, IT'S THE BIZMARKIAN MIND-SWAPPER! WITH THIS BEAUTY STRAIGHT FROM NEBULA ZED, YOU CAN ZAP ANYONE'S MIND INTO ANYTHING, BE IT ANIMAL, VEGETABLE, OR MINERAL!
OH, BUT HOW TO CHOOSE? THEY'RE ALL SO DELIGHTFULLY LETHAL.
SERIOUSLY, ZIM, HOW MANY TIMES HAVE YOU TRIED THIS?

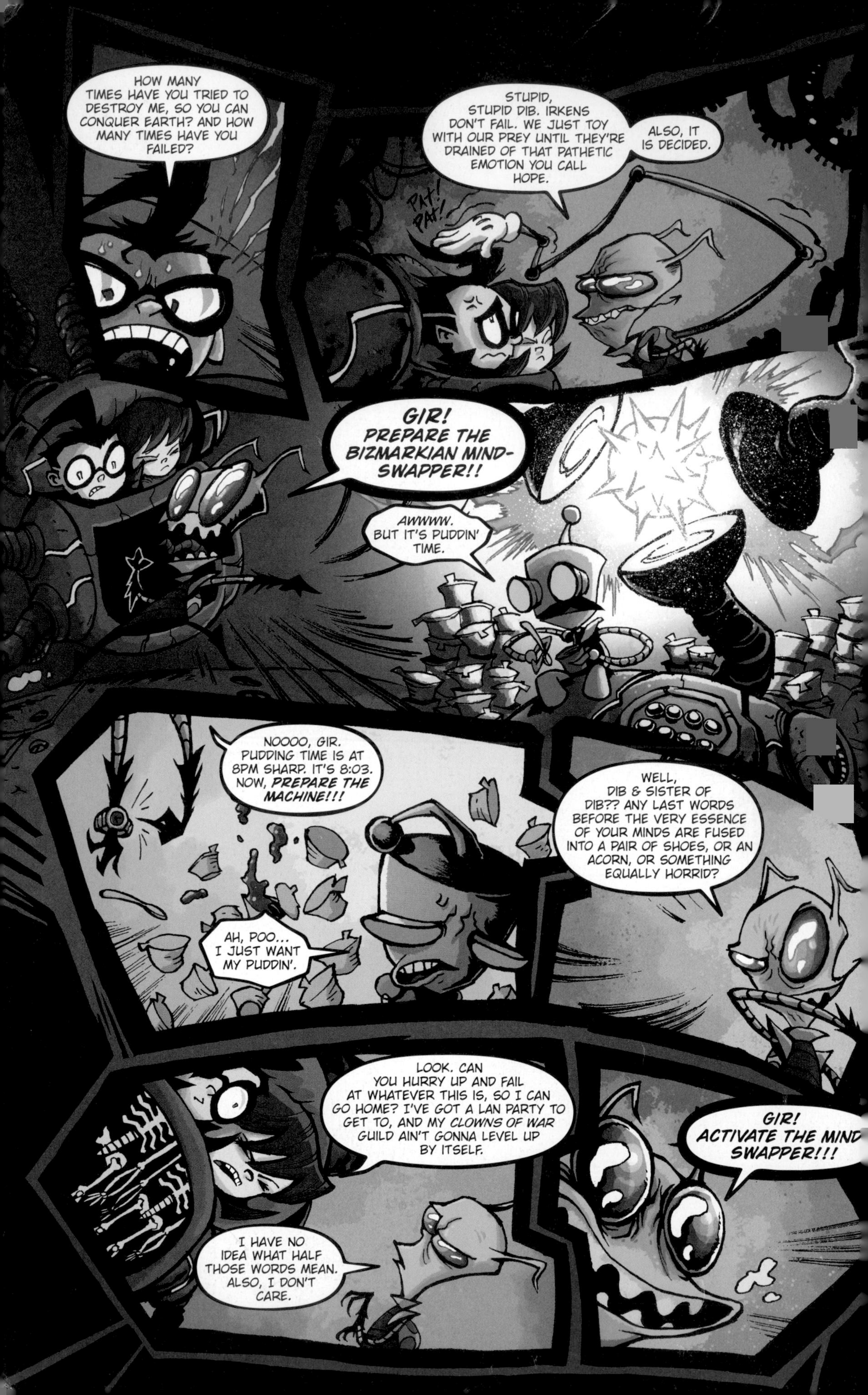
HOW MANY TIMES HAVE YOU TRIED TO DESTROY ME, SO YOU CAN CONQUER EARTH? AND HOW MANY TIMES HAVE YOU FAILED?
STUPID, STUPID DIB. IRKENS DON'T FAIL. WE JUST TOY WITH OUR PREY UNTIL THEY'RE DRAINED OF THAT PATHETIC EMOTION YOU CALL HOPE.
ALSO, IT IS DECIDED.
PAT! PAT!
GIR! PREPARE THE BIZMARKIAN MIND-SWAPPER!!
AWWWW. BUT IT'S PUDDIN' TIME.
NOOOO, GIR. PUDDING TIME IS AT 8PM SHARP. IT'S 8:03. NOW, PREPARE THE MACHINE!!!
AH, POO... I JUST WANT MY PUDDIN'.
WELL, DIB & SISTER OF DIB?? ANY LAST WORDS BEFORE THE VERY ESSENCE OF YOUR MINDS ARE FUSED INTO A PAIR OF SHOES, OR AN ACORN, OR SOMETHING EQUALLY HORRID?
LOOK. CAN YOU HURRY UP AND FAIL AT WHATEVER THIS IS, SO I CAN GO HOME? I'VE GOT A LAN PARTY TO GET TO, AND MY CLOWNS OF WAR GUILD AIN'T GONNA LEVEL UP BY ITSELF.
I HAVE NO IDEA WHAT HALF THOSE WORDS MEAN. ALSO, I DON'T CARE.
GIR! ACTIVATE THE MIND SWAPPER!!!

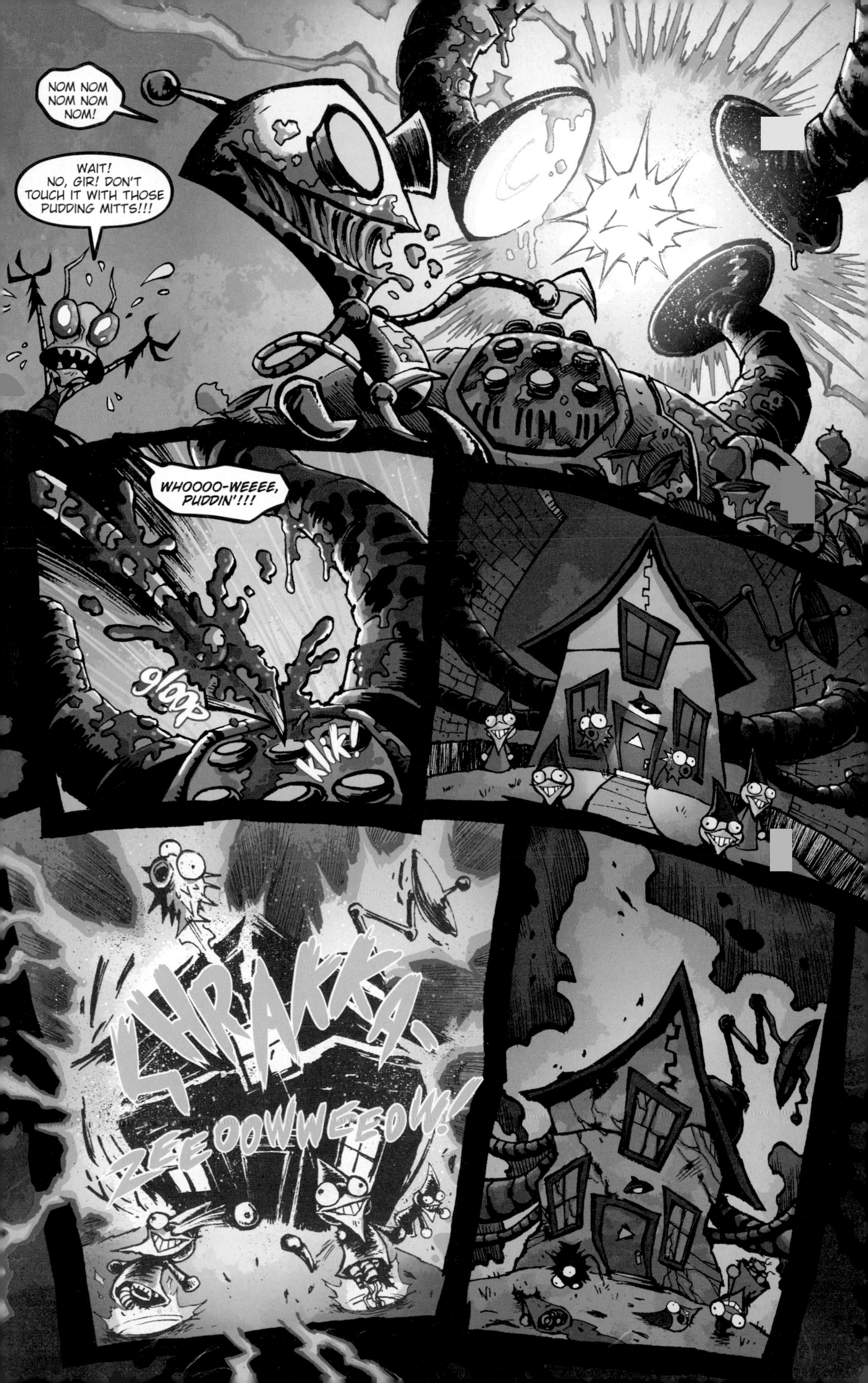
NOM NOM NOM NOM NOM!
WAIT! NO, GIR! DON'T TOUCH IT WITH THOSE PUDDING MITTS!!!
WHOOOO-WEEEE, PUDDIN'!!!
gloop
klik!
CHRAKKA.
ZEEOOWWEEOW!

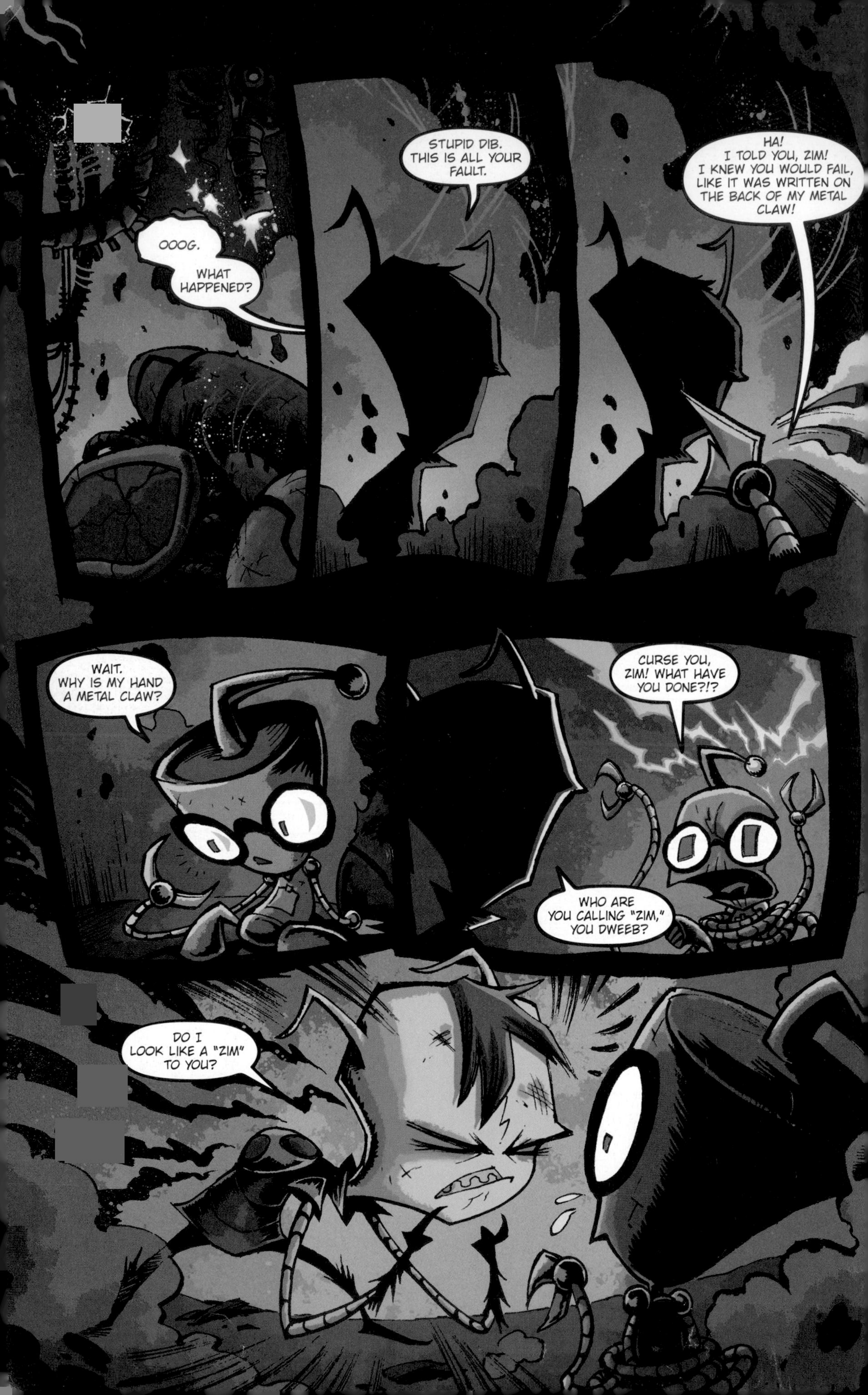
OOOG.
WHAT HAPPENED?
STUPID DIB. THIS IS ALL YOUR FAULT.
HA! I TOLD YOU, ZIM! I KNEW YOU WOULD FAIL, LIKE IT WAS WRITTEN ON THE BACK OF MY METAL CLAW!
WAIT. WHY IS MY HAND A METAL CLAW?
CURSE YOU, ZIM! WHAT HAVE YOU DONE?!?
WHO ARE YOU CALLING "ZIM," YOU DWEEB?
DO I LOOK LIKE A "ZIM" TO YOU?

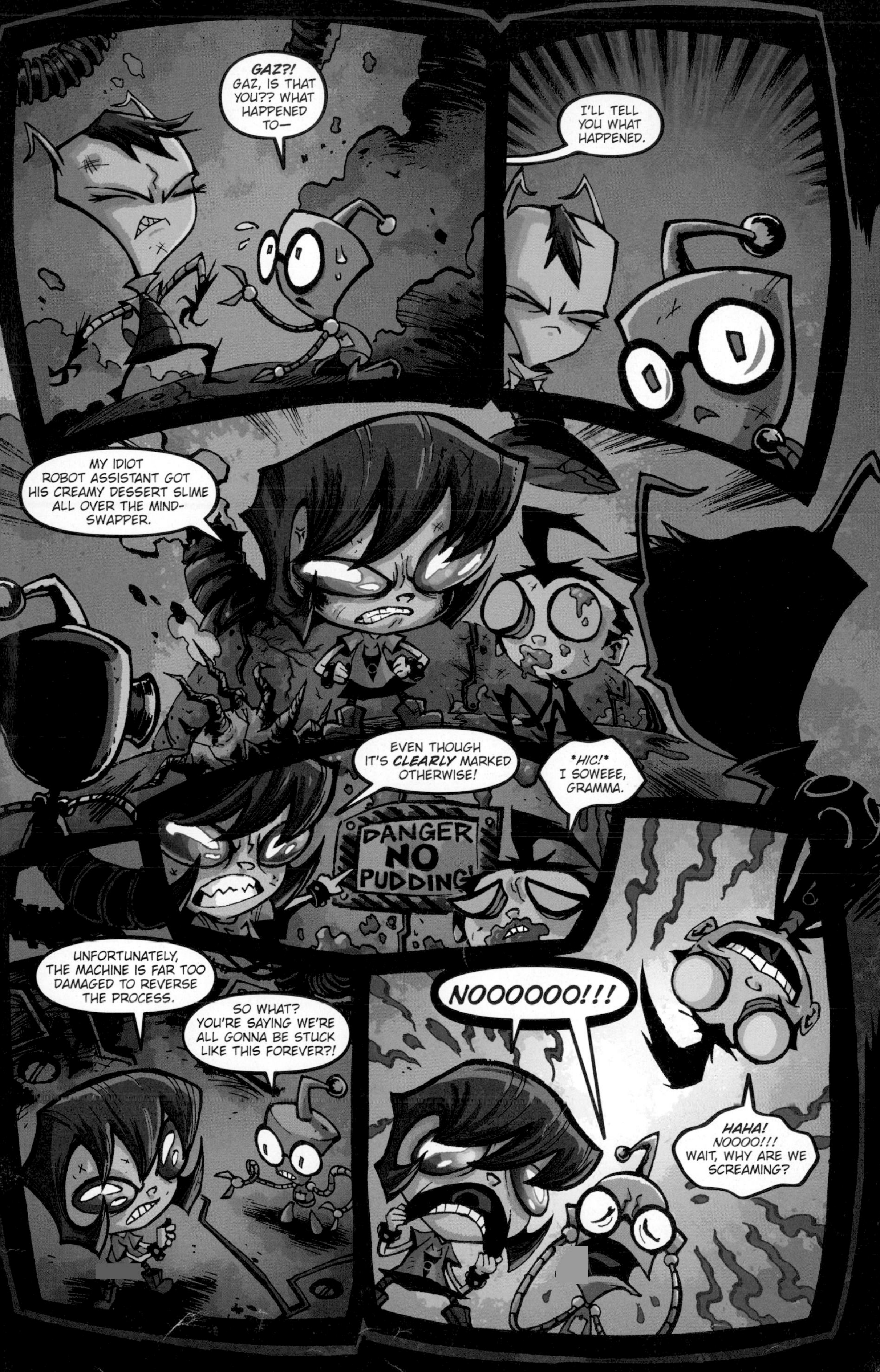
GAZ?! GAZ, IS THAT YOU?? WHAT HAPPENED TO—
I'LL TELL YOU WHAT HAPPENED.
MY IDIOT ROBOT ASSISTANT GOT HIS CREAMY DESSERT SLIME ALL OVER THE MIND-SWAPPER.
EVEN THOUGH IT'S CLEARLY MARKED OTHERWISE!
HIC! I SOWEEE, GRAMMA.
DANGER NO PUDDING
UNFORTUNATELY, THE MACHINE IS FAR TOO DAMAGED TO REVERSE THE PROCESS.
SO WHAT? YOU'RE SAYING WE'RE ALL GONNA BE STUCK LIKE THIS FOREVER?!
NOOOOOO!!!
HAHA! NOOOO!!! WAIT, WHY ARE WE SCREAMING?

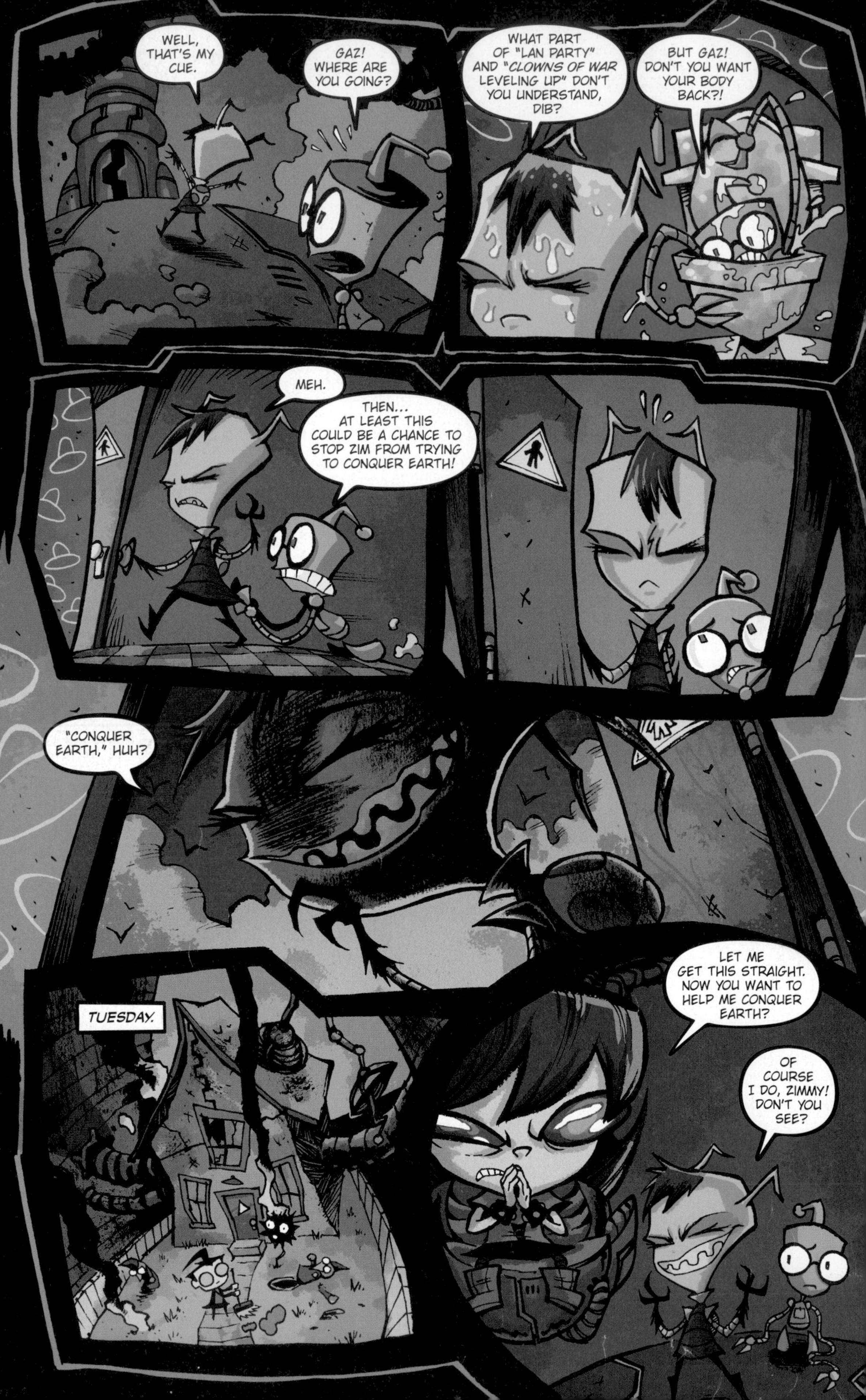
WELL, THAT'S MY CUE.
GAZ! WHERE ARE YOU GOING?
WHAT PART OF "LAN PARTY" AND "CLOWNS OF WAR LEVELING UP" DON'T YOU UNDERSTAND, DIB?
BUT GAZ! DON'T YOU WANT YOUR BODY BACK?!
MEH.
THEN... AT LEAST THIS COULD BE A CHANCE TO STOP ZIM FROM TRYING TO CONQUER EARTH!
"CONQUER EARTH," HUH?
TUESDAY.
LET ME GET THIS STRAIGHT. NOW YOU WANT TO HELP ME CONQUER EARTH?
OF COURSE I DO, ZIMMY! DON'T YOU SEE?

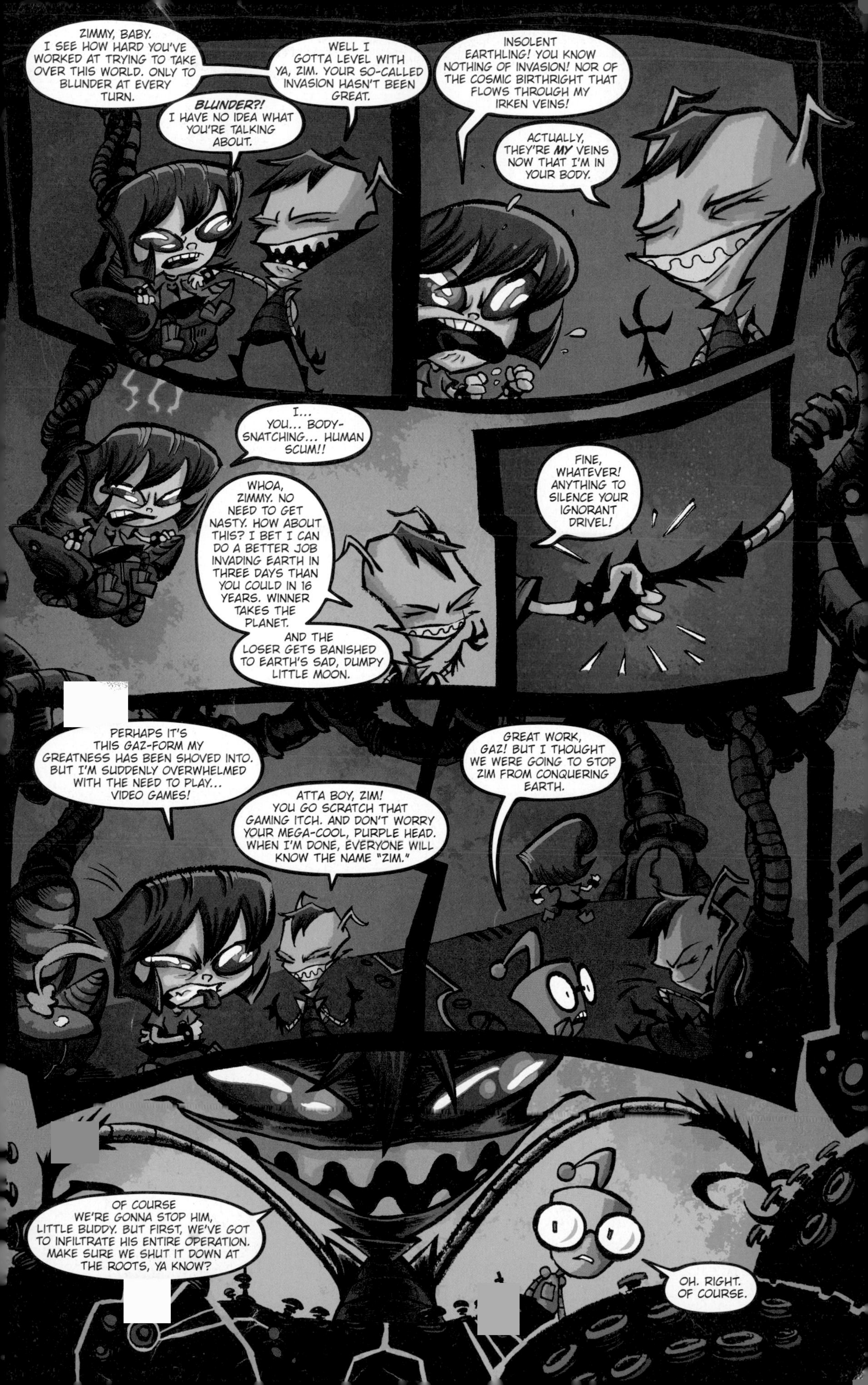
ZIMMY, BABY. I SEE HOW HARD YOU'VE WORKED AT TRYING TO TAKE OVER THIS WORLD. ONLY TO BLUNDER AT EVERY TURN.
BLUNDER?! I HAVE NO IDEA WHAT YOU'RE TALKING ABOUT.
WELL I GOTTA LEVEL WITH YA, ZIM. YOUR SO-CALLED INVASION HASN'T BEEN GREAT.
INSOLENT EARTHLING! YOU KNOW NOTHING OF INVASION! NOR OF THE COSMIC BIRTHRIGHT THAT FLOWS THROUGH MY IRKEN VEINS!
ACTUALLY, THEY'RE MY VEINS NOW THAT I'M IN YOUR BODY.
I... YOU... BODY-SNATCHING... HUMAN SCUM!!
WHOA, ZIMMY. NO NEED TO GET NASTY. HOW ABOUT THIS? I BET I CAN DO A BETTER JOB INVADING EARTH IN THREE DAYS THAN YOU COULD IN 16 YEARS. WINNER TAKES THE PLANET.
AND THE LOSER GETS BANISHED TO EARTH'S SAD, DUMPY LITTLE MOON.
FINE, WHATEVER! ANYTHING TO SILENCE YOUR IGNORANT DRIVEL!
PERHAPS IT'S THIS GAZ-FORM MY GREATNESS HAS BEEN SHOVED INTO. BUT I'M SUDDENLY OVERWHELMED WITH THE NEED TO PLAY... VIDEO GAMES!
ATTA BOY, ZIM! YOU GO SCRATCH THAT GAMING ITCH. AND DON'T WORRY YOUR MEGA-COOL, PURPLE HEAD. WHEN I'M DONE, EVERYONE WILL KNOW THE NAME "ZIM."
GREAT WORK, GAZ! BUT I THOUGHT WE WERE GOING TO STOP ZIM FROM CONQUERING EARTH.
OF COURSE WE'RE GONNA STOP HIM, LITTLE BUDDY. BUT FIRST, WE'VE GOT TO INFILTRATE HIS ENTIRE OPERATION. MAKE SURE WE SHUT IT DOWN AT THE ROOTS, YA KNOW?
OH. RIGHT. OF COURSE.

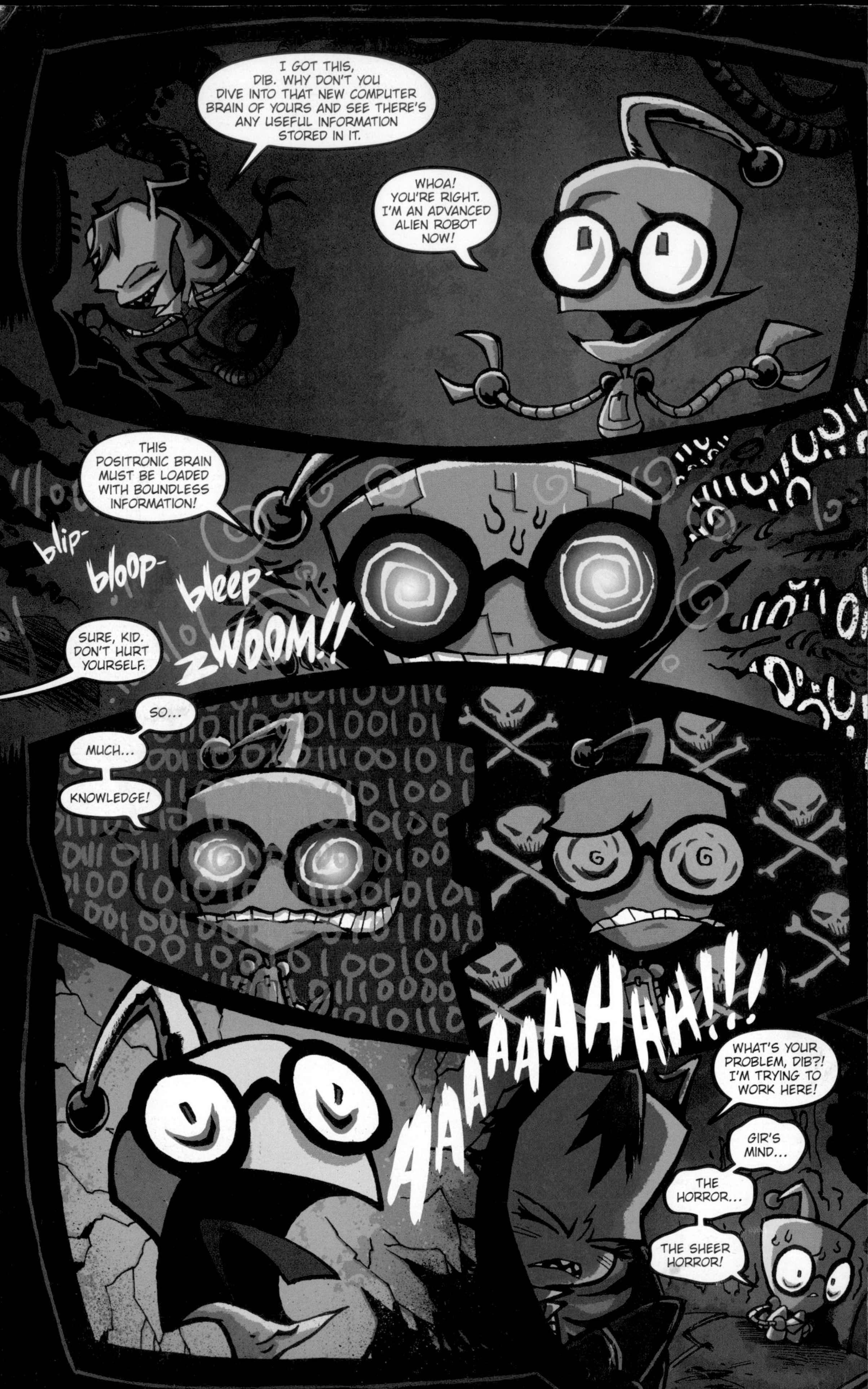
I GOT THIS, DIB. WHY DON'T YOU DIVE INTO THAT NEW COMPUTER BRAIN OF YOURS AND SEE THERE'S ANY USEFUL INFORMATION STORED IN IT.
WHOA! YOU'RE RIGHT. I'M AN ADVANCED ALIEN ROBOT NOW!
THIS POSITRONIC BRAIN MUST BE LOADED WITH BOUNDLESS INFORMATION!
blip-
bloop-
bleep-
ZWOOM!!
SURE, KID. DON'T HURT YOURSELF.
SO...
MUCH...
KNOWLEDGE!
AAAAAAAAHH!!!
WHAT'S YOUR PROBLEM, DIB?! I'M TRYING TO WORK HERE!
GIR'S MIND...
THE HORROR...
THE SHEER HORROR!

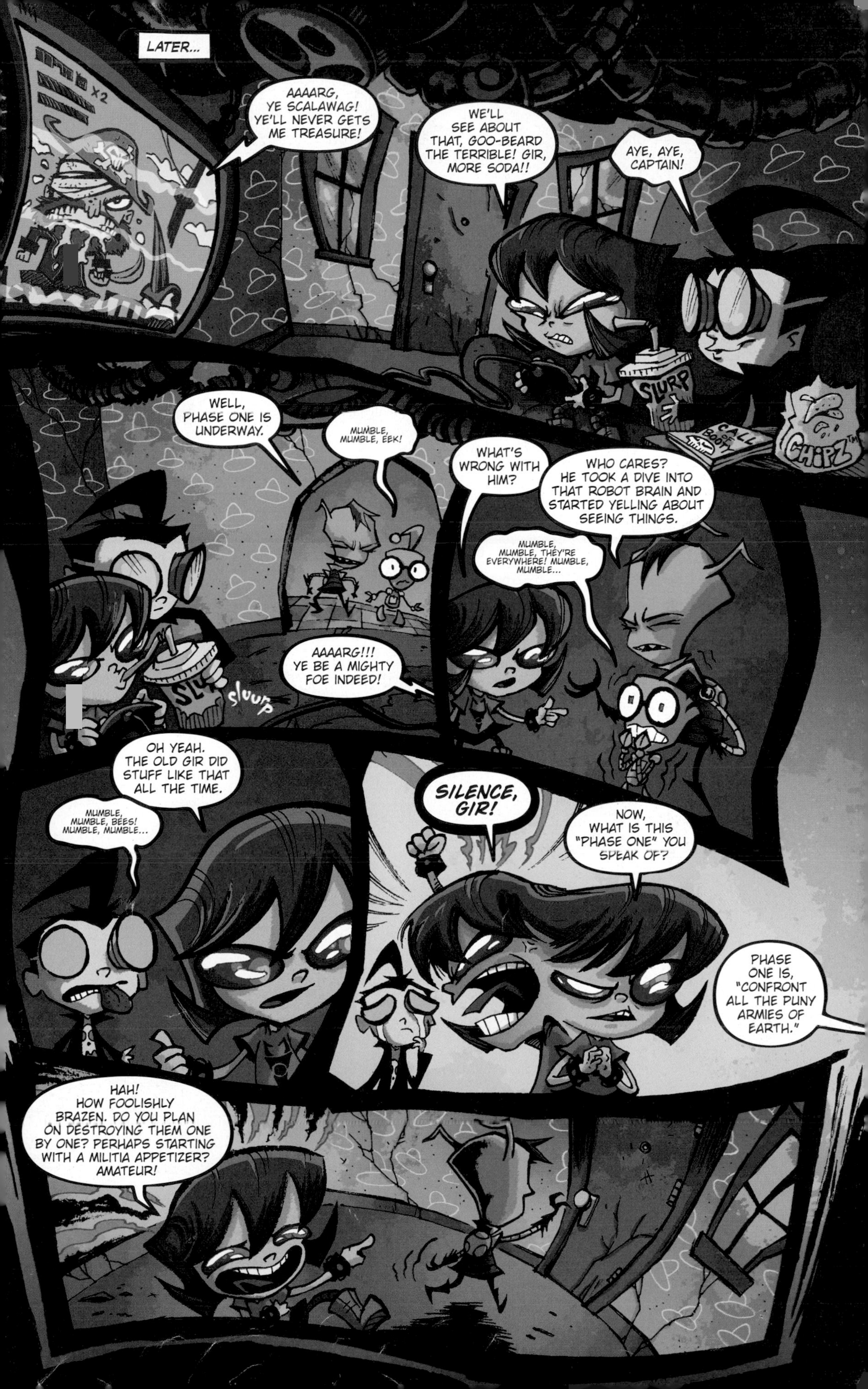
LATER...
AAAARG, YE SCALAWAG! YE'LL NEVER GETS ME TREASURE!
WE'LL SEE ABOUT THAT, GOO-BEARD THE TERRIBLE! GIR, MORE SODA!!
AYE, AYE, CAPTAIN!
SLURP
CALL OF BOOTY
CHIPZ™
WELL, PHASE ONE IS UNDERWAY.
MUMBLE, MUMBLE, EEK!
AAAARG!!! YE BE A MIGHTY FOE INDEED!
sluurp
WHAT'S WRONG WITH HIM?
WHO CARES? HE TOOK A DIVE INTO THAT ROBOT BRAIN AND STARTED YELLING ABOUT SEEING THINGS.
MUMBLE, MUMBLE, THEY'RE EVERYWHERE! MUMBLE, MUMBLE...
OH YEAH. THE OLD GIR DID STUFF LIKE THAT ALL THE TIME.
MUMBLE, MUMBLE, BEES! MUMBLE, MUMBLE...
SILENCE, GIR!
NOW, WHAT IS THIS "PHASE ONE" YOU SPEAK OF?
PHASE ONE IS, "CONFRONT ALL THE PUNY ARMIES OF EARTH."
HAH! HOW FOOLISHLY BRAZEN. DO YOU PLAN ON DESTROYING THEM ONE BY ONE? PERHAPS STARTING WITH A MILITIA APPETIZER? AMATEUR!

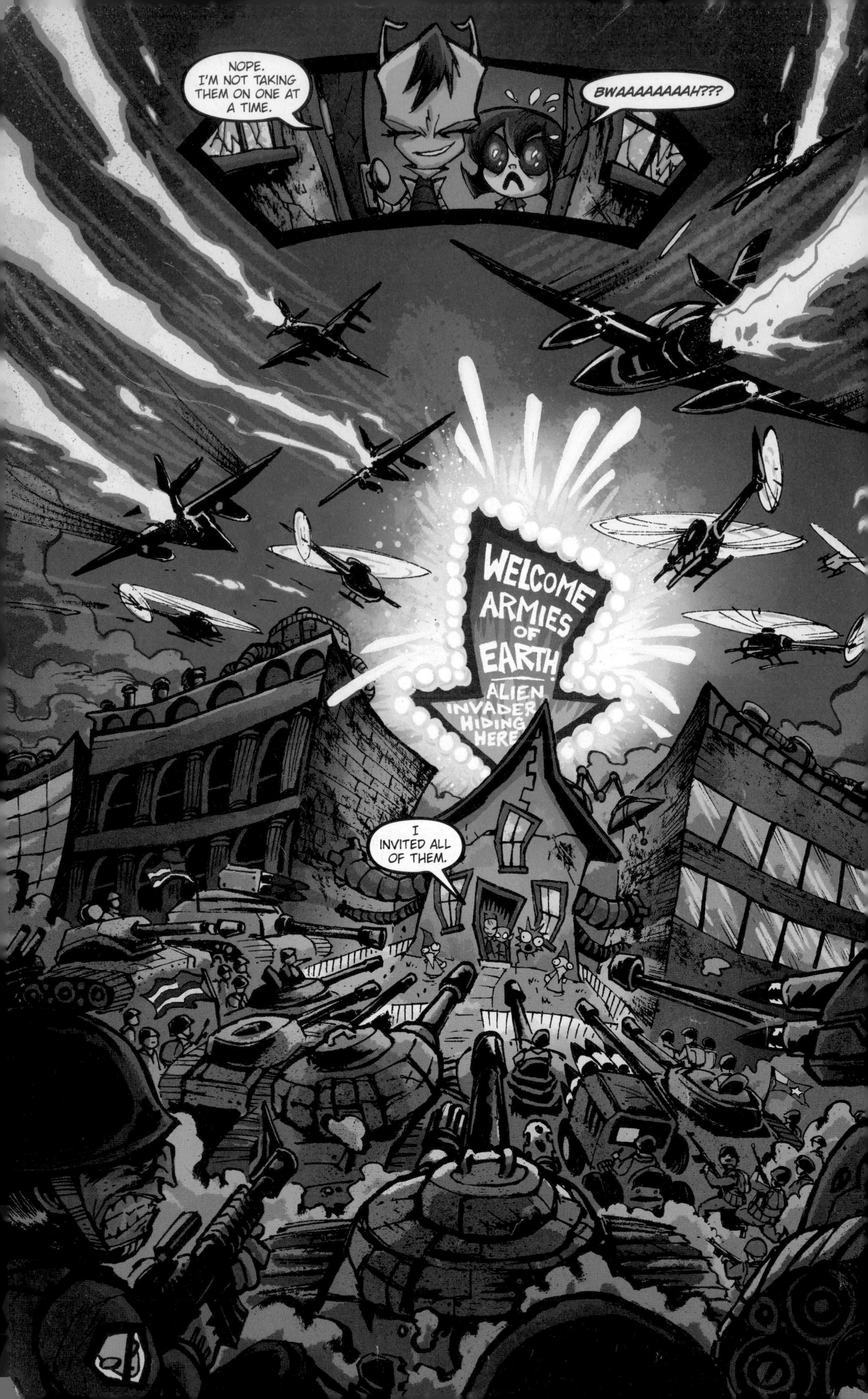
NOPE. I'M NOT TAKING THEM ON ONE AT A TIME.
BWAAAAAAAAAH???
WELCOME ARMIES OF EARTH
ALIEN INVADER HIDING HERE
I INVITED ALL OF THEM.

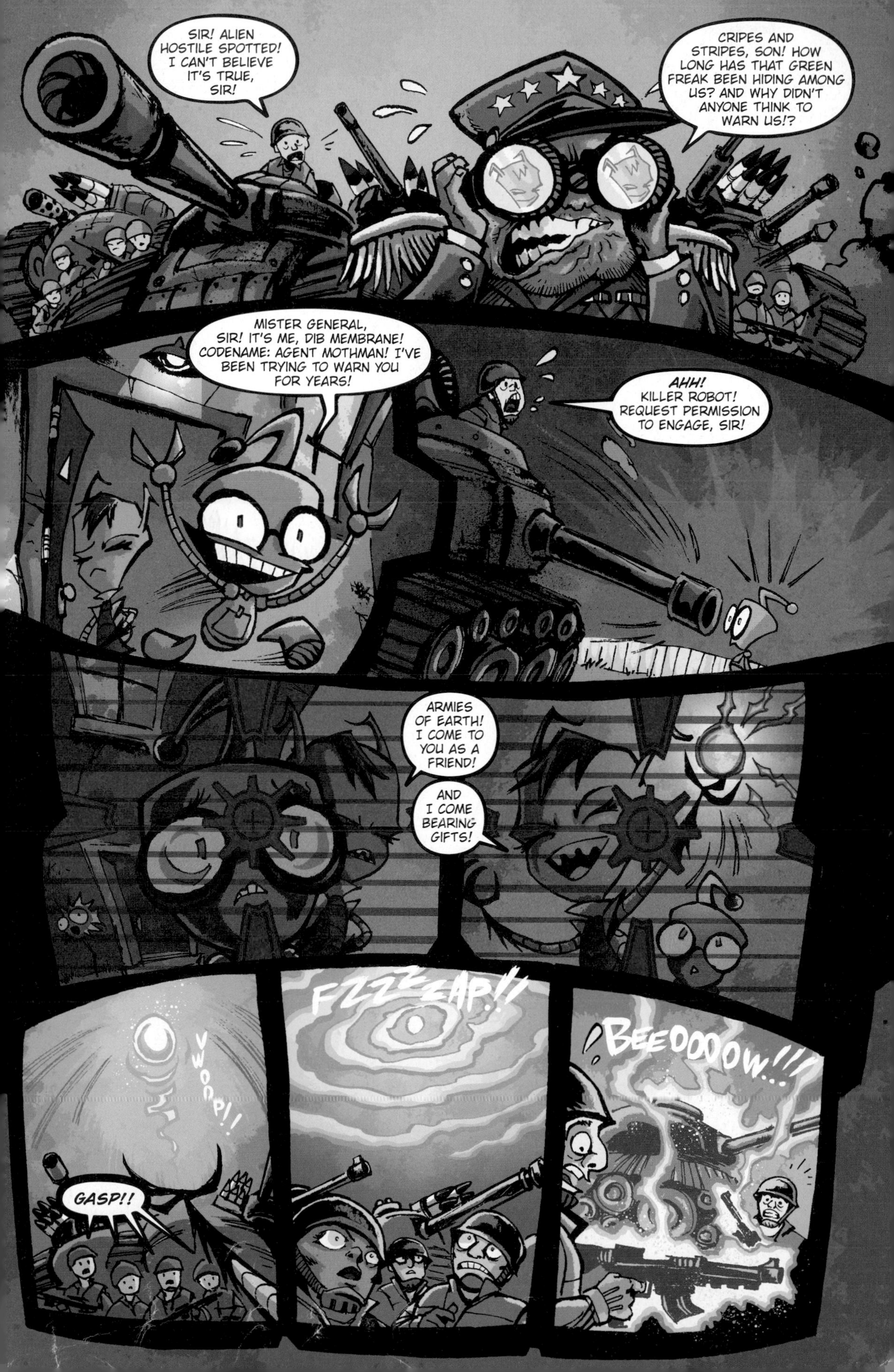
SIR! ALIEN HOSTILE SPOTTED! I CAN'T BELIEVE IT'S TRUE, SIR!
CRIPES AND STRIPES, SON! HOW LONG HAS THAT GREEN FREAK BEEN HIDING AMONG US? AND WHY DIDN'T ANYONE THINK TO WARN US!?
MISTER GENERAL, SIR! IT'S ME, DIB MEMBRANE! CODENAME: AGENT MOTHMAN! I'VE BEEN TRYING TO WARN YOU FOR YEARS!
AHH! KILLER ROBOT! REQUEST PERMISSION TO ENGAGE, SIR!
ARMIES OF EARTH! I COME TO YOU AS A FRIEND!
AND I COME BEARING GIFTS!
VWOOP!!
GASP!!
FZZZZZAP!!
BEEOOOOW...!!!

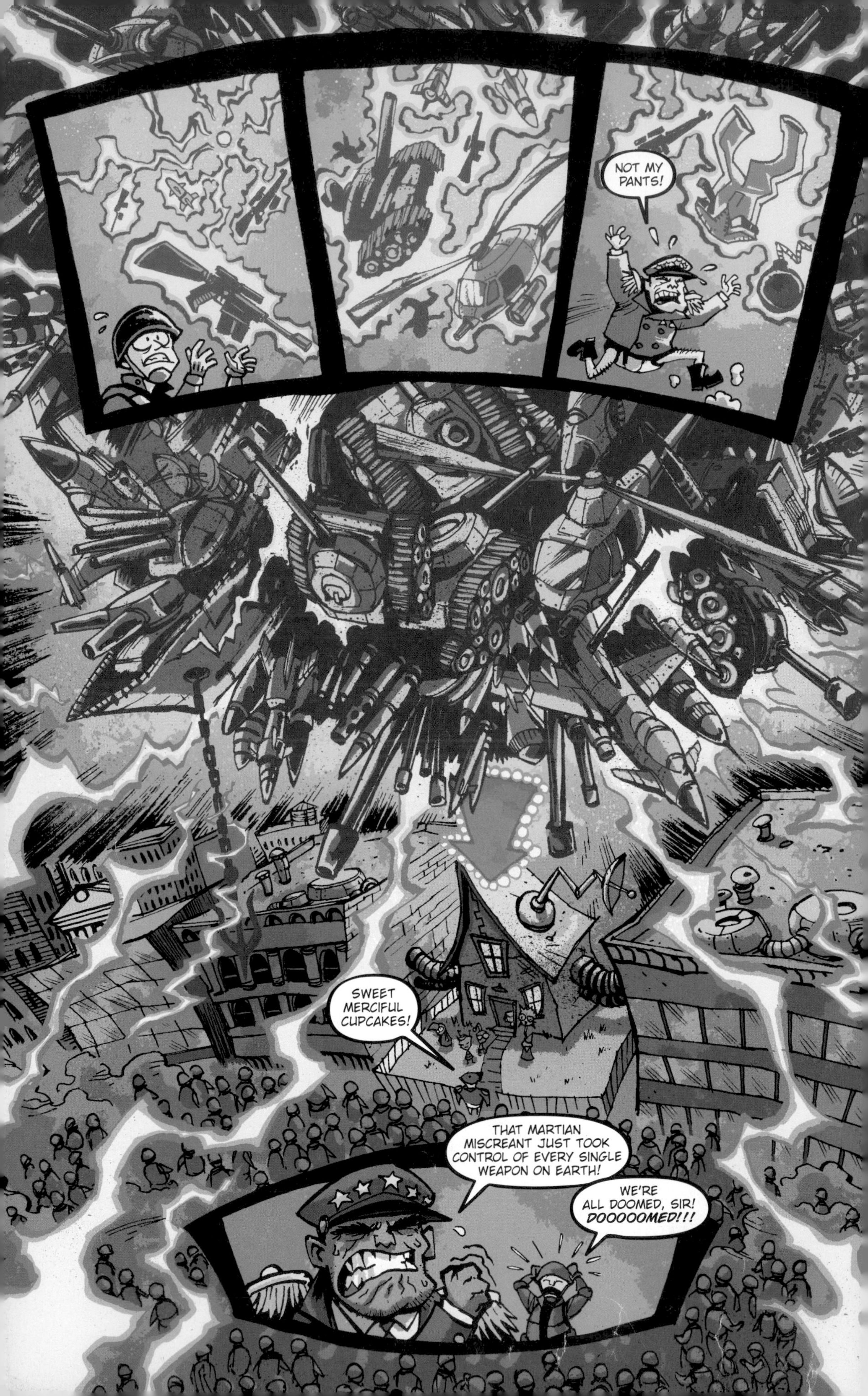
NOT MY PANTS!
SWEET MERCIFUL CUPCAKES!
THAT MARTIAN MISCREANT JUST TOOK CONTROL OF EVERY SINGLE WEAPON ON EARTH!
WE'RE ALL DOOMED, SIR! ***DOOOOMED!!!***

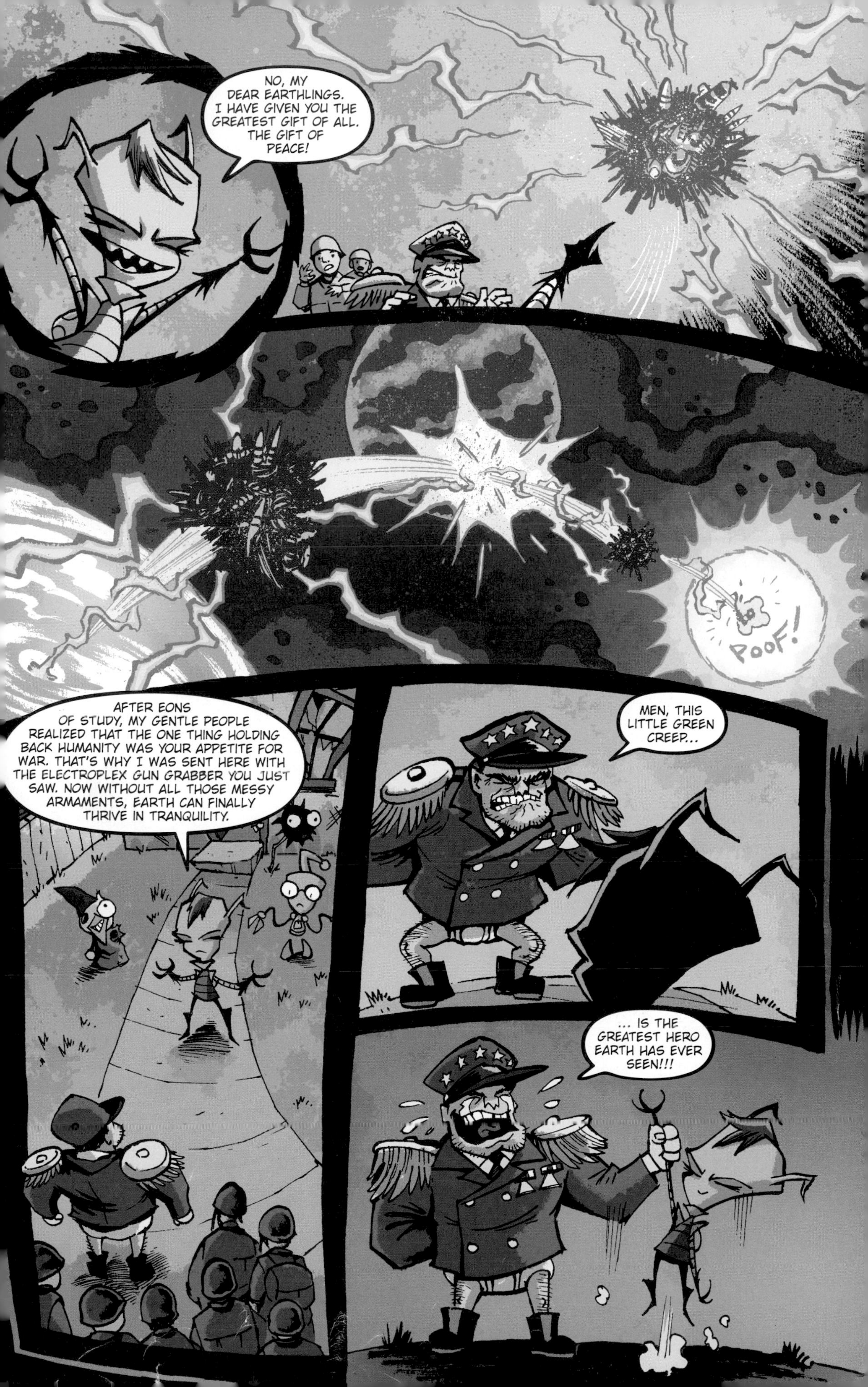
NO, MY DEAR EARTHLINGS. I HAVE GIVEN YOU THE GREATEST GIFT OF ALL. THE GIFT OF PEACE!
POOF!
AFTER EONS OF STUDY, MY GENTLE PEOPLE REALIZED THAT THE ONE THING HOLDING BACK HUMANITY WAS YOUR APPETITE FOR WAR. THAT'S WHY I WAS SENT HERE WITH THE ELECTROPLEX GUN GRABBER YOU JUST SAW. NOW WITHOUT ALL THOSE MESSY ARMAMENTS, EARTH CAN FINALLY THRIVE IN TRANQUILITY.
MEN, THIS LITTLE GREEN CREEP...
... IS THE GREATEST HERO EARTH HAS EVER SEEN!!!

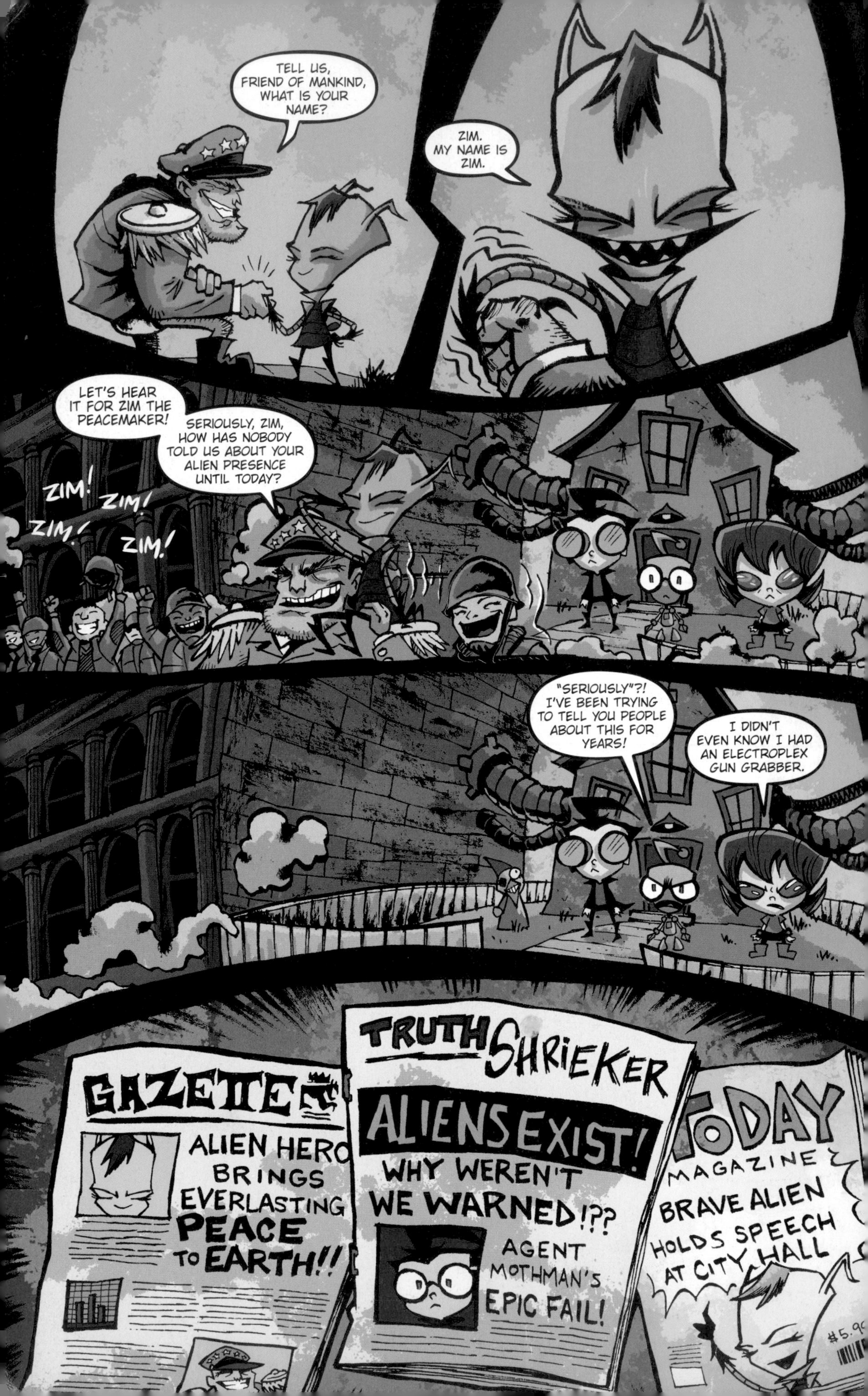
TELL US, FRIEND OF MANKIND, WHAT IS YOUR NAME?
ZIM. MY NAME IS ZIM.
LET'S HEAR IT FOR ZIM THE PEACEMAKER!
SERIOUSLY, ZIM, HOW HAS NOBODY TOLD US ABOUT YOUR ALIEN PRESENCE UNTIL TODAY?
ZIM! ZIM! ZIM! ZIM!
"SERIOUSLY"?! I'VE BEEN TRYING TO TELL YOU PEOPLE ABOUT THIS FOR YEARS!
I DIDN'T EVEN KNOW I HAD AN ELECTROPLEX GUN GRABBER.
GAZETTE
ALIEN HERO BRINGS EVERLASTING PEACE TO EARTH!!
TRUTH SHRIEKER
ALIENS EXIST!
WHY WEREN'T WE WARNED!??
AGENT MOTHMAN'S EPIC FAIL!
TODAY MAGAZINE
BRAVE ALIEN HOLDS SPEECH AT CITY HALL

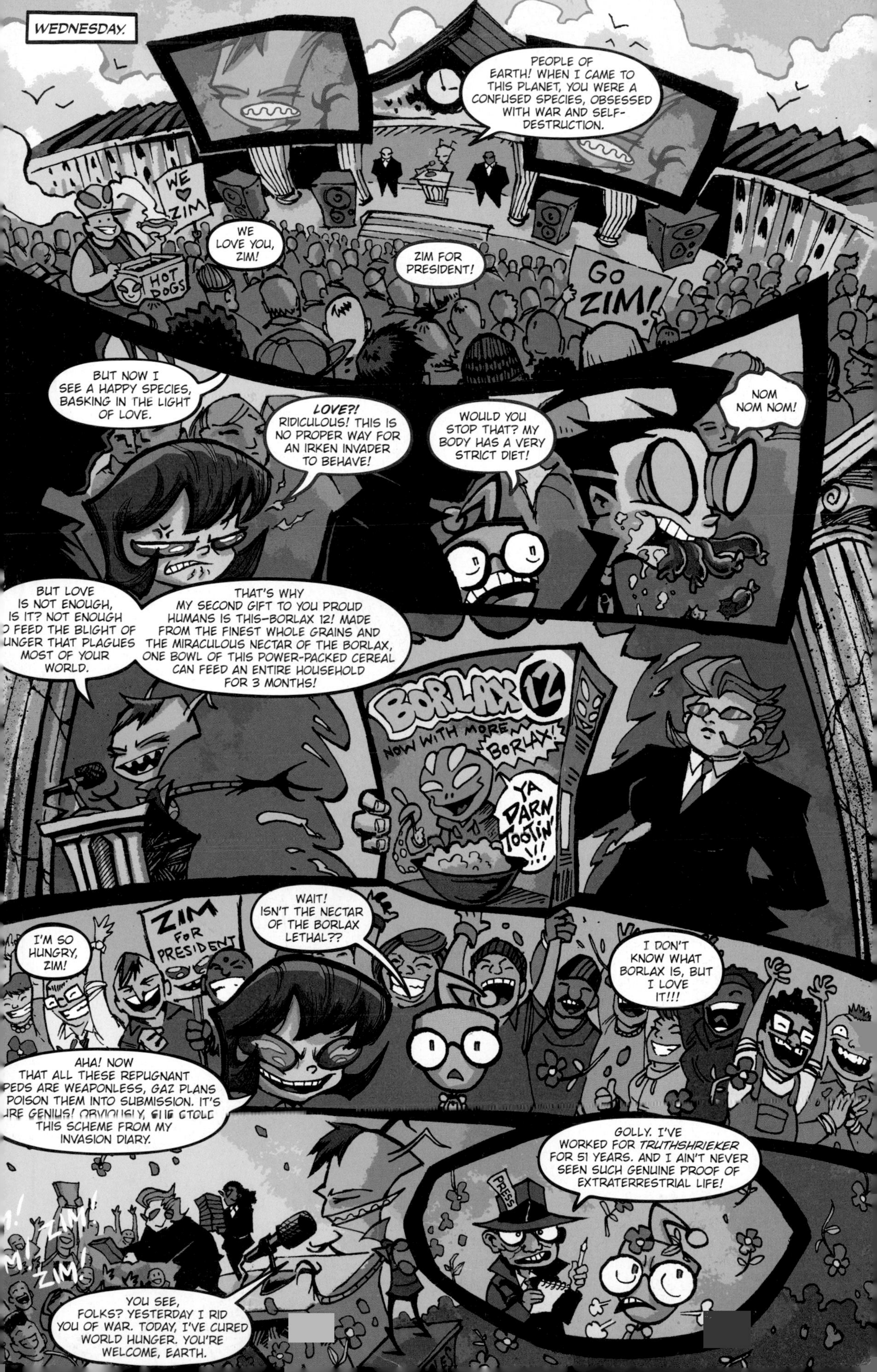
WEDNESDAY.
PEOPLE OF EARTH! WHEN I CAME TO THIS PLANET, YOU WERE A CONFUSED SPECIES, OBSESSED WITH WAR AND SELF-DESTRUCTION.
WE ♥ ZIM
HOT DOGS
WE LOVE YOU, ZIM!
ZIM FOR PRESIDENT!
GO ZIM!
BUT NOW I SEE A HAPPY SPECIES, BASKING IN THE LIGHT OF LOVE.
LOVE?! RIDICULOUS! THIS IS NO PROPER WAY FOR AN IRKEN INVADER TO BEHAVE!
WOULD YOU STOP THAT? MY BODY HAS A VERY STRICT DIET!
NOM NOM NOM!
BUT LOVE IS NOT ENOUGH, IS IT? NOT ENOUGH O FEED THE BLIGHT OF UNGER THAT PLAGUES MOST OF YOUR WORLD.
THAT'S WHY MY SECOND GIFT TO YOU PROUD HUMANS IS THIS–BORLAX 12! MADE FROM THE FINEST WHOLE GRAINS AND THE MIRACULOUS NECTAR OF THE BORLAX, ONE BOWL OF THIS POWER-PACKED CEREAL CAN FEED AN ENTIRE HOUSEHOLD FOR 3 MONTHS!
BORLAX 12
NOW WITH MORE BORLAX!
YA DARN TOOTIN'!!!
ZIM FOR PRESIDENT
I'M SO HUNGRY, ZIM!
WAIT! ISN'T THE NECTAR OF THE BORLAX LETHAL??
I DON'T KNOW WHAT BORLAX IS, BUT I LOVE IT!!!
AHA! NOW THAT ALL THESE REPUGNANT PEDS ARE WEAPONLESS, GAZ PLANS POISON THEM INTO SUBMISSION. IT'S RE GENIUS! OBVIOUSLY, SHE STOLE THIS SCHEME FROM MY INVASION DIARY.
GOLLY. I'VE WORKED FOR *TRUTHSHRIEKER* FOR 51 YEARS. AND I AIN'T NEVER SEEN SUCH GENUINE PROOF OF EXTRATERRESTRIAL LIFE!
PRESS
ZIM! ZIM! ZIM!
YOU SEE, FOLKS? YESTERDAY I RID YOU OF WAR. TODAY, I'VE CURED WORLD HUNGER. YOU'RE WELCOME, EARTH.

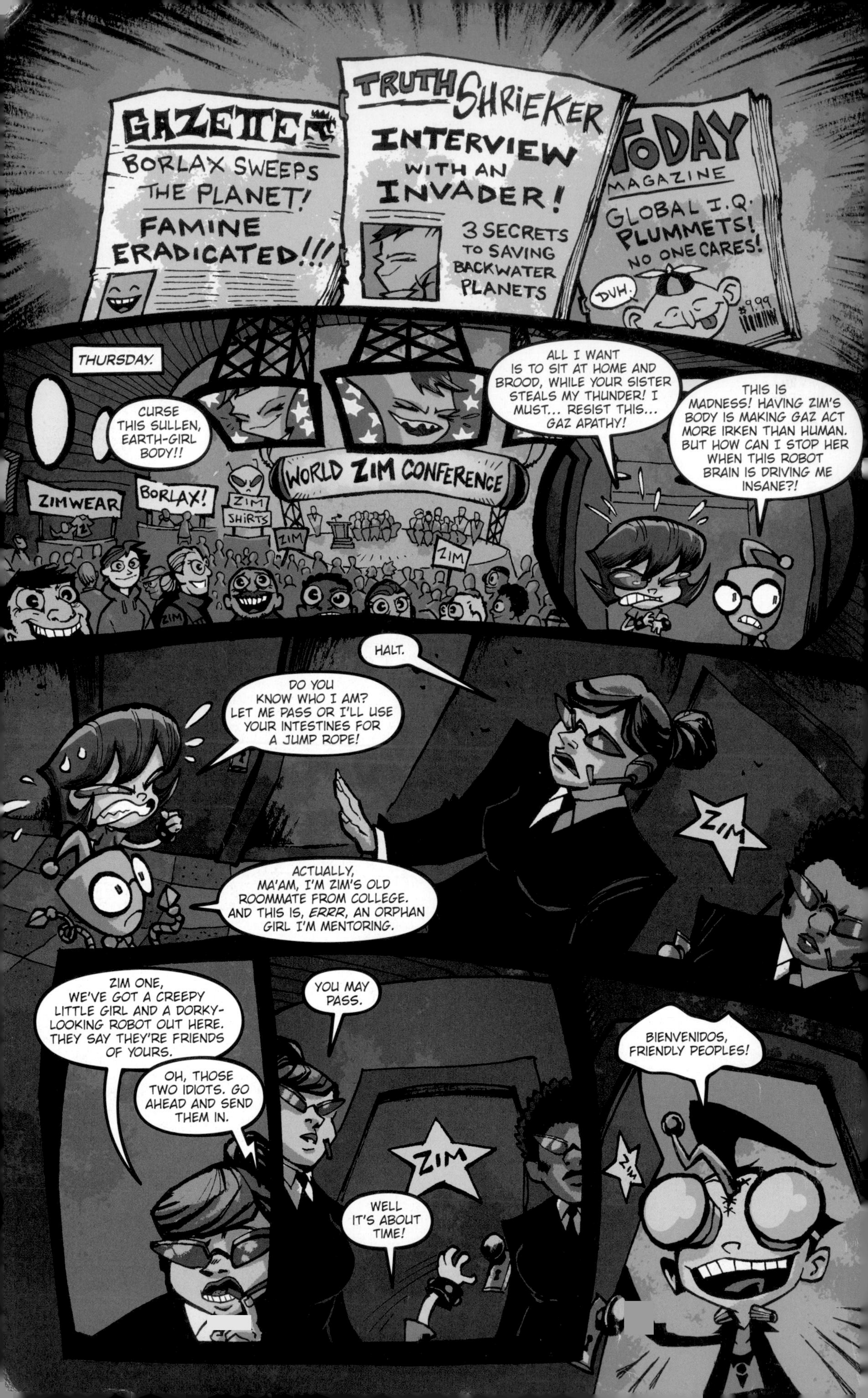
GAZETTE
BORLAX SWEEPS THE PLANET!
FAMINE ERADICATED!!!
TRUTH SHRIEKER
INTERVIEW WITH AN INVADER!
3 SECRETS TO SAVING BACKWATER PLANETS
TODAY MAGAZINE
GLOBAL I.Q. PLUMMETS! NO ONE CARES!
DUH.
$9.99
THURSDAY.
CURSE THIS SULLEN, EARTH-GIRL BODY!!
WORLD ZIM CONFERENCE
ZIMWEAR
BORLAX!
ZIM SHIRTS
ZIM
ZIM
ALL I WANT IS TO SIT AT HOME AND BROOD, WHILE YOUR SISTER STEALS MY THUNDER! I MUST... RESIST THIS... GAZ APATHY!
THIS IS MADNESS! HAVING ZIM'S BODY IS MAKING GAZ ACT MORE IRKEN THAN HUMAN. BUT HOW CAN I STOP HER WHEN THIS ROBOT BRAIN IS DRIVING ME INSANE?!
HALT.
DO YOU KNOW WHO I AM? LET ME PASS OR I'LL USE YOUR INTESTINES FOR A JUMP ROPE!
ZIM
ACTUALLY, MA'AM, I'M ZIM'S OLD ROOMMATE FROM COLLEGE. AND THIS IS, ERRR, AN ORPHAN GIRL I'M MENTORING.
ZIM ONE, WE'VE GOT A CREEPY LITTLE GIRL AND A DORKY-LOOKING ROBOT OUT HERE. THEY SAY THEY'RE FRIENDS OF YOURS.
OH, THOSE TWO IDIOTS. GO AHEAD AND SEND THEM IN.
YOU MAY PASS.
ZIM
WELL IT'S ABOUT TIME!
BIENVENIDOS, FRIENDLY PEOPLES!
ZIM

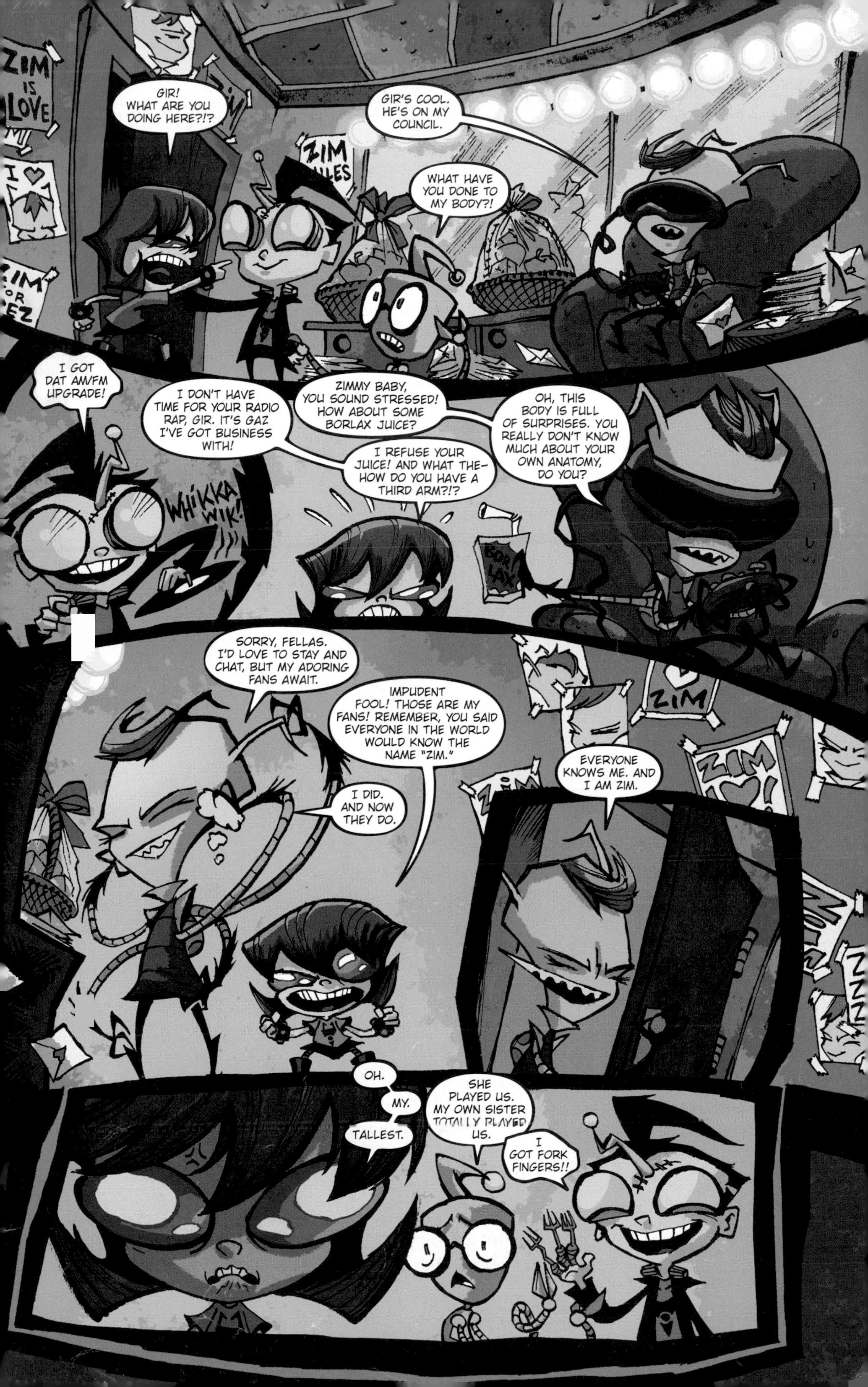
ZIM IS LOVE
GIR! WHAT ARE YOU DOING HERE?!?
ZIM RULES
GIR'S COOL. HE'S ON MY COUNCIL.
WHAT HAVE YOU DONE TO MY BODY?!
I GOT DAT AM/FM UPGRADE!
I DON'T HAVE TIME FOR YOUR RADIO RAP, GIR. IT'S GAZ I'VE GOT BUSINESS WITH!
ZIMMY BABY, YOU SOUND STRESSED! HOW ABOUT SOME BORLAX JUICE?
I REFUSE YOUR JUICE! AND WHAT THE- HOW DO YOU HAVE A THIRD ARM?!?
OH, THIS BODY IS FULL OF SURPRISES. YOU REALLY DON'T KNOW MUCH ABOUT YOUR OWN ANATOMY, DO YOU?
WHIKKA WIK!
BORLAX
SORRY, FELLAS. I'D LOVE TO STAY AND CHAT, BUT MY ADORING FANS AWAIT.
IMPUDENT FOOL! THOSE ARE MY FANS! REMEMBER, YOU SAID EVERYONE IN THE WORLD WOULD KNOW THE NAME "ZIM."
I DID. AND NOW THEY DO.
EVERYONE KNOWS ME. AND I AM ZIM.
ZIM
OH.
MY.
TALLEST.
SHE PLAYED US. MY OWN SISTER TOTALLY PLAYED US.
I GOT FORK FINGERS!!

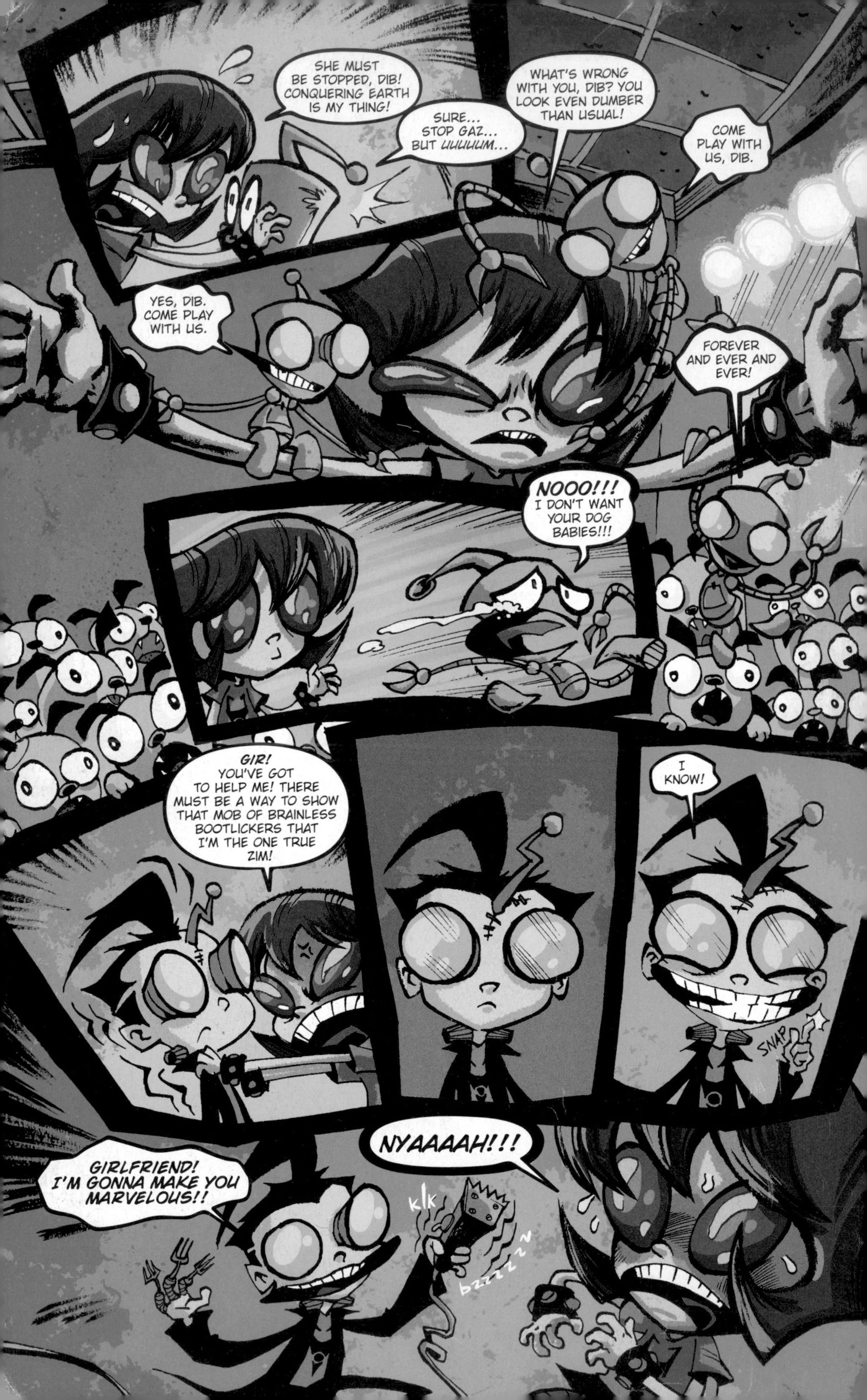
SHE MUST BE STOPPED, DIB! CONQUERING EARTH IS MY THING!
SURE... STOP GAZ... BUT UUUUUM...
WHAT'S WRONG WITH YOU, DIB? YOU LOOK EVEN DUMBER THAN USUAL!
COME PLAY WITH US, DIB.
YES, DIB. COME PLAY WITH US.
FOREVER AND EVER AND EVER!
NOOO!!! I DON'T WANT YOUR DOG BABIES!!!
GIR! YOU'VE GOT TO HELP ME! THERE MUST BE A WAY TO SHOW THAT MOB OF BRAINLESS BOOTLICKERS THAT I'M THE ONE TRUE ZIM!
I KNOW!
SNAP
GIRLFRIEND! I'M GONNA MAKE YOU MARVELOUS!!
NYAAAAH!!!
KLK
bzzzzz

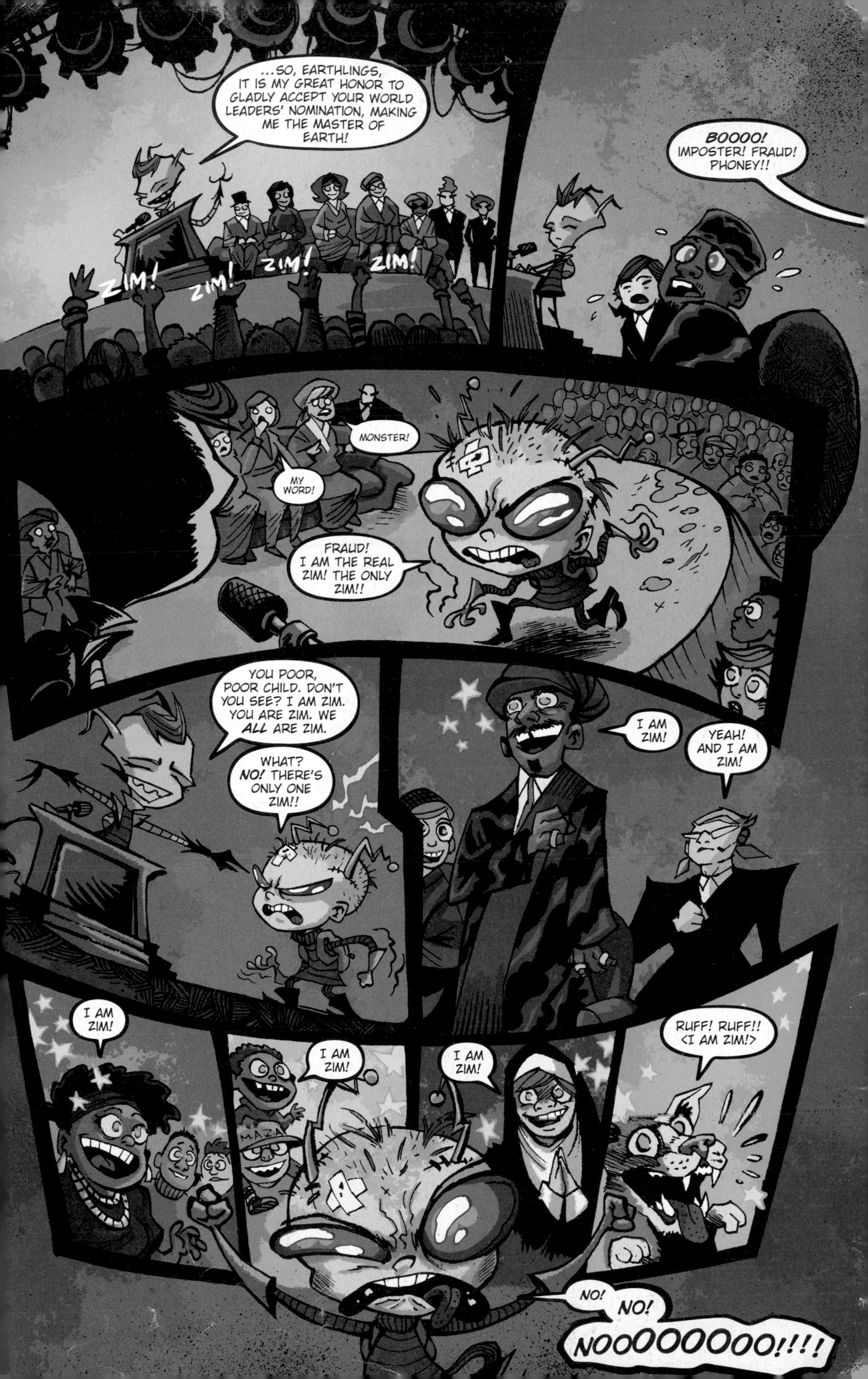
...SO, EARTHLINGS, IT IS MY GREAT HONOR TO GLADLY ACCEPT YOUR WORLD LEADERS' NOMINATION, MAKING ME THE MASTER OF EARTH!
ZIM!
ZIM!
ZIM!
ZIM!
BOOOO! IMPOSTER! FRAUD! PHONEY!!
MONSTER!
MY WORD!
FRAUD! I AM THE REAL ZIM! THE ONLY ZIM!!
YOU POOR, POOR CHILD. DON'T YOU SEE? I AM ZIM. YOU ARE ZIM. WE ALL ARE ZIM.
WHAT? NO! THERE'S ONLY ONE ZIM!!
I AM ZIM!
YEAH! AND I AM ZIM!
I AM ZIM!
I AM ZIM!
I AM ZIM!
RUFF! RUFF!! <I AM ZIM!>
NO!
NO!
NOOOOOOOO!!!!

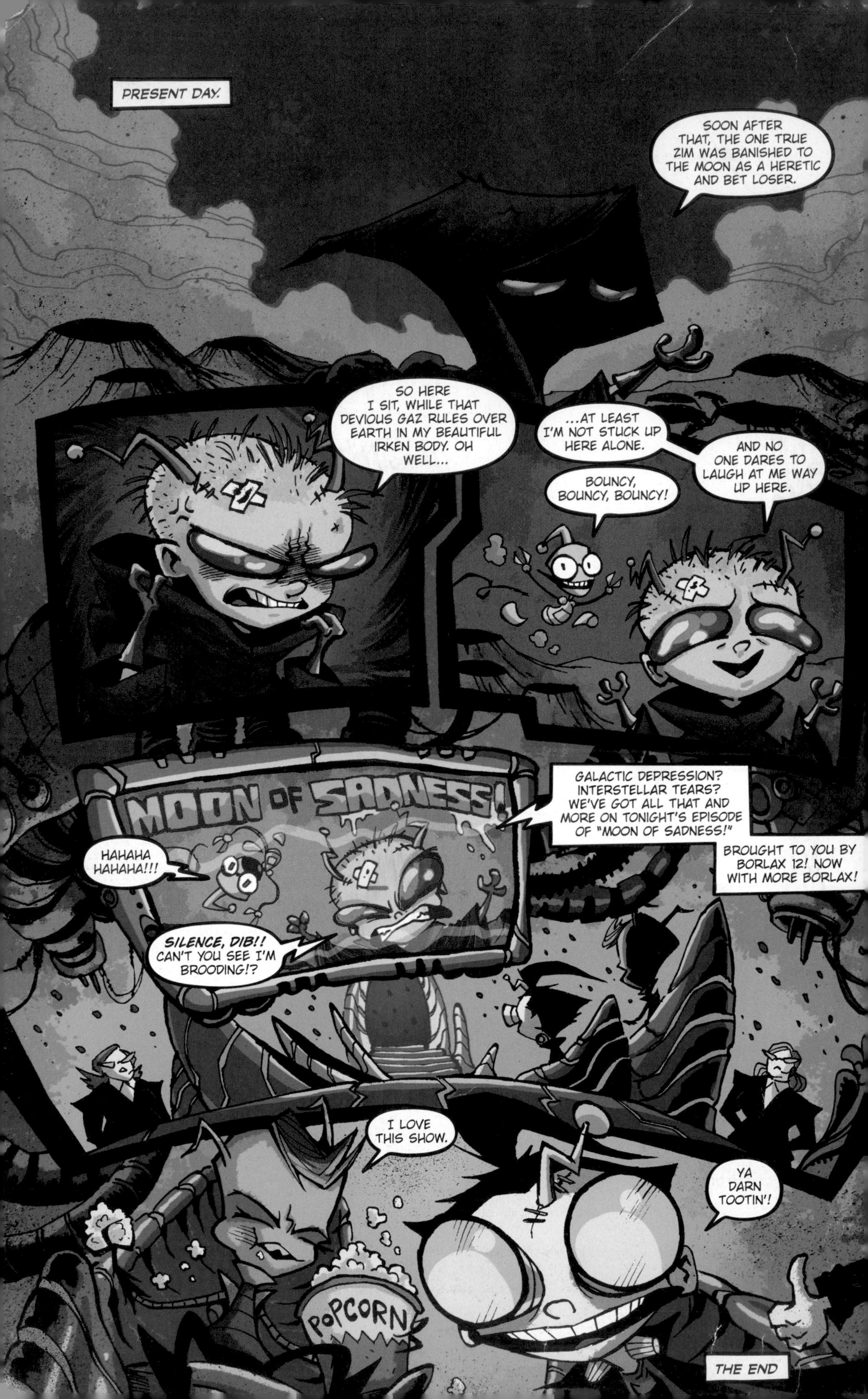
PRESENT DAY.
SOON AFTER THAT, THE ONE TRUE ZIM WAS BANISHED TO THE MOON AS A HERETIC AND BET LOSER.
SO HERE I SIT, WHILE THAT DEVIOUS GAZ RULES OVER EARTH IN MY BEAUTIFUL IRKEN BODY. OH WELL...
...AT LEAST I'M NOT STUCK UP HERE ALONE.
AND NO ONE DARES TO LAUGH AT ME WAY UP HERE.
BOUNCY, BOUNCY, BOUNCY!
MOON OF SADNESS!
GALACTIC DEPRESSION? INTERSTELLAR TEARS? WE'VE GOT ALL THAT AND MORE ON TONIGHT'S EPISODE OF "MOON OF SADNESS!"
BROUGHT TO YOU BY BORLAX 12! NOW WITH MORE BORLAX!
HAHAHA HAHAHA!!!
SILENCE, DIB!! CAN'T YOU SEE I'M BROODING!?
I LOVE THIS SHOW.
YA DARN TOOTIN'!
POPCORN
THE END

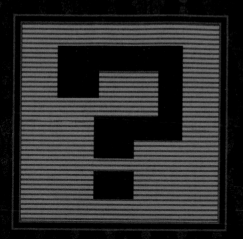

@JhonenV

JHONEN VASQUEZ

Jhonen Vasquez is a writer and artist who walks in many worlds, not unlike Blade, only without having to drink blood-serum to survive the curse that is also his greatest power (still talking about Blade here). He's worked in comics and animation and is the creator of *Invader ZIM*, a fact that haunts him to this day.

@erictrueheart

ERIC TRUEHEART

Eric Trueheart was one of the original writers on the *Invader ZIM* television series back when there was a thing called "television." Since then, he's made a living writing moderately-inappropriate things for people who make entertainment for children, including Dreamworks Animation, Cartoon Network, Disney TV, PBS, Hasbro and others. Upon reading this list, he now thinks he maybe should have become a dentist, and he hates teeth.

WARREN WUCINICH

Warren Wucinich an illustrator, colorist and part-time carny currently living in Durham, NC. When not making comics he can usually be found watching old *Twilight Zone* episodes and eating large amounts of pie.

@warrenwucinich

DAVE CROSLAND

Dave Crosland was born in Buffalo, NY and fought his way through the baneful hordes to adulthood in Los Angeles, CA. He's created art for comics, cartoons, concert posters, video games and more. Along with *Invader ZIM*, his memorable projects include *Randy Cunningham: 9th Grade Ninja*, *Scarface: Scarred for Life*, *Everybody's DEAD*, *Yo Gabba Gabba* and his autobio comic *EGO REHAB*. When he isn't drinking rum from the skulls of his foes, Dave can be found hoarding pets and eating all your peanut butter.

@DaveCrosland

FRED C. STRESING

Fred C. Stresing is a colorist, artist, writer, and letterer for a variety of comics. You may recognize his work from *Invader ZIM*, the comic you are holding. He has been making comics his whole life, from the age of six. He has gotten much better since then. He currently resides in Savannah, Georgia with his wife and 2 cats. He doesn't know how the cats got there, they are not his.

@FredCStresing